APRIL FOOL

BOOKS BY WILLIAM DEVERELL

FICTION

Needles

High Crimes

Mecca

The Dance of Shiva

Platinum Blues

Mindfield

Kill All the Lawyers

Street Legal: The Betrayal

Trial of Passion

Slander

The Laughing Falcon

Mind Games

April Fool

NON-FICTION

A Life on Trial

WILLIAM DEVERELL

APRIL FOOL

M&S

Library and Archives Canada Cataloguing in Publication

Deverell, William, 1937–
April fool / William Deverell.

ISBN 13: 978-0-7710-2711-6
ISBN 10: 0-7710-2711-7

I. Title.

PS8557.E8775A68 2005   C813'.54   C2005-903173-5

We acknowledge the financial support of the Government of Canada through the Book Publishing Industry Development Program and that of the Government of Ontario through the Ontario Media Development Corporation's Ontario Book Initiative. We further acknowledge the support of the Canada Council for the Arts and the Ontario Arts Council for our publishing program.

Typeset in Bembo by M&S, Toronto
Printed and bound in Canada

This book is printed on acid-free paper that is 100% recycled, ancient-forest friendly (100% post-consumer recycled).

McClelland & Stewart Ltd.
75 Sherbourne Street
Toronto, Ontario
M5A 2P9
www.mcclelland.com

2 3 4 5 6   09 08 07 06 05

*To the Sierra Legal Defence Fund and
all defenders of our natural heritage . . .*

AUTHOR'S NOTE

Many fans tell me they delight in taking sightings, somewhat in the manner of avid birders, of several of my characters who flit from one plot to another, but in *April Fool* I have finally succumbed to urgings to recreate a protagonist. Returning to the scene of the crime is Arthur Beauchamp, the fusty Latin-rapping dean of West Coast criminal lawyers. He earns this role for having aided and abetted *Trial of Passion* to become the first Canadian winner of the Dashiell Hammett Prize for Literary Excellence in Crime Writing.

Many friends old and new must be thanked: cops and robbers and lawyers, environmentalists and forensic scientists.

RCMP Sgt. Trent Rolfe, with his wide experience in the Unsolved Crimes Unit, helped provide an insider view of current crime-scene techniques and the handling of exhibits. RCMP forensic scientist Stefano Mazzega was of critical assistance with DNA profiling procedures. As to human profiles, novelist Ann Ireland helped enrich many facets of that embattled seeker of love, Arthur Ramsgate Beauchamp, Q.C., as he grapples with the ineffable mystery of the female psyche.

Senior defence counsel Peter Jensen helped me to navigate current courtroom procedures, as did federal prosecutor Peter Hogg. (Though I've used my literary licence to tweak slightly the rules of court).

Help on environmental issues came from Jerry DeMarco, former lead counsel for the Sierra Legal Defence Fund, and from Jan Kirkby, landscape ecologist with the Canadian Wildlife Service. Mort Ransen's documentary *Ah, the Money, the Money, the Money*, about an island rising to the challenge of the clear-cutters was the inspiration for the subplot.

Some years ago, I spent a couple of stimulating days with Dwight Erickson, once the world's number-five jewel thief, who demonstrated his art and provided a wealth of useful tips.

Thanks to all.

PART ONE

". . . the uncertain glory of an April day."

— Two Gentlemen of Verona

1

Nick the Owl Faloon is sitting beside a stone fox by the name of Eve Winters, who is apparently some kind of shrink. They're scoffing up fresh-caught sockeye, sharing a long table with four couples from Topeka, Kansas, who are up here on a wet spring holiday. In spite of all the happy talk, the Owl picks up there is an edge to this dinner, the men regretting they brought their wives along. A fishing extravaganza that put them back a few yards each, and they bring their wives when they'd rather get plotzed and bond.

Though square, they are nice average people, and Faloon hopes they're well insured so he's not going to feel bad about the coming night's *entreprise risquée*, his plan to whack their rooms out. Two weeks ago, while here on a previous dining experience, he made a clean play for the master key, slipping it off its hook long enough to wax it. He also checked a typical room, there was no nighter to secure the door from inside, just a security chain.

"And are you a sports fisher too?"

It's Eve Winters, she has finally become aware of his existence, maybe assuming the little owl-like creature to her left can't possibly be as boring as the other guy beside her, a condominium developer with a spiel of corny jokes. She is somewhere in her thirties, very tall and slender, ash blond, looking in good health – she has done the trail, Faloon overheard her say that, six gruelling days. Sports fisher, she's politically correct, a feminist.

3

"No, ma'am, I run a little lodge down the hill. Less expensive than this here establishment, but to be honest my food isn't as good."

The Owl is speaking of the Nitinat Lodge, which is on a back street in this two-bit town of Bamfield without much of a view, and mostly gets backpackers and low-rental weekenders. The Breakers Inn, looking over the Pacific Ocean, survives on its summer fat and still, in March, gets the fishers from Topeka or Indianapolis. And the way these tourists are spending tonight, that'll pay the chef's salary for the month. Faloon had to lay off his own cook for the off-season.

"But I would imagine you have a more exotic clientele." Eve Winters says in a clear, liquid voice, maybe so her other seatmate can get the point. She has marked down the condo developer as a chauvinist bore, with his story about the fisherman and the mermaid. What is interesting about this guy, to Faloon anyway, is that adding to the bulge of his size forty-eight kitchen is a thick moneybelt.

Faloon tells Eve Winters how he bought his small lodge a year and a half ago, and how he caters to hikers mostly; he likes vigorous outdoorspeople, finds them interesting. That gets this lovely creature talking about her six days on the West Coast Trail with three friends. He enjoys the refined way she expresses herself: "I had a sense of eternity out there, the wind in the pines, and the wild relentless surf."

It isn't easy to concentrate on tonight's job, Operation Breakers Inn, because he feels a little hypnotized by the soft grey eyes of Eve Winters, who doesn't take on sharp outline, she's like an Impressionist painting. The Owl, who is starting to wonder if he needs his eyes checked, senses her aura, a silver haze floating about her head. No makeup, but none needed, her face tanned gently by the wind and whatever sun you get this time of year on the West Coast. Dressed casually, jeans and light sweater.

Hardly anyone does the trail so early in spring, when it's still a swamp. This has meant a near-zero occupancy rate at the Nitinat since last fall, and by now, the final day of March, he is two months behind in his mortgage payments. His financial adviser, Freddy Jacoby, also his fence, warned him, you'll get three months' business max, maybe four if it don't piss in June. The Nitinat Lodge was his retirement program, cash in on the tourist trade, accommodate wayfarers in the middle of what turned out to be nowhere or, more accurately, the western shore of Vancouver Island – you can only get here by logging roads or the local packet freighter, the *Lady Rose*.

Eve Winters says she supposes he's walked the West Coast Trail many times, and he replies no, not once, and it's one of his greatest sorrows. A skiing accident prevented him from pursuing his passion for the outdoors, he gets along with two pins in his right leg. That isn't the honest truth, which is that the Owl doesn't like walking more than he has to. Faloon is an easy person to talk to, he brings people out – he's curious by nature, an information-gatherer. So he urges her on about how she found Bamfield "unspeakably funky" and stayed on for a week after her three girlfriends left on the *Lady Rose*.

What Faloon finds unspeakably funky about Bamfield, permanent population three hundred and something, is that it's almost useless to have a car – you take a water taxi to go anywhere, an inlet splits the town in two, and the terrain on this side is sort of impenetrable. This is the pretty side, though, West Bamfield, with its boardwalks rimming the shore, resorts and craft stores, eye-popping beaches a stroll away, but East Bamfield has the only saloon. The most attractive thing about the town, though, is the RCMP detachment is a couple of hours away by boat or car, in Port Alberni.

The lady lets drop that her full title is Dr. Eve Winters, and according to the card she gives him she has a Ph.D., her angle being something complicated, a "relationship analyst." He gets the impression he's supposed to have heard of her. And maybe he has, he remembers something in one of the papers, a weekly column with her picture, like Ann Landers. She's not staying here at the Breakers, but renting a cottage down by Brady Beach. The Owl assumes, without asking, that Dr. Winters is alone there. The Cotters' Cottage, locals call it, is owned by an old couple in East Bam.

"So tell me – is there any entertainment in town on a Friday night?"

The Owl has the fleeting thought that she's asking him for a date, but then he realizes how absurd that would be. April Fool's Day is tomorrow, maybe she's practising for it. Yet he plays with a daydream of escorting her to the Bam Pub, walking in, displaying her. This is quickly interrupted by an image of Claudette glaring from behind the bar. Claudette St. John, bold of tongue and broad of beam, is obtainable, achievable. Eve Winters is infinitely not.

He tells her there's a jazz quartet from Nanaimo at the Bam Pub, as the Owl and the other locals call it. She says she is a jazz aficionada, pronouncing that obscure word correctly, he assumes.

He explains bluntly, lest there be any confusion, that his girlfriend works in that bar, Claudette, and she'll be happy to know you met Nick Faloon and will make you feel at home. As he describes how to get the water taxi and find her way, Dr. Winters seems to be casing him, and this makes him uncomfortable. Does she read his mind, does she know things are getting on him, that he's been sleepwalking, that two nights ago he woke up outside the lodge in his underwear?

"How unfortunate that your friend, Claudette, isn't with you tonight."

He doesn't know how to take that – is he seen as cheesy, he doesn't take his girlfriend to this expensive restaurant? Or is that an opener, she wants to analyze their relationship. Maybe she divines it's been rocky lately with him and Claudette. He never should have made out with that logging-camp whore.

"Yeah, unhappily she works late on Fridays, and has to stay over in East Bamfield." Which has an upside, he won't have to explain to Claudette he was on a prowl tonight. "You go over there, you should introduce yourself, she'll protect you from the loggers that will be hitting on you."

He hopes Eve Winters sees that as more a compliment than suggestive, and apparently so, because she offers a smile with clean white teeth and thanks him. She passes on the dessert and rises. Many eyes are on her as she glides out.

With this leggy creature gone, some of the tension eases, the men stop preening, the wives relax, and another two bottles of wine are ordered. The Owl, who is on the dry tonight, is pleased that all eight are consuming to excess, though the downside is people get up at night to piss.

These tourists are of the capitalist class, the men ordering top-of-the-line Cabernet and Bordeaux, the women with their pearls and gold bracelets, and they all came in by chartered plane. He is taking a calculated risk having dinner with them – though Sergeant Flynn will try to finger him anyway – but he has to take stock of these prospective customers, see if the game is worth the play, find out what rooms they're staying in – which he's already done, he scanned the registry.

In the meantime he's still feeling remorseful – he'd sworn to go straight after becoming a local businessman. He isn't one to mire himself in guilt, despite the fourteen catches on his sheet, and never mind the ones he beat. But he's got to square the bank, he's being forced out of retirement to do so.

When the Owl says something complimentary to the waiter about the sockeye steak, the man opposite says that what Faloon just ate was caught by him this morning. It turns out this guy is a retired insurance exec, and the Owl admits he's retired too, running a little inn nearby.

"What did you do before that?" The tone says he's not really interested.

Faloon says, "Jewellery."

He thinks about entertaining him, telling him the secrets of knowing a good stone. The Owl had been a class jewel thief in his prime, once ranked as number seven in the world. But loose lips sink ships, and it is time for Nick Faloon to leave, and he says his adieus, pays his bill, and Mr. and Mrs. Galloway wave him goodbye at the door.

The best rooms at the Breakers Inn are on the third floor, with balcony views of ocean, beach, and craggy outcroppings that are worth the extra they charge, and it is here that all the Topekans are staying. From where he's hiding, a darkened alcove with mops and brooms, the Owl can hear muffled snores. He's been crouching here for two hours, after slipping back into the Breakers while the hosts were serving Kahlua and coffee.

He checked out this alcove a few weeks ago, his last visit here, when he excused himself for the john. That's when he got hold of the master, palming it into soft wax. He took a couple of days off, down to Vancouver, where Iggie Nichols ground out a dupe in his shop and got paid with five bottles of cognac the Owl deep-pocketed from a liquor store.

The Owl is hoping he has retained his touch. A hot prowl holds out many perils for a fifty-four-year-old, out-of-practice thief armed only with latex gloves and Hush Puppies. Even if the play runs smooth, the Owl will be the first object of suspicion – Sergeant Flynn will have him immediately in mind. That was the one glitch in assembling a new life – Jasper Flynn showed up last year from Alberni to smell him out. "You cause any trouble, I'll flatten you like roadkill." That was fair, and to Faloon's great shock the cop didn't spread the word there was a felon in everyone's midst, not to mention his conviction for sexual assault, the serious kind they used to call rape.

Nick Faloon will do a long bounce if this caper doesn't pan out, worse maybe than the ten-spot he drew on that rape because of a cold-blooded but brilliant liar. That was a career-threatening event, it caused the Owl to lose faith in the justice system. His lawyer, the great Arthur Ramsgate Beauchamp, looked so dejected that Faloon had to cheer him up, reminding Mr. Beauchamp he got him off about a dozen real beefs, he was due, things balance out.

The Owl did the fat six years before parole kicked in, worked his tail off to build another stake, a European tour where his French is handy, hitting five-star hotel rooms, jewellery shops, working with two stalls, sometimes three. Over time he retained some gorgeous women to stall for him, Cat McAllister the all-time titleholder, her shtick being to hike her skirt, adjust her stockings, and the sales manager has his eyes on her thighs as the key to the display case disappears.

He was famous for his stagecraft, his detailed set-ups. Like that time in Beverly Hills – he showed up at a gem store as a window cleaner in white coveralls, with ladder, buckets, and squeegees, the staff paying no attention, the blowtorch below their field of vision anyway. When you heat those plate windows, a linoleum knife cuts through them like cheese, a neat hole bypassing the alarm. A mechanic's claw does the rest.

Faloon wonders if he's still the class act for which he gained fame in some of the best circles, the hotel industry, the insurance industry, Interpol. A spontaneous actor, he always had a gift of the gab and the bluff. Your eyes can give you away, you can't jerk, you got to have flow. It's all angles, reaching in under the salesgirl's arm, or the high-low trick when there's a tall case: "I'd like to see that piece," and the clerk reaches up and you grab from below. Timing is everything, and little edges like garlic on your breath. When all plans fail, you got to be able to wing it. Your feet are the last line of defence.

But in the end it's the fence who gets the hog, which is why Freddy Jacoby is always ready to pay Faloon's legal bills, to return him to the street, so the Owl can pay off his debt, a vicious circle.

It is half past one as he emerges from the alcove, half past one on what is now April Fool's Day, maybe a good omen, maybe bad, he isn't sure. He should wait until they are in deep sleep, but he's antsy, primed.

Only the hall light is on, a wall fixture, and he reaches up and twists the bulb loose and lets his eyes adjust to the darkness. He chooses door number five – the twirl inserts cleanly and the bolt releases with a soft thud. The door opens a few inches before the security chain takes hold. He loops an elastic band onto it, jiggles it free. He waits a minute or two, then enters. Light dimly penetrates from outside, below, where the Galloways always keep the porch lamp on.

The male sleeper is on his back, smelling of Cabernet, snoring, his partner curled on her side. He remembers her – a pushed-up bosom graced by a strand of shimmering pearls. And here they are, hanging from the dresser mirror, brazenly set out for the Owl – and for alternate eveningwear, a gold necklace with matching earrings. He'll pass, though, he is more interested in the trousers hanging from a chair. In the wallet, he finds about six U.S. large. He pockets a couple, returns the wallet, and quietly exits.

It never pays in Faloon's business to give in to greed. Enough to piece off the whining bank and get himself square, that's all the contributions he's seeking. Sometimes they don't notice, they shake their heads and ask themselves, "Did we blow that much?" Sometimes they blame the staff. Sometimes they don't complain to the cops, they don't want to be hauled back here for a trial.

Hitting the next two rooms, Faloon finds more heavy sleepers and has no trouble with the wallets, and manages to triple his score – six grand is already a good night's work.

When he enters the final room, silently closing the door, making out the shapes, he becomes aware something is amiss. That something is an absent condominium developer, Coolidge is his name, the guy who turned off Eve Winters with his lack of charm, the guy with the heavy moneybelt. The wife is alone in the bed, no sounds from the bathroom, which is dark.

He is frozen in mid-step. The teller of bad jokes is out on a walking tour of Bamfield? Fishing for salmon at two in the morning? He listens for footsteps in the hall, hears nothing. A quick look about reveals no poke in view anyway, obviously he took his moneybelt.

But now he sees a strap of, possibly, that very moneybelt peeking out from under a headless pillow. The Owl does some instant calculations – a developer, Coolidge occasionally chances on some tax-free cash, takes a fishing vacation in Canada to fritter it away, stashes his earnings under his pillow for his late-night ramble because he isn't going to risk being mugged.

He advances, gently clouts the moneybelt from under the pillow. It's thick with notes – a quick riffle hints at close to fifty Ks, an unexpected bonanza. Figuring this is dirty money and its loss may not be reported, Faloon yields to temptation and takes half. He replaces the belt and floats out, down the hall, down the stairs, out the back door into the rain.

And just in time. Coming up the walk is Coolidge, huddled into a slicker. Faloon crouches behind a garbage bin. When he peeks around it, the guy is just standing there, swaying a little, like he's drunk. Then he makes his way to the front door.

Faloon waits thirty seconds, then slips away with the night's profits, thirty-one big ones in a zip-lock bag. The whole operation has taken half an hour, and at 2 a.m. he is on the winding path down from the Breakers Inn. The village is dark except for street lamps and the Marine

Sciences Centre across the inlet. It's raining hard, but that's not a particularly rare phenomenon on these great Pacific shores.

There's a fine view from here in the day, you can see the way the bay opens up to Barkley Sound, and the Deer Islands, and the green humps of hills rolling down into the endless sea, and even now there's enough ambient light so the Owl can make out the merging misty shapes, the promontories that anchor the beaches, the white-flecked breakers.

Partway down, he detours fifty yards into the bush and stashes his profits in a hole beneath the root of a cedar tree that he'd hollowed out for this contingency. After covering the opening with rocks and dirt and leaves, he returns to the path.

The way you get from the Breakers to the Nitinat Lodge is by a forested trail, then you branch to the left where the Brady Beach sign shows under a street lamp. And quickly you come upon a cozy log building with four small rooms and a couple of cabins that leak. This property is about the first thing the Owl ever paid for. Going straight has turned out to be a disaster.

He makes for the back door of his darkened building, then pauses, wondering if Eve Winters, the jazz aficionada, enjoyed herself at the Bam Pub tonight. Maybe he should stroll down to Cotters' Cottage and ask her about that. Just a thought.

2

The Owl rises at nine, weary but okay, and decides to stroll down to the Clayoquot Café for a cappuccino, this being a Saturday routine. The rain has settled to a soft mist, and fog shrouds the slopes of hemlock and cedar, strands of it drifting among the warehouses and docks across the way in East Bam, settling on the saltchuck, where fishing boats work their way out of the inlet.

No one's around the landing pier, so he tosses the plastic gloves into the water, weighted with the duplicate key and some rocks. From there it's a two-minute walk to the canopied deck of the Clayoquot. A tree-huggers' coffee bar, with rustic willow-wand chairs, tables outside with umbrellas.

Usually he meets a few friends here, hippies, Greenpeaceniks, a community that for some reason has latched onto the Owl, finding him droll. One such person, who helps with whale-watching tours, is Bill Links, a stringy ponytailed guy, and he asks if Faloon has heard about the robbery. "Someone at the Breakers had forty grand lifted from his moneybelt last night."

The Owl tries not to show emotion, but is chagrined that his night's work has so quickly become the day's news. He raises the coffee mug to his lips, feels the hot liquid slide down his throat, wipes the foam from his lips. Maybe he should have realized a guy who sleeps with his moneybelt checks it every morning. Forty grand? The developer wildly exaggerated his loss.

The law is already here from Alberni – Bill Links points to the RCMP boat moored at the coast guard dock. The Owl expresses eager interest in the matter, and Links says he was talking to Mrs. Galloway, who rang the bulls after a firestorm of complaints from her peeved guests – they seemed to think management was to blame, someone had to have a key.

They speculate for a while it was an inside job, maybe the new waiter, maybe the girl who cleans for them. Bill Links doesn't know the Owl is a retired outlaw, but soon the whole town will know, because Sergeant Jasper Flynn knows.

Though rankled by the burden of hassles to come, he'll brazen it out – there's nothing to hang on him but the coincidence of having dined at the Breakers. But Jasper Flynn, figuring nothing will stick, might want to act out that roadkill scenario. At best, Faloon would be ridden out of town, at worst ridden over, with permanent tire marks on his ass.

As he's settling his mind to that dire prospect, he observes a commotion racing up the boardwalk in the form of Meredith Broadfeather, a militant of the Huu-ay-aht Nation, her hair flying, her arms waving, and she is yelling, and matters turn monumentally serious as Faloon finally makes her words out: "There's been a murder at Brady Beach!"

Faloon's heart stalls, then starts pounding, as Meredith pulls up puffing, catching her breath. Now she is supposed to yell, "April Fool!" but she doesn't, she shouts a name: Eve Winters, a doctor from Vancouver. "I saw her," she says, trembling – she is in almost as bad a state as Faloon, except that he's hiding it. Raped and murdered, Meredith says in a shocked voice.

A strange feeling comes over him, partly anguish, partly a premonition of doom, but also something heavy and confusing. He listens with no show of emotion to the tale told by Meredith Broadfeather.

She saw Jasper Flynn and two other cops heading by foot down the Brady Beach Road, and out of curiosity went with them to Cotters' Cottage. She looked through the bedroom window before they could stop her – Eve Winters's naked body was on a bed, and it looked like something white was stuffed in her mouth, it might have been her panties. The cops suspect the same guy who ripped off those Americans. Sergeant Jasper Flynn has summoned Forensics from Alberni, by float plane, and more cops are arriving by road.

The Owl does his magic disappearing act, takes the wooden staircase up to the back street, to his lodge, trying not to seem in a hurry. He's not sure what he'll do, he's in a fog of anxiety.

His four rental units are on the main floor, and Faloon keeps the upper storey to himself, his bedroom and a kind of den and his own bath. He stares at his reflection in the mirror above the sink, and for a moment isn't sure what he's looking at – this can't be him, the former seventh-best jewel thief in the world, it's someone else. He thinks about posing as French, but he hasn't got good papers. He decides on Gertrude. He'll be a Dutch tourist.

He shaves off his moustache and goes over his face once again, then hauls out the trunk with his favourite old getups. He weeds through the women's outfits – dresses, skirts, blouses, flared jeans, hairpieces, bras with felt padding, and he is having trouble deciding despite the urgency. He was arrested in a dress once, after a heist in Barcelona, so he can only pray these local bulls are not as sharp-eyed. He opts for the outdoors look, the jeans with the padding around the hips and bottom, a denim shirt, an orange scarf for flair.

He paints his lips, combs out the brunette wig with the bangs and sticks it on, then fills a backpack with food from the fridge. Frazzled, he almost forgets the passport, Gertrude Heeredam from The Hague. Other items are stuck in the pages, a driver's licence, a health card, quality material crafted by Nellie Chin at her backdoor shop in Vancouver's Chinatown.

He transfers money from his wallet to the pack, half a yard and change. He finds Dr. Winters's card she gave him last night, rips it, flushes it. He pulls on a pair of boots that he hardly ever wears, then peers out the window, sees no one, and heads out, taking the staircase down, not even thinking about trying to collect the stashed loot.

He is thinking more clearly now, but is horrified by pictures that come to him of Dr. Eve Winters being raped, shoved off, she was a class person, beautiful, with breeding and a good turn of phrase. He remembers how she had a sense of eternity on the West Coast Trail. He remembers how she didn't sneer down at him, how she preferred him to the condo developer, Coolidge.

And what was *he* doing out at two in the morning? On a hot prowl of his own? Faloon remembers how he was rubbernecking at Dr. Winters, trying to come on.

The Owl is in danger of being poked in the eye twice by the fickle finger of fate. He was already done once for a serious beef he didn't commit, and he isn't about to test the accuracy of the justice system this time. He's not going to stick around on a gamble that the heat has another target, that they're on to Coolidge already, or some wrong character she picked up at the pub, a drifter. Which might have happened if she didn't follow Faloon's advice to strike up with Claudette.

Near the bottom of the stairs, he almost runs into Hattie Mills coming out of her gallery in a hurry, but she doesn't give him much of a look and dashes past. The disguise works with others too, on the boardwalk, where there's a buzz, people standing outside their shops, conversing.

Fortunately, the water taxi has just tied up at one of the lodges, but when he heads that way he suddenly staggers to a stop. Getting off is someone he knows too well, Claudette St. John, with two friends, all talking loudly about the murder. As she glances at him, he turns his face, but no damage is done, she ignores him.

He gets into the outboard, hiding under his rain cape, as the women race off. Now he's feeling hope, once he gets across the water he's on the road out, though he has more sense than to try for his beat-up Impala, parked behind the motel. He'll flag a ride, a middle-aged lady hitchhiker who's just done the West Coast Trail stands a chance of getting to Nanaimo today, maybe in time for the last Vancouver ferry.

It's sprinkling again as the boat furrows slowly to the government dock. He wonders if he should call Beauchamp from a pay phone to tell him of his unhappy predicament, but remembers he retired from the courts to be a gentleman farmer.

He tries to piece together the likely chain of events: this morning, the developer awakes to find his moneybelt half as heavy as it should be, and wonders if it's an April Fool's joke in bad taste. On conferring with his colleagues, he learns they also suffered losses. The RCMP race over here, question the Galloways and their staff, and the names come up of the two extra guests for dinner. For some inexplicable reason, the feet look for Dr. Winters first instead of honing in on the prime suspect.

The boat collides softly with the bumpers on the dock, and Faloon puffs up the hill past the Bamfield Trails Motel and the smattering of shops, and gains the road to Pachena Bay, a click and a half away – that's where he intends to start hitching, as if he's just come off the trail.

His feet are soon sore – he is not used to these boots, they are stiff with lack of use. There's not much traffic, none going his way except for one barrelling logging truck, working overtime on a Saturday. Then he hears the siren, and it's an RCMP four-wheel running hot, tearing up the mud and gravel. Cold-looking faces stare at him from the windows, but the vehicle speeds on.

He is limping as he takes in a spectacular view of Pachena Bay, a flat beach a half-mile long at the foot of a long Pacific funnel. Pachena is also the northern terminus of the West Coast Trail, or what is called Shipwreck Trail for the many wooden vessels lost on the rocks out there, but the Owl's only interest right now is the old logging road that will get him to the safety of a city. He detours through the shore shrubbery to the beach, where he gets a long view up the road as it bends east into the mountains. There, to his dismay, he sees a road-block. A cruiser straddles the highway, a couple of uniforms checking out a campervan for possible escaping perpetrators.

Faloon retreats to the refuge of a makeshift shelter some hippies must have built from driftwood. Here he stares out at the deserted beach, at the churning clouds breaking apart above the ocean, and then he sets out, slogging through the understory of third-growth timber and clumps of bracken and salal. When he finally ventures near the road again, his feet are killing him. But a warming sun has broken through, and he is maybe half a mile beyond the roadblock.

He begins to thumb, and as luck would have it, the first vehicle stops – it's a Crown Zellerbach crew cab, a bearded, burly sixty-something driving, a foreman probably, a bull of the woods.

Faloon climbs in and says in a husky voice, just breathing the words, "Thanks you. I speaks not good English." He throws his pack behind the seat, beside a chainsaw and tools and a six-pack of Canadian.

The driver pulls back onto the road. "You just come off the trail? Where you from?"

"Der Nederland. Gertrude."

Folks around here call him Grizzly, he says, and Faloon can see why. He carries on about how he's a yard supervisor, and he's going to Lake Cowichan. Faloon says, "Thanks you." He means it, Cowichan is a fair-sized town with a bus station.

Faloon is hoping his poor English will discourage conversation, but Grizzly needs to talk, explaining – slowly, so Gertrude can follow – how he doesn't normally pick up hitchhikers because of company policy, but a lady by herself could be in danger here. "You talk to police at roadblock?" He is speaking Tarzan English so Gertrude can understand.

"Yah, very bad happening."

He nods. "They say the killer did many other crimes. His name is Faloon, small man but strong like a cougar. He is crazy." He wiggles an index finger at his head. "Psycho sex fiend."

The Owl sits rigidly as Grizzly describes in this basic English what he would do to Faloon if he had his way, slime like him should be castrated before some slippery lawyer gets him off on a technicality. But after an hour of not receiving much response, Grizzly peters out, enabling the Owl to relax a little as he pretends to sleep.

They follow rivers along the way, raging in the spring, they pass by tree farms and clear-cuts, the sun pulling mists from ditches and road pools. The Owl is starting to see hope rising too. He could slip over to Vancouver, hide himself in the bowels of the east side, maybe call a good mouth who doesn't sell out clients. He will inquire if the horsemen found someone else's prints or DNA, and if not he will seek greener pastures. Again comes·an image of that fine-looking woman in death, but he quickly blots it out.

Though his eyes are closed, he senses Grizzly reaching behind for something, hears the hiss of beer as a cap is unscrewed, a gurgle, a belch. Thankfully this old bull, with his dangerous views on castration, doesn't have great powers of observation, and the Owl is gaining in optimism.

So far, this has been a miracle escape, right out of a war movie, he crossed the enemy lines and he's already planning for the future. He'll try for a couple of quick scores in Vancouver and elsewhere, enough to get out of the country. Europe probably or some enlightened land where the cops suck up to tourists, maybe Greece or Turkey or Lebanon, where he emigrated from as a child.

On the other side of the Nitinat bridge, Grizzly pulls off, asking the Owl to excuse him, he has to relieve himself. The sight of water gushing over rocks and waterfalls forces Faloon to recognize the same compelling urge, and he climbs from the passenger side and goes behind a tree.

Tired, consumed by worry, he forgets he's Gertrude Heeredam, and instead of squatting, he pulls out his oscar while standing, letting go a hot arcing stream. He is not quite finished when he glances up and sees Grizzly staring at him from behind a salmonberry bush across the road, his mouth agape, an expression that turns to rage as Faloon hurriedly tucks in.

Fearing an episode of curbside justice, Faloon sprints to the idling crew cab, clambers behind the wheel, locks the driver's door, shifts, spits rocks. But now Grizzly is right on him, at the side of the truck, and he feels a lurch as he vaults into the back.

The Owl is convinced now that fate has it in for him this April Fool's Day. What a chump, with his mental meltdown. He's afraid his rider will try to kick in the rear window and strangle the cross-dressing psycho sex fiend, or maybe grab the chainsaw and decapitate him. But Grizzly doesn't seem ready to do these things, just glaring at him from the rear-view, sitting on a sheet of plywood, nursing an elbow he banged.

The road is winding and ribbed with ridges, so Faloon can't pour the juice on, but he doesn't dare slow. He can keep going until he runs out of gas, and then the yard super will castrate him. As the road dips by the river, he dares a risky play, slowing almost to a stop so Grizzly can maybe drop the tailgate and clamber out, deciding not to be brave, content to be left alone on the road and not take chances with a psycho killer. But Grizzly doesn't move, and there's even an evil smile on his face, as if he knows what Faloon is up to.

Getting up speed again, he sees shimmering blue waters in the distance, log rafts assembled on it, and the road descends until it comes to a fork by the western lip of Cowichan Lake. When he rounds a curve, he is suddenly aware of flashing lights, officers lounging beside a blinking cruiser – another roadblock.

This he greets with mixed emotions, almost welcoming the sight of an officer furiously waving him to stop – horsemen do not as a rule remove your body parts. As the Owl brakes, he turns fatalistic, this has not been his day, not at all. He switches off the engine and listens to Grizzly, outside, loudly ratting on him.

When a constable approaches him to seek clarification of these accusations, he rolls down his window and produces Gertrude Heeredam's driver's licence.

"You make an ugly woman, Faloon," he says.

3

With envy, Arthur Beauchamp watches juncos mating in the raspberry patch. A bumblebee tests a daffodil. There is lust in his garden, spring's vitality. Maybe his sap will start flowing again too, and the lazy lout below will rise from flaccid hibernation. The desire is there, but the equipment faulty. When was his last erection — a month ago? A half-hearted attempt at takeoff. But he knows he must accept and move on. We age, faculties rust. Some men lose their hair. In compensation, Arthur has kept his, a thick grey thatch.

No one is around — Margaret is at one of her interminable Save Gwendolyn meetings — so he's unembarrassed to rasp, to no recognizable tune, the song of Autolycus: "April, the sweet o' the year, when the merry daffodils appear." He mangles the verse. His memory has begun to wear at the edges, like his coveralls. There was a time when he could trumpet, even when in his cups, in that former wasted life, the entire madrigal.

He lays down his trowel, straightens, his back creaking like a rusting gate. Is it the somnolent country life that brings on this decay? Yet he is only sixty-eight. Doc Dooley, who holds the secret of Arthur's high cholesterol and balky heart, is eighty-five and runs in the Garibaldi Island marathon. Run, jog, walk, he orders, and if you can do little else, wobble.

He closes the garden gate, washes his hands by the tap behind his country house — two storeys, 1920s gingerbread — and contemplates playing hooky with rod and reel. Below the house, where mown grass gives way to white-scrubbed drift logs and the rippled wash of Blunder Bay, his outboard beckons from his sagging dock.

But no, he must hike, must stay faithful to Doc Dooley's regimen, a mile and a quarter up Potter's Road and down Centre Road to Hopeless Bay, to load his rucksack with mail, skim milk, olive oil, and . . . what else was on Margaret's list? Three tomatoes and two lemons. No need to write everything down.

She is keeping him on a strict diet. She blames herself for the minor stroke he suffered two years ago, attributing it to her over-bounteous table. "Eat light, Beauchamp, and avoid fats," said Doc Dooley.

He skirts the upper pasture to look for holes in the cedar fence. Occasionally, and by no evident means, the goats escape under, over, or through it — wise locals drive carefully along Potter's Road. Some thirty kids are expected at Blunder Bay Farm — Margaret has a way of knowing these things — so it will be a busy month. Other residents include chickens, geese, a horse called Barney, Slappy the dog, and a pair of cats named Shiftless and Underfoot.

The path descends to an alder bottom, then rises to a dry fir forest before joining the road. He is puffing a little, his nostrils filled with the soft scents of a pleasant spring day.

Avoid stress. Another of Doc Dooley's prescriptions. Isn't that why he fled to Garibaldi Island? To escape the city's ferment, the law's wounding duels? He was fat and foundering, lonely and ill, about to be divorced by a faithless wife. Arthur is a farmer now, he hasn't seen the inside of a courtroom for half a dozen years. Life has taken on a rosier hue since he fell in love with Garibaldi Island, then, just as quickly, with his neighbour, Margaret Blake, organic farmer, environmental activist.

She gave him eyes to see nature's artistry after six decades of city blindness, when gazing at concrete, not conifers, at shop windows, not still ponds, seemed the natural way of humankind. Arthur's milieu was more conservative than conservationist. "Let's save *this* environment," a fellow member of the Confederation Club once chortled.

But rural life comes with its cracks and stains. For one, he didn't anticipate living with Margaret would be so hectic. For three of their five years together, she served as Garibaldi's elected trustee, volatile, disputatious, scaring people with her gingery tongue. Now her ire is focused on the proposed development at Gwendolyn Bay, its threatened deforestation. On that issue, this is an island divided. Friendships have been broken in heated debate at permit hearings. Locals driving by still wave, but many no longer smile.

Arthur's annual pursuit of tomatoes, carrots, and cabbage has kindled in him a love of green and growing things, refreshed each spring with the new life about him. He supposes he's an environmentalist, but sees it as a lost cause, the earth warming, overpopulating, racing toward one of those messy epochal crossroads, maybe another mass extinction. Arthur would rather not think about this. He imagines there's not much one can do about it. There's no one to take to court. The whole thing lacks the sweet simplicity of a murder trial, a clean verdict at the end, freedom or punishment.

He sees two more houses being framed on Centre Road, view sites snapped up by weekenders from the city, the island changing too quickly, its population doubling in six years. The loudest supporters of the Gwendolyn development are these new people, who want "progress" and "conveniences," who lug to the country as much of the city as they can, SUVs and gas barbecues and lawn mowers. Arthur has to forgive them. He too was a newcomer, he didn't understand rural things – though he had a sense there was more to life than starting off the day in a crowded elevator at parking level five.

He suspects it's unfair to deny others the right to live here, to pull up the drawbridge. He doesn't know how anyway, it's beyond him, it's politics. Arthur is not a political person, not a joiner. Alcoholics Anonymous on Tuesdays, Tai Chi irregularly on Thursdays, bit roles with the Garibaldi Players, that's his limited social docket. He leaves high matters of state to Margaret, who is a member of some twenty groups, Farmers' Institute, Garibaldi Protection Society, Library

Board, Parks Commission, Field Naturalists . . . When does she stop?

Across the road, just past the ferry turnoff, a pixie is hitchhiking – it's the third time he's seen her in the last several days – olive-skinned, big mischievous eyes, wide mouth, a classic beauty. A different kind of newcomer, a hippie, the kind you see at demonstrations. Spiked hair. Denim jacket with peace symbols and a Cuban flag. A smile and a wave, which he tentatively answers, a tip of his hand to his John Deere cap.

As he chuffs up the rise below Breadloaf Hill, he sees about thirty vehicles parked by the community hall. The Save Gwendolyn Society. He thinks he hears Margaret's voice exhorting action. Yes, there is her aging spaniel, Slappy, listening at the door, ears perked. Arthur hopes no one will see him slip past, he doesn't want to be dragged in there. He doesn't even want to think about Gwendolyn Valley. There's nothing these people can do about saving it.

Todd Clearihue, the boyish ever-smiling developer, speeds by in his Audi convertible, honks, waves. Beside him is the pixie. She waves too. Clearihue is the president of Garibaldi Lands Inc., which has title to Gwendolyn Valley. Margaret calls him a sociopath.

Coming into view, where the road descends to the docks of Hopeless Bay, is the General Store, *circa* 1904, paint peeling from the boards of its high-windowed false front. A flatbed pulls away, three men in the cab with takeout coffees, and as they pass by, Arthur reads the logo: Gulf Sustainable Logging. They are strangers and do not wave. Maybe they were offended by the notice posted by the door: "Chainsaws must be left in your truck. We are not responsible."

The store (Abraham Makepeace, proprietor) connects to a warehouse on piles, and groans within of groceries, tools, and the various odds and sods that support civilization on this cranky island. It also serves as post office (Abraham Makepeace, postmaster), coffee lounge, and, ever since the Brig Tavern burned down, illegal source of spirits (Abraham Makepeace, bootlegger).

Staring out the windows of the enclosed porch are several local idlers in their tractor caps, work shirts, and patched jeans. The porch serves as a lounge, chairs in haphazard array around a wood-fired Jøtul, coffee in the pot, an honour jar heavy with dollar coins. Arthur exchanges greetings, obligatory remarks on the weather, and steps up to the mail counter.

Makepeace, tall, skeletal, the face of a depressive bloodhound, is slow to hand him the mail, a final possessive inspection of letters and magazines. "Your subscription to this here *London Review of Books* is due. Bill from the vet. An offer from a phone company, they want to give us the Internet on local calls. They say we can't live without it."

"Who says?"

"Well, practically everyone."

"I have lived sixty-eight years without it."

Makepeace too has been slow to catch up to the electronic revolution, last year buying his first fax machine, a dollar a page to send or receive. But he's debt-ridden from tabs unpaid. He is fatalistic about the Gwendolyn development, which will include an efficient store, with chrome and fluorescent lighting and grocery buggies. A beer-and-wine outlet, a restaurant and bar, a real-estate office.

Makepeace pulls the island weekly, *The Bleat*, from Arthur's mail slot and folds it open to the letters page. "Guess you want to read Margaret's latest." Arthur pats his pockets for his reading glasses, he remembered to bring them.

"'Pirates,' she calls them." This is Baldy Johansson, the terminally unemployed electrician, who has got up for a refill. "That ain't so bad, but 'ecological Nazis' – ain't that carrying it too far? Can't they charge her for slander, Arthur?"

Arthur must regularly parry such elusive questions of law, has found ways to divert them. "There's no law against hyperbole." Arthur can tell no one quite understands that word.

The Bleat, renamed from *The Echo* as a salute to the island's many sheep farmers, causes Arthur anxiety when it appears, usually about midweek. Its editor seems not to have heard of the laws of libel, and makes no effort to restrain his most regular correspondent. This latest letter of Margaret's seems inflammatory to excess, "environmental wrecking crew" being the epithet most softly put. She has already been warned by Garibaldi Lands Inc. (locally known as Garlinc) that "remedial" action might be taken. The horrors of a defamation trial.

"That there wife of yours is pissing in the wind," says Ernie Priposki, the alcoholic farmhand. "They own the land, they can do what they want with it, ain't that the law, Arthur?"

"People have rights in this fair and democratic land. Trees do not."

"Can't stop progress."

Arthur pours himself a coffee, turns to the front page, the main story, under the byline of Nelson Forbish, publisher, editor, and entire workforce. "It is rumoured that logging of Gwendolyn Bay is to begin this week, which has caused foment on our beautiful island."

A smiling photograph of Todd Clearihue (lately seen zooming by with the hitching pixie) in close embrace with Island Trustee Kurt Zoller, who is brandishing a cheque. "Garlinc boss donates $300,000 for new fire truck."

"You got to look on the good side," Priposki says. "It means jobs, there's a lot of guys out of work on this rock. Garlinc ain't doing a clear-cut, they're going to leave some trees, people want their lots to be nice. I'll have another little hit."

Makepeace brings out a bagged bottle, pours a dollop of rum into Priposki's coffee. "Not you, Arthur, I suppose."

"Thank you, no." He catches a whiff of alcohol and tenses.

"Blame the government," says Jeff "Gomer" Goulet, the crab fisher. "They could've made it a park."

Garlinc paid $8 million for Gwendolyn Valley, an estate sale, the land sold too quickly, before anyone could object. Margaret organized petitions, besieged Ottawa to add Gwendolyn Valley to the scatter of lands composing the Gulf Islands National Park. All to nought.

"No government's got no business seizing nobody's private land." A heroic triple negative from Baldy Johansson. "We got rights, don't we, Arthur?"

"I didn't know you owned land, Baldy."

"Well, if I did."

Arthur buys a two-day-old *Vancouver Sun*, sits down with his coffee, spreads the front page open. Immediately a story catches his eye: "CROWN SEEKS PSYCH HEARING FOR RAPE-MURDER SUSPECT." Below that, a related article: "FRIENDS MOURN DEATH OF DR. WINTERS." Her photograph, blond, smiling, attractive. But it's another photo that holds him, a forlorn face in a police cruiser.

Nick the Owl Faloon. How could this be? Arthur dares not count the times he defended this mannerly rascal, and a deep sadness comes. He doesn't want to read further, not now, so he quickly finishes his coffee and makes his purchases.

He decides to return home by the Gwendolyn Bluffs, though that means a long detour, at least another hour. But it might be the last time he will see this valley clothed in green. They plan a hundred and fifty lots with, according to the glossy handout, "driveways, power, cable, sewer, and water in." There will be a resort, shoreline condos. To attract city commuters, a hovercraft service.

Though the trail to Gwendolyn Bay crosses private land, the owners, the Sproules, are well-regarded old-timers who resist the blandishments of the fly-by-night loggers who infest these islands. They allow Garibaldians to use it, but the secret is kept from uncountrified visitors who tend to leave gates open or tramp on the chocolate lilies. The path also provides clandestine entry into upper Gwendolyn Valley, its lovely pond.

Arthur feels winded but in no distress as he climbs from sheep pastures into dense cedar forest, to a mossy mesa with thick-waisted Douglas firs, a swirling ballet of green-leafed arbutus, groves of Garry oaks, twisted and fat of bud. Below, through gaps, can be seen the rocky beach and the strait, and beyond, the perilously close shores of vast, busy Vancouver Island.

As he nears the Garlinc property – ill-protected by rusting fence wire – he hears a distant hammering, and wonders if a crew is already working on the road access. The valley is guarded on either side by high rock faces, and the only opening, known as Gwendolyn Gap, or just the Gap, is too narrow for a road. But the developers have been given a blasting permit. Arthur shudders, recoils from the ugliness of it, of man and his machines and his explosive devices.

He exerts himself over one last rise, takes in a soul-shuddering view of valley, sea, and distant snow-coned mountains, and realizes he has forgotten to buy lemons. What causes this Lethean forgetfulness?

Maybe it's the bizarre murder charge against Nick Faloon, churning darkly in his mind.

He sits on the grass against a boulder, a cautious twenty feet from the lip of the precipice above the Gap. He pulls out the newspaper and his glasses and his old Peterson bent, and as he stuffs it with tobacco, he looks down upon Gwendolyn Pond at the buffleheads and mallards gliding among the water lilies. He is overcome by a feeling of helplessness.

Living in the country, living with Margaret, has connected him with the earth in ways that remain elusive, made him aware that an ancient, more beautiful time is gone. Forever, he fears. He can't see the Save Gwendolyn Society preserving even this tiny speck of the planet.

"Don't get yourself tangled in politics on this crazy island, Beauchamp," Doc Dooley counselled. "It's an invitation to the grave."

Arthur lights up, reads a précis of events in a sleepy outport four days ago – dubbed by the press the April Fool's Day murder. Several sports fishers robbed, Dr. Winters raped, choked to death on her own underwear. He had heard nothing on the radio, but it is regularly tuned to classical music. He won't have a television set.

The victim of this slaying is "a well-known psychologist and relationship therapist" whom he vaguely remembers smiling at him from the newspapers, a syndicated column, *Doctor Eve*. Indeed, he admits to having furtively read her advice. She was no pseudo-expert in the manner of Ann Landers, held a Ph.D. in counselling psychology.

"Nicholas Faloon, 54, proprietor of a local inn, was arrested while attempting to flee the area dressed as a woman." This seems a Faloonish touch. He insisted, on being arraigned, that his name was Gertrude Heeredam, and demanded a Dutch interpreter. Thus the psychiatric assessment.

It is inconceivable that Faloon will pull this off. Has he not got a lawyer? Arthur wonders if he should urge a friend to take on his case, someone competent, experienced.

He looks away from the newspaper, listens again to the sound of hammering. Probably a woodpecker. Clouds, wet and gloomy, are rolling in. A kingfisher chatters by the pond. Two bald eagles make lazy loops above him, then one sails toward a perch on a Douglas fir. He makes out a clump of twigs there: an old nest.

He returns to his newspaper. "Sources say Faloon is known to the police." That seems an understatement. Faloon is a kleptomaniac who, in brave acceptance of his disability, put his compulsion to profitable use from an early age. Arthur first acted for him in a juvenile case involving a missing box of rare comic books.

Faloon's last trial, the rape, still causes acid to burn in Arthur's gut, the low point of his courtroom career, the only wrongful conviction to besmirch his forty-year record. Ten years for a sexual assault Faloon did not commit. Arthur invariably rejected consent rape defences, the defendant often a brute, the woman twice victimized. But this mild-mannered thief would be as likely to attack a woman as a pumpkin to sprout wings and fly.

Arthur still takes on the burden of the failed defence, excoriates himself. He didn't penetrate the armour of the complainant, Adeline Angella, an attention-seeking magazine writer who tearfully described to a jury how an interview with a celebrated jewel thief evolved into a rape extorted by a knife to her throat.

Angella sent out a plea to Women Against Violence to fill the court. Who in that hostile arena was going to believe that Nick Faloon succumbed to Angella's lure? Arthur wasn't able to put a firm finger on her motive for making a false complaint. Publicity? Profit? After the trial and appeal, her blunt account of her courtroom ordeal appeared in a major women's monthly.

The article in the *Sun* quotes Staff Sergeant Jasper Flynn: "The theory we're working on is the victim met her fate after resisting an intruder intent on robbing her." "Met her fate" – a shy euphemism from a veteran cop. He declined to say whether anything was stolen from her. How absurd to think Faloon would engineer a lucrative robbery of hotel rooms, then compromise his success by targeting, in the dead of night, a visiting psychologist. But that seems the official view.

Surely, he's again a victim of circumstances, of coincidence, a man in the wrong place at the worst of possible times, an obvious target. The police zeroed in on him, ignoring other possibilities. An act of rape is alleged, so there is likely to be DNA from the attacker's semen – the test results surely will exonerate poor Nick.

The last time they met was after Faloon was given day parole. He came to Arthur's office bearing a gift, a box of Cuban cigars, which Arthur accepted guiltily, not wanting to offend the man he'd failed so grievously.

"Did I not hear you tell the parole board you've mended your ways?" he asked.

"Almost, Mr. Beauchamp. I'm just putting together a little poke, and then I'm certified street legal."

Something in the tourist industry, he said. A bed-and-breakfast. Arthur had encouraged him, but held little hope.

It has begun to rain. The two eagles are in the air again: a display of aerobatics, cartwheels and swoops, one in pursuit of the other. Arthur is awed: this is their famed nuptial display – he can hardly wait to tell Margaret. After the eagles gambol away behind a hill, he folds his newspaper, packs away his pipe, rises, and casts a last look below. Gwendolyn Bay is on the other side of the island from Blunder Bay. He will not have to look at the damage they will do here.

◆

He arrives home drenched. His apology draws from Margaret a look between disbelief and exasperation. "Jesus, Arthur, I don't care about the damn lemons, I care about your health." She's fifteen years younger than Arthur, a feisty survivor of the 1960s – that's when her commune set up shop on the island. It didn't last; Margaret did.

This gracile, lithe, and energetic activist is leagues apart, in substance and style, from his first wife, Annabelle, chic and city-slick, artistic director of an opera company. She broke his heart, capping a series of affairs by absconding with a conductor. The sole child of that sad union, Deborah, a divorced single parent, is in Australia, a school principal. Arthur's parents also went their separate ways. Leeches of incompatibility lurk in the mud of the Beauchamp gene pool.

Arthur worries that Margaret, in turn, may yet find a bad fit with a Beauchamp, will find it intolerable living with this forgetful soliloquizing bore. Pompous, donnish A.R. Beauchamp, a poor lover, frequently unavailable.

After he tells Margaret of the eagles' conjugal dance, she rushes to the phone to call her friend Zoë, the local minister's wife. "The eagles are mating!" Her bell-like voice, breathless and triumphant.

Arthur turns on the six o'clock news as he undresses for a bath, and garlic scents waft from the kitchen. He hopes there will be pie – he harvested young rhubarb, left the tender red stalks in the kitchen as a hint. But Margaret has become stingy with her desserts. He might be a few pounds overweight, but the flesh hangs well enough on his tall frame. His most attractive feature, says Margaret, presumably joking, is the commanding nose. Cyrano, friends call him.

On the radio, he hears that Nick Faloon has appeared in court on a psychiatric remand. A judge has ordered the appointment of a legal-aid counsel.

That will not do. Arthur climbs into the tub with the phone and leaves a message at Pomeroy Macarthur Brovak and Sage, criminal lawyers. Any one of them will do, though he'd prefer the brittle but oftentimes brilliant Brian Pomeroy – if he's at the top of his game and not struggling through another nervous breakdown.

Arthur spends much of the evening nodding sympathetically over poached salmon and greens, then rhubarb pie and tea, then in the comfort of his club chair by the fire, as Margaret holds forth. "There's old growth in there, Arthur, because there's never been a road. Now they're going to cut a swath sixty yards wide through it. Pavement! Power lines! Next will be a bridge – we won't be an island any more, we'll be a bedroom. Is that what you want?"

This is one of her rhetorical flourishes, not a question. He has learned it's unwise to argue, so he pronounces his loyalty, and she is satisfied with that and carries on.

Much of her fire tonight is directed at Garibaldi's trustees, who rezoned Gwendolyn, who "buddied up" to the developers, traded in this island's wild heritage – "for fifty acres of public park and a fire truck that we were raising funds for anyway." She rejected such gifts when she was trustee, then was narrowly defeated in the last campaign.

"They're going to start tomorrow, Arthur. They're blasting the Gap. There are some three-hundred-year-old firs in there. How can you sit there and let that happen?" She immediately regrets that challenge, comes behind him, folds her arms around his neck, her brown, close-cropped hair tickling his ear. "Come on, Arthur, you've got to stop being such a doornail. You can't live on Garibaldi and be a political recluse. We're not asking much . . . some legal help, that's all."

"In what sense?" He has always managed to tiptoe away from such requests: to assent means to get involved. Political meetings. Contention. That's not why he came to Garibaldi.

"We have to take some risks. Direct action."

An expression that encompasses sins like civil disobedience, a concept in which he's never found much favour. Laws should be changed, not broken. "Surely you're not hammering spikes into trees."

The phone rings. "We'll talk about it tonight when I get back." She picks up the receiver: "Hi, what's up? . . . Twelve more bodies, right on." She hangs up.

"Twelve bodies?"

"Don't worry, they're alive."

Shrugging on her coat, she says, "Remember to look in on the Woofers" and races off, abandoning the recluse. Arthur is smarting, but he's also troubled: direct action hints of illegality and sorry consequences.

After he tends to the dishes, he strolls over to Margaret's former residence – their farms have been consolidated – to check on the Woofers boarding there. Willing Workers on Organic Farms: they come from lands near and far, they exchange labour for lodging and food, they stay for a few weeks, they go. Blunder Bay has had as many as five, but currently only two: Paavo, a forestry student from Helsinki, and Kim Lee, a Korean nutritionist. Communication is faulty. Paavo struggles in English, and the Korean girl is beyond comprehension.

Sign language, however, makes do, though it demands skill at slapstick. Clucking and flapping ensures the chickens are fed; a pantomime of two-handed masturbation gets the goats milked. These efforts are usually greeted by uproarious laughter. Though the Woofers often create more work than they do, they are good kids, adventurous, travelling the world. Arthur enjoys sharing chores with them, swapping language lessons, brushing up on his French or German, learning a little Finnish or Korean or Japanese in exchange for English and Latin and ancient Greek.

No one is about but Kim Lee, a fresh-faced twenty-year-old. "Where is Paavo?" he asks.

"Go. Help. Save." A sweeping motion, raising her arms high, then circling what may be the trunk of a tree. Arthur gathers Margaret has commandeered Paavo for her surreptitious project.

She doesn't return until after midnight, waking him briefly as she slides into bed. He seeks to caress her, but she denies him, rolls onto her stomach. Arthur has trouble resuming sleep.

4

Arthur is awakened by a clattering outside. When he sits up he is blinded by the sun streaming through his window. He finds his glasses and makes out Stoney and Dog throwing tools into the back of his pickup. Margaret's own truck has gone, and she with it – her side of the bed is empty. A memory of last night, her coolness, causes an ache in the chest, like heartburn.

He hollers, "Don't do anything. I'm getting dressed." Stoney is a habitual borrower of his beloved 1969 Fargo, though that's partly Arthur's fault: he leaves the keys on the dashboard. The last time Stoney drove off with it, Arthur went two weeks without a vehicle – other than his Rolls, on blocks, under cover. Stoney sold him the Fargo, so perhaps he feels some inherent right to its use. He and Dog exercise a similar claim to the garage they built for Arthur, who once surprised them inside assembling a still.

Stoney – alias Bob Stonewell – is a supposed master of many trades: mechanics, carpentry, and a specialized form of horticulture – and is usually reeking of its well-smoked essences. His accomplice, who seems to bear no other name than Dog, is built like a fireplug and speaks about as often. Somehow, these two stalwarts have become part of Arthur's life, like extra appendages that one must learn to live with, however non-functional.

As he steps into his gumboots, Arthur sees Dog toss a tree-climbing harness into the cab of the truck. Closer observation reveals that

Stoney's jacket is speckled with saw chips. Both seem exhausted, dirty as if from hard work, however unlikely that would be on this pleasant April morning.

"You fellows are up early."

"Haven't been to bed." Stoney extends a can of beer. "You drinking these days, Arthur?"

"Afraid not." Why is it generally assumed that Arthur must one day, after fifteen years, finally succumb? "What have you gentlemen been up to?"

"First off, we're celebrating our new company, Island Landscraping. You heard that Dog and me, we bought a backhoe, eh? Kind of used and beat up, but we got it running smooth as silk." However tired, Stoney is a tireless gabber, especially when under the influence of Garibaldi's infamous main crop. "I'm in hock for the parts, though, and I was thinking, that low spot over there, where all you got is horsetails, what you need is a pool – that's the only thing this property lacks."

"We already have a pond." Back of the barn, where the geese nest.

"Full of weeds. I'm talking about going down fifteen, twenty feet, for swimming."

Stoney probably overheard him and Margaret talking about a swimming hole. "It's still rainy season, Stoney, but if Island Landscraping survives as a going concern until August, we shall then consider its bid." The low spot is saturated with spring runoff; he has visions of a backhoe sitting forever in a wet hole a hundred yards from the house.

"Naw, you want to do it early, so it fills up, otherwise you got an ugly hole for four months. I know where I can lay my hands on a pump, it just needs an overhaul. That's all clay down there, eh? The walls will hold real good even in April. Anyway, what's happening is we had a little stall just up the road, and the flatbed's full of tools we've got to return to the other volunteers. We can be back in an hour with this old fella." He pats the hood of the Fargo, a fond gesture, proprietary.

"I will drive you." Stoney and Dog climb in beside him, and they head off. "You have not spent the whole night idly. What else were you celebrating?" A tribal rite, perhaps, in which one's head is sprinkled with sawdust and fir needles.

"Project Eagle. Dog and me are up there with the ringleaders. We may need to retain you in case we get in shit. Don't think it wasn't a death-defying experience, eh? It got dark, and all we had was flashlights and a kerosene lamp. Dog did the finishing touches, the barrier, he can go up them trees like a squirrel. I did the roof. We had all the pieces pre-assembled, sent 'em up on ropes and pulleys."

Arthur is still not fully awake, not following this. Project Eagle?

"I hammered in my last shake just as it was getting dawn. I told everyone, if I'm up here, I might as well stick around, but that got vetoed, they claim I ain't got enough staying power. They were drawing lots about who would go up there when me and Dog left to drop off the tools. Actually, we stopped off at Honk Gilmore's, he's got some primordial bud, man."

Arthur's anxiety grows with every word. "Pause here, Stoney. They were drawing *lots*? To go where?"

"We had about thirty people hammering away there. The Gap. Right in the middle of the road that ain't going to happen if we got a breath left in us, right, Dog?"

Dog nods, half-asleep. They have now pulled up to Stoney's two-ton flatbed. Arthur makes out, under a torn canvas, saws, shovels, grapples, pulleys, wheelbarrows, a generator.

"Let me understand this, Stoney. You are describing some kind of tree house?"

"Not some kid's tree house, a fort, a *real* fort. We're talking, oh, maybe eighty feet up."

"Eighty?" That was the hammering Arthur heard.

"It's a palace, man. It's even got a chemical shitter." He jostles Dog awake, and they get out.

"I suggest you fellows hide those tools for now, deep in the bush."

He presses the accelerator too hard, and the Fargo bucks and spits gravel. He takes the old bypass, up by the deserted vineyard, a project surrendered to birds and broom. He senses that his worst fears are about to be confirmed.

As he approaches Centre Road, Margaret's full-sized diesel Toyota passes the other way, Paavo driving, no Margaret. Distracted, swerving, he almost clips the Hamiltons' roadside stand and its piled cartons of eggs. A hysterical chicken flaps past his front wheel. Slow down, he tells himself, everything's going to be all right. Progress is retarded, in any event, by an empty logging truck that leads him on a winding climb. As he passes the old granite quarry, a glimpse in the rear-view reveals a fat figure astride a midget car – it's Nelson Forbish, editor of *The Bleat* ("Covering the Island, Covering Up for No One"), on his all-terrain vehicle.

Centre Road climbs steeply to the Lower Gap Trail, where another logging truck sits, along with a king cab, a bulldozer, and an excavator. Down the hill is a straggling line of parked vehicles, curious locals approaching by foot. Arthur wedges his truck behind a fresh stump – an acre of trees is down, a field of amputated trunks. But the crew of Gulf Sustainable Logging are now standing by idly. As Arthur stares at the carnage, he feels a sickness, again comes that sense of helplessness.

"Hop on, Mr. Beauchamp," Nelson says. He prefers to address Arthur formally, but after six years still mispronounces his name, anglicized beyond repair centuries ago as "Beechem."

Arthur risks a perch behind Nelson's ample girth, grasping the straps of his camera bag. Nelson goes slowly up the Gap Trail, his horn making tinny beeps, encouraging pedestrians to give way. "Press vehicle," he calls out, then grumbles, "Nobody tells me anything till the last minute. Any idea what's going on up here, Mr. Beauchamp?"

"I intend to find out."

"You want to give me a good quote for later?"

"Not now, Nelson." So many of Arthur's quotes to *The Bleat* have been so garbled that he has begun creating fictions. Last month, Nelson printed his canard that the Northwest Nude Bathers Society was planning an anti-logging protest here on April first.

"How's the program?" Arthur asks.

"I'm down to two hundred and eighty, and it's killing me. I get hallucinations. I dreamed I was in chains and there was a pork roast sitting in front of me."

After a few minutes they come to narrowest part of the Gap, where sound is muffled by the forest and only an occasional spear of sunshine penetrates the canopy. It's made darker still by the sheer rock walls. Here, Douglas firs rooted centuries ago, and found the sun – many are massive, covered by thick slabs of ancient bark. Delicate moss fronds hang from lower limbs, and tiny birds cavort in them, kinglets.

Slappy bounds up to Arthur, tail wagging, as he dismounts at a small clearing made soft by a carpet of needles, with cones and dead branches raked neatly to the side. Among those gathered here is Reverend Al Noggins, ringleader of the Save Gwendolyn Society. He's in the far corner of the clearing, an alcove, talking with the attractive gamin Arthur saw hitchhiking, the five-foot-two hippie.

The star of this show is a venerable Douglas fir eight feet wide at the base, dwarfing even Nelson Forbish as he gapes upward. Arthur calculates the platform as not eighty feet high, as Stoney claimed, more like fifty, the height of eight tall men. It girds the entire trunk and is protected by a sturdy guard rail. A shake roof, supported by diagonal beams, is held to the trunk with foot-long bolts. Canvas rain blinds that can be lowered. Affixed to the beams, a fan of poles, sharpened at the ends like spears: the Dog-built barrier.

He calls, "Are you up there, Margaret?"

She appears over the railing, shouts down, "Here I am." An expressive shrug, arms held out as if she's about to take wing. "I didn't plan it. My name was pulled from a hat."

"And how long will you stay?"

"We're provisioned for . . . well, three weeks. That's the plan."

Arthur stares up dumbly as the kinglets flit and cheep in the boughs above her. Two more heads appear. Cudworth Brown, the dissolute poet manqué, and his teenaged current interest, Felicity Jones. Margaret gathers them in a hug.

"We have sleeping bags, a little Bunsen stove, books to read – I may finally get to *War and Peace*."

"I'm not quite sure what to say."

"I can't hear you."

—

37

He shouts. "It's a shock." What means her bold and naked smile? There's no apology here, no misgiving.

"Arthur, I know this will seem extreme to you." Extreme? To stable, steady Beauchamp? "I put my name in the hat with five others, I can't renege, I have to do it. This is about finally taking a stand. If we don't, we surrender. I can't live with surrender."

Nelson is transcribing every word. Cameras are also at work: Flim Flam Films, a Saltspring Island company. By now, fifty friends and neighbours have arrived. Trustee Kurt Zoller is here. Striding anxiously into the clearing comes the CEO of Garlinc, Todd Clearihue.

Last seen, he was giving a lift to the pixie. Arthur massages a crick from his neck, glances over at her, olive complexion under spikes of black hair. A row of rings in an ear and one in her lip. A jacket open to Che Guevara on her T-shirt, an exhortation: "Rise Up!"

"Three weeks, did you say, Margaret?" Though shouted over the increasing ambient noise, it sounds of snivelling.

"That's the plan, we're doing shifts. Will you remember to put out the bird food? The vet's bill has to be paid, and you'll have to get in some feed."

"What about the kids, the goats?"

"Edna Sproule will help with the birthing. I want you to eat at the Woofer house. Kim Lee is a knowledgeable cook, and you ought to be on a vegetarian diet anyway."

The hidden text: He's helpless. He will be spoonfed lentil soup and tofu. Margaret looks proud and beautiful, Rapunzel in her tower. Removed, remote, unreachable.

Everyone is listening breathlessly to these disclosures of Arthur's helplessness and dietary needs. He will seem a worrywart to boot if he broadcasts his fears for Margaret's safety. Not to mention her mental health, after three weeks living with this pair.

Cudworth Brown is a former ironworker, runs the recycling depot. Most call him Cud, which is reflective of the slow, chewing motions of the ruminant creator that he is. He's been writing poetry for the last dozen of his forty-two years, and has finally been published: *Liquor Balls*, a thin volume of lusty verse. The local literary celebrity has attracted, in Felicity Jones, his first groupie, an eighteen-year-old naïf repeating her final year at Saltspring High.

"I can't conceive of how you got up there, Margaret. How will you ever get down?"

Reverend Al Noggins finally brings this neck-wrenching tête-à-tête to a close, moving Arthur away. "Have to keep the banter brief, Arthur." The reverend, everyone calls him, or Reverend Al, a short, bearded, energetic Welshman, twenty years of preaching the gospel at the local Anglican church. "We have a nesting eagle pair over there." He points to a Douglas fir thirty feet away. "We had an engineer design the platform, old boy, it's built to specs. For emergencies they have a rope ladder with a safety line."

Todd Clearihue comes striding up, but before he can speak, Reverend Al says, "Todd, we're not moving until you send away the logging crew. In addition to humans, there's another species up there we propose to protect. Bald eagles. There's a nest." A sonorous voice, well suited to the pulpit.

"Aw, come on, Al, don't try to pull that off on us. How would you know?" The air is thick with friction, but Clearihue maintains his smile.

"Take a hike up the bluffs, old fellow. You can see the nest, it must weigh half a ton."

Clearihue turns to Arthur, sensing he's more malleable. "I can't believe this is happening in my community." Though his family remains in Vancouver, he has bought waterfront property and joined several community groups, but retains the pasty look of one unused to rambling down wooded paths. "This is going to cost us at least twenty thousand a day."

Garlinc didn't have to borrow to buy the land, so Arthur suspects it has the resources to hold out. A private corporation with several partners, though Clearihue is reputed to be the majority shareholder, old money from precious minerals. "I'd sure like to figure a way to avoid going to court," he says.

Arthur is thinking about court, about the eagle's nest. He saw the mating eagles yesterday, above the Gap. He's not sure if they're on the protected list. He's not sure if there *is* a protected list.

Trustee Zoller descends. "What's the law here, Arthur? Couldn't they go to jail for squatting?" He operates the water taxi service and in the last election squeaked in by two votes, cashing in on his popularity as an accordion player. An odd fellow with his twitches and flinches and hints of paranoia. "I hope you're not part of this underground operation."

"Of course he's not," says Clearihue. "This must really be embarrassing for him. Any ideas, Arthur?"

"I suggest we wait for Corporal Ivanchuk." Who's absent because it's Tai Chi Thursday at the hall.

Arthur thinks about the Confederation Club, his old chums carrying on about how he married a 1960s back-to-the-lander, now she's become an eco-terrorist.

Corporal Al Ivanchuk finally trudges up, Corporal Al, as he is known so as not to be confused with Reverend Al. He's an easygoing giant who instructs Tai Chi and is the local Cub and Scoutmaster.

"What have we here?" he says.

"A blind man could see what we have," says Zoller, snappish. "There has been unseen activity going on under your very nose while you're dancing the Tai Chi." Arthur tries to work his way through this abstraction. He thinks of three weeks of vegetarian dinners.

"That's a pretty good piece of work," says Corporal Al, gazing up at the tree fort.

"How are you going to handle this, corporal?" Clearihue asks. "I'd hate to see them criminally charged, they're friends, but this is costing us big time."

"Money is only something printed on paper — seems to me our first concern should be for people's safety." He calls, "You folks okay up there? Last thing we want is an accident."

Cud Brown answers: "Boom-shaka-laka, we're living large, man, but I can't get cell reception. Can you call Felicity's old lady? I don't think she knows."

"Not good. She's going to be very upset."

"Capiche, there were only supposed to be two of us."

"Tell her I'm fine," Felicity yells. "I was just going to visit, but I'm staying. It's super up here."

"I'll break it to her. You guys need anything else?"

"Thanks, Corporal Al, we're great," Margaret says. Gleeful. Arthur doesn't like the way she was hugging Cud, he's thankful Felicity is there to share his cot or whatever they'll sleep on. A hairy-armed brute with tattoos. A nose broken in a storied fight at the old Brig Tavern. His satiric nickname: Cuddles.

"What I see going on here," says Zoller, working his way into one of his convolutions, "is that conspirators are being turned a blind eye to because one of them is the wife of a prominent lawyer."

"Civil matter, out of my jurisdiction," Corporal Al says. He is on his radio, trying to get a message through to Felicity's mother, obviously not relishing the task. Tabatha Jones is displeased that her daughter is seeing a man twenty-two years older who is said to have deflowered many local maidens.

Arthur looks up at his smiling reckless wife, her arms defiantly folded. She is enjoying this far too much. She asked the recluse for legal help, and has cleverly compelled him to give it. He feels manipulated, a sensation seared into memory from his years with Annabelle.

The girl in the Rise Up top is looking knives at Clearihue, who's making an effort not to see her. "This is ridiculous, Arthur," he says. "We're going to have reporters – do we really want that here?"

He's counting on Arthur being embarrassed by Margaret's direct action: he is well known from his years in the courtroom. A book has been written about him, his important trials. And yes, he feels embarrassment, but it pales against a fear for his wife, for her safety.

"When the reporters come, Todd, I can only hope we offer our island's traditional hospitality."

The media might find novelty here, a reprieve from the catastrophe-laden six o'clock newscast. *Next up, we'll meet some feisty tree-sitting Gulf Islanders.* But comedy will spiral into tragedy when the defendants are enjoined to stop trespassing or face damages, costs, and possibly jail.

Noggins beckons him. "Someone I want you to meet, Arthur."

"I'll be there presently, Reverend Al." His given name is Aloysius, but no one can pronounce it. He is ruddy, fifty-five, and was a life-long bachelor until the island's most careless carpenter winged his way to heaven after falling off the church roof. Bequeathing to the pastor not just guilt but his widow, Zoë.

The someone-to-meet would be the dark-haired gamin, who is grinning jauntily at Arthur, her T-shirt challenging him to rise up. One of those radicals who infest good causes with their banners and slogans — how is it she is friendly with the Anglican minister? Reverend Al may be a conservationist, but he is a Tory.

Arthur isn't looking forward to this encounter. For the time being, he's saved by a squad of reporters — tipped off, it would seem, to catch the morning ferry — who emerge from the woods like guerrillas, armed with cameras and microphones. They zero in on Todd Clearihue, who, Arthur senses, wants to rush off to seek his restraining order.

"Mr. Clearihue, what's your next move?"

"Cooler heads will prevail, I am sure. One of the parties up there, Margaret Blake, she's a fine lady, I have a lot of respect for her. Oh, you may not know her husband — this is Arthur Beauchamp, the lawyer."

"Mr. Beauchamp! I covered the Hogarty double murder, remember me?"

"Of course I do."

"What's your reaction to this, Mr. Beauchamp?"

Arthur raises his noble nose above the half-circle of microphones, points it at the platform, at Margaret. He wants to ask, What *is* my reaction, my dear? She puckers her lips and pops him a kiss. He feels a thump, message received, her need to do this. *I can't live with surrender.*

"Pride is my reaction. Pride in my wife and in my community. What you are witnessing is the brave and predictable response of the good, honest, caring folk of Garibaldi Island, angered by the prospect of the rape of a virgin forest. It ought to be added to the national park system, a gift of nature for all the people of Canada."

This brings applause from the Gwendolers. Arthur is a little amazed by what he has just said, but the words came naturally, unforced, unrehearsed. He hopes the press won't assume he's a spokesman for the protesters.

Nelson Forbish is at his ear, tugging his arm. "Save some for me, Mr. Beauchamp."

"In your next headline, Nelson, you might call it the Battle of the Gap."

Nelson jots that down. A reporter asks, "Mr. Beauchamp, how do you feel about your wife being up there?"

"I love her deeply, naturally I have a concern for her well-being. Of significant, though lesser concern is my stomach. Margaret is a cook of unparalleled artistry." He gets his laugh. He's playing to the jury, it's an ingrained habit.

The microphones swing away, seeking an alternative point of view. Zoller puts a comb to his hair. He has positioned himself well, but is being ignored in favour of Corporal Al.

"Officer, what do you see as your role?"

"Well, I see my job as keeping a low energy level." Todd Clearihue is on the move, but Corporal Al spots him. "Todd, I understand there's dynamite in one of those trucks by the road, and I'd like it parked at the quarry until you can drive it off the island."

"Let's see what the courts have to say about that." His ire is starting to show.

"Todd, I'm taking responsibility for lives here, you ought to be too."

"Sure, you're right, I'll look after it."

And Clearihue strides off, past Reverend Al, past the pixie, who taunts him: "Speaking of lives, Clearihue, get one." That provokes no response, and she hollers after him, "Thanks for the ride, sorry I couldn't fulfill your fantasies."

The media avoid her, sensing, like Arthur, that danger lurks here, a left-wing crank, a loose and libellous tongue. A reporter asks Corporal Al, "Will you be calling for reinforcements?"

"No, that's just going to *raise* the energy level. No need to, as long as everyone acts responsibly."

Reverend Al engages the press, a tutorial on saving green spaces, a list of species harboured in Gwendolyn, the Garry Oak, the Phantom

Orchid. He ends with a touch of rhetoric about the eagles: "the national symbol of our friends and neighbours in the United States of America."

A land not far. Arthur can see the San Juan Islands of Washington from his farm, the white pinnacles of the Olympics. This story could wedge its way into the news there, human interest to stir the patriotic heart. In design, in timing, this has been a well-orchestrated media event that somehow seems beyond the production skills of his fellow Garibaldians. There was outside help.

Felicity Jones calls from above. "I would now like to read a poem I wrote." She shoves Cud playfully. "Without any help from *you*. It's called 'I Am a Tree.'" The imagery is priapic, the tree as penis, stately, wedded to the earth, sap rising from its roots. Arthur endures – the poem is too simple to be banal.

As the recital ends, Felicity's mother strides into the clearing, looks about, and whacks Nelson's camera away when he attempts to catch her grim expression.

"Felicity Jones, I want you down from there right now. You are *not* repeating another year of school."

Tabatha is a weaver, a single mother, fiercely protective. Her daughter is in equally fierce rebellion. Arthur has a sense that the Save Gwendolers are about to suffer a minor publicity setback.

Tabatha waves a finger at Cud, yelling, "You are *out* of her life. Last weekend she came home at two o'clock smelling of, of . . . I don't know what."

"Tequila, my love. Maybe some pot."

Reverend Al moves to dampen this embarrassing debacle, puts an arm around Tabatha, murmuring, "A quiet moment of reflection."

A rope ladder flutters from the platform. Felicity clips onto a safety line and morosely begins her descent. Watching her causes Arthur's stomach to tumble, and he allows Reverend Al to pull him away. "Hard to believe, but I've been missing your croaky voice at hymns."

Arthur apologizes: the weather was too pleasant last Sunday. He casts a look up: Felicity halfway down, Margaret bent over the railing, Cud Brown positioned behind her buttocks. This repellent scene is blocked by foliage as Arthur is led to the priest's young guest, perched on a windfall cedar, fusshing with a cellphone. "Name is Lotis Rudnicki," says Reverend Al. "Member of your tribe, old fellow."

What tribe? A Polish surname, but one makes out brushstrokes of Africa and Asia. The international woman maybe, her genes fed from many streams. Under the spike hair, energetic oval eyes that betray the arrogance of youth. Rose-petal lips, marred by the lip ring. As the current argot has it, she is in your face, with Che Guevara and her revolutionary slogan. She snaps her phone shut, flashes Arthur a practised smile.

"Lotis is our mouthpiece," Reverend Al says. "She's with Sierra Legal Defence."

"You're a lawyer . . . ?" Arthur can't hide a hint of incredulity.

"Almost." A large confident voice from this small package.

"How does one be almost a lawyer?"

"I wilt under cross-examination, I get called to the bar in May." A mocking drawl, an indifferent shrug.

"I trust I won't be premature in offering congratulations." Why has Arthur taken on this formal tone? He is almost icy. It's not the T-shirt, not the lip ring (but why would she want to mar those plump smiling lips?). It's the youth. That is what's in his face, the whole bag of youth and hope and naïveté and boldness and ill-understood idealism wrapped up in this cheeky little woman.

"She's been staying in our cottage," says Reverend Al. "Giving us advice."

"Ah, yes, tutorials in direct action."

"Eco-guerrilla warfare," Rudnicki says. "Fought with sound bites and close-ups." She cranks the handle of an imaginary antique camera. "Angle on Felicity Jones as she blows her hero a kiss, then follows her mother out of the frame."

"In my day, Ms. Rudnicki, lawyers became involved after the fact, not at the planning stage of a tort." He says this with an intimidating smile, challenging her. This snip has been devising scenarios to get her environmental law group in the news. Arthur understands now why he's so displeased with her – she is the agent of a broken home at Blunder Bay.

Her look is more scornful than hurt, and she fires back. "What do you think Garlinc's lawyers were doing, playing with their dinks? They were at the planning stage of a fucking *crime*. The rape of a virgin forest, isn't that how you put it, Mr. Arthur Ramsgate Beauchamp?"

She stands, defiant, hands on hips. *Rise Up!* her bosom cries. An abrasively theatrical young woman, American accent, Californian in manner. Reverend Al shifts nervously, not daring to come between them.

"Have you done some scripting on the next scene as well, Ms. Rudnicki? It plays out in a courtroom." He wants to know what she's made of, this mouthpiece for the Save Gwendolyn Society who is young enough to be his granddaughter. But not as young as he first thought. Late twenties.

"We've thought about it."

"Who's we?"

"We are me and Selwyn Loo. Lead counsel for Sierra Legal." Seeing his blank expression, she adds, "He turned down a Rhodes to work with Sierra. He's a ranked chess player. He can take on half a dozen tables in a blindfold match."

"This is not a game, Ms. Rudnicki. We are not contending for a trophy."

She gives him a tired look. "I'm going to light a hump, anyone mind?"

Arthur isn't sure if he minds. Then he realizes she means a Camel's cigarette – she brings out a pack. The smoking environmentalist.

She takes a long pull, exhales. "Okay, I'm now ready to say something to you, Arthur Beauchamp. I don't mind the hostility, I shed it like a duck sheds rain. But maybe you should get with the program. There's your partner, a tough, beautiful, fantastic lady, putting herself on the line, holding off the barbarians at the Gap, while you, this great icon of the courtroom, are displaying a totally shallow attitude, complaining about losing a good cook. What is she, your *employee*?"

That comes like a slap. Before Arthur can devise a face-saving response, Reverend Al does crisis counselling, signalling Rudnicki to rein herself in, putting an arm on Arthur's shoulder. "You're upset, old boy, and you have every reason to be. As I would be had Zoë's name been pulled. You're welcome any night to share our home and our table."

They have exposed the great icon for what he is, selfish, concerned about his comforts and his stomach. He must stop feeling sorry for himself. Poor Margaret, three weeks of enduring the gross inanities of the local literary lion.

He can barely meet Rudnicki's eye. "Sierra Legal is rendering its services pro bono, I presume – on a matter of grave importance to our island. I should not have been unwelcoming. I apologize, Ms. Rudnicki. Your first name is Lotus?"

"L-o-t-i-s. Lotis Morningstar Rudnicki."

Counter-culture parents with a spelling disability? Or named after the nymph Lotis – who, to escape Priapus, god of fertility, turned herself into a flower? When Arthur feels awkward, he will often spout Latin, and does so now, pompously, a line from Terence that he hastily interprets: "Many a time have great friendships sprung from bad beginnings."

Lotis smiles widely, amused by this Latin-rapping stuffed shirt. "Okay, sorry I cracked on you. Anyway, you're right, Selwyn and I don't have much courtroom experience. We're hoping you'll join us at counsel table."

"I regret to say, Lotis, that I am retired. My role will be to applaud vigorously from the sidelines."

She hesitates, as if considering a further appeal. "I heard you saw the eagles' mating display. Will you sign an affidavit?"

"Of course, if it will serve a purpose." He finds himself echoing a local refrain: "What *is* the law?"

"Section thirty-four of the Wildlife Act makes it an offence to take, injure, molest, or destroy the nest of an eagle, peregrine falcon, gyrfalcon, osprey, heron or burrowing owl, or, for that matter – subsection c – *any* nest if it's occupied by a bird or an egg."

Recited from memory, it would seem. Arthur entertains a hope that a brain lurks beneath that horror-show hairdo. But he cannot remotely imagine her or this Loo fellow defending Margaret. He will hire a leading barrister, a battle-scarred labour lawyer at ease with injunctions.

Arthur calls to Slappy, but the dog returns to his station at the tree and lies down. *Semper fidelis.* Arthur must get back. There are arrangements to be made, chores to be done. Life will be lived differently for a while.

5

Nick Faloon is relieved to have wormed out of the main block to what they call Protective Custody, the wing for dangerous sexual offenders, the DSOs, as they call them, plus other unpopular people like gays and trannies and squealers doing a reduced bounce for co-operating with Her Majesty.

The deputy warden was not entirely convinced by the Owl's exaggerations that a barbarian in the main wing threatened to cut his balls off, but the deputy didn't want to take a chance on this prized catch, didn't want to deliver him up to the courts without all his parts. Also helping Faloon's cause was being a possible nutcase, though the deputy wasn't buying that. Nor was the couch doctor who analyzed him a few days ago, a young guy, Dr. Dare, who was onto Faloon's game, he brought a Dutch interpreter with him. Faloon didn't try to come out as Gertrude, it would have blown up in his face. The shrinker spent fifteen minutes with him, asking a few questions that seemed innocuous but were probably loaded with double meaning, and walked out laughing.

Among the advantages to PC in addition to not getting castrated is that there's a decent lounge for visitors, and some of the other guests are interesting and intelligent people. There's a defrocked priest in here who has a problem with underage boys, and they talk about religion, Faloon playing along that he's a Christian, and there's a former jail guard waiting sentencing, looking to do both hands for manslaughter or, in his case, wifeslaughter. Faloon gets called Gertie by the gay guys.

Though he has a hope that DNA fingerprinting will clear him, he can see himself eating pressed turkey for all Christmases to come. He shouldn't have panicked in Bamfield, should have brazened it out, now he's dug a hole for himself with this Gertrude Heeredam act.

The only thing looking up is that he has a lawyer. Faloon asked Willy the Hook Houston to scratch around for one, but in the meantime out of nowhere Mr. Brian Pomeroy phoned, and he's coming by this afternoon. He may not be in the league of Arthur Beauchamp, but comes highly recommended in the joint – though you have to look at the source of such endorsements, Mr. Pomeroy didn't get *them* off. According to Willy, who is raising a defence fund, he's a good talker, smart without being sleazy.

Claudette St. John hasn't visited yet, but she sent a teary letter saying she knows he's innocent. Faloon is buoyed by that, Claudie being so true-blue despite her suspicions about his night with Holly Hoover, the logging-camp tramp. He kicks himself for that mistake, Claudette's a superior woman, he's never known anyone with such an open heart.

He hasn't been sleeping well, and a couple of nights ago he found himself sleepwalking again, banging into the cell door while unconsciously going out to the deck of the Nitinat Lodge to take a piss.

It is just after the morning count that his new mouth shows up, and the screws let them have an isolated table in the lounge. Pomeroy's face is somehow familiar, maybe Faloon has seen him in court. He's forty-five or so, looks a little depraved, maybe because of all the character lines in his face.

After opening courtesies, Faloon asks why Pomeroy has taken an interest in him, and learns a "concerned gentleman left a message." Faloon doesn't feel invited to inquire further, assumes it must be Jacoby, his financial adviser.

"I've been following your career," Pomeroy says. "Impressive."

"Thank you."

"I'm hoping there's a psychological basis for Gertrude, it's not just a hustle."

"I thought it was worth a try, Mr. Pomeroy. I lost my head."

"I don't want to hear that. I want to hear that you *became* Gertrude. Where did you get the women's clothes?"

"Well, my job is a thief, and I keep different outfits depending on the occasion. I was arrested in a dress once before."

Mr. Pomeroy was looking fairly bored, but now lightens. "Have any friends seen you playing dress-up?"

"I can probably locate some."

"How are you fixed for funds?"

The lawyer is one who goes direct to the heart of things. Faloon tells him some allies are raising working capital. Freddy Jacoby in particular, who has got fat off the Owl over the years, with his fifty to eighty per cent lion's share.

"Multiple personality is the old term, these days it's dissociative identity disorder." Pomeroy swings his briefcase up, pulls out papers that look like psychological studies. "Okay, assuming you have this disorder, I think it's important that you understand it. Important if you're to be cured."

The fixer doesn't wink, but might as well have. What he's really saying is, I hope you're a fast learner, because, it turns out, another psychiatrist is coming to see him this afternoon, Dr. Endicott Sloan. What Pomeroy wants, though he's too ethical to say it outright, is for the Owl to read these case studies, learn the symptoms, get into the role.

Faloon tells him of his brief ordeal with Dr. Dare, who walked out breaking a gut.

"I'll deal with Dr. Dare."

"Let me ask you, Mr. Pomeroy, in the remote possibility this is going to work, where does it get me in the end?"

"The ding ward instead of the big house. You're in a deep hole, Nick, especially since you've already been convicted of one attack on a woman. I watched some of that in court, by the way. The jury was lapping it up, she did an artful job on you."

That's where Faloon saw him, the Adeline Angella fiasco, lawyers would wander in and watch Beauchamp in action. He wants to ask Pomeroy what's the story on the Topeka condo developer who was out till 2 a.m., and are there other suspects, but the counsellor is off on this insanity sidetrack.

"A reasonable scenario – you'll correct me if I'm wrong – goes like this: You're at that outdoors café having a coffee. Word comes down about the murder, you go into a panic state, you lose your real identity. The stress causes you to retreat into the role of Gertrude Heeredam. Again."

"Again?"

"Like the night before."

Faloon feels a chill. "I am carefully listening to this. Is our theory that the victim was snuffed by Gertrude Heeredam, and that's going to make Nick Faloon not guilty?"

"You have a better idea?"

"Aren't you going to ask if I did it?"

"I don't want to ask."

"I am anxious you should know. I am as innocent as an angel, Mr. Pomeroy, at least the murder part."

"Okay, then you had better explain how your sperm managed to find its way into her vagina."

Faloon goes into shock.

"You see, Nick, the Crown particulars have the semen coming up DNA-positive for you."

Faloon can't find words, his mouth opens and shuts like a hooked, landed fish. He feels woozy. "That's not . . . Mr. Pomeroy, there's got to be a mistake! Or someone else has got the same DNA!"

"Do you have an identical twin, Nick?"

"No."

"Then the chance of coincidence is roughly on a par with your winning this year's Miss Universe Pageant. Let's get back to Dr. Sloan. He'll conclude it's not important you don't know Dutch, and that you're probably fragmented into different women, as in this first case study . . ."

Distantly, Faloon hears the clanging of a cell door closing.

◆

Fear concentrates the mind, and Faloon is absorbing his lessons, getting ready for Dr. Sloan. He's even starting to think he may be sharing, as the text says, "two or more distinct identities that recurrently take control of the patient's behaviour."

This insanity bit might be his only hope. Guilty means the whole book. Pomeroy told him he could get out of the shrink tank after maybe a five-spot on condition he stays on Prozac, or whatever keeps you from dissociating.

Dark thoughts intrude. Was it truly his DNA? What if there *is* a murderer inside the Owl, unrecognized, crawling from his skin? A rapist . . . He tells himself to get real. But this is far worse than the other false charge, Adeline Angella, the magazine writer. She inveigled to meet him in a bar after Beauchamp got him off the Kashmir Sapphire caper, wanted to know all about "the fascinating world of the jewel thief," as if he was going to tell her. How had he been so sappy as to go up to her apartment?

In the lounge, where he's reading the last of the case studies, Faloon is interrupted by the defrocked priest, a cherubic sixty-year-old, Father Réchard, who originally comes from Quebec and is impressed with Faloon's French – his parents spoke it at home. "Something seems to be troubling you, my son."

He wants to tell him Satan has fucked him from behind. Someone *had* to be lying about the DNA. Why?

"Should there be any troubles you want to relieve yourself of, I will be happy to extend an ear."

Faloon likes Father Réchard, despite his disability, likes the well-mannered way he has of talking. He thinks of confessing to him. But to what? He's not particularly religious, though he prayed to the Prophet, Jesus, Buddha, you name it, Krishna, to send him an angel. Hoping it might be Beauchamp.

"Faloon!" a guard calls out. "Medical visit!"

He is led through a series of buzzing doors to the clinic, where Dr. Sloan is reading a poster about correct condom use. He is overweight, has the jaded look of a man who hasn't gone far in his choice of career. Faloon is urged onto a plastic chair – everything is fixed to the wall or floor, maybe in case of tantrums.

Sloan doesn't want to waste time, the hearing is tomorrow, he has to get his report written tonight. He asks Faloon about his medical history, which is uneventful until the shrinker asks him about any strange occurrences in his past. Faloon explains he has been bothered since a teenager about a series of lapses – he isn't sure what to call them – in which he found himself wearing women's clothes.

He knows the shrinker will test this against other evidence, and when asked about witnesses to these episodes he gives a couple of names he already supplied to Pomeroy, old friends. Sloan wants to know about his parents.

"There's only me, I lost my . . . it's something I'd rather not talk about."

Sloan's appetite is whetted, so Faloon tells him the story, haltingly, as he fights emotion, about how when he was a child in Lebanon, the Falange came into his village and shot all the men, including his father. Only the women escaped. Sloan's brow furrows, and he begins making notes.

"But many were raped, including my mother . . . I'm sorry, I can't, I . . . Oh, goodness, he does carry on, that weakling."

Upon hearing this feminine lilt, Sloan looks up. Faloon can't tell from his expression if he's buying or not, but ploughs on. "He just has no spine, can't face the harsh realities. That's why he became a crook, doctor, without his parents there was no moral upbringing."

"Who are you right now?" Sloan is squinting at him.

"I'm Samantha, I think . . . I'm confused." He begins shaking.

"Mr. Faloon . . ."

The Owl perks up. "Yes, doctor?"

"Who are you?"

"Same guy I've always been."

"Did you just have one of those, as you call them, lapses?"

"Not that I'm aware. Except I forgot what we were talking about."

Sloan pulls some diagrams from his briefcase. "I'm going to put you through some tests."

As Faloon stares at an ink blot, he wonders if he should add about the sleepwalking, but decides not to press it.

"I'd say that looks like a woman dancing."

"Hmm," says Sloan.

◆

That evening, the Owl is in the lounge watching the news with the guard who threw his wife off a balcony and one of the squealers. The violent images from the Middle East disturb him, make him queasy. Another suicide bombing.

"Fucking Arabs," says the guard.

"They don't respect life," says Faloon, who doesn't advertise his heritage in these difficult times.

He is happy when the TV switches to local news, a bunch of people waving placards that read, "Save Gwendolyn." His seatmates are bored by this and start talking, so he doesn't pick up why Gwendolyn needs saving, maybe she's also up on false charges.

"What was all that shit you were studying?" asks the squealer, whose name is Mario, and they call him Lanza. Except to be polite, Faloon doesn't make efforts to relate to him, a guy who's looking to get reduced to a deuce for ratting on a big-time dealer in nose product.

"Correspondence course."

"Look at those horses' asses," says the guard.

Faloon focuses on the image on the screen, two people up in some kind of tree fort, the announcer carrying on about an injunction tomorrow. Then he is startled to see Arthur Beauchamp, in ragged coveralls, sitting on a small tractor, being interviewed, the ocean behind him, a nice house.

"Clem Keddidlehopper," says the guard.

Faloon sends him a nasty look.

"I will be there to support her," Mr. Beauchamp is saying.

"Will you be defending her in person, sir?" asks the interviewer.

"No, it is always a wise practice to hire lawyers for this sort of thing. I am a simple farmer." Faloon knows he'll have to give up on any daydreams that Mr. Beauchamp will come to his rescue.

6

Arthur rises late after a night of tossing, of dreaming of Margaret as a tree, growing out of sight. He grabs a suit and tie from the recesses of his closet, then races to his Fargo, hoping he won't miss the early ferry. He finds time to buy a muffin from the Winnebagel, the ferry roadside stand, because the boat is late by twenty minutes: a problem with the engines this time.

As the *Queen of Prince George* limps toward the dock, he examines his suit for moth damage. He finds none, but it's unfamiliar wear, he feels strange in it. He forgot his brogues; he'd slipped on his worn loafers. Again he wonders if his brain is not working to former capacity.

On the upper deck, armed with a cup of glutinous coffee from the dispensing machine, Arthur tamps tobacco into his pipe and watches the gulls glide in the slipstream. He wonders how long this hiatus in his comfortable routines will last. He will soon tire of tofu. Again he chides himself. Margaret will be eating dried cereal for twenty-one days, while putting up with a buffoon. (How are their sleeping quarters set up? He'd like to see the blueprints for this platform.)

The affidavits filed by Selwyn Loo, whom Arthur has yet to meet, seem competently prepared, but he's had his ticket for only six years. "We're green but mean," said the spike-haired imp, Lotis Rudnicki. She has ginger, stood toe-to-toe with the right-wing opposition, the shallow icon Arthur Beauchamp. A former actress, he's learned, minor Hollywood roles.

For now, Arthur has decided against hiring an old hand – he doesn't want to be seen as demanding special attention for Margaret. Nor would she want it.

It's Friday, day two of the Battle of the Gap. The loggers are still waiting by the trail. Reporters are squeezing out every saccharine droplet of human interest: Felicity, grounded but in a state of doe-eyed devotion for her Lord Byron, and a stuffed shirt stoutly defending his tree-hugging wife. Yesterday, Arthur escaped from a TV crew on his old John Deere.

He hopes the judge will be fair-tempered, and not one of the many he offended in the course of boisterous debate. He hasn't been in a courtroom for years, but feels the old tension, his heart working harder. He tells himself to relax, he will be but a spectator today.

Chugging down the street to a loud thrum of engine – his muffler is loose – Arthur arrives in the capital of British Columbia. Victoria is lush with flowering plum and cherry trees, gardeners sprucing up the boulevards for the Americans and Japanese who will flock here in season to imbibe the floral gardens, winding streets, and tea rooms serving scones and Devonshire cream.

The courthouse is a drab, boxy affair, six storeys on half a city block. Arthur has defended many cases here, but he can't bring any quickly to mind: yes, the bribery scandal, of course. The Beacon Park murder. But his triumphs are starting to lose shape, to blur in memory.

He hurries through a side door, avoiding the news cameras at the front. He utters a mild epithet on reading the posted docket: Edward Santorini is presiding in contested chambers – former chief Crown Attorney, loser of five straight murders against him. One time, while racked with a ferocious hangover, Arthur lashed out at Santorini, called him a horse's ass.

He glances over the criminal list, sees Nicholas Faloon's name, murder in the first degree, Provincial Courtroom 5. The crush of events has squeezed Faloon from his thoughts – this must be the mental fitness hearing.

Brian Pomeroy was on the answering machine: "I'll do what I can, Arthur, but I'm afraid Nick's deoxyribonucleic acid was found in a most inconvenient place." Arthur is pleased Brian jumped to the task but dismayed that somehow – impossibly, absurdly – the DNA fingerprinting found a match in Faloon. He wonders if there'll be time to pop down to the criminal courts. But in the meantime he's late for the Gwendolyn hearing.

Todd Clearihue is in the corridor, speaking to a reporter, promoting Garlinc's case but seeming anxious to return to court. He beats Arthur to the door, cracks it open. "They got started twenty minutes ago." A friendly punch on the arm. "Hey, Arthur, I know we'll be toking the peace pipe when this is all over. Listen, help me. Who's the looker working your side? Damn, she's familiar."

"Lotis Rudnicki. The young lady you picked up hitchhiking." *Sorry I couldn't fulfill your fantasies.*

Clearihue blanches.

The room is crowded – mostly environmentalists, Arthur supposes. Counsel for Garlinc is Paul Prudhomme, a silver-haired patrician, old money, privately schooled, unambitious. He is fielding questions from the judge.

"Why can't you go around that tree?"

Prudhomme is about to answer but is distracted by Arthur striding up the aisle – the grand entrance is an old habit, a show of control and confidence. He exchanges nods with Prudhomme, with Santorini, and eases his creaking back onto a chair behind lynx-eyed Lotis Morningstar Rudnicki. She looks almost unrecognizable in a chic pantsuit, with her hair brushed. No wonder Clearihue had trouble placing her. Beside her is an angular young man in a long ponytail, obviously Selwyn Loo. Arthur is confounded to see a white cane at his table. Dark glasses. The blindfold chess champion.

Selwyn turns to him, as if aware of his nearness through highly tuned senses. Arthur leans forward, but before he can introduce himself, Selwyn says, "Good morning, Mr. Beauchamp."

"How did you know?"

"I've heard you smoke a pipe."

Arthur's suit must smell of it, the pipe in his pocket. He earns a brisk handshake, then cannot retreat as Selwyn tugs him into a chair at counsel table, whispering, "I need all the help I can get – the judge is a nincompoop."

Prudhomme struggles to pick up where he left off. "As I was saying . . ."

"Before you say what you were saying, what if the eagles raise a family in that tree? That's their only argument that I can see." Santorini is cranky. "You can't do in their nest."

"Milord, we've done helicopter searches, dozens of passes over two days, and no eagle has been seen in that tree. There's an old nest, but it has been without tenants for years. I think you'll find the relevant material in affidavit J."

Selwyn stands. "Surely, the nest is protected under section 34 even if it has been abandoned for a decade . . ."

"Mr. Loo, we already had that argument, and I'm against you. It's absurd to think a valuable timber tree can't be harvested because there's an old, falling-apart nest in it. No, I'll need some proof it's a viable nest. Eggs, Mr. Loo, I need to see eggs."

"The eggs might come along a lot sooner, milord, if we put a stop to these so-called aerial searches, which seem intended to scare the eagles away. Has your Lordship had a chance to look at the counter-petition filed this morning?"

Santorini is not on top of things, and shuffles through his file. "Counter . . . Yes, let's see, you want to restrain these flights – why? They're just bird-watching, in a manner of speaking."

"Because it's not a search, it's deliberate harassment of eagles to prevent them from nesting."

Santorini frowns over the Wildlife Act, then turns again to Prudhomme. "Why is this tree such a bother? Can't they go in some other way? Over the hill?"

"If your Lordship will look at the topographical map, appended to Exhibit M, you will see what an imposing task that is. According to the engineer's report, it's hugely expensive and would be environmentally destructive."

"And we wouldn't want that." Selwyn's barbed tone. Arthur wonders how long he's been without sight – has he ever seen nature in her glory? He tries to imagine absorbing beauty through other, enhanced senses, the chatter of wrens, the smell of the humid forest, the feel of a fern leaf.

"What about going in by barge from the ocean," Santorini says. "At least until after nesting season. Or have you thought of helicopter logging? I know something about this, I worked on a few logging crews in my time, summer jobs – I didn't get my degree handed on a silver platter."

Prudhomme explains politely how each of these helpful hints, in turn, are prohibitively dear.

"What about this business with all the air traffic around the nest, they say you're trying to scare the eagles." He abruptly focuses on Arthur. "What's your position, Mr. Beauchamp?"

"I would be delighted to state my position were I counsel, milord. However – happily for the defendants – I'm not." But he cannot resist: "The rule, as your Lordship is abundantly aware, is that the applicant must come to court with clean hands."

"Are you asking me to assume they're trying to forcibly evict a bird?"

"A pair of them. I can attest to having seen them, in fact. As my affidavit indicates, they were showing the typical indicia of being in love."

"Didn't know you were such an expert, Arthur."

"In birds or love?"

Poorly smothered laughter from Lotis Rudnicki. Maybe she thinks it's absurd that this old gaffer might be an expert on love. Proving she's capable of the sin of compromise, at least in a courtroom, there's no lip ring, no gel in the hair.

Santorini is chuckling too. "Well, the real question is whether those eagles are nesting there or not. I'm going to adjourn this for a couple of days. I want a sighting – not just an eagle, a nesting eagle, eggs – and I'd like photographs."

After adjournment, Santorini's clerk corrals the lawyers. "The judge wants to see counsel. Especially you, Mr. Beauchamp." She leans to his ear. "Even in those shoes."

Arthur reluctantly parades behind the others, finds Ed Santorini at his desk in shirtsleeves, his feet up, a benign smile that hides an intention to talk hard business.

"You're looking in great shape, Arthur. Ten years younger than when I last saw you, if you want the truth. Must be the country air. Goddamn, come here, you old son of a bitch." He stands, and Arthur moves toward him with hand extended, but is met by the full Italian embrace. "Best fucking lawyer on these Pacific shores. Bruised me up a few times."

"You're looking remarkably ageless yourself, Ed."

"I don't want any jokes about bald eagles."

"Nonsense, you look good without your feathers."

Santorini laughs again. "You reprobate. Hey, as we were carrying on in there, I started wondering, How do those birds mate on the wing? Must be something to see." Selwyn Loo smiles pleasantly as a heavy silence sets in.

Santorini resumes his seat, proceeds briskly. "Okay, I'm not going to detain anyone, I just want this thing settled as painlessly as possible. Arthur, you've got your wife up that tree. Good-looking woman, from the pictures I've seen, and I'll bet she's a hell of a great gal. I don't want her arrested – I don't want anyone arrested here – and I don't want anyone thrown in jail or fined. I just want those people off that tree, eagles or not, and I'm going to insist there be no logging until we straighten that out."

"What about the air surveillance, sir?" says Selwyn.

"Okay, I want to be fair, let's hold off on that for a while. Any problems with that, Paul?"

Prudhomme agrees to advise his clients to comply.

"And in that spirit, let's see if the defendants can bend a little too, climb down from their perch. Will you talk to them, Arthur?"

"What do you suggest I say?" He wants to tell Santorini that Margaret Blake doesn't climb down from anything easily.

"Christ, Arthur, use your famous velvet tongue, explain to your good wife I'm letting her off the hook – the other guy as well. I'll protect their interests as long as they co-operate with me."

To Arthur, that sounds of disguised bullying. "Communications are not simple. One shouts."

"Heard you do it many times."

Twenty years ago, for instance, in open court – Arthur can't remember all the words he used in describing Santorini. Only the expression *horse's ass* lingers.

"Eddie, I do not intend to counsel persons, whether they be clients, friends, or wives, by shouting into half the nation's microphones."

"Then go up the tree on that . . . what have they got, a rope ladder?" Santorini's bonhomie has faded under Arthur's gently scornful gaze, and he is flustered now, aware he is making demands that are patently unreasonable.

"Perhaps I could swing like Tarzan through the boughs."

Lotis Rudnicki snorts with laughter. Santorini forces a stiff smile, studies her for a moment. "You're sure we haven't met, Miss Rudnicki?"

"Not in the flesh, milord."

The comment demands elaboration, but Santorini opts not to seek it. "Arthur, I take it you're not involved in this . . . this escapade. The plaintiff alleges a conspiracy, I'd hate to see you named in a writ. Along with whoever built that platform."

He stands. "Okay, we'll use the weekend as a cooling-off time and meet again on Monday. No, I have a judges' seminar. Tuesday. I want a response to my offer of clemency. I don't care how you lay down the law to your wife, Arthur, but I don't want to see her with a criminal record."

Arthur plays with the concept of laying down the law to Margaret Blake as Santorini walks him out, an arm around his shoulder. "You old fox, it's great to see you back in a courtroom. I remember when you referred to me as the backside of a horse." He guffaws. "Hell, I know you didn't mean that."

"Of course not, Eddie."

Arthur gets one last friendly poke in the ribs before he returns to the courtroom. Santorini is famously unpredictable, maybe he can be worked on.

He proposes lunch to Selwyn and Lotis – these two thin lawyers might enjoy a treat at Nouveau Chez Forget, where his old friend Pierre Forget serves his matelot de sole à la campagnarde occasionally spiced with a tantrum. His offer is accepted, and they will meet there at one o'clock.

As Arthur follows them from the courtroom, he marvels at how keen Selwyn's sense of direction is – a flick and a tap with his cane on a bench, then he walks assuredly up the aisle, and easily finds the door.

Arthur feels impelled to drop in on Nick Faloon's fitness hearing, but hopes it will have ended, that he won't have to witness the charade of an insanity defence.

The Provincial Courts are located on the ground floor, and there he comes upon a radio reporter working to deadline, reciting into his cellphone. "A contrary opinion was given by Dr. Endicott Sloan . . ." A forensic specialist who believes what he's paid to believe, and regurgitates it credibly in court. Is the defence so desperate that Brian Pomeroy must ally himself with a charlatan?

This time, Arthur makes no loud entrance, and waits at the back. Brian is standing, arms folded, a rangy man with that wrecked, slightly dissolute look that many women seem to find attractive. Nick Faloon is in the dock, passive and depressed, showing his age, thick of waist, thin of hair.

Dr. Sloan is still in the witness stand, a nasal voice, a litany of learned phrases. "In most cases of dissociative identity disorder, the primary identity is passive, dependent, and depressed. I found Mr. Faloon to fit those qualifications."

The judge, a young woman – Iris Takahashi, according to the list – breaks in: "Against that, I have the written opinion of your colleague, Dr. Dare." He is here too, Timothy Dare, sitting at the front, arms crossed, staring icily at Sloan.

She reads aloud from Dare's report: " 'Mr. Faloon presented himself in a fraudulent manner, and I have no doubt he is capable of conducting his defence. The only illness he's suffering is a severe case of malingering.' " Takahashi looks down at Dr. Sloan. "You seem to be poles apart."

"I can't speak for Dr. Dare, I can only give my best professional opinion."

"Summarize it for me."

"Simply, Mr. Faloon from time to time retreats to the safety of a world that may seem fantastical, but for him is credible and real. His disorder reflects a failure to integrate various aspects of his identity, memory, and consciousness. In short, Mr. Faloon takes on the personas of the various women who inhabit his body, and thus evidences the classical personality features of the dissociative personality. It is what we may call an escape mechanism."

The judge asks, "Exactly what was he escaping from?"

"The threat by a member of the RCMP that he would be roadkill. You'll see that mentioned in my report."

"But not mentioned in Dr. Dare's," says Brian. "He spent fifteen minutes with my client and produced two paragraphs, as against the seven pages from Dr. Sloan."

Would that justice could be so easily measured. Arthur has little doubt that the astute Dr. Timothy Dare is on the mark. The young judge is clearly unfamiliar with Sloan's shabby reputation.

"More to the point," Brian says, "Dr. Dare was totally unaware of the childhood trauma that spawned this disorder, the murder of his father."

Dare heaves himself to his feet with a cynical smile and walks to the door. Before leaving he winks at Arthur, as if they are witnesses to a cheap burlesque.

"Unless anyone strenuously disagrees," says Takahashi, "I would like to order a further thirty-day psychiatric remand at VI."

The Vancouver Island Forensic Clinic, a way station for the criminally insane. Arthur wonders if his wily former client can maintain his pretence through a month of observation. Now Faloon notices him, his expression evolving to surprise, then brightness and, to Arthur's dismay, hope. He nods to Faloon, then flees like a coward as court is recessed.

As he hurries out to his truck, he tries to blot away Faloon's last crestfallen look. Arthur's major weakness as a lawyer was that he cared for his clients, even the most blameworthy. And Faloon was among his favourite villains. He feels conscience-stricken, helpless in retirement.

His drive to Pierre's is interrupted by a brief encounter with the law, a matter involving his muffler and a warning. The restaurant is in a converted Victorian-era country home – he hasn't been there since its opening two years ago. Pierre moved his business from Vancouver after an incident with a restaurant reviewer that culminated in the dumping of asparagus en sauce chanterelle on his head.

He finds Lotis smoking outside. Selwyn is in the lineup; the wait could be twenty minutes. But Pierre has spotted him through the window and comes outside. "Ah, it is Beauchamp. For two years you do not come to my restaurant. You are not deserved to be here, a traitor to my table."

For a moment he fixes on Lotis, not quite ogling her, studying her, then urges them past the other waiting patrons. One of them makes a complaining noise. Pierre says, "This is Beauchamp." He approaches a couple lingering over coffee and dessert. "Please, will you be so kind as to finish your flan at the bar. Your bill is paid." He calls to a waiter: "Henri, c'est Beauchamp."

Pierre refuses Arthur's request to see a menu. "For your friends, I advise the tossed spinach salad, then the curried shrimp, it is exquisite. But for Beauchamp, who likes his meat, l'entrôcote à la Bordelaise." Arthur feels his taste buds quivering and reminds himself steak isn't on the diet.

"I think something lighter."

"Not to eat what I bring is an affront."

Lotis Rudnicki, activist in the struggle for the classless society, expresses shock at the favouritism, the jumping of the line. Arthur explains that for many years he was diner-in-residence at the old Chez Forget. He'd also got Pierre out of some legal scrapes.

Over salad, Arthur makes bold to ask about Selwyn's blindness, and learns he was sighted until fourteen, when a virus attacked his optic nerves. A dedicated man who has only the memory of beauty seen – Arthur finds much sadness in that, but more wonder.

He compliments Selwyn for his showing in court: a victory, the logging and the overflights have been put on hold. But Selwyn is gloomy, frets that the judge is pro-logging, clearly against them.

"Selwyn, you're a grouch potato," Lotis says. "You have to stop being so irrepressibly *bleak*." He does seem a sad fellow. In counterpoint she's cocky, a schemer, the brains behind the impasse at Gwendolyn Gap. "We have a secret weapon, Justice Santorini's extreme need for Arthur's love. If he asks this judge to drop his pants, he'll drop his pants. That gives us stalling time."

She causes Arthur discomfort with her bawdy analogies. According to Reverend Al, she has a history of leading student demonstrations. "International stuff as well, old boy. Anti-globalization. I suspect she's an anarchist. Doubtless an atheist." He spoke in awe, fascinated by rebels and disbelievers. Arthur has never met an anarchist, has never wanted to.

Lotis entertains with a chilling tale of the perils of hitching on Garibaldi. She was in a hurry to get to the Save Gwendolyn meeting on Wednesday. "I passed on the local serial killer, a two-ton gorilla in a one-ton truck. Gave a thumbs-down to three rapists in an Unsustainable Logging crew cab." She performs, sticking out a thumb, making doltish faces. A comedic actor. One would consider her well tuned to the modern world, perceptive, were she not immersed in the dog-eared politics of the Left.

"I thought I'd be safer with the baby-faced suit in the burgundy Audi V8 guzzler. This massively unhip guy turns out to be Todd Clearihue. We'd never met, he didn't know me from Mother Jones. Thought he'd impress me with his mall and marina and condos. 'His vision,' he called it — as if it's something creative as opposed to an extension of his cock. Reminded me of my last producer blowing on about the umpteenth sequel of *Scream*."

"That is where I saw you," says Pierre, hovering while a waiter serves the curried shrimp and entrôcote. "That scene, where you are naked, hiding from the slasher. Magnifique."

"I'll wait for the video," Selwyn says, dry, unsmiling. He rarely smiles.

"*The Return of the Slasher*. Starring Todd Clear-cut, disguised as good old country boy. He dug my peace symbols. 'Cool,' he said.

Cool? He's a liberal, he's hip to peace and civil rights." She fakes a male voice: "'Taking a little shakedown cruise Saturday on the boat, think you might enjoy that?' When I drew his attention to the ring on his hand, he said his wife was in the city. I said, 'Drop me off, I think I'm going to be sick.'"

◆

As the Fargo chugs off the Garibaldi ferry ramp, Arthur is talking to himself again, reciting Shelley as a salve to his irritation. The ferry sailed three hours late, it's half past seven, too late to lay down the law to Margaret. Anyway, he won't run panting after her. She has Slappy, she doesn't need another old dog hanging around.

He still feels his stomach complaining about the unaccustomed rich food. He ought not to have had the coeur à la crème d'Angers.

Also plaguing him is a feeling of uselessness as Nick Faloon blunders his way to a life sentence for murder. But is Arthur harbouring an illusion as to Nick's innocence? Maybe Nick is capable of acts of vast evil, was guilty of the first assault, as well. Arthur can find little sustenance in that theory.

Stoney's flatbed is still immobile at the side of Potter's Road, but the tools and wheelbarrows have disappeared. Arthur's muffler is in its death throes by the time he nears Blunder Bay, and the roar startles a goat escaping up the road. The fence will have to be mended again. Tomatoes must be repotted in the greenhouse. Bills must be paid. He has to keep on top of things.

7

After spending the morning with Paavo, helping him shore up the fence, Arthur visits the Woofer house to find Kim Lee at a wok, stirring chop suey.

"I." She has trouble with that vowel, points to her chest. "Make. Out-take." Takeout. She's prepared a lunch for Margaret and Cud, to be hoisted to their tree fortress. Arthur sniffs at the wok. "I. Take. Tree house." He doesn't relish the idea of feeding Cuddles as well.

He must drop by the gas station on the way back, ask them to replace the muffler. He doesn't trust Stoney, who still hasn't got his own truck running. Arthur can see it on Potter's Road — its hood up, the self-proclaimed best mechanic on the island fiddling with the engine.

He strolls there to find Stoney splicing ignition wires.

"Where did you put the tools, Stoney?"

"What tools?" he says, barely looking up.

"The ones used to build the tree platform."

"Oh, them. Hey, I heard you have a muffler problem. I think I can get you a spare in good shape."

"The tools, Stoney. You don't want them traced to you."

Stoney emerges, grease patches on his face. "Well, the good news is they're all safe and accounted for. Dog is guarding them. Now."

The little adverb hints that Stoney has engineered another calamity. Arthur isn't sure if he wants to hear the bad news yet, he isn't emotionally prepared.

"Hey, Arthur, I got a crisis here with the starter. Dog and me, we got to get them tools back to their rightful owners, so could we maybe borrow your truck for the day? I'll fix the muffler, charge you only for parts, bring it right back."

Arthur will let him have the Fargo; he'll take Margaret's diesel. As they walk back, a goose follows Stoney, hissing.

"Arthur, this low area over here screams, Dig me, man, dig me ten feet down, fill me with water. You really got to think about that swimming pond. Put in a dock, one of them rubber boats, loll around reading your Greek classics and shit."

"Stoney, you have something to tell me."

"Well, to tell the truth, there was this lady hanging around, eh? With a fancy camera, I figured she was one of the news photographers."

"And she followed you into the bush where the tools were hidden. And took pictures."

"Right. Except for one detail. They weren't in the bush."

That detail is resolved when Arthur spies Dog sleeping under a blanket behind the garage. A glance through the window reveals climbing harnesses, saws, hammers, wheelbarrows, generator, even scale plans for the tree platform.

Arthur has visions of writs flying. *Garlinc versus Arthur Ramsgate Beauchamp*, warehouseman for the conspiracy. *Plaintiff further alleges the defendant's vehicle was used to remove the incriminating items.* He thinks about explaining to Ed Santorini how he has been victimized by the Garibaldi gremlins.

A few brisk, pointed words persuade Stoney that the tools must be hauled away within the hour, under canvas. Arthur secures the plans. Built-in table, shelves, benches. A privacy partition for the chemical toilet. Where do they shower? "One foamy here," says a scribble. No mention of another.

What nonsense to entertain such low suspicions. Margaret and Cud? How absurd, she's never had much time for the fellow, with his unbounded lack of class. ("Want to see the peace symbol on my ass?" She looks up, bored with Tolstoy. "Why not?") An irrational anxiety is creating seamy imaginings, an ugly habit learned during a long career as cuckold.

Early this morning, midnight for her, Deborah called from Melbourne, shocked and delighted to have seen her father on the late news, a brief clip. "The kind of item they throw in for a chuckle to soften you up for the ads," she said. "Nicky said you looked a little pompous." His fourteen-year-old grandson.

Deborah viewed the protest as a lark, refused to give ear to his complaints. "Dad, you're perfectly capable of making your own sandwiches . . . You're miffed because she's on the podium and you're second fiddle . . . *Do* something, get active, there's more to life than growing radishes. You were a big-time lawyer when she met you. What have you done to impress her since?"

✦

At the Gap Trail, the logging trucks are gone, press vans in their place. A sign reserves a roped-off area for Garlinc employees, a table with its glossy brochures, "In Harmony with Nature." Todd Clearihue's Audi is there. Another two dozen vehicles are strung down the road. Among the stumps, a banner, "Operation Eagle." Tents have been erected. A Greenpeace information table. A Rainforest Alliance booth.

Corporal Al is on foot patrol and pulls Beauchamp over. "Let me take this rig off your hands, Arthur, or you'll have an uphill hike. Everyone's assembling to go to the heights to look for eagles, that's why all the cars." He leans into the cab. "Sure smells good." Essences of soya and garlic waft from the cartons.

"War rations."

"Actually a lot of folks are taking turns sending up hot meals." He takes Arthur's place in the Toyota. "Don't see you much at Tai Chi these days."

"I've been remiss."

A six-minute hike brings him to the Gap. Clearihue is conferring with a woman, an investigator perhaps, making notes for court, taking pictures.

The regulars of the Save Gwendolyn Society are assembling with cameras and binoculars. They want to hear about the court proceedings. They want Arthur to be honorary patron for the fundraising drive. They talk about auctions and bake sales, garage sales. Garlinc paid $8 million for this property. The last bake sale brought in $258.

But support for the protest is growing. Selwyn gave a strong interview on national television. Donations have started to flow to the Save Gwendolyn Society.

Hammocks have been strung up on the tree platform – Margaret is gently swinging in one, reading. Cud is leaning over the railing, lowering a rope to Felicity Jones. She puts a few pages in a basket. Love verses? *I am a flower waiting to be plucked . . .*

Slappy tries to jump into the basket, and Felicity has to wrestle him out. Cud waits until the chop suey is added to the cargo, then pulls it up. Arthur fights off a surge of resentment that Margaret is sharing a high-rise apartment with this versifying quack. *An original voice from the bush. Bawdy and muscular.* The reviewers of *Liquor Balls* were cautious, as if in fear such a ruffianly poet might harm them if they panned the book.

One foamy here. He feels reverberations, echoes of fears instilled through long conditioning. Annabelle, his socially energetic ex-wife, banished him to hell, to cuckoldom, alcoholism, impotence, he was writhing with jealousy. He came to Garibaldi six years ago less to retire from law than to escape the pain, the shame, the sniggers. He does not intend to go through that again.

"Arthur, you made *lunch?*" Margaret has risen and joined Cud. Comrades. Shoulder to shoulder.

"You must thank Kim Lee."

She seems disappointed in him. "Any eggs?"

"Yes, ten this morning. The hens are beginning to lay again. No nanny goats have dropped their burdens." Reporters have sidled up, recording these homely shouted moments for their mass audiences.

"Arthur, after I finish *War and Peace*, I think I'll need something lighter."

72

"I shall bring you some mysteries, you have earned the right to forbidden tastes." She devours such books. He'll keep her busy reading.

"I forgot to tell you, get Barney out of the lower pasture before he explodes. You need a gas mask for his farts."

Here comes Reverend Al, intent on breaking up this talkfest.

"My dear, I have been instructed to have a deep, personal conversation with you, but I'm not quite sure how that could come about."

"How about a conjugal visit?"

"If only I had the wings of Icarus." A camera is in his face, capturing his foolish smile.

"No hassle, man," Cud says, "I'll send down the elevator."

"Do it," says Felicity. "It's awesome up there."

Arthur has a crick in his neck from looking up. Icarus flew too close to the sun, fell to his death. He reminds himself that Stoney and Dog were among the building crew. He is leery of the rope ladder, though Felicity managed it well enough. But he can see himself tanglefooted in the rungs, hanging upside down.

He glances at Doc Dooley, who is about to set out with the eagle-spotting party. Dooley shakes a warning finger. Avoid stress.

"Margaret, the judge will forgive all sins if you evacuate the tree."

"Fat chance," she says. Slappy punctuates this with an emphatic bark.

Margaret seems far too pleased with her situation, her central role in this protest. Life with Arthur has paled, she has found a richer passion. A stout tree she can hug all day. How might Arthur urge her to give another volunteer a turn? He can't just shout it – that would only stiffen her resolve.

"Write her a letter." Reverend Al, a mind reader. Then he joins the eagle seekers as they take up packsacks and cameras.

Arthur tags along too, but is bearded by Todd Clearihue. "Hey, Arthur, can we pause for a friendly confab?" From his pocket, he produces several photographs – interiors of Arthur's garage, the tools, a close-up of the plans. "I'll be candid, Arthur, these were taken yesterday."

"By your trespassing private investigator. Todd, I suspect we may *not* be friends when this is over. Especially if I'm forced to sue for defamation should I hear the merest hint that I was in league with the parties who hid them there."

"Okay, let's put that aside. I can't believe you would do anything improper like that."

The intimation of blackmail has Arthur fighting an impulse to stalk off, but that would put past to any hope of negotiation. "Todd, you cannot deny that Gwendolyn Bay is a natural park. Nor that there is a hue and cry among the public. What an admirable gesture it would be to donate these lands – a brilliant coup of public relations."

Arthur expects no more than to soften up Garlinc for fair compensation – they will not throw away the $8 million paid for the land, will want other outlays covered. Clearihue carries on about anticipated profits, investment could be trebled, he has shareholders to answer to: a cynical mantra, the majority stock is held by his family.

"Suggest a figure," Arthur says.

"Sixteen million on quick turnover. The property is worth that alone in timber and recreational potential."

"That's double what you paid."

"Everyone knows the owners undervalued it."

"Outrageous." Ten thousand bake sales later . . .

"Arthur, let me be sincere with you – I'm just one shareholder. The other guys don't give a shit about Gwendolyn." A lowered voice. "I don't want this to get back to them. I'm with you on this deal. I live here, this is my now-and-forever home, I want to see parkland. For me, my kids." An intense look, he hungers to be believed.

"Fine, then give me your bottom figure."

"Fourteen and a half." Barely a whisper. "But it has to be quick, because if Justice Santorini switches on the green light, we're driving into Gwendolyn. I don't want to, but I don't have an option."

◆

Winded, Arthur lies on the moss, watching the troops disperse as they seek vantages to photograph a nest obscured by foliage. The structure is a massive thicket of sticks; the search crew can find no high point that might reveal if a female is nesting there.

One solitary eagle is on the wing, floating on the thermals. Below Arthur lie Gwendolyn Valley and the cup-shaped bay. As the eagle floats off behind a ridge, a pair of vultures come into view, as if with glum augury: the expedition is futile and must fail. The few members of the press who joined the trek are already heading down the trail; there is no story here.

They miss stout Flora Henderson tripping over her dog and ending up with her bottom wedged in a rift between rocks. Baldy Johansson cracks his shin trying to pull her out. Arthur is glad to see Baldy here – he was one of the naysayers hanging around the General Store.

Far down the beach, a determined otter forages among the driftwood. There are cliff swallows here, returning migrants, swooping like darts – where will they go when the walls of the Gap come down? And what is this? A little clump of ghost-white leaves and flowers. It may be the Phantom Orchid that lives off fungi, threatened in its northern range. He pictures the forest stripped to nakedness.

Arthur has always run from causes, distrustful of zealots with their hard opinions, but he's been feeling his despair turn to anger, the fuel that drives one to . . . social action, Lotis Rudnicki calls it. She taunted him again in the restaurant. Get on message, get on board, get involved. She remains stubbornly unwilling to tremble in his presence, enjoys defying the old crustacean and his calcified values.

He has been shoved about from all sides – Margaret, Deborah, the militant pixie – and it's wearing him down. He'll give these young lawyers a hand. He'll advise, he'll take a more active role in court. He'll go that far. For Margaret.

◆

On his way home, he stops at the General Store for his mail. The usual table of hard-drinking citizenry is here, as is Nelson Forbish, sticking copies of *The Bleat* in the mail slots, a special edition under the headline, "BOTTLE OF THE GAP DRAWS WORLD ATTENTION."

"'Bottle of the Gap?'" says Ernie Priposki, staring at the front page over his fortified coffee.

"Rush job of proofreading," Nelson says.

Arthur retrieves a copy: a photograph of two blurred, distant figures up a tree. Closer inspection informs that one of them is "prominent citizen Margaret Blake, wife of a former distinguished lawyer." What is he going to say to Ed Santorini? The judge will not be satisfied with a fat chance.

"Can't stop progress," Priposki says. "They're gonna have a fancy lounge in that development, with TV and cocktail waitresses."

Abraham Makepeace, heretofore not known to have a sense of humour, says, "Would you be happier if I wore a dress?" He fondles each article of Arthur's mail. "Here's your pension cheque, that's about all the good news. Card from a Woofer who's cancelling, going to business school. Margaret's got her David Suzuki newsletter. Invitation to subscribe to *Time*, with a free electronic pocket organizer. This here looks like it's from a law office."

Arthur tears it open. A few lines from Brian Pomeroy acknowledging he has the Faloon file well in hand, and inviting Arthur to join him in the defence. Fat chance.

"Hey, Arthur, you finding life on the homestead a little lonely these days?" The throaty chuckle of Emily Lemay, who managed the Brig Tavern until that fateful day when the kitchen grease caught fire. "Want me to come by and change the bedding?"

"He ain't that desperate," says Priposki.

"If I ever am, Emily, you'll be the first person I call."

"You got my number, case you need solace." Her Rubensesque figure quivers as she chortles. "Cuddles likes them young, but he ain't choosy. Randier than a five-legged dog."

She winks at Priposki, who joins in the ribbing: "Did I hear right he gave a librarian the clap on one of them reading tours?"

Arthur grins, he's a good sport.

Miraculously, yesterday's newspapers have arrived, and he buys a *Sun*, reads about the memorial service for Dr. Eve Winters, about the tributes for this caring marital healer. No children, and the story doesn't mention a consort. She was something of an athlete: tennis, swimming, bicycling.

On an inside page he sees his own picture: blowing Margaret a kiss from beneath the tree. How mawkish.

He picks out several mysteries from the used-book shelves, buys a new can opener – he has no idea where Margaret stored the old one. The coffee tin was empty – or was it the sugar tin? He buys both. He isn't sure what else the house is lacking – Margaret usually gives him a list.

He studies a bag of whole wheat flour. Yes, and yeast, he'll make his own bread. He's not a greenhorn in the kitchen, just out of practice ever since, on another April day, the widow next door came by looking for a lost lamb, finding one in Arthur. He succumbed hopelessly to love, remains its pathetic prisoner to this day. He feels hollow without her, incomplete.

He's not sure how much of his feelings she returns. "Arthur, I love you," she will say, but brightly, playfully. On their last night together, she shunned his touch in bed. She'd been deeply in love with popular, outgoing, fiddle-playing Chris Blake, who died untimely of a heart attack three years before Arthur plodded onto the scene. His ghost still haunts Blunder Bay, flitting in through bedroom windows, hovering, watching, judging.

Beauchamp returns home to an unbearable echoing silence. He misses Margaret's bell-like voice, on the phone, rallying the troops. He misses their evening walks with Slappy, his diligent inspection of every rock and bush and turd. He has company in misery – Shiftless, the yellow cat, is pouting on her mistress's reading chair.

Brian Pomeroy is on the answering machine: "When I saw you sneak out of court the other day, Arthur, I was overcome with a concept of staggering grandeur: a majestic piece of theatre, Arthur Beauchamp's comeback . . . Please call me. I'm falling apart here, I'm suicidal, only you can talk me down."

He seems in one of his demented moods, or well into the sauce. Arthur isn't up to dealing with Brian tonight. He has chores to do. He must confer with the Woofers (tofu burgers again, tonight) about the mystery of the escaping goats. Fat, farting Barney must be exiled to rockier pastures.

He enjoys these duties – he has known no life as placid and reward-ing as being the hired hand to Margaret Blake. The thought of even brief banishment from these shady vales and daisy-speckled fields causes him gloom. Gearing up for a trial, firing the engine, the huge mental and emotional toll – the prospect sends a shudder up his spine.

◆

"Face it, Beauchamp, you've lost the quickness. You have become old and forgetful. You haven't read a Supreme Court case in years, the law has moved beyond you." Arthur is talking to no audience but Barney and Shiftless, on a trek to the upper pasture. "You've lost the fire."

He has never understood why he succeeded so well in court – he is not disputatious by nature, and every client's trial was almost as severe a trial for him. A shy man when not on stage – but when he donned his robe: behold the confident persona. Arthur hasn't been able to figure out the mechanics of that – call it a dissociative disor-der. *The primary identity is passive, dependent, and depressed.*

After Blunder Bay is tucked in for the night, he sets a fire, and is about to snuggle into his club chair with the *Satires* of Juvenal when the peace is disturbed by the phone: Brian Pomeroy, boister-ous and drunk.

"Arturo, maestro, hero to all who struggle to fill the void since you left."

"Dispense with the blarney. The answer is no."

"I sympathize. You've got an ecological disaster on your hands and your wife is five flights up a tree – by the way, that's such a heart-warming story that I cried watching you on TV. You're looking great, in fighting trim."

"Too long out of training, Brian. I shall not be auditioning for your majestic piece of theatre."

"Give me half an hour of your miserable, lonely time, Arthur. *Audi alteram partem*, the first rule of fairness: listen to the other side."

"*Nolo episcopari.*"

"What's that?"

"The first rule of Beauchamp. I am declining to serve."

"Tomorrow's Sunday, and I'm catching the morning ferry and I'm coming over there to pitch you with a few friends in tow. Please don't tell me you have to be in church or milking cows or some other lame excuse, just give me the directions."

A few friends in tow. Arthur doesn't know quite what to expect. Friends adept at the arts of persuasion? He will not bend, even under torture. He doesn't owe Nick Faloon anything, he'd done his best. "Brian, you're most welcome, but . . ."

"I hear you're still off booze, congratulations, remind me to ask how one does that. Now I learn you're not supposed to drink when you're doing Prozac."

"Follow the signs to Potter's Road and Blunder Point . . . Never mind – I'll meet you at the ferry. How are the children?" Three of them, adopted when toddlers, Central American orphans.

"They're beautiful."

"And Caroline?" His equally acerbic wife, an English professor.

"That's why I'm taking the Prozac. I, too, choked on a pair of panties. Ciao"

Arthur isn't able to decode that. Brian's affairs are infamous, his separations with Caroline noisy. He's famously neurotic, but Arthur always enjoyed sharing courtrooms with him; he has a cutting wit.

He eases himself into his venerable chair – it has long accommodated itself to the shape of his body – adjusts his glasses, leafs through the *Satires*, reading the poetry aloud, then pausing with eyes closed to translate from the Latin: "'Conceived by a girl ashine with Iulian blood, and not from one who weaves for hire by the windswept walls.' Isn't that lovely, darling?"

Only silence greets that unanswerable question.

8

Because the ferry takes a meandering multi-island run on this sunny Sunday, it is one o'clock when the *Queen of Prince George* shudders into the Garibaldi dock, sending pigeons fluttering. Lounging by the Winnebagel, behind a faceful of cheese-burger, is the editor of *The Bleat*, who pauses mid-bite to watch a classic fin-tailed Cadillac convertible sweep off the ramp, bearing four off-islanders already looking lost.

Arthur signals them to pull over. Brian Pomeroy climbs out, lights a cigarette. "I have a grisly hangover. The air smells too clean here, I'm not adapted for it." He looks wan and unhealthy.

The others are cronies of Faloon. Willy the Hook Houston, who must be in his seventies now, a grey spry Brit, distinguished in bearing and appearance. Cat McAllister, Faloon's stall for many years, in her early forties, still exquisitely formed, a tight cerise dress, platinum hair. At the wheel is Freddy Jacoby, expensive suit, well filled out, a seller of financial advice and a buyer of suspect goods, whose handsome retainers often graced Arthur's desk.

Now advancing is Nelson Forbish, licking mustard from his fingers. Arthur beckons to Brian to join him in his truck, waves to Jacoby to follow. But Brian takes too long savouring his cigarette, and Nelson's cherubic face fills the driver's window. "What's up?"

"Not now, Nelson."

"There gonna be some action?" His voice lowers. "Looks like you're bringing the boys in."

"These are not boys."

"The muscle, the weight."

"They are merely film producers, Nelson."

"What film?"

"That fellow driving? You've likely caught him on TV. Academy Awards."

Nelson looks at Arthur suspiciously: he has been fooled before, Arthur's little joke about the nudist protest. "They gonna shoot a movie here?"

As Brian gets in, Arthur leans to Nelson and whispers, "I'll give you an exclusive in good time." He heads off, the Cadillac following.

Brian stares bleakly out the window. "By some mysterious form of random mimicry, on the same day Doctor Eve choked on her white nickers, someone stuck red bikinis in my jacket pocket. If it's Brovak, as I suspect, he won't own up to it and he's a prick. When I tried to tell Caroline it was an April Fool's joke, she laughed her head off, then kicked me out. I'm staying at the Ritz."

No wonder Brian is making a botch of the Faloon case. He got roaring drunk last night with no cause to celebrate. If this man isn't having a breakdown, he's teetering at the edge.

"You've got a marriage that works, Arthur. You and Margaret fit like comfortable shoes. Tell me how you do it."

Instead, Arthur attempts to introduce his island, pointing out the sites, the tiny steepled church, the dowdy island graveyard, but Brian expresses little interest. He is finally roused from his moping by his cellphone, a chime, a few chords from the *Fourth Brandenburg*.

"Hello ... Gabby? ... I love you too, Gabby ... I don't know, honey, whenever Mommy lets me come back."

To Arthur's utter discomfort, Brian begins to cry. He hopes that Brian, in this sensitive state, will not be too wounded by his critique of the Faloon defence strategy.

◆

There is much nervous shuffling in the house as his guests crane to watch Arthur pull a loaf from the oven. He can hear Brian on his phone in the next room. "Caroline? Pick up, Caroline, it's me. I'm coming to see the kids tomorrow."

"Cat, will you take the vegetables and the dip outside – since the day is mild, I think we ought to sit on the deck. I can offer coffee, tea, or a very good local apple juice. You will forgive the bread its concave shape."

"We are obliged that you would put yourself out in such a big manner, Mr. Beauchamp." Freddy Jacoby, the appointed spokesperson. "I want to say on behalf of everyone it is an honour to have us at your home."

"You're most kind. Cat McAllister, you are looking lovelier than ever. It must be twelve years since I last had the pleasure."

"They took me out of circulation for a while, Mr. Beauchamp, over a tiny swindle thing." As Arthur leads her to the deck, she catches a high heel on a loose board.

"And Willy Houston – have I heard right that you've retired?"

"Yes, sir, I'm not much into the game any more. I have a little set aside, and can throw in something for the defence." One could mistake him for a retired banker, polite, well spoken, though he's Cockney born and bred.

"You must try my wife's goat cheese. Very low in fat."

They shuffle into chairs around his warped cedar table. Brian says, "You start, Freddy."

Jacoby shakes his head woefully. "For me, I got to admit I don't think he's as *meshuga* as he's putting out, Mr. Beauchamp. As to the robberies, I couldn't put it past him, but I honestly don't believe Nick shoved off that lady psychiatrist." He takes a breath, then delivers his prepared text: "We know you and him go back a long time, and he always talks with great admiration, like you're his mentor and he owes his career to you. We know you were disappointed in the last outcome, and on the basis of that we hope Nick deserves one last chance to clear hisself."

"Also, he's in a bad way," says Brian, cueing him – he has obviously rehearsed this show.

"Right," says Jacoby. "Nick, he's – I'll be honest, Mr. Beauchamp, he's suicidal. Sitting out there in the spook house with all sorts of dangerous psychos, it's doing something to his head. You wanna add to that, Willy?"

"He got on the phone to me from VI," says Willy the Hook. "There are some very depressive blokes in that joint. They're getting to him. He's afraid he'll never graduate from there, and he's thinking of finding an easier way out."

Cat chimes in. "He was framed already once, Mr. Beauchamp. A rape he couldn't of done. Now someone's trying to set him up again."

"My best estimate," says Jacoby, "is the bulls faked the DNA test, figuring he owes for past offences. The ones you beat for him, Mr. Beauchamp."

"They got somebody in the science lab to sign off on it," says Willy.

"Or maybe the killer doped up the corpse with his semen," says Cat. "To frame him."

Arthur feels a tingle. Nick Faloon, framed for murder . . . They have found his tender spot, written a clever script, however awkward and forced in delivery.

"We took up a little collection here." Freddy Jacoby produces a wad of bills. "Just to get you started. And we chipped in and got you this for your wife." A velvet padded box opens to reveal a Piaget watch. "On my honour, it is legitimate and can't be traced nowhere. Also, we all commend your wife for what she is doing. We are for saving the trees."

Arthur is thinking about false incrimination. He cannot imagine that police scientists could be corrupted – but might others have motives? Adeline Angella, who sold her story to *Real Women Magazine* . . .

"I worked with Nick for a dozen years, Mr. Beauchamp," says Cat. "He never once made a pass. Okay, once, but I tickled him and he stopped. Nick don't attack women. Nick don't kill. He's been jobbed."

Everyone turns to Brian, who is rubbing his forehead, trying to knead a headache away. He speaks wearily, "Fact is, Arthur, we couldn't help notice your interest in this case. You called my office to get him help. You showed up in court. Don't pretend you don't give a shit. Because *I* give a shit, and I've got three kids and a marriage counsellor to support and I'm turning down good money. There's a hundred and ten thousand dollars in that bundle."

"To get you going, Mr. Beauchamp," says Jacoby. "Business ventures are pending that will scrape up more."

"The question of fees doesn't weigh on me right now," Arthur says.

"Because something else does," Brian says, remorseless. "That rape conviction still galls, doesn't it? What was it – thirty straight wins?"

"To be precise, thirty-three."

"I sat in on some of that trial. I saw Angella's touching performance on the stand. Now she's written another article about her lasting trauma as a victim. She's making a living out of it, she's on the lecture circuit. What I propose is this: I'll undertake to repair that blotch on your record . . . Arthur, can we go outside for a smoke?"

"We are outside."

Brian looks around, as if needing to make sure. "Okay, can we go farther outside?"

"Have your talk," says Jacoby, "while we partake of this refreshment. The dip is undeniable, Mr. Beauchamp."

Brian continues to pitch Arthur as they walk toward the barn. "I have access to Angella – who, by the way, has a record for making spurious complaints about stalkers, bus-stop butt squeezers. She was hanging around court a couple of days ago watching me finish a sex assault, and now she wants to interview me. She has an assignment from *Real Women* to obsess over rape again. She wants to get the defence lawyer's point of view. 'Balance,' she calls it."

"I would suggest staying clear of her, or next you'll be asking me to act for *you*."

"While I take on Angella, you take on Nick Faloon." Brian leans on a fencepost, drags hungrily on his cigarette. "Where can I lie down? Any freshly dug hole will do."

Arthur leads him to a sunny patch of spring grass by the barn. Brian briefly inspects it for livestock droppings, then subsides onto his back. "Nice spread, Arthur, but I heard people get taken off these islands in straitjackets. The boredom finally causes them to snap." He is about to light another cigarette, then realizes he has one going. "Apart from the odd forest blockade, does anything really *happen* here?"

"You have no idea what happens here."

As if to illustrate, the proprietor of Island Landscraping is coming up Arthur's driveway on a backhoe, Dog following in Arthur's still-mufflerless Fargo. "Excuse me while I tend to some business."

Stoney parks his machine out of sight of the road, behind the flared skirts of a cedar windbreak. Dismounting, he pats a fender. "A beauty, eh? I drove a hard bargain with Honk Gilmore, got it cheap considering it's just been overhauled with all new parts. Sorry, didn't know you had company – I came by basically to ask for some legal advice. How do I plead not guilty to a mechanic's lien? They want half of what I bought it for."

The nature of this visit comes clear. Stoney got the machine cheap because Honk Gilmore never paid for the overhaul and the new parts; now Island Landscraping seeks to hide it from creditors. "Stoney, I'm not about to conceal a wanted backhoe in my front yard."

"That's not the way I work, Arthur, you know me, I wouldn't dream of it. I came here to do a test dig – free, no obligation, a loss leader – and if I hit clay as I suspect, then we know the pool will hold. I'd start now, but I don't want to disturb your guests. I heard they're in the movie business – if they need any help building sets, you know who to call." Garibaldi's town crier has been busy spreading the word. "Okay, Dog's gonna drive us back so I can get to work on that muffler. We'll return when you're not so busy."

Stoney doesn't allow further protest. He is already in the Fargo's cab with Dog, waving at the film producers as he drives off. Arthur dismisses the notion of going after them in hot pursuit. The backhoe will be evicted tomorrow.

He returns to Brian. "Two of the local malefactors. Not quite in Nick Faloon's league." He sits and packs his pipe. "Where do you think you're going with his case, Brian?"

He's still on his back, chewing a grass stem, playing with another cigarette. "I'm not going to pull it off, am I, Arthur?"

Arthur coaxes a burn from his Peterson bent, and decides to go straight to the nub. "Insanity makes a dangerous mix with alibi. Jurors who might otherwise entertain reasonable doubt do not take chances on alleged insane murderers. This Gertrude Heeredam business can only blow up in your face. That you have got this far is a tribute to the mendacity of Dr. Endicott Sloan."

"I thought I'd throw it in the pot. It was a backup if I couldn't find a real defence."

"Act quickly on this, Brian. Get him out of VI before they find out his father is still alive."

Brian sits up too suddenly, grabs his head. "He *is*?"

"Mr. Faloon is a senior civil servant in Lebanon. He flew here not ten years ago to visit his son. When I met him, he showed no signs of having been shot by the Falange."

"Oh, shit."

"It's a story Nick has told so many times it has become accepted legend. The child refugee, anxious, bewildered, thrust into a new world, unable to withstand its temptations. It won him many suspended sentences. He was three years old when his parents emigrated from Beirut. They have since returned. All this will be discovered if the authorities dig into citizenship and immigration records."

"God, I'm fucking up so badly I've become a menace to my client. My last lucid moment was nine days ago, on April Fool's Day, when I innocently pulled a pair of foreign panties from my jacket pocket while Caroline was bundling the kids for a walk. I got up this morning after two hours' sleep so I could come over here and show you what shape I'm in. I can't do this trial alone. So forget insanity, let's move on to greener pastures." Brian does just that, collapsing on the grass again.

"What else do we have?" *We* – Arthur let slip that troubling pronoun.

"To start, there's nothing to tie him to the scene but his semen. No prints – but you'd expect Faloon to wear gloves. No hairs, fingernail scrapings, blood. The only signs the victim resisted are a chipped front tooth and some redness on the lower abdomen and the wrists. That could have come from tight clothing worn on the trail. No apparent means of illegal entry, so she may have let Nick in."

This hints of another problem – Brian lacks faith in his client. "Or whoever did it."

"Right, of course."

"At an odd hour of the night – what was the pathologist's best estimate?"

"Around 2 a.m. Also at that time, one Harvey Coolidge from Kansas, a teller of bad dinner-table jokes, was out of bed too. He couldn't sleep, wasn't digesting well, went out to get some air."

"He dined with Faloon and Winters?"

"And was looking cross-eyed at her all night."

"How strong are those four counts of theft?"

"They can't make him on those, there's not a thimble of proof. Forensics vacuumed the rooms, Faloon didn't leave a hair. Mind you, he did it, all right, buried the loot somewhere."

"Anything stolen from Dr. Winters?"

"No. She had a fanny pouch, four hundred and change, credit cards, all untouched."

"Earlier, she was at the local bar?"

"Listening to a jazz band."

"In anyone's company?"

Brian is onto his fourth cigarette, his voice hoarse. "Came in alone, took a barstool, hung around for almost an hour, drank two glasses of wine. Another woman had some chit-chat with her, Holly Hoover, unemployed, single, a local. Winters left during the last set, about eleven o'clock."

"And returned to her cottage how?"

"No one knows. She would've had to be boated across. The cops can't figure that one out – no one's come forward."

"The murder weapon was unusual."

"White cotton standard-brand underwear. Her other clothes – bra, jeans, sweater – were on a chair by the fireplace. A bath towel was at the foot of the bed. A fair theory is she just got out of the shower when she was surprised by her attacker."

"In the meantime, of course, the authorities are focused on their all-too-handy prime suspect while other trails go cold."

"They've got his DNA prints, Arthur."

"That's a stickler."

"But circumstantial. DNA doesn't prove he raped or killed her. It's consistent with the rational theory that Faloon was simply invited to her bed at some point."

"*Rational* theory?" Arthur finds it inconceivable that he could urge it on the jury with a straight face. Who would believe that Eve Winters found this Peter Lorre lookalike of romantic interest?

"At least let's be creative with the concept. Doctor Eve may have wanted to try . . . something different."

"Were the sperm motile?"

"No, but the swab didn't get to the lab till late in the day."

"Cat McAllister makes a case that Nick was framed, that someone might have had a sample of his semen."

"And we're back to Adeline Angella."

Arthur nods, and they smoke quietly for a while. "She wants to interview you for a magazine piece. Why you, Brian? Was your assault trial controversial in any manner?"

"Not really. Sales manager gropes secretary in the stockroom, rips her dress, she calls the cops."

"And was that *after* you were on record as Faloon's counsel?"

A pause for thought, then he nods. "Okay, that's why she targeted me."

"I would be very careful with her."

"All I need to make my world complete is a false accusation of rape." He repeats his offer: "I'm willing to do my part, Arturo, if you do yours."

This case has the desperate smell of a loser. Yet Arthur's pride is in play. If Nick Faloon were to be wrongly convicted again, this time for murder, it would be an egregious insult to Themis, goddess of justice . . .

Not for the first time today, his thoughts scamper squirrel-like up a tree. Where proudly stands, waving to the cameras, the smiling, defiant spouse. In contrast to her, we have the doornail sitting in his club chair with his dead poets. *You were a famous lawyer when she met you. What have you done since to impress her?* Deborah's words echo harshly.

He suddenly feels weightless, like Atlas upon Hercules relieving him of heaven's burden. His shoulders straighten. "Take up Angella's invitation. I'll want to visit Bamfield, particularly to meet the woman who engaged Dr. Winters in the bar. In the meantime, we must have *all* laboratory tests – they may have examined the wrong material, confused their exhibits. And let's get Nick out of that asylum."

A smile blooms on Brian's crooked, ravaged face. "The return of Cyrano." His cellphone rings again. He answers, "Last Round-Up Funeral Home. How may we help you?" Arthur retreats. His senses quicken as he approaches the support group. He is no longer a local yokel, he's a lawyer again. Margaret will understand. He'll seek her consent, of course, that's the right thing to do.

The three faces shine expectantly at him as he slices more bread from his bowbacked loaf. He must complain to Abraham Makepeace that he's stocking old and impotent yeast. The only sound is produced by Jacoby, playing with the bundle of bills, snapping the elastic. Finally, he says, "We are waiting with bated breath for your verdict, Mr. Beauchamp."

"I'll do it if I have permission from my wife." Yes, he'll explain to Margaret that he faces a challenge of his own. *I have to do this.* Faloon's trial will be many months away. He can do much of the preparation at home.

Cat plants a kiss on his forehead, her breasts brushing his chin. Arthur is assailed by a nosegay of . . . not perfume, the scent of her sex. He feels a blush of embarrassment.

Brian rejoins them, still on the phone. "Okay, sweetie, I'll see you tomorrow. Kiss, kiss." He pockets the phone. "Expenses will be high, gentlemen. The maestro comes higher." In a more sanguine mood, relieved of the burden of the trial, he plucks the packet of bills from Jacoby. "Will you be putting this under your pillow, Arthur, or should I deposit it?"

"In a trust account." Arthur has long stopped worrying where his fees come from – the legal profession would be in dire straits without thieves and swindlers.

Brian places the money in a case, and draws from it an expansion folder, the Faloon file. "I told these good people you don't come in for under thirty thousand a day plus disbursements, based on a ten-day trial, more if it goes longer." Nobody blanches, they are smiling.

Arthur is glad Brian dealt with the fees, shielding him from that discomfort. Three hundred thousand dollars will provide a hefty boost to the Save Gwendolyn fund.

Jacoby raises his glass. "I would like to toast Mr. Beauchamp for making this bold decision."

Others murmur assent, but Brian wants to celebrate with other than apple juice. "Is there a liquor store here, Arthur?"

✦

At the General Store, only two of the usual idlers are about: Emily Lemay and Gomer Goulet. Makepeace is in the aisles helping Winnie Gillicuddy, who is a hundred and three and can't see well, yet walks to the store almost every day. "No, no, Winnie," he says, "you give me the list, I'll get someone to drive by with the whole shebang."

"I don't want a shebang, I want what's on this list, and twenty dollars on Lotto 6/49." Winnie resists Makepeace's attempt to wrest away her shopping basket and heads down the aisle.

Jacoby says, "I assume we will not be looking at any bottles of champagne in this fine establishment."

"Not much call for that here."

As they settle on a bottle of rye whisky, Emily sashays to the counter. "Aren't you going to introduce me to your friend from Hollywood, Arthur?" The long-reigning Garibaldi sex goddess decides not to wait for such politeness, thrusts out her hand. Jacoby takes it uncertainly.

"Frederick R. Jacoby, ma'am."

"I love your movies. We're so excited that you're going to do one on little Garibaldi."

Jacoby looks sideways at Arthur. "So far, ma'am, we're keeping everything ambiguous."

"You think you might find room for me on the casting couch, Mr. Jacoby?"

"Wouldn't be room for anyone else," says Goulet.

Winnie calls from the back. "You call this shrivelled thing a grapefruit? Where in tarnation have you hid the tea?"

◆

The afternoon is waning as Arthur leads the group, merry with drink, to the ferry.

"If you desire any help with these developers," says Jacoby, "to make them see reason, I am aware of certain persons you can call upon."

"Very kind of you, but that will not be necessary."

After seeing them off, he hastens to the Gap. To reduce traffic in the forest, all demonstrators have moved their tents to the acre of clear-cut by the road. Stump Town, they call it. A banner has been strung up: "Is This What You Want on the Gulf Islands?"

The several reporters here look happy with their item of the day: Reverend Al performed an elaborate ritual this morning – not to be found in the Anglican canons – consecrating the site, proclaiming the protest tree a holy gift of nature. Henceforth it's to be called the Holy Tree.

Arthur cannot avoid Trustee Zoller, who comes close to his ear. "In case you got the wrong impression that I'm not entirely unsympathetic to saving this forest, you're wrong." As Arthur tries to dig through this weedy garden of negatives, Zoller adds to the confusion: "I'm more useful working from the outside. As an insider."

"I'm glad you're coming around, Kurt."

"They say it's going to be an epic, with Sean Penn and Woody Harrelson. Somebody told me they pay extras two hundred a day." Arthur hurries up the trail, Zoller clinging to him. "Maybe you could put in a word."

The rumours have also scaled the Holy Tree, with added distortions. After their shouted words of greeting, Margaret asks if it's true he was rehearsing the bedroom scene with that platinum floozy he was seen with earlier. She has a big laugh over this. She continues to be in fine spirits up there, smiling royally down at her subjects. The press like her. *Plucky* is the overused adjective.

"All will be revealed tomorrow when I post a letter." It will include a polite plea to give someone else a turn.

Margaret posts her own letter, a paper glider. It's a list: fresh underwear, socks, pyjamas. Arthur will fetch her robe too – he doesn't want her parading about in nightwear in front of Cudworth. Ground observers are guarding against Felicity sneaking him booze or pot. Stimulants have been known to cause the oaf to lose his veneer of civilization.

One supposes he pries and spies, denying her privacy. Where do they change clothes? *Hey, you got your bra strap twisted.* They must constantly be in each other's hair – one table between them, one desk, one potty. Arthur can't imagine what they do all day, how they exercise. Yoga maybe. *Hold that position. Now stick out the butt.*

Cud appears, shirtless, brushing his teeth. He lets go a spume of white spit that arcs past Zoller. "Oh, sorry, man, didn't see you down there." Once more, Arthur dismisses any notion that Margaret might find this fellow of romantic interest.

9

Faloon is learning the routines at VI, one of which is sitting around in the lounge after lunch, him and a bunch of sedated zombies, watching the cartoon channel. He wonders who came up with this brilliant idea of a forced diet of Porky Pig, they probably think the inmates can't handle anything more complex, or you're supposed to laugh, a kind of therapy.

But no one cracks a grin, the humour lost on, for instance, the two oxen sitting over there, both killers, one of them chopped up his mother-in-law and the other put down a neighbour on orders from God, and has an erect dick tattooed on his forearm. But the real fun guy was the Nazi punk, who took an irrational dislike to Faloon on first encounter, and kept whispering things like, "I'm going to eviscerate you, Jew boy." Fortunately he was taken away the next morning for what Faloon hopes was a lobotomy.

It's two o'clock on an average Sunday in the ding ward. An hour to wait for Claudette St. John, who got herself a visitors' pass, who is finally coming from Bamfield to see him. Her letters are the only warm spot, she believes in him.

This is gratifying because he and Claudette were on the outs after the incident with Holly Hoover, who caught him in a weak moment. Holly was about to do a circuit of the logging camps and needed a room for the night, plus she's a very hot product, terrific body, and they ended up trading. Claudette got wind and accusations flew. Despite Faloon's lies, things didn't go well for a long time.

But Faloon isn't much cheered by Claudette's support – for him hope is gone. The air went out of him like a flat tire when Arthur Beauchamp walked out of that courtroom, looking grim and severe, like he was disappointed in the Owl, somehow betrayed.

If he beats the rap on account of insanity, this is his future, right here – the Owl will be spending the rest of his life where every day you got to worry there's been a goof-up, they forgot to trank down Weird Harold, who's decided the quivering lump of jelly over there is reading his inner thoughts. "Tell me why you feel threatened," the local head fixer said, who spent most of that session cleaning his glasses and working at his crockery with a toothpick.

The Owl silently cheers on the Roadrunner, who makes another miraculous escape from Wily Coyote. Faloon has been studying the ventilation ducts, trying to decide if he's small enough to squeeze into them, wiggle his way somewhere, the laundry room, then over the fence to the street. It seems a better plan than to overcome the six-and-a-half-foot warder who stands by the door.

A break for commercials, and the ape with the blue veiner tattooed on his arm is no longer riveted to the screen. He is sizing up the Owl. The tranks are wearing off, God is whispering that Faloon is trying to control his mind. The other one is staring at him now too, the mother-in-law chopper, whose preferred tool was a cleaver. In such an atmosphere, Faloon has decided not to offend anyone with Gertrude Heeredam demonstrations.

Anyway, he has practically given up on the multiple identity theory, a play born of desperation. The psychiatric nurse isn't buying it, a shrewd and unsympathetic woman. Nurse Thompson has been assigned to "work" with him, as she puts it. Now she wants to run him through a lie detector. His current counsel, Brian Pomeroy, says definitely not, it would put the final kibosh to the whole deal. She'd check into his father, discover he returned to the old country after his business folded, and is ten thousand miles away.

His parents don't have happy memories of Canada, their boy a delinquent, always running away from home. In school, he was the little Arab kid who got stepped on. He had to stand up to them, show them something, so as a dare he stole the principal's briefcase and entertained his new friends with the *Playboy* in it. That gave him honour and respect. It was the turning point of his life.

A child psychologist told his parents he suffered from kleptomania, and wrongly assured them he'd grow out of it, the problem wouldn't grip him for life. The only side benefit was it got him some cheap sentences; Mr. Beauchamp has even been known to wring tears out of his disability.

Mr. Pomeroy lacks the satin touch and seems kind of scattered, but he has other qualities. For instance, he's got the nuts of Godzilla. Adeline Angella has made contact with him. She wants to interview him at a quiet place for dinner. Since the same modus operandi happened in Faloon's case, the spider inviting the fly, he tried to warn Mr. Pomeroy off, but he's going ahead with it.

The lawyer wanted to know all about Faloon's ill-fated date, and made detailed notes, once pausing to compliment him on his powers of observation. Faloon explained it's how he made his living.

It was at the Kashmir Sapphire trial where Faloon first saw Angella, at the press table, giving him the eye while Mr. Beauchamp destroyed the main Crown eyewitness, who it turned out could hardly see, let alone read, the calendar on the courtroom wall. After Faloon was cleared, Angella accosted him outside, giving him the pitch about her being a magazine writer and she would love to know about the fascinating world of the jewel thief.

To his everlasting sorrow, Faloon was intrigued, everyone wants a little fame and recognition. He could spin her, his friends would have a laugh reading the story. But of course he got into the sauce before meeting her, celebrating with Cat and Willy – the Kashmir had been a three-handed play, a lawn party, a visiting maharaja, a replica in paste, two months of planning.

Angella suggested a restaurant at the Four Seasons, and Faloon had to admit he was banned from that chain, so they settled on a Spanish place in her neighbourhood, El Torro, where he continued to get oiled, with sangria then wine. She wanted to know about the Kashmir

Sapphire, and he told her it was too delicate a subject right now. He laid on a lot of baloney instead, stuff like he was raised in a family of trapeze artists, and how he filched the Persian Goddess from the Constantinople Museum by swinging on a rope.

The fact is the Owl is really not a movie-hero kind of guy who swings from ropes and chandeliers and leaps over laser beams, he has always left that sort of stuff to Clint Eastwood. He doesn't like the physical stuff, relies on nimble fingers and swift feet.

The Angella woman was better than passing grade, but not top shelf. Full-beam headlights, though. Breastacula. The Owl wasn't counting on any sexual involvement until he picked up that she was coming on to him – leaning forward, all audience, an "Oh, goodness" here and a gasp there, her hands fluttering over her breasts. She had this way of staring intently at him as she dipped her tongue in her wineglass before taking a sip. If the idea was to make him horny, it was working. "Cognacs?" she said. "I'm just around the corner."

Finally, on the TV there's something for the level above five-year-olds, *The Simpsons*, but when it opens to Homer presiding over a family dinner, Weird Harold rises, points to the screen, and shouts, "That's him! That's Gary! May you rot in hell!"

The warder presses a button, sirens sound, and lights flash, and the warder is moving toward this unbalanced individual with a straitjacket, and they wrestle. Now the guy who dismembered his neighbour is again fixed on Faloon. But before the nightmare can ignite into some epic bloody climax, reinforcements pour in, syringes in hand.

Faloon looks at those ventilation ducts again.

✦

The booths in the visiting area are full on a Sunday, but it's a non-contact zone, the visitors separated by a window, with a kind of walkie-talkie setup that is probably bugged. Claudette approaches, smiling. She had her hair cut, it makes her look a lot younger than fifty, at which age she's still table grade. You've got to be someone who likes a little extra, though.

They were a regular team for over a year, except for that brief outage over the logging whore. Until he got busted, Faloon was planning to propose she give up her rental, make Nitinat Lodge her home. He kind of thinks he loves her, and vice versa, but neither of them have committed themselves to that concept.

As endearments fly, it floods in on him how much he is going to miss her, she is the only woman not in the trade he has ever opened up with. Because he's so scrawny and generally homely he feels privileged that she's fond of him. She's enamoured about him being an outlaw, a jewel thief, but has this habit of encouraging him to be straight. "Isn't it fun running a business?" "Don't you feel good about yourself when you're doing honest work?" As he's swabbing out the toilets at the Nitinat Lodge.

Claudette is Nova Scotian. She cut out of school early and meandered across the country – apple picker, cocktail waitress, road flagger, patty flipper – but she had to stop at Bamfield, it was the end of Canada, and she's been slinging pints at the Bam Pub for the last six years.

She asks, "You got my letters?"

"Read every one ten times, but you got to cut down on the scented paper, the tears smear it up."

"Oh, Nick, I'm gonna fall apart. What are you doing in here, you're not crazy."

"Yeah, but don't say that – they're listening. For the record, I am innocent."

"I explained that to Jasper Flynn till I'm blue in the face. You hate violence. I told him how you look down on robbers who use weapons. I don't believe those DNA tests, scientists are always making mistakes, testing the wrong samples, stuff like that. Either that or they're lying, and the cops are trying to set you up."

"Claudette, when it comes to coppers, I have no enemy. I never met one who don't like me. We're tough competitors, just on different teams. There's got to be some other answer. They ought to drill that condo developer with a few more questions."

"Maybe you want to think about Holly Hoover."

A name he never thought she'd mention without a profanity. This is the hooker who, three months ago, traded him sex for a free room. Lying about that to Claudette was about the hardest thing he's ever done.

"Honey, are you sure you didn't screw her?"

He gulps and nods. He's going to live with this lie if lightning strikes. He waves her to be silent, mimes that she should just mouth what she wants to say – he's good at lip reading.

The gist of what he makes out is this – while Claudette was working the bar at the Bam Pub, she saw Dr. Eve Winters and Holly, tight together on stools, talking about what, she doesn't know. Some flirtatious signals started happening, heavy eye contact, a squeeze of the hand, a pat.

Faloon nods, a picture forming of Claudette watching the harlot through narrowed eyes, her every touch and wink, watching the two women hit on each other. To Holly, a jane is as good as a john, she's a pro, she's not gender-biased. He tries this new slant on Dr. Winters, remembers how when the Topeka fishermen were undressing her over their salmon, she chose the Owl to talk to as less offensive.

Holly left the bar first, then Dr. Winters followed ten minutes later. Claudette does a charade of her yawning, looking at her watch. Faloon doesn't know what he should make of this, but he can't see Holly knocking someone over. She may know something, though, and isn't talking.

He holds Pomeroy's business card to the glass, Claudette nodding, she'll pass this bit to the lawyer. He mouths, Have you told the cops?

She nods, then shrugs elaborately. Faloon gathers they didn't seem interested.

After they go on air again, Claudette tries to cheer him up with Bamfield vignettes. Rumours have spread that Faloon's take from the Breakers Inn is buried somewhere in town, so half the population is wandering around with shovels. Faloon misses Bamfield. Despite slowly going broke there, it was an okay joint, he beat his habit for a while. It felt weird going straight, but he might have adapted if he hung in. Because there was Claudette.

He feels buoyed by her, and as he watches her fight tears while being so perky and stand-up, he figures he's in love with her, though he's not sure because he's never experienced it before. He says it anyway. "I feel like I'm in love with you."

"Oh, Nick, I think I love you too." The floodgates open.

✦

He's playing with being in love, enjoying the idea, even as Nurse Thompson puts him through a personality test about whether he has anti-societal feelings. She's trying to get him to say the first thing that comes to his mind after loaded words.

He's not very good at this game, his attention wandering because he unhappily recalls, in all the tears and excitement with Claudette, promising to get her a diamond as big as a walnut. It had the jarring ring of commitment. Engagement. Marriage.

"Blood."

"Nose."

"Nose? Why a nose?"

"Because I walked into a wall last night, and had a nosebleed."

"Sleep."

"Walk." The nurse frowns, not happy with these results. "Because I was sleepwalking when I walked into the wall."

"Death."

"Suicide." Faloon has already told her about his feelings in that direction.

"Anger."

"Love."

"Woman."

"Love."

Nurse Thompson gives him this distrustful look. "Is that all you can come up with?"

"On account of maybe I'm in love."

"Why are you staring at me?"

Faloon worries she may think his feelings are for her, and explains about Claudette. How though it wasn't at first sight, it ballooned into a romance, and how she is so big-hearted and has faith in him.

Nurse Thompson looks like she doesn't believe him. Or isn't equipped to deal with love.

◆

On Monday, Brian Pomeroy drops in unannounced. Having asked around in the joint, Faloon has learned this counsellor is hitched but has a reputation for affairs that get him in shit. He's courting extreme danger by planning to go out with Adeline Angella, and the Owl is impressed by that.

Since lawyers don't usually make house calls except with bad news, he assumes there has been a wrong turn in his fortunes. But no, Mr. Pomeroy comes into the little interview room with one of his rare smiles.

"Are you holding up okay?"

"Basically, I'm in love. How about you?"

"I'm on Prozac. You're lucky to have Claudette cheering for you. *I* should be so lucky to have such a partner. She tells me Holly Hoover is very outdoorsy for a hooker, has a big boat, also a canoe. No one saw them, but they may have gone for a romantic paddle in the drizzle. Maybe across the inlet. I gather Ms. Hoover rents a place not far from Brady Beach."

"Ever since maybe a month ago. A trailer."

"I want you to tell me, Nick, man to man – ever get it on with Holly Hoover?"

"I am committed to another woman." Faloon must brazen it out, he can't trust loose mouths not to talk, especially this one, with the smell of yesterday's whisky on his breath.

"Holly stayed overnight at your place. Good-looking woman, I hear."

"Whatever you're insinuating, Mr. Pomeroy, I am in denial. She just rented a room."

Pomeroy grins in a winking, skeptical way, then jolts him with good news: "Arthur Beauchamp is going to take you on."

It's as if the clouds have parted and the sun is shining on Faloon. In this elated state, he listens to how some of his colleagues visited Beauchamp and pleaded his case. Coming out of retirement for Faloon is such an honour he feels a lump in his throat.

"We're bringing you back to court tomorrow. I may not be able to help him much, because I'm having a few family problems."

"I figured it was something like that, Mr. Pomeroy. You never even got around to asking if I did it. I never even . . ."

His hand says halt. "I want you to listen carefully, Nick, because I'm going to put a situation to you. It goes like this: Nick Faloon and Eve Winters strike up a conversation over dinner at the Breakers. She finds him droll, interesting, a character. Maybe he's not a stud, but as a psychologist she sees beneath the surface. She wants to celebrate her strenuous hike with something more interesting than amateur night at the local, she wants to do something quirky and daring and totally off the wall, because she's that kind of gal: she's into experimenting, she's innovative, curious, fascinated by all aspects of human sexual behaviour. So she asks Nick to wander by later to share a bottle of wine. And of course they get it on."

"Only a baboon's going to buy that, Mr. Pomeroy." He wonders how much Prozac this fixer has been doing. "This was a very refined lady. No way she would stoop to hustling a low-class citizen like me."

Pomeroy keeps on with his scenario. "She forgets to lock the door when Nick leaves, and the prowler strikes." Finally, his voice trails off with the absurdity of the proposition.

"Mr. Pomeroy, I don't even want Claudette to know that idea ever got mentioned. Not to be personal, but . . . maybe you should be getting help with your marriage? Like, ah, maybe a relationship analyst like Dr. Winters?"

"Thanks, we have one. Except that I'm the outsider in *their* relationship." The lawyer is showing emotion and has to pull himself together. "Anyway, this brings us to the ironical possibility that you, too, were victimized on April Fool's Day."

"I am listening."

"Someone may have planted your seed in the victim. The someone we have in mind is Adeline Angella."

Faloon isn't startled, he'd played with the thought but rejected it — there wasn't much sense to it, or any motive. Unless Angella was offended by what he testified in court, implying that after the big sexual come-on she wasn't that hot in bed.

"You used a rubber, right, Nick? That's what you said in court."

"She says not, but on God's word, Mr. Pomeroy, she provided it. She went to the bathroom, came back with a Trojan."

"Her version is that she begged you to put on a condom as you held a knife to her throat, and you refused."

"What I was holding was not a knife."

"And what happened to the skin?"

"I don't know, it was the wrong size, too big. If you have to know, Mr. Pomeroy, I don't have very much circumference in that department. Somehow it kind of slipped off and got stuck up there."

"Up her pussy?"

"I guess. I never saw it again."

"Nor did the cops. A doctor examines her an hour later, takes a couple of swabs, and not surprisingly they've got your come on it. Meanwhile Angella has fished out the safe and put it in the freezer with the ice cream."

This theory showed almost as many gaping holes as the scenario of Faloon making it with Dr. Winters. Why would Angella have kept some of his discharge? Only madness would drive her to a deed like this, a murder, trying to hang it on him.

After the lawyer leaves, he tries out that word again. Madness . . .

Maybe he didn't see that side of her because he was blinded by lust, it was three years since he went to bed with a woman. But she practically offered it on a spoon, took him to a small apartment that was so clean it didn't seem lived in. The first thing she did after pouring him a snifter was show him her book of clippings, stories she wrote, which were mostly for low-rent publications, not regular magazines.

Again, she asked him for the inside story of the Kashmir Sapphire, and he kept putting her off, saying maybe some other time. He continued to make up fables instead, Angella purring, "How exciting, it's just like a Cary Grant film." She had a taste for old caper flicks, Cary Grant, Errol Flynn. Somehow they got onto the romantic side of such movies, then sexual fantasies involving masked intruders, and that's when Faloon started to feel strange about her, she seemed to want to act out a movie role, scripted.

She put out the lights until there was just a glow from the bedroom like an invitation, and that's when he asked if he could kiss her.

"You're not supposed to ask," she said.

10

Arthur rises early this morning to assemble himself for the courtroom, feeling ill prepared after his long hiatus. He remembers his brogues, and selects a poorly fitting suit of a cut he hopes has returned to vogue after a decade. Brian will meet him at the Victoria ferry terminus, so he'll go as a foot passenger. The Faloon hearing ought not to take long, a few housecleaning items, sweeping out the garbage that has collected around the case, the claim of insanity.

The Gwendolyn injunction is also set for hearing this morning. Arthur will wander in when he can: he doesn't want Santorini thrusting him into the role of counsel – Selwyn Loo is more than capable, though his larder of arguments is growing bare. He has filed photographs of the nest, of a solitary eagle on a nearby branch. The Save Gwendolers are worried – why has its mate not been seen for several days? Selwyn will plead for more time.

Arthur sent ten handwritten pages up the dumb waiter yesterday, a collage of farm concerns – they're down to one Woofer – a denial of the rumours of film stardom, a ponderous explanation about owing a debt to Nick Faloon, and an obliquely worded invitation to come to ground. He sought reaction as Margaret read it. Was she relieved he'd stopped being a doornail? Irritated to have been shunted onto a sidetrack and having to share the family spotlight? She looked startled for a moment, but it was only the onset of a sneeze.

In the end, she deflated every expectation with a shrug. "Why even think about it? If you feel strongly, go for it." The inference was inescapable: she's not about to abandon her post. Still, like Minerva on her throne, who gave Ulysses strength, Margaret blessed this project. And, like Ulysses, Arthur has set sail for the Isles of the Blest, fully aware the legend is unclear whether he reached those shores or capsized.

He dusts off his elderly, sagging briefcase, and gathers up the Faloon file, its pages scattered to every reach of the dining-room table. He spent a day absorbing witness statements, exhibit lists, synopses of laboratory tests. It will take him months to bone up on recent law and forensics. DNA profiling was in its infancy when he quit practice.

Staff Sergeant Jasper Flynn wrote up the file in typically stilted police prose: "The scene of the incident is the property of Gerald and Inez Cotter, 85 and 79 respectively, who reside in East Bamfield, and advertise said cottage for rent."

The Cotters knew Faloon casually, but "suspect never visited them or had access to the key to their cottage." Twenty-four fingerprint lifts were taken, "none matching suspect, twenty-two others identified as known individuals." Not known to the defence, however. Intriguingly, there were two unidentified prints.

Eve Winters stayed there four days, after hiking the West Coast Trail with three women friends, who batched with her one night, then returned to Vancouver. The inelegant Sergeant Flynn refers to two of them as "admitted lesbians." Professional women: an anaesthetist and an accountant. The third is a graduate student in history at the University of British Columbia.

The pathologist's report discloses no external injuries, other than the chipped front tooth, abrasions to the undersurface of both wrists, and light bruising around the mouth, possibly from the panties being forced into it. The few tiny cuts and sores on her body were days old and consistent with scratches and sore feet earned during a wearying hike. Why didn't Winters resist more forcefully? The Crown may have a problem rationalizing that – the jury, too, as they look upon the meek, runty figure in the prisoner's dock. Eve Winters was five inches taller, and fit.

But Adeline Angella doesn't weigh much more than Faloon – how could *she* have taken on the athletic Doctor Eve without suffering the worst of it? Unless a weapon was used – Winters yielding to the threat of a gun, allowing herself to be tied. This would account for the abrasions on the wrists. No rope or cord was found.

Harvey Coolidge is the Topekan developer who went for a walk to settle his stomach. His wife, a heavy sleeper, has only a dim memory of him rising from bed, then returning. He denies being anywhere near Brady Beach; he was strolling the deserted town. No one seems to have asked him why he would take so much money to a fishing resort in an isolated village and keep it under his pillow. He was duplicitous enough to have exaggerated his loss, probably for insurance reasons.

Another person of interest is a woman in the sex trade. Brian telephoned last night to tell him Claudette St. John suspects there was an apparent liaison between Winters and Holly Hoover.

"Apparently she swings either way, and Eve has similar inclinations."

"Were these observations reported to the police?"

"Claudette spoke to Jasper Flynn. But his attitude was, don't bother me with trivia, don't complicate matters, the Mounties already got their man."

In all seven pages of Flynn's summary of evidence, the interview with Claudette St. John merited not even a footnote. Arthur finds this either lazy or negligent. Holly Hoover earned two sentences. "Witness was talking at the bar with deceased about music, hiking, and the weather. She was thrilled to meet her, having read her column." No hint of romantic overtures, no mention that Holly Hoover practices the ancient profession. Truly, this is a mind settled.

Briefcase in hand, Arthur emerges into the grey April day. It will feel odd returning to the arena; he can only hope he can slip into the routines, as one slips into old shoes, with remembered ease.

Outside the Woofer house, Kim Lee is changing the tire on her bicycle.

"Kim, you, me, drive ferry."

"You dry very?" She extends a water bottle.

"Drive. To ferry."

"Ah, *very* . . . Very good?"

Kim joins him in the truck's passenger seat. On the way, Arthur gives monosyllabic pointers about keeping Blunder Bay Farm afloat for the day. She nods, smiles, a lovely, open, innocent face, like a sunflower.

When he parks and hands her the key, Kim looks confused. "I no dry."

"You don't drive?"

Kim shakes her head. Not understanding what Arthur wanted, she accompanied him out of politeness. She will have to hitch back, someone else will retrieve the truck, Paavo — no, he left last night. Arthur foresees confusion reigning at Blunder Bay, but he can't dally, the *Queen of Prince George* is pulling in.

He will try to get back early to sort things out.

A rubber toy squeaks as Arthur climbs into a well-used family Honda. "Sorry about the kids' mess," Brian says. "Caroline has custody of the Saab." He snaps his cellphone shut. "I just got word that the state has assigned one of its top slingers, Buddy Svabo, to the case." Senior Crown Buddy Svabo, who occasionally mismanages his anger, will be a headache, but an over-reaching prosecutor wins no popularity contests with juries.

"Something else you should know. I just got the lab reports. They did a screen for Rohypnol, and found some traces in Doctor Eve's bloodstream."

"A mood elevator?"

"You've been out of commission too long, Arturo. Rohypnol, rochies, roofies, Mexican Valium. Little white tabs from the friendly folks at Roche Pharmaceuticals. Powerful intoxicant, ten times the strength of Librium, odourless, colourless, tasteless. It's one of the hot date-rape drugs."

Opening up an absorbing array of possibilities. "It causes the victim to lose consciousness?"

"Can do. Takes effect in twenty minutes, reaches a peak in about an hour. Amnesia afterwards, the victim doesn't know who, when, where, or how."

"I assume no such pills were found in the rented cottage?"

"Nor at Faloon's lodge."

"How available are they?"

"Illegal here, but you can get them easily, from Mexico, off the Internet."

Angella's researches must have acquainted her with Rohypnol. Now there is a clue as to how she might have overpowered Doctor Eve. But, still, why would she?

They are moving with the traffic down Pat Bay Highway, where the farmland peters out and the malls and condos multiply. Brian is driving well enough, no sign of a hangover. Arthur dreads another teary spectacle, but politeness demands he ask after his family.

Brian responds calmly, in the manner of one sedated, telling of his Sunday outing with his daughter and two sons. "They've learned to turn the situation to their advantage. 'Mommy lets us do that' is one of the refrains." His cellphone interrupts. "Oh, *really*? How fun." Pleasure animates his voice, but he makes a sour face. "Fine and dandy then, we'll hook up."

He tosses the phone into the back seat, where it clatters among the plastic animals. "Angella. She's in Victoria, meeting our new prosecutor. Third call this week, and it's what – Tuesday? Our date is this weekend. Meanwhile, I am to look up her Web site, which has the entire article from *Real Women* on it, how she got raped and how you were so mean to her in court."

He has more immediate concerns. "I'm a damn good father, Arthur. I don't try to turn them against Caroline, I speak of her only to praise her. But from Antonio – he's the seven-year-old – I got, 'Why does Mommy call you a rooster?'"

He sniffs, fumbles for the sunglasses behind the vizor. "You're going to have to get someone else to junior you, Arthur. I'm liable to snap. I can't handle it." He bangs his hand on the steering wheel. "A rooster! To my kids! I've been straight! For almost two years . . ."

Arthur finds it hard to sympathize. He's been straight all his life. His thoughts flip to Margaret, up in her roost with the roostering, roistering original voice from the bush. Arthur once went to a reading by that posturing poetaster. His "earthy muscular renderings" (*Capilano Review*). More like barnyard grunts.

✦

Outside the courtroom, they come upon Buddy Svabo, who dons a mask of delight. "Here comes trouble." Early forties, short, compact, a bent nose – he was an amateur boxer. With him is a burly man, obviously the case officer. "Told you, Jasper, they're desperate, they're bringing in the artillery."

Staff Sergeant Jasper Flynn heartily takes Arthur's hand. "Looking forward to seeing you in action, sir." Thick-necked, forty, attractive in a square-chinned, barrel-like way. Premature hair loss is compensated for by a handsome, curling moustache.

"Beautiful area, the Alberni Inlet," Arthur says. "I don't suppose you get many murders out that way, Sergeant."

"No, sir, but I've only done six months there, filling in for the head of Major Crimes, he's on sick leave. Now they want to move me back to Vancouver to push paper."

"That makes for a rather short stint."

"Yes, but thanks to your client, I get to stick around while I run this file and chase a few salmon. Tell him I appreciate it."

Brian searches in vain through pockets and briefcase for the cellphone he left in the car. Finally he marches down the hall to a public phone.

Buddy asks, "How long are you going to maintain this pretence your guy's insane, Artie?"

Arthur hates that diminutive – it's like artsy, used of one who is tasteless and imitative. "Evidence mounts," he says. "We have a trail of dissociative identity disorder going back to childhood."

"I'm no expert," says Flynn, "but I'd say he's as crazy as a fox. Otherwise, he's as normal as you and me."

Buddy seems annoyed by the officer's flip attitude. "He's freaking *ab*normal."

"And that's our position too," says Arthur. He draws Buddy to an alcove.

"Yeah, Flynn *should* be pushing paper," Buddy says, glaring at the officer. "That guy's in deep doodoo. He had a dangerous ex-con in his jurisdiction, a thief, a rapist, and he didn't warn the community. That's why the head honchos plan to shift him out of Alberni, sooner than he thinks. There's already been heat, we've been getting it from women's groups too."

"I'll try not to add to your burden. Do we have full particulars?"

"Why? Is there anything missing? Nothing to hide, that's the way I always work. Did you get the latest analysis? Rohypnol, you slip it into a girl's glass of wine, and pretty soon she just can't say no."

"I want the names of the known individuals whose prints were in Cotters' Cottage."

"Her three girlfriends, the owners, a previous tenant, and a couple of dumb cops who didn't wear gloves. One of them *that* brilliant sleuth." A nod in Flynn's direction.

"None of Harvey Coolidge, I presume." The condo developer.

"You've got to be kidding. The guy's straight as an arrow, solid pillar of Topeka."

"What about the two unidentified prints?" Perhaps Holly Hoover, perhaps Adeline Angella, though he doesn't want to alert Buddy that she's of interest.

"Who knows? Eve was there for almost a week, she probably had visitors, hikers. There was a bottle of Chablis on the table, uncorked, three-fifths empty. The prints on it were deliberately smeared. Two glasses in the sink, washed. They didn't analyze for Rohypnol, but that's how he did it."

"And who had keys?"

"Owners had a spare set. Ask your client, maybe he made a copy. It's pretty freaking obvious that's how he got into the rooms at the Breakers."

"Let me finish my shopping list, Buddy. I would like the laboratory reports in their entirety, including the Rohypnol test. As to the main exhibit, the semen sample — may that be released to us for an independent analysis?"

"Not. You'll have to get a court order. There isn't enough material left to give out free samples. What's all this about? I thought you were going on insanity. You managed to push it this far, you've got nothing else."

"I want all bases covered."

"If you're thinking of defending the main issue, whether Faloon actually did it, I'm going to have to call Adeline Angella – I guess you remember her. Previous rape, it shows a pattern, the similar fact rule applies."

"I will be strenuously opposing."

"I like a good fight." Buddy affects a boxing stance. "Seriously, I can't go easy on your guy, Artie. I have to get him off the streets, there's a huge amount of pressure on me."

Arthur watches Brian talk animatedly at a pay phone. Caroline, maybe, or their counsellor.

"Let us have some give and take, Buddy. You consent to my independent analysis and abandon the idea of calling Ms. Angella, and I will not argue insanity."

Buddy's eyes narrow in suspicion. "You're willing to throw away the one hope you've got?"

"An insanity verdict means a mental institution. Could be forever, who knows. A pyrrhic victory for us but a loss for the Crown."

"I smell a rat. If you're that scared of Angella, I'm hanging on to her."

Ultimately, Buddy consents to further testing of the diminishing sample of Faloon's precious bodily fluid. Arthur will abandon insanity.

A stirring from the press table as Arthur enters court. The provincial judge, Iris Takahashi, is working her way through a long list, the daily menu of remands, bail applications, and guilty pleas. She nods at Arthur as if recognizing him, though he can't remember where they met.

"That worked out very well," he tells Brian as they settle on the chairs reserved for counsel. "He's going to give me a second chance at Adeline Angella."

"Don't look now, but she's third row from the back, on your left."
Arthur resists an itch to turn.

"Regina versus Faloon," the clerk calls.

Arthur's client comes into the room blinking. As his eyes settle on Arthur, a puckish smile.

Brian rises. "Your Honour, I had this case brought forward so I could apply to withdraw as counsel. A matter has arisen . . . I can't say more, let's just say there are some friendly differences of opinion between counsel."

A fine, understated performance for Angella. Arthur comes forward. "May it please the court, I apply to go on record as counsel." There is not usually such rigorous formality in the changing of the guard in criminal matters, but he has decided to milk it. "Arthur R. Beauchamp of Tragger, Inglis, Bullingham."

"I know," Takahashi says. "I articled there, Mr. Beauchamp. You tutored me in criminal law."

It comes to him just in time. "Ah, yes, the studious young woman at the back – more observant than her tutor, it must be admitted." She smiles. More proof of his decrepitude, he once had an acute memory for faces.

"Very well, Mr. Pomeroy, you are discharged."

Arthur chances a look at Angella as Brian leaves. She packs away her notepad and rises in pursuit of him. A short-legged woman with a penguinlike waddle. Late thirties – ten years older than when he last saw her – smartly dressed and coiffed, not a hair out of place. So earnest and self-effacing when she was on the stand.

"May I also put on record that the defence of insanity is being withdrawn. In its stead, I shall be seeking a full verdict of not guilty. Circumstances have come to light that impel me in that direction."

Reporters write furiously. Buddy, unhappy that Arthur has got the first punch in, must be prodded to record his consent to the independent analysis of the semen sample.

A date for the preliminary hearing is set, the last two weeks of June. The trial itself will likely be another six months away. Arthur will rent a comfortable suite, persuade Margaret to accompany him, a break from the farm. Assuming she's down from her tree. ("DAY SIX!" cried the *Times-Colonist* in its daily front-page countdown. Such encouragement could incite her to stay up there in perpetuity.)

A van awaits to convey his client away, so Arthur has only a few moments with him in the cells. Faloon apologizes for dragging Arthur from his life of ease, and hopes his friends didn't lean on him too hard. He will be in Arthur's debt "for all eternity, and then some." He adds: "I like Mr. Pomeroy, don't get me wrong, but maybe he's a little too imaginative when he's falling apart like that."

"I understand your friend, Claudette, is being very supportive."

"Non-stop. It would be a lot better if we didn't have to meet in the nut house."

"We'll get you out of there within the week."

Arthur will interview him at length another day, but now must hurry off to the injunction hearing – it is probably long over now, but he wants to learn the result.

As he emerges from the elevator, he hears a voice call out, "Here he is." Santorini's agitated clerk. She hurries him into the courtroom. "The judge is fit to be tied. This was to have come on at ten o'clock."

Confused, Arthur makes his way toward the counsel table. Selwyn Loo again picks up his presence from imperceptible clues. "Good morning, Arthur. The judge seems to think we can't go on without you."

"He wants you to get a grip on your wife," says Lotis, deadpan. No challenging hairdo, a touch of makeup today. Ankle-length fawn dress. This petite actress ("*actor*," she insists) knows she must dress for the role if the revolution is to be won.

When court assembles, Santorini fixes on him icily: "You had more important business, Mr. Beauchamp?"

"Merely a murder case. I wasn't aware I was required here. I still don't know why."

"To explain *this*." Santorini hold up a page of newspaper. "'Fat Chance, Says Tree Sitter.' I take it that is Mrs. Beauchamp's response to my offer?"

Arthur wonders if he lost at golf yesterday. "Margaret Blake made an unguarded comment, not intended to offend."

Selwyn rises. "Milord, no harm is done if the defendants remain where they are. Logging can't proceed anyway – that's clear from the act. An eagle habitat cannot be disturbed."

Garlinc's counsel, Prudhomme, rises wearily. "It's not a habitat if the nest is abandoned, the court has already ruled that."

"Milord, eagles don't easily abandon nests that have been maintained over the years . . ."

Santorini interrupts. "Eagles *aren't* the problem. The problem is I've held out the hand of conciliation, and it has been summarily rejected. I'm going to give the respondents two more days, and I want you to know, Mr. Beauchamp, that my patience is wearing thin."

The matter is being taken as a personal slight; Arthur is the blameworthy party, he has failed to govern his wife.

"I mean it. There's a serious contempt-of-court issue here. I won't be afraid to order incarceration. And if anyone else tries to go up that tree, I'll have him or her arrested on the spot." Santorini slams his desk book shut and walks out.

Santorini's ultimatum will get Margaret's back up; Arthur has a discomforting vision of her in the women's lockup, stubborn, refusing to apologize and purge the contempt.

In the barristers' lounge, Lotis seeks the bright side. "We bought two more days."

"Eagles mate for life," Selwyn says. "A solitary parent can't raise a brood. These developers may not be beyond shooting one. Even if we have a nesting pair, that only wins us the summer. The fledglings leave the nest in September, in go the loggers."

"Selwyn, stop being a bringdown." Lotis brushes hair from her eyes. Arthur wants to send her off to a salon, or buy her a clip. "This is guerrilla warfare, man, you've got to fire up the troops."

After Selwyn heads off to a meeting, she says, "He hates shrinks, won't do tranks. Generalized anxiety disorder. I talked to him about it, you can see where it comes from. His mom was a Chinatown junkie, a hooker. Throw in the blindness. Throw in extreme environmental angst. I shouldn't be so hard on him."

Arthur doesn't know what to say but express sympathy – he understands anxiety. His chauffeur, Brian Pomeroy, has unaccountably disappeared from the courthouse – cornered by Angella? – so he invites Lotis to join him in a taxi to the ferry terminal.

"Yeah, I can make the three o'clock." Unenthusiastic.

"You do have a residence on the mainland? Or do you live out of that?" A heavy packsack.

"Got evicted last week. Too many meetings, too much shouting. I couch-surf."

Arthur assumes there's some kind of radical underground where beds are freely available to itinerant urban guerrillas. He remains leery of this woman, distrustful – revolutionaries reject that most precious of concepts, the rule of law.

Still, he needs a sounding board, and en route to Chez Forget – his boat doesn't leave until three-fifteen – he shares with Lotis the burdens of wifelessness on the farm, being forced to eat tofu, Woofers leaving, kid goats coming.

"Sounds ghastly."

Denied sympathy, he turns the topic to her, admits a curiosity about her acting career.

"My total pitiful output was three teeners, three screamers, two soaps, a comedy series that never made the cut, and numerous acts of prostitution."

"Acts of . . . I'm sorry, what?"

"Commercials, dah–ling. How I got through law school."

Arthur doesn't prompt her, but she's unreserved in talking about her Hollywood career, its collapse. A bad love affair, a stop at an abortion clinic, a breakdown. She decided to start fresh, immigrate to her favourite city – she'd done film work in Vancouver – and arm herself with a law degree. To her, a weapon in the struggle.

Again, Chez Forget is crowded, but Pierre sits them at an outside table in the warming April sun. "It is *intolerable*. This is not the Burger

King, here you need reservations. I will start you with the foie gras." With a bow, he places before Lotis a small vase with a single red rose. "For you, mademoiselle, who is so beautiful."

She blows him a kiss. "Oo-la-la."

Lotis refuses the foie gras with the proletarian disdain Arthur has come to expect from her, and Arthur is made to feel badly not just about the homeless and hungry but about geese and their ill treatment. Still, he's finding this relationship less prickly, as if a form of accommodation has been reached. He was expecting more vanity from an actress. Actor.

Pierre presents Arthur with a telephone. "Normally, I would say go to hell, Beauchamp is dining. But it is Pomeroy, returning your call."

Brian is in his car. "Sorry I missed you, I was having a few nervous moments with Angella. She wanted a ride to Vancouver, I made a lame excuse about having to visit my uncle in jail. I won't be ready for her until I'm wearing a body pack."

"When will that likely be?"

"We're on for Thursday night. Adeline asked if I like paella, so it's back to El Torro, where Nick made his error in judgment. She still lives nearby in the same apartment. Maybe she wants to re-enact the event, slip me some Rohypnol, stuff underpants down my throat. Won't Caroline be sorry then."

"Did she ask about your sudden exit from the case?"

"I said it was an ethical problem. 'I make it a rule never to represent the guilty.' That actually came out with a straight face. She asked, 'How do you know he's guilty?' I said, 'Solicitor-client privilege.' She nodded, impressed with my formidable grasp of ethics."

◆

Arthur stands fast against dessert, orders coffee, while Lotis, who ate like a bird, plays with a fallen petal from the rose Pierre gave her. It's so pleasant, the sun beating down, robins singing, that he's sorry they must soon leave. He's enjoying a healthy venting about his murder case. Lotis seems easily entertained, wide-eyed, attentive – she doesn't treat Winters's death as a casual act of brutality dwarfed by the evils of our rapacious economic structures. She's curious about the case, a diligent if skeptical listener, though seems to regard it as a badly plotted screenplay.

She's unafraid to criticize Arthur's defence of ten years ago, his effort to persuade a jury that Angella seduced a felon, then cried rape. "Could anyone be *that* desperate to get published?"

"She tried to impress Faloon with her poor catalogue of clippings. It may not be desperation but obsession. Mental disease could be at play."

Arthur's magazines are replete with ads for writing schools and vanity presses. He suspects that being published is, for some, the central fantasy of their lives, in the extreme case, neurotic, all-consuming. (Cud Brown once told him he would kill to get published. Though that was several years ago, and he was drunk.)

"When was that rape trial?"

"Ten years ago. The appeal process went on for several years." Dead-ending at the Supreme Court of Canada: *Our job isn't to second-guess the jury, Mr. Beauchamp.*

Lotis finds it incredible that Angella would save Faloon's semen. "On the off chance she might want to incriminate Nick again? Sorry, the theory leaves me underwhelmed, it's beyond unlikely."

Arthur is wounded by her casual rejection of the theory. He had hoped it at least skimmed the surface of plausibility. "My dear, murder itself is unlikely, especially when planned, a rare event. The motives that propel it are just as unusual." He's lecturing, as if to a student, a donnish habit from his days of giving tutorials.

Lotis relents. "Okay, she's a borderline personality, she's twilight zone, she has a weird reason for deep-freezing the semen. Was she on birth control?"

"Nick was wearing a condom."

"Arthur, the ugly truth about condoms . . ."

She pauses, looking at him bright-eyed, as if expecting him to understand the obvious.

"They break. Take it from me. That's how I ended up in my friendly neighbourhood pregnancy termination clinic – a dried-out safe my partner found in his trinket drawer. Ex-partner."

"Actually, Faloon said the condom slipped off . . ."

"During intercourse?"

"As he was . . . yes." Arthur reddens. "It was too large for him."

"You are so . . . I don't know, *Arthurian*. Victorian. You're actually blushing. Whoa. Stop." Her lynx eyes widen, her mouth forms a perfect oval. "I just had a flash how this could've played out. On close personal inspection, Angella finds that Nick has deposited more in her than in the safe. She starts freaking about disease and pregnancy. She flies off the hinges, calls the cops."

Arthur finds it helpful to reassemble the facts in that light. Angella finding the recreant condom, hiding it in panic, calling 911. The idea of a tell-all magazine article comes later, as a bonus. It is a logical scenario, and one he should have urged on the jury.

Arthur orders the poires au chocolat. Relax, he tells himself, there's another ferry sailing at six, and Lotis is offering useful insight into eccentric Adeline Angella.

"She's some kind of polyester queen?"

"A fair depiction, I think."

"Was she in a relationship at the time?"

"No. She has lived alone for her adult life."

"Religious?"

"Catholic."

"Anti-abortion?"

"She wrote newsletters for a pro-life organization."

"Well, there you are."

She's on the mark. Fear of pregnancy, the massive dilemma it posed – add religious guilt to this toxic mix, and Faloon becomes the luckless victim of an ill-fitting Trojan.

Lotis brushes hair from her face, leans forward to sniff the rose, in its slender vase. A picture deserving of a camera. Behind this portrait of nose and rose and wayward hair, an agile and (dare he say) youthful mind is at work. Compensating for the cocky, in-your-face demeanour, for her naïve notions of building a classless society.

"Another problem dogs me. Should I dare you to come up with one last brilliance?" That's taunting, maybe even mocking. "I'm sorry,

I'll shut up about the case." A flock of starlings is raucously announcing the coming of evening. He gestures for the cheque.

"You've got me utterly fucking engrossed in this case, let's talk on the way to Garibaldi."

"You're not going to Vancouver?"

"No. I'm going to be your new Woofer."

She's a kidder. "You're crashing at Reverend Al's cottage?" He knows the lingo, he's cool, he does Tai Chi.

"I'm broke, I'm earning peanuts. I'm ready to woof. Save on rent and food, help with the chores, sounds cool. In my free time I prep for my bar exams and help steer Operation Eagle."

Arthur doesn't like the feel of this. She would be up his nose all day. "Have you ever lived on a farm?"

"No, but it can't be that complicated." She perseveres in the face of Arthur's smile of incredulity. "Okay, I'm a creature of the city, I dwell with the struggling masses. I wanted to do poverty law, but there were no jobs. But hey, the environment's a critical part of the struggle. Like the marijuanistas say, overgrow the government. I like Garibaldi, it's the most accidentally hip place I've ever been to. Clean air, good smoke. And I'm totally, totally wrapped in the Gwendolyn campaign."

What might Margaret feel about Lotis moving into Bungle Bay? A tinge of jealousy, perhaps, that might persuade her to climb down from her perch?

"I hope you'll enjoy your stay."

She rises. "Put me on pause while I go to the can."

Now what has he got himself into? He can see the Woofer house becoming headquarters for the Anarchist League. The woman was thrown out of her last place for having raucous meetings.

Lotis is still in the washroom when Pierre pulls up in his Peugeot. "When the cat's away, eh, Beauchamp?" He kisses his own fingertips. "Belle enchanteresse. I will drive to the ferry and you will add it to the tip."

Arthur doesn't respond to his insinuations, though he takes pleasure from them.

Pierre holds open a door for Lotis, bowing like a courtier of the House of Bourbon. "Which sleazy motel would you and M. Beauchamp prefer?"

"I think we can hold out until we get home," she says, frightening Arthur, giving him a squeeze. He can smell washroom soap. She's a hippie again, the makeup is gone, the lip ring back. She's in jeans, a work shirt with burn holes.

◆

On the *Queen of Prince George*, they climb to the upper deck to watch the sun go down. Grebes and cormorants fish the bays, fir trees glow bright green with new spring skirts, the vivid yellow of flowering broom in clear-cuts and view corridors.

Soon all these islands will be city playgrounds, he doesn't see how that can be avoided. *You can't stop progress.* You can't stop humankind from its headlong rush to its overcrowded extinction. He doesn't share Lotis Rudnicki's belief that the world can put the brakes on.

She asks, "What's the one last brilliance you wanted from me?"

Arthur has been filling his pipe and is lost for a moment. "Ah, yes, Adeline Angella. Your diagnoses have been faultless to this point, so let me test you with this: what motive, however twisted, would drive her to implicate Nick Faloon in a murder?"

"To discourage the police from looking elsewhere. It's beyond gorgeous out here. Fade out into a Cecil B. deMille sunset."

The dying sun burnishes the forested islets to the east, and overhead the clouds are the hues of wild roses, and to the west, scarlet. Arthur is staring at this display but isn't seeing it. "To discourage the police . . . Please expand on that."

"The big question could be: What motive did she have to murder Dr. Winters? Maybe Angella was one of her patients, something bizarre developed between them."

This comes with the sudden thud of revelation, and Arthur spills tobacco. He works so clumsily at getting his pipe lit that he burns his thumb. He must talk to Winters's secretary, or subpoena her clinical records. Why had he not considered such a link? His brain has become flabby, he must get it in trim or he may bungle this case. Alzheimer's, that's his fear.

✦

On Garibaldi, Arthur finds the Toyota still at the dock, the Fargo still in Stoney's yard, and the backhoe still in Arthur's, its scoop in the air like a claw. It hasn't seen recent duty, the loss-leader pond remains undug. At least the tools are gone from the garage.

While Kim Lee helps Lotis settle into the Woofer house, he heads to his own. The first of the kids must have arrived today: Edna Sproule's truck is on the upper road, and flashlights are active in the goat corral. Edna is a fourth-generation islander, owner of Boris, billy-goat sperm donor. Arthur will join her after he changes into country clothes.

From the bathroom window, as he finishes showering, he hears a shriek of delight: "Whoa, he's adorabubble." Lotis Morningstar Rudnicki has seen her first kid birth.

Arthur feels the threat of heartburn, his stomach gurgling, he ought not to have had the poires au chocolat. He decides to rest a bit. Soon he is asleep in his club chair. He dreams of Margaret in a birdcage. "Day five hundred!" the judge shouts. He's in court naked and unprepared. He cannot think of a question. He has lost his touch, lost his memory, lost everything.

11

At the Woofer house, over Kim Lee's breakfast, a hot gluey substance with seeds, Arthur plans his day. There will be extra chores with the kids — four so far. Edna Sproule's truck is in the yard, and though he knows he should help her, he feels depleted — April has been a cruel month.

He hears Lotis coming down the creaky stairs, late, she slept through the crowing cocks. She is clad in her sleeping garb, an oversized T-shirt that covers only the bare essentials. It urges, "Support the Sicamous Seven," whoever they may be.

She squints at the wall clock. "Oops, didn't realize there was a seven-thirty call. Sorry, I had trouble falling asleep. Kept hearing a maniac laughing outside. Crept downstairs to check if the house was safe, and none of the doors was locked."

Steadfastly averting his eyes from the junction of thigh and T-shirt, Arthur explains that the keys have been long lost, that what she heard was likely a screech owl.

"Drink coffee, yes?" Kim Lee extends a mug.

"Thank you, Sister Kim, is that birdseed porridge? I think I'll settle for a Tijuana breakfast: coffee and a hump." She opens a window wide, lights her hump, sits on the sill, has the delicacy to cross her legs. "What's on the list of chores?"

"Have you ever milked a goat?"

"No, but I can fake it."

Edna Sproule has midwived twin kids by the time Arthur and Lotis join her. "Udderly fantastic," Lotis says, looking awed at these sucking, wobbly-kneed progeny of hard-working Boris.

Edna frowns. "Where *have* I seen you before."

"*Scream Seven*. Still available on video."

"No . . . that commercial. Where the wife comes home to find her husband did the laundry, and there's a mountain of suds."

"And I say, 'Did you use enough soap, dear?'"

"Yes, that just breaks me up! You're the one in the ad! Oh, my. Oh, my." She seems overcome.

"Girl's got to get through college." Lotis seems to need to explain.

After the goat-milking demonstration, he shows her how to raid the chicken shed for eggs, introduces her to the greenhouse and vegetable garden, explains the uses of fork and hoe, shows her what a thistle looks like. Before the morning is over, she has managed to douse herself with the hose, wade into a bed of stinging nettles, and tear her jeans on barbed wire. Arthur enjoys every minute.

He will now take her up to the Gap, the highlight of the day. Margaret will learn he has a new playmate at Bungle Bay. The cat's away, and the mouse will play. Madam has the poet, after all, with whom to stay.

As Lotis is changing, a vehicle purrs up the driveway. Miraculously, it's the formerly mufflerless Fargo. Stoney has succumbed to a spate of initiative – the new muffler works well, except for a wheezing sound. He turns off the engine, takes a pull from a beer can.

"I straightened out that legal technicality with the backhoe, they're gonna give me a few more weeks because of this contract. So I'm gonna start on your pool like I promised, I'm a man of my word."

To deny the existence of any contract would take too much effort. Arthur will let Stoney dig the pool. What damage can he do so far from the house?

"Got a muffler off Myron's old Chev, kind of had to bang her in place. Should hold until the next crisis. Told you I'd do it for free, but there's fuel costs, eh, and I'm in a kind of debit situation . . ."

Arthur reaches into his wallet, fans out some twenties.

"If you're going to take the old girl out for a spin, man, you may want to gas up." Stoney sets to work, the backhoe chuffing into life.

Lotis returns, in black tights, distracting Stoney, who misdirects the machine into a thicket of salal.

"You are watching the birth of a pool."

"Will it have a swim-up bar?"

"It will be shared by frogs and salamanders."

"Glad I didn't bring my suit." She pulls out a cigarette.

"I thought you were quitting."

"After my carton runs out." Brushes the hair from her almond eyes.

Their first stop is the three-pump gas station – the gauge was hovering below empty – the second is Hopeless Bay. Not Now Nelson Forbish is leaving the store, eating Cheezies. He's doing the rounds, delivering this week's *Bleat* on his ATV.

He extends a cheese-and-salt-coated hand to Lotis. "I don't think I've had the pleasure of the movie star."

"I'd recall it if you had."

Nelson brings out pencil and pad. "I heard you may be auditioning for Arthur's movie."

Lotis looks perplexed. "Duh . . . what?"

"Not now, Nelson. We have a busy schedule."

"A picture."

Lotis hugs Arthur around the middle, and he starts like a nervous horse. Such embraces are natural to her – she's a performer, expansive, American – but foreign to him, rarely enjoyed even as a child. He's not sure what his reaction should be, and stands like a scarecrow, arms akimbo. Nelson says, "Another." The feel of her supple body brings blood rushing, Eros rising from the ashes of disuse. Accompanied, of course, by shame.

Hattie Weekes, the island's most fearsome gossip, is on the deck, squinting, capturing this. Arthur decides he may as well wrest advantage from the situation – word will go like the wind to the Holy Tree. He holds the door for Lotis. Hattie is already at the coin phone, stirring her wallet for a quarter. *A word once sent abroad*, said the great Horace, *flies irrevocably.*

A pile of *Bleats* sits on the counter. "HERE COMES HOLLYWOOD!" shouts the front page. Nelson has relegated the Battle of the Gap to the inside. "An uneasy truce holds at the protest site, while lawyers rush off to court, the results of which aren't known at press time."

Arthur tells Makepeace, "Ms. Rudnicki may charge anything to my account but cigarettes."

The postmaster hands him a small sack. "If you're going by the Gap, this is for the preacher. Fifties and or hundreds, here and there, mostly cheques. This here's a generous one." Makepeace holds an envelope to the light. "Two thousand on a bank in Chicago."

"Someone said they seen her barenaked in a movie called *Bodice Ripper*." This is Joe Rosekeeper, lascivious retiree, who's staring at Lotis through the plate window.

"Not Arthur's type," Emily Lemay says. "No meat on her. Come over some evening, handsome, I'll serve you up some steak and potatoes." She chortles, enjoys seeing him turn red. She's been flirting more boldly since breaking up with Handyman Sam.

Emily has just ferried from the city and brought today's paper: "DAY SEVEN!" Santorini's irate outburst has earned front page. A sidebar describes Arthur and Santorini as "former courtroom foes." Arthur's streak of notable wins against the former chief Crown is mentioned, along with their imbroglio in court many years ago. Here is the horse's ass quote, the full text returning to him now, a reference to "kitchen cockroach ethics."

Arthur imagines Santorini reading the paper over breakfast, his rage. He may go off the deep end when the hearing resumes tomorrow; Arthur must be alert for grounds of appeal.

Hattie Weekes is still on the phone, presumably describing the sordid scene of lust between the deserted husband and the brassy young snip. Let Margaret speculate. Let Nelson publish his photo: an aging Don Juan whose magnetic appeal lures the young and desirable.

✦

125

At Stump Town there are more tents, more volunteers – about a dozen young pilgrims arrived this morning. Kurt Zoller is passing out business cards, and presses one into Arthur's palm. His water taxi service – "it's literally been running me into the ground" – now has prospects, but his compulsive wearing of life jackets inspires little consumer trust.

"Garibaldi isn't just a blob on the map now," he tells Arthur. "More crowds are trickling in every day." He has taken the measure of new political winds: "I've gone three hundred and sixty degrees on this one."

"But that means you're back where you started, Kurt." He leaves Zoller to redo his calculations.

Lotis has already gone up the Gap trail. He's relieved to be away from her high energy – she exhausts him. He joins Reverend Al, who is on a walkie-talkie with his spouse, Zoë, one of the watchers on the uplands.

"Still just the one bird, honey," she says.

"Cheese and rice." Jesus Christ. Reverend Al has an unhappy penchant for euphemism.

Arthur hands him the donations. "It's starting to roll in."

"The judge wants eggs. We're running out of time."

The deadline is tomorrow. Santorini's clerk has notified all parties that the hearing must move to Vancouver, where the judge is stuck with a multicount corporate fraud. The ferry involves a three-hour ordeal, so Arthur and Lotis will risk Syd-Air, "Serving Our Islands" with an aging Beaver. Arthur will carry on to Bamfield. Lotis will gather clothes and essentials from her last city hideout before returning to Garibaldi.

When Arthur arrives at the Holy Tree he sees Margaret filling a bird feeder and Cud grunting as he ties a "Save Gwendolyn" banner to a branch. Lotis is below them, bending to Slappy, who licks her face. "And who is this cute little Woofer?" she says, then looks up, rewards the cameras of Flim Flam Films with a wink and a smile.

Margaret isn't smiling. He calls up, jocular: "Has Lotis told you she's taken a position at Bungle Bay?"

"I hope she'll work out." A definite chill in her voice.

"She had a splendid start."

"Yeah, I nearly ripped my crotch open on barbed wire." Lotis gives Slappy a neck rub.

"Oh, dear." Coated with ice.

"Darling, I'm sorry, but duty calls. I'll be off-island for the next few days."

"I see. Well, you know where I'll be."

"The Faloon matter will take a fair bite of my time."

"And what about Garlinc versus Gwendolyn? Will you be spending any time on that?"

"I'll be in court for you, of course."

"Not just for me, I hope. For all of us, for Gwendolyn."

It strikes him that it's not Lotis that she resents, it's his rinky-dink role in the injunction. This has the makings of a marital row.

Cud returns from his bough, scuttles out of view, fearing to be entangled in this. Lotis drifts away. Husband and wife are one on one. He wants to shout, *Damn it, I love you, can't you see that?* Instead, he sulks. Reverend Al is on the scene now, making a slicing motion across a finger: cut this short.

Chickadees flit about the bird feeder. One lands on Margaret's outstretched hand. She waits until it flies off, then calls, "I heard the judge was pissed off at me."

"The judge wants – well, you know what he wants." He isn't about to make a public plea for Margaret to relent – what kind of message would it send? Santorini has made the situation worse with his brusque demand.

"I don't know how he can properly decide anything without coming here to see for himself."

"The courts don't work that way, my dear."

"Well, they bloody should."

She's right. Damn it, he must stop apologizing for the system of laws and rules that he blindly cherishes.

Down comes a bag of laundry, which he dodges as it plops at his feet. "You might send up some fresh sheets and towels."

She's steaming behind a stoic mask – the last time Arthur saw this face was when the decaying victim of a forgotten mouse trap stank up the pantry. This is not the time to admit he has no idea how to operate the washer and dryer.

As she returns to her bird feeder, he entertains the shuddering thought that he could lose this woman. He knows what she wants as proof of love: stop being a feckless noncombatant. Be a proud defender of Lady Gwendolyn. Fight for her as he would for any innocent client facing life.

"Tell Mr. Santorini to come here, Arthur. Tell him to smell the air of the forest and listen to the birds. We had a purple finch here yesterday."

Arthur doesn't expect Justice Santorini will be interested in a purple finch.

"And if he still wants me to come down," she says with a shrug, "tell him he can climb up here and get me."

That evening Arthur is still flustered and bewildered by Margaret's chilly reception. (Guiltily, he found himself examining Margaret's sheets, on the growing mountain in the laundry room, for suspicious stains.) He calls Australia for help. Three years ago, his daughter Deborah fled a boring marriage. Three years before that, her mother ended hers with Arthur. It's said that infelicitous events occur in cycles of three – is it Margaret's turn to break free?

He rails on to Deborah about the louche poet, about the cruel teasing he's been getting, the misfiring of Operation Morningstar, the negative vibrations from the high pulpit of the Holy Tree. "You told me to get active, impress her, make a famous return to the courts. Now she's miffed at me for ignoring her."

"Okay, Dad, but her irritation has a lot to do with that hot little number you were squiring about. Margaret's human. You probably do have ideas, you rogue."

"Nonsense. Margaret was affronted at my cavalier assumption I could make her jealous. Oddly, she seems even more put out that I'm running off to do a murder trial – though earlier she gave approval. The older I get, the less I am able to comprehend the female mind."

He can hear her take a deep breath. "Okay, Dad, there's a romantic side to Margaret you seem oblivious to. She wants you to be her knight, her chevalier. A situation has arisen where she has become the classic maiden in distress. Galahad is being called upon to save her from the clutches of the inquisition, swoop her in his arms, and carry her off. But who does he gallop off to rescue? A thief. A habitual criminal."

After a long pause: "I see." Margaret feels jilted not for Lotis Morningstar Rudnicki but for Nick Faloon. "Then why would she make my task harder by daring the judge to climb the tree?"

"She's putting you on the spot. You're going to perform like Galahad or else."

12

The floats of Syd's Beaver wobble unsteadily, throwing up curls of spray as it lifts from Blunder Bay. Rain, visibility poor. Arthur's farm retreats below, a hazy splotch of beach and pasture. He hopes he won't return to find a potted landscraper crushed under his own backhoe. Yesterday, having struck clay, Stoney celebrated by smoking a joint, then left, claiming unspecified emergencies.

The dark waters of Georgia Strait give way to the Fraser's muddy outflow. Canada's Pacific metropolis arrives quickly, absurdly, like a giant foot thrusting from the mainland, the city bottled in by sea and river. Grey towers looming from the mist. Cars backed up for a mile across Lion's Gate Bridge.

"Epic pileup on the bridge," says Lotis, looking down as the aircraft banks. She is in her long fawn dress, her courtroom guise. In counterbalance, neon-bright vermilion lipstick.

They throttle down past the cranes and container ships to the seaplane docks at Coal Harbour. Arthur alights from the plane feeling ill equipped for urban survival. This city of his birth feels oppressive with its clamour and fury: a wail of siren, a squeal of brakes, unmusical complaints from a passing car – hip hop, he thinks they call it.

A taxi brings them to the glass-panelled faux arboretum that is the Vancouver Law Courts Building, and they enter the Great Hall, sheltered by fifty thousand square feet of angled skylight, tinted blue, resting on a network of aluminum trusses. Vines trail from the concrete abutments that sheath the tiers of terraces and courtrooms.

Arthur has a sense of foreboding. He is beyond praying that Santorini, by some Jovian miracle, will decide to smell the air of the forest. This judge seems to have lost his robust sense of humour.

Tell him he can climb up here and get me. It's Cyrano to the rescue. Saving Roxanne from the evil Compte de Guiche so she may love her false poet. Arthur played the role as a teen, his student drama club. He knows the plot, cringes at the thought it's being re-enacted.

On the third level, lawyers and litigants are milling about, impatient, clocks ticking at hundreds of dollars per minute. In Room 32, reporters shuffle and grumble. Paul Prudhomme is pacing. Selwyn Loo has undone his ponytail, and his black hair cascades over his shoulders, a look that makes him seem in grieving. Anxiety disorder. Arthur takes a chair beside him.

"I am on message," Arthur says. "I'll be proud to share counsel table with you."

"Welcome aboard. Next stop is probably the Appeal Court."

"In which case, I defer to you. I'm the new boy on the team." This is the young lawyer's case to argue – he has earned it

The clerk finishes a call to Santorini. "His Lordship finally made it off the bridge and is on his way." He lives across the inlet in the aeries of West Vancouver, was a victim of the epic pileup.

Arthur tries the meditation exercises Corporal Al taught him – they ease the strain of waiting – while Lotis chats with Selwyn about the delights of Garibaldi, insisting he pay a weekend visit.

When court is finally called, Santorini enters rigidly, white-faced in black and crimson robes, recalling to mind Virgil's Tisiphone: *a robe this Fury wore, with all the pomp of horror, dyed in gore.*

"I'm not even going to apologize, because . . . Madam clerk, I want the Highways minister on the line. Later, call that damn injunction, let me get this can of worms out of the way. I take it there's been no movement, except that this ring-dang-do has become some kind of media circus. The courts are not going to be mocked, we live under the rule of *law*." He bangs his fist on his daybook, sending a pen aloft and papers fluttering.

The pricey lawyers for the corporate wrongdoers look nervous: they're next.

Selwyn rises. "Surely, milord . . ."

"I want to hear from Mr. Beauchamp!"

Arthur rises wearily. "*Ego homo nullius coloris.*"

Santorini says nothing for a few moments, but surrenders. "Okay, what's that mean?"

" 'I am a man without words.' Strictly translated, a man without colour, in that he is incapable of the art of argument." Arthur can see the way this is going, his best hope is to provoke him into reversible error.

"You put this into Latin, Mr. Beauchamp. Or Greek, if you want, or ancient Hebrew, it's all going to come out the same. I am giving that eagle two more days. In the meantime, the defendants are in contempt of court. I am sentencing each of them to a five-thousand-dollar fine and seven days in jail."

Prudhomme starts to rise, presumably to advise the judge he missed a few procedural steps.

"I'm not through! That's for today! Tomorrow, I double it, ten thousand and fourteen days. And the day after, double again. And it's going to keep doubling until the defendants obey this court! Call the next case!"

◆

As Arthur ushers Selwyn and Lotis to a taxi, he still hears the echoes of the judge's wrath. It's not healthy to let oneself go that way – he remembers how old, irascible Judge Kincaid succumbed to a coronary in heated debate, a death that still pricks Arthur's conscience.

The Appeal Court is uncharted ground for these young Sierra lawyers, no precedents, no experience, so Arthur escorts them to the Bank of Montreal complex where Tragger Inglis Bullingham's oiled machinery, he assures them, will spit out the notice of appeal in the time it takes to change a flat tire.

He may also find counsel here to help him prepare for the Faloon case. He'll welcome Brian Pomeroy back if he ever resolves his marital crisis, but in the meantime he needs a good detail person. Surely a 130-lawyer firm can provide someone competent, a woman preferably, attuned to nuances Arthur might miss.

On the thirty-ninth floor, Arthur leads Selwyn and Lotis past a bank of four receptionists, and they pass through a vast oak portal to the inner sanctum. Secretaries and law clerks make way for the procession, the senior staff greeting Arthur: "Good to see you, sir." "You're looking well, indeed, Mr. Beauchamp." Lawyers wave from their glassed cubicles on this, the sweatshop floor.

Escalators take them three storeys higher, the domain of the upper castes, estate specialists, corporate advisers, senior counsel, posh offices with views. Above, on the forty-third floor, reside the partners, a score of them. From his own office there, Arthur often looked out upon distant islands in the gulf, wondering what life might be like on those mysterious green humps.

"I shall park you in the library, where you may review the law of contempt." They enter the vaulted, tiered room – gothic in design, a spiral staircase leading to the upper floor, glowering dead partners staring from the heights. "Those portraits can cause a deep depression if one gets absorbed in them too long."

"I'll try to ignore them," Selwyn says.

Lotis leads Selwyn on a tour of the stacks. Arthur wonders how he researches, few texts are in Braille. He looks up to the sound of a throat being cleared, sees Roy Bullingham on the upper balcony, a spindly wraith leaning on his cane, eighty-nine years old. He is known as Bully, though only an anointed few address him so.

"Then the reports are true." A wheezing voice, like the Fargo's replacement muffler. "You have returned from the hinterland. I knew you wouldn't last."

"Ah, Bully, just the man I want to see."

Bullingham seems about to descend the stairs on those gimpy knees, so Arthur goes up, taking the stairs two at a time.

Bully extends a bony hand. "You're too damn healthy, Arthur. I don't like to see that, it's a sign of a man not putting in his hours at his desk. I understand your wife has been treed, as it were, I suppose that's what all this is about. This nonsense reflects poorly on the firm — people still think you're associated with our institution."

"As indeed I am. My name remains on the letterhead, so I assume it still brings business."

They proceed into a suite of gleaming offices, Arthur hunting down Doris Isbister, the secretary who bravely put up with him for thirty years, and who knows more law and procedure than many with degrees. "Good grief, it's Mr. B." She rises from her desk, enfolds him in her bosom.

"And what are you up to currently, Doris?" Her desk is piled high with court documents.

"Something for yesterday that can wait for tomorrow. I heard Justice Santorini blew his top. You're appealing?"

"Not half as appealing as you, my dear." It's an old joke, how easily the routines come back. "I've scribbled out the affidavit material." Scrawls on the back of an envelope, indecipherable to all but Doris. "And as a precedent you might dig out . . . what's that file called? Where that old fool Watson tried to cite me."

"Yates and Ellery, the Gastown riot."

"Who, might I ask, shall we be billing for this?" says Bully, a devotee of strict accounting practices — he and his two departed pioneers began the firm on a shoestring at the end of the Great Depression.

"Think of it as a donation to a worthy cause, Bully. A drop in the bucket compared to the several hundred thousand I shall be asking the firm to pledge."

Bully freezes.

"Charitable gift to the Save Gwendolyn Society, a very nice tax break. Pays for itself in good publicity."

Bully leads him to his office, making soft sounds, profanity or whining, and settles into his throne. Wainscoting and furnishings are from various endangered tropical trees. The room has a view north and east, the snow-topped North Shore peaks, the fertile plains of the Fraser. The mists have dispersed, the sun has made a brave appearance.

"I'm contributing at least three hundred thousand myself, Bully, a fee. I've been arm-twisted into taking a murder."

"I am aware of it. You've been prominent in the news. As it happens, we have a dead file on the victim."

"Dr. Eve Winters?"

"Talk to Cleaver, he remembers advising her a couple of years ago. Thin file, didn't go to court. Therapeutic malpractice, or some such animal."

"I presume the firm can fit me out with junior counsel. Perhaps some rising star, a woman . . ." Arthur trails off as he sees Bully looking at him blankly. An unwritten policy to discourage the ambitions of female barristers has apparently not changed. Bully believes their place is at a desk.

Arthur drops the matter but continues to pry open the purse for the Save Gwendolyn Society, a ten-minute sermon, and is startled by the result. Bully will recommend a sizable grant if Arthur's donation can be run through the office as an additional tax deduction. "That way we claw back fifty-five per cent of the total." Bully's brain is a calculating machine.

After the appeal is sent off to be filed, served, and put on tomorrow's list, Arthur returns to the library to find that Doris has disinterred the Gastown Riot file. She has also fetched old Riley, a bespectacled gnome from the fortieth floor, to help with the research. Lotis has been reading from a case to Selwyn.

"Give me that case again," Selwyn says.

"Queen and Polk, House of Lords."

"Page number."

"Two-hundred nineteen."

"Let me make sure I have it." He recites from memory an entire paragraph of Lord Sankey's judgment, with hardly a word misplaced.

Doris stares at him with astonishment. "My *goodness.*"

"Photographic memory," Selwyn says in his sad, dry way.

"Mr. B, I've arranged for your lunch with Brian Pomeroy and Gowan Cleaver at the El Beau Room. Gowan will bring his file on Dr. Winters."

Lotis's eyes turn bright. "Am I invited?"

She's intrigued by the mystery of who killed Eve. She still gives the impression of having descended from some other planet, but he's unable to deny his growing regard for her. She's only one month shy of being gowned. She'll have her ticket by the time the preliminary opens in June. She has a quickness of mind lacking in many barristers already broken in, an energy that hasn't been corrupted or burned out. Yes, she's an extremist, can be a headache, and comes without risk insurance, but . . .

"Lotis, would you be interested in taking a break from saving the planet to save a thief?"

"I'm having a duh moment."

"I'm in desperate need of a junior to do the grunt work – research, interviews, interfacing with the Crown. There will be a reasonable salary."

"Whoa, the only accused I've ever defended is myself."

"What was the charge?"

"Unlawful assembly. An alleged riot in Seattle."

"Did you get off?"

"You bet."

"That's all I need to know." Arthur can't see this ambitious, theatrical young woman turning down such an offer, but she hesitates. Arthur detects a slight slippage of her majestic self-assurance.

"What about Gwendolyn? My project."

"No reason you can't carry on with it. I suggest you assign your articles to me – if Selwyn concurs." She already occupies a fat slice of his life as tenant-farmer and local protest leader; she may as well be wholly indentured to him.

"Okay. I'm down for doing it." Confidence has returned.

◆

While Selwyn works up his submission with old Riley, Arthur and Lotis walk down to El Beau Room, a dark, dank hotel saloon, long the haunt of the city's barristers, a place to drown away the many injustices done them in court.

By the time they arrive, Arthur has sketched for her Brian Pomeroy's scheme to get Adeline Angella loose and talkative and to steal off with a set of fingerprints to compare with the unknowns from the cottage. Brian will be joining their table later – Arthur spots him at the bar with his marriage counsellor, Lila Chow-Thomas.

Over salads and the house-special pasta – nothing else today, Arthur is made of steel – he charges his new assistant with her first duties: interviewing Winters's hiking companions, overseeing the independent analysis of the semen sample, gathering information about Rohypnol. Buddy Svabo has been playing coy with the many files police carted from Eve Winters's office. (*Nothing to hide – that's the way I always work.*). There will be a disclosure hearing Monday at which they will demand he produce them.

Lotis makes notes, head bowed, brushing hair from her eyes that soon take up their former place. "I still don't see Angella stashing the semen. Is there some kind of DNA pecker-track vault where they keep ten-year-old smears?"

"They usually discard old exhibits after appeals, or after a sentence has run its course."

"So here's a different thought: Someone from Forensics could have planted Nick's ejaculate in Winters. Or a cop."

"Planted how?"

She shrugs. "Soak the old swab in distilled water, squeeze it out, douche the corpse with a syringe or a turkey baster. Grade-school chemistry."

"It would be quite a reach to prove that."

"How many people have access to the exhibit lockers? Don't they have to sign some kind of register?"

Arthur can't keep up with the questions. Her scenarios are improbable – an analyst stealing, an exhibits clerk switching samples – far less credible than the Adeline Angella theory. Still, he must not, like the police, become fixated. He will follow the trail of these exhibits, seek a gap in continuity, evidence of mishandling. A known sample of Faloon's DNA may have accidentally mixed with the test sample.

Now comes Gowan Cleaver, pinched nose and pencil moustache – an austere man whose suits never wrinkle. "Welcome back to the lists, Arthur." He calls to the waiter, "Just a whiff of vermouth, Samson."

Hands are shaken. "This is my indefatigable assistant, Lotis Rudnicki. Gowan is one of our leading barristers." A slight exaggeration – his main handicap as counsel is his caustic manner.

Cleaver accepts his martini, a double. "Quick power lunch, then back to court. Are we waiting for Pomeroy?"

At the bar, Brian's marriage counsellor gives him an exasperated look that suggests she's losing patience, then finishes her mineral water, looks at her watch, and excuses herself. Brian slumps, orders another glass of wine.

Cleaver produces a file folder with several handwritten sheets. "Dr. Eve Winters's notes on some silly dame who hated her father and thus got fucked up in life and went frigid. Winters came to me because she started ranting on the phone, threatening defamation, fraud, breach of ethics, invasion of privacy, every tort in the book."

He dips into the folder for a cassette tape. "Here's some of it, recorded off her machine. I told her to wait it out, not stir up any hornets' nests. Didn't matter, never went anywhere."

"What was the nub of the complaint?"

"Okay, she comes to Dr. Winters with a problem – she can't get it up, she's frigid."

"Sexual arousal disorder," Lotis says.

Cleaver reacts as he might to a child who should only be seen. "I stand politically corrected. I assume you have expertise in the area." Lotis tosses her hair, unchastened.

Brian brings his wine, straddles a chair. "In case anyone's interested, I'm having a marriage breakdown."

"Obviously," Cleaver says. "I see you're using Chow-Thomas."

"Is she any good?"

"Usual feminist bias. Mind you, my marriage was beyond saving."

"I think Caroline has got to her."

Lotis mimes a gag reflex.

Cleaver continues. "Dr. Winters's patient is hung up on men, she flirts, gets into awkward situations when her bluff is called. Can't do it, backs out, freaks out. Another relationship in the wastebasket. Winters saw her twice, encountered blocks galore, got stood up for the next appointment. Their last contact was a month later, when this sexual-arousal-disordered person got on the blower to Winters with a rant about how she was going to sue her ass off. That was after this came out in *The Post*."

Cleaver reads from a photocopy of the Doctor Eve column: "'A strict religious upbringing has barred the doors of awareness for this sad woman, who has painted herself into a lonely corner. She has a desperate need to examine her sexuality, to discover inclinations which may be truer to her heart.' Winters changed the name, of course, and identifying details, called her Lorelei."

The siren of the Rhine, who lures and leaves men to their fate. A silence as Arthur exchanges glances with Lotis and Brian, then asks, "Would the woman's name be Adeline Angella?"

Cleaver looks at him oddly. "Yeah, I think that's it." He studies the notes. "Angella."

Three pair of eyes grow large around the table. "This was when?" Arthur asks.

"Two years and two weeks ago."

"Do you remember the Faloon rape?"

"Vaguely, it didn't connect." Cleaver rises. "Hope I've been of help."

"Your lunch is on me." Arthur decides to order the apple pie – but only one scoop of ice cream.

Brian groans. "I am looking forward with unimaginable delight to having dinner with this flirtatious ball-crunching iceberg. I intend to protect my ass." He snaps open a cellphone. "Latest Japanese gimmick – wireless relay to the recorder in my crotch. I just did a tester."

He presses various buttons on the phone. A women's voice. *Brian, that is an extremely sexist comment, and I find it quite cheapening to have to meet you in a public bar. Goodbye.*

"Loud and clear," Lotis says.

Brian looks at her. "I think you're weird."

"Back at you."

✦

That night, Arthur is awakened in his hotel suite by Brian's haunted, inebriated voice. "Arturo, we've got to talk, it was right out of Stephen King, I had to pull a last-minute el foldo."

Arthur manages only a sleepy grunt.

"What time is it? Chris' almighty, it's after midnight? Sorry, I'll come by for breakfast . . . No, I'll be too hungover, let's make it lunch." He hangs up before Arthur can croak a response.

13

Arthur sees no hangmen on this morning's Appeal Court roster. The three judges are a liberal lot, the chief justice himself presiding, Selden Horowitz, shrewd but kind, on the cusp of retirement at seventy-four.

Arthur eases himself into a chair, weary. He slept poorly, missing the softness of a Garibaldi night, unused to the clanging city. Selwyn Loo's table is almost bare, the seat beside him empty: Lotis is off arranging for the DNA analysis. She will visit Faloon, introduce herself. She is not to mention the Lorelei business yet – institutional walls have ears.

Selwyn is on his feet for only ten minutes, a performance that seems to startle the court, a précis of facts and law without a wasted word. "On page 401, Justice Duff affirms the principle that an unfair hearing has no legal force." At that point, Horowitz asks him to pause, and the three judges huddle and whisper.

"Mr. Prudhomme," says the Chief Justice, "it would seem that the judge below was in a fit of pique."

"Got up on the wrong side of the bed," says a fellow justice.

And with that, Arthur understands that the day has been won. Prudhomme can't find an opening; the third judge chimes in. "Yes, he forgot that an accused party has the right to be heard before conviction and sentence. And what's this nonsense about doubling the fine and jail term every day? After three weeks, by my rough calculations, that comes to $3 billion and forty thousand years in jail."

"Well, milords," Prudhomme begins, then stalls, past hope.

"We will hear you, of course," says Horowitz, making a point of extending the courtesy Santorini withheld.

Prudhomme sighs. "Out of discretion, I'll simply ask that the matter be remitted to Justice Santorini for reconsideration."

That results in a debate about whether it's fair to return the matter to a mind apparently settled, but Arthur rises and whispers to Selwyn, "Stick with Santorini."

Later, the appeal allowed, the matter sent back, Selwyn asks Arthur, "Why Santorini?"

"Better the devil you know. This makes him malleable – Eddie's terrified of the court of appeal." Equally important, they have bought Gwendolyn more time.

◆

Brian is red-eyed and haggard as he joins Arthur in his suite. He is garrulous nonetheless, and paces, smoking. They are in Arthur's favourite small hotel, overlooking English Bay, sailboats dwarfed by hulking anchored freighters.

"Brovak's just back from Mexico. He acted insulted that I accused him of pulling that prank with the panties. The guilt on his face was as obvious as your nose, Arthur. 'At least cover for me,' I begged him. 'Tell Caroline you did it.' But he won't, and he's lost a friend. I may even leave the firm."

Arthur understands he must listen to the commercials before the feature begins. But he can empathize with Brian, his marriage crisis. Between the two of them, they have as much understanding of women as they have of the mechanics of gamma-ray bursters.

"You've been through it, Arturo. How does it fall apart?"

What has Brian heard? Has Margaret given a press conference? *Cud and I are deeply in love* . . . It dawns he's speaking of Annabelle, relief floods in. "Hardly made in heaven. I wore the horns."

"But who came out the winner in the end? The great Cyrano met an eco-suffragette with whom he has an abnormally non-fractious relationship. How do you do it? What is the answer, my adored master?"

Arthur takes that as rhetorical. He doesn't have an answer anyway. To sit around like a lump, accept whatever fate deals – that's his traditional response. At least Brian is actively fighting for his marriage. It may be messy, but there's life in it, excitement.

"One of the factors contributing to the debacle of last night was my hostile hearing from the marital fixer – you saw her, Lila Chow-Thomas." Brian relates this between bites of room-service sandwiches, washed down with beer from the mini-bar. "Thin-skinned woman, offended because I asked to meet in a bar. Only because I wanted to talk to her alone, without Caroline running interference. I made the mistake of asking if being attractive was a handicap to her work. I wasn't flirting, but she flounced out. Afterwards, at what my bar dares call happy hour, I had a couple of doubles, smoothing the way for a historic bad trip, which, by the way, El Torro is the perfect locale for, shit-coloured brick, bullfight posters, dental office music."

Arthur works his way through this thicket of words and images as he watches Brian set up a laptop computer. Arthur has remained, and vows he ever will be, computer illiterate, leery of this contrivance and its baffling lexicon of disks and bits and ports and prompts. Clearly, this one will be used as a playback device, the evening's events copied to it from the recorder that spent last evening in Brian's crotch.

"She's already there when I roll in, looking as if she just stepped out of HMS *Pinafore*, navy jacket and knee-length tartan skirt and leggings. The lady may be aesthetically challenged, but she's attractive in a 1950s-movie sort of way, a notable feature being her two thrusting vital statistics. Heavy makeup, hot lipstick, her hair in bangs and bows. She has a *copa de vino* going, I'm about to learn she's a bit of a juicer. There's some innocuous chat about wine, about how the sangria at El Torro is, as she puts it, fun. A lot of sangria is what Nick drank here ten years ago, but I go along with it, tell the waiter to bring a pitcher – I'm reckless, already hammered. Let me take you on location . . ."

From the computer's speakers come the opening bars of a bolero. Lights blink and flicker on the screen, an inscrutable message appears: "Right click to pause."

I thought you might not show up. Afraid of what I might write.

Why?

Well, defending that sort of people . . . Criminals, sexual predators, it's hard to paint a sympathetic picture . . . All right, I have to admit I'm biased.

You have a right to be. I know what you've been through. I looked up your Web site.

Brian pauses the recording, lights another cigarette. "Maybe she picked up a pornographic undertone, because she gave me a startled look. You looked up my *what*? She was primping, flirty nuances, playing with her hair."

What does it feel like when you ask them if they enjoyed it?

Come again?

When you're cross-examining. That's what Mr. Beauchamp asked me, or almost. He accused me of being a willing party.

"Okay, pause again, here's where she introduces the topic of you, Senior Queen's Counsel Arthur Ramsgate Beauchamp, the defender of her rapist. This is where it starts to get chilling, because in a spooky way that trial was the highlight of her life. She's slugging up the sangria as she recounts the horrors of the witness stand."

Arthur can hear the bolero louder, an accelerating pulse, like a heart keeping beat.

Are you friendly with Mr. Beauchamp?

He runs in different circles. Hasn't been the same man since your trial. Basically, that was the end of his practice, he quit soon after.

He was so . . . I wanted to kill him.

Brian stops the recording. "I miss a prawn with my fork, it clangs against the dish. She wanted to kill you, Arturo. What was I to say? Goodness, my dear, you had every right to feel that way."

Arthur wonders if he ought to shrug off such a harsh remark from this prim, mannered woman. No doubt many others spoke as angrily after feeling the whip of his cross-examinations, but after ten years this was hardly spontaneous.

"She starts doodling instead of making notes – she doesn't want to interview me, she wants to talk. About her interview with Buddy Svabo, about how she must relive the horrible ordeal – as if she hasn't been dining off it for the last ten years — about Faloon, about the Winters murder. Burbling away as I top up the sangrias."

"Do not underestimate her. I wouldn't be surprised if she tried to get you soused enough to reveal her name has been bandied about." Arthur opens the window to let out the smoke, and he can see grey prominences above the horizon, the Gulf Islands, that world impossibly distant. This is not the last time, he suspects, he'll feel twinges of regret about taking on this case. He can't back out, but he'd rather be fishing.

"Fast-forwarding here, because she toddles off to the loo. The one thing she doesn't mention is going to Winters for therapeutic advice, how she threatened to sue her."

A significant omission. The cassette from Dr. Winters's answering machine was teeming with insults. *You're an unprincipled, unethical bitch. Wait till I see my lawyer, you bitch. I hate you.*

"She comes back smelling like a hothouse flower, drenched in something called Fantaisie, which I'm later to learn is her *parfum de goût*. In the meantime, I'm on the verge of a nervous breakdown. And I'm drunk, Arthur, and I start to pour it out, how I'm a victim of a cruel joke, how I haven't been home for twelve days. And I'm getting an audience — she exudes sympathy, she's human, she isn't a psychopathic monster after all. In the meantime, I'm in such a state of flotation that I've let chances slip by, the waiter has grabbed her empty glass with all her fingerprints. I turn the subject to her, expressing wonder that this femme fatal remains unpartnered. We pick up here."

I will never repeat my mother's mistake. She's . . . well, she's free of him now, in a better world. I refuse to speak of my father.

Arthur distinctly hears a sniffle. "But she *does* speak of him," Brian says, "and out comes the tissue, and she gets up a head of steam, comes off the rails a little."

He used to scoff at my ambitions, said I'd never be a writer . . . Oh, no, he was the writer, two self-published novels that went nowhere. He never gave me affection, he never hugged. He thought I wasn't in the house one time, and I heard him tell Mother they should have just gone ahead and terminated the pregnancy . . .

Another pause in the recording. "Here I am, honest to God, holding her fucking *hand*. I'm thinking fingerprints, I'm stuffing her used tissues into my pocket. Fingerprints on tissue? Anyway, it turns out that her literary loser of a father snuffed himself, put a bullet in his head. I wanted to explore this, but suddenly the heart-rending episode is over, the clouds break, the sun comes out, rainbows appear."

I'm being such a goose. I usually don't drink this much. I've just had my first work of fiction published. Would you be interested in reading it? I'm just around the corner.

I'll walk you home.

"Her flat is in an unhip metal-grey stack of units. She's been fifteen years in the same apartment, which somehow doesn't seem normal. I find myself entering the elevator with her – I'm a robot, programmed to follow a path to catastrophe. Her place has three locks, it smells of disinfectant, the décor is so square it's cubic, with doilies. There's a balcony with a kind of viewette of a strip mall. Sitting prominently on a table: a metre-high pile of movie magazines and about a dozen copies of this."

He passes Arthur a copy of *Tales of Passion*, April edition. The cover illustration is of a well-muscled man outside a window, a woman in a nightie peering out. Readers are invited to turn to page twenty-eight, a story by Adeline Angella, "You're Not Supposed to Ask."

"She wanted to read it *aloud*. Over cognac. On her couch. The evening continues to morph into high surrealism."

Mind if I visit the little boy's room?

Yes, of course, freshen up.

"Note, Arturo. I do not say, 'I have to go to the washroom.' I am regressing. I am talking *her* language. I rummage in the medicine cabinet, looking for a secret stash of rochies. *Nada.* The bedroom door is ajar, and I can't help glancing in as I pass by, and there she is on the bed, pulling off her leggings, and she gives me this chiding tease, 'You're not supposed to *lo-ook.*'

"I study the situation in the living room, where we have a soft light, cheesy piano music on the stereo, *Tales of Passion* open to her story. Cognac in liqueur glasses. Unthinkingly, I pick mine up, sip, and I'm overcome by a delusion that it's been doctored with ten milligrams of Rohypnol. Angella comes out in bare feet, pink toenails, sits catlike on the sofa, pats a spot beside her, tells me it's only twelve pages, and I should sit. I'm about to take a rain check on the literary reading when a paranoid rush hits: I've got *my* fingerprints all over everything, her cosmetics, her Parfum Fantaisie. Why not go all the way, leave a sample of my semen? I'm panicking, Adeline is tugging at me to sit down. Here are the final few minutes."

Don't be a silly. It's early. We can watch the Tonight Show *after.*

I'm feeling ill. I'm allergic to Clorox. Let me borrow this, I really want to read your story . . .

Arthur hears chimes from the laptop, the theme from the Fourth Brandenburg. This is an evil thing, Arthur thinks, the cellular phone. To keep one is never to escape the great sticky web of social inter-course, never to be alone.

My goodness, Adeline, who would be calling me this late?

Sit, sit.

Boilershop Investments. To listen to our easy terms, Press one . . . Jesus . . . Well, hi!

"Calling me at this ungodly moment, honest to God, was Professor Caroline L. Pomeroy. She knows it's late, but she can't sleep. 'I want to hear your easy terms,' she says. I am standing. I have the phone crooked between ear and shoulder while I fumble for a cigarette and struggle for the perfect nuanced response. Angella tries to grab the lighter from my hand. I nearly fall on her as we tug for control of it. Her liqueur sloshes all over the reading copy of *Tales of Passion*."

You're not supposed to smo-oke. Ouch! Your knee!

Brian demonstrates, going on his knees onto the couch, clutching his cellphone and a package of cigarettes. "The recorder not only picked up Angella's heavy breathing but Caroline's icy hang-up line." From the computer, clear and sharp: *I presume I've called at an awkward time.* A click.

That was a client, Adeline, he's threatening to jump from Lions Gate Bridge!

Don't forget the magazine! Call me!

I will.

Promise?

The sound of locks being released, the door opening, closing, a fast retreat.

"As soon as I was safely down, I phoned Caroline back. No answer. This morning I phoned again. Caroline's machine said, 'Don't bother.'"

He sighs, picks up *Tales of Passion*. That's when Arthur notices the residue of fingerprint powder. "The forensics lab I use took eight lifts off it, couldn't match any with the unknowns in Cotters' Cottage."

A letdown, but Arthur isn't surprised.

"After I left the lab this morning, I actually sat down and *read* 'You're Not Supposed to Ask.' Within its gooey pages is a subterranean rape motif, a touching tale of how handsome Harry loses his key and has to go in though a back window, and it's the wrong townhouse. You're not supposed to ask, you're not supposed to look, you're not supposed to smoke, but you are supposed to fuck."

"Might we pause here, Brian? Did you happen to ask Angella where she was at two o'clock on April Fool's morning?"

Brian sags. "Shit, I forgot."

14

Risking Syd-Air again, Arthur is above the knobby spine of Vancouver Island and can see, through gaps in the mist, the open ocean, its inlets and beaches. This will be Arthur's first visit to Bamfield – a hamlet so remote it has been spared the uglier benefits of tourism. Claudette St. John, who has quit her job at the bar to run Faloon's lodge, has agreed to show him about.

He will be looking for the *vestigia* of Adeline Angella: metaphorical footprints, traces of an April Fool's visit. Brian Pomeroy's strange encounter has persuaded Arthur the woman is truly ill – it was as if she was re-enacting the great drama of her life. Maybe to make it seem authentic. He hopes Brian can be prevailed upon to nourish this relationship, to find out if she has an alibi. *You're not supposed to ask . . .*

Lotis Rudnicki is taking briefs from Winters's three hiking mates today – they've invited her for lunch. She has also retained a distinguished scientist, head of biotechnology at the University of Victoria, to do a second DNA test of the incriminating semen.

Arthur asks Syd to circle around Bamfield, for a mental mapping. The inner hills and valleys are a checkerboard of clear-cuts, but a strip along the ocean has been spared, Pacific Rim National Park: forest, lakes and bogs, the fjord called Pachena, and its wide, shallow, log-rimmed beach.

Bamfield is picturesque from the air, a village Venice, cleaved in half by an inlet sheltered behind a thickly wooded peninsula. On the seaward side lies Brady Beach, guarded by high promontories. North of that, at the tip of the peninsula, is the Breakers Inn, advertised by large red letters on the roof.

There is one venerable building in East Bamfield, the former Pacific cable station, now the Marine Sciences Centre; elsewhere, a scattering of dwellings, a motel, the pub. But his aircraft is coasting to a dock on the more interesting western shore, with its rustic cedar buildings by a raised boardwalk, artisans' shops, shingled homes, gardens with daffodils and Red-flowering Currants.

Greeting him at the dock is a plump woman with a dimpled smile: Claudette St. John. "Nick says you're the best thing that happened to him since God made sin. Come along, love, I've made us a lunch." She wrestles for his bag, and he is no match for her. "I don't know if you heard – Nick and I are getting married."

Arthur feels the burden of her cheerfulness, her faith in his skills, and has a fretful moment – they're becoming more frequent – when he prays he hasn't come out of retirement to end his career in failure.

The Nitinat Lodge is a two-storey log building with a trim lawn and early tulips, augmented by a few cabins tucked into a cedar forest. Several young hikers are on the grass, throwing a Frisbee.

Faloon had problems running his inn, Claudette confides – maybe because of his limited experience in honest business. Or because his heart wasn't in it. She shows him her new brochure – "Bed and breakfast in the forest, off-season rates, eco-friendly."

"I hired a Native girl to hand them out to hikers on the trail. Nick will go nuts when he sees we got a going concern here."

"I suppose you come across a lot of wildlife." Arthur has in mind cougars, bears, and wolves, he has a slight phobia in that regard. Gentle Garibaldi offers no such dangers.

"We had animals poking around the garbage a while ago, raccoons maybe, probably a bear – they get pretty hungry in the spring. Had a couple of cougar sightings."

Arthur shivers. "And what would those folks over there be up to?" Several men in the adjoining field, labouring with spades, throwing up hillocks of dirt and grass.

"Treasure hunters. Jasper Flynn let drop the stolen money is buried somewhere, and he's got all the town idlers working up a sweat. I got them to turn over Nick's garden for free. Careful of these stairs, love, Nick tripped there in the middle of the night. Mind you, he was sleepwalking."

She serves up a steaming beef stew. Arthur can see why Faloon is endeared of this woman – she is frank and guileless. But he is bothered about the sleepwalking, and asks about it.

"Maybe it's the phases of the moon, whatever, sometimes he just finds himself barefoot in the yard. Usually I wake him up, and he laughs it off and comes right back to bed, but once he walked off my deck into the blackberries, and lucky he was only scratched."

Faloon has never mentioned this tendency. Not once. That's troubling in itself.

Claudette still hasn't been able to pin down Holly Hoover – she has a trailer nearby, but has rarely shown her face since the murder. She's in town, though, was seen in the Bam Pub today, buying a six-pack of cider.

"If she's not in her trailer, check on her cabin cruiser, the *Holly Golly*. You'll recognize her by the explosion hairdo, black curls."

Arthur can't bring himself to ask if she suspects Faloon slept with Hoover. His bowl of stew is empty, and it would be impolite to refuse the second helping Claudette urges on him.

"I want you to meet Meredith Broadfeather, it's about a mystery boat. Say no more, you'll hear it from her. Whisper a secret over lunch, and it's all through town by dinner."

"I'm familiar with the process." He produces a photo of Angella. Might Claudette have seen this woman in Bamfield? In the bar?

"A lot of strange people wander through . . . Is she a drinker, then?"

"It would seem so."

"To be honest, I can't say. I see too many faces, dear, they start to blur."

Arthur tells her who it is, and Claudette looks more closely. "So this is the shameless hussy." Though she must be curious, she asks no questions. A long-time bartender, she understands discretion.

Arthur rises from the table, thanking her profusely. He must repair to his lodgings.

"I'd love you to stay, but I'm full up right now. I just hope you'll be comfortable in Cotters' Cottage, given what happened there."

"But I've reserved for the Breakers."

Claudette seems as confused as he. "Mrs. Cotter told me they were expecting you, I saw her just this morning."

"This is a bit of a rigmarole." The Cotter couple, two decades retired, let out the hideaway at Brady Beach where Eve Winters drew her last breath. He'd phoned them, asking to see it. Mr. Cotter, who seemed hard of hearing, said, "Yesiree, when can we expect you?"

"Tomorrow," Arthur said, but he shouldn't have ended the conversation there. It will be awkward straightening matters out.

Claudette joins him on the hilly fifteen-minute hike to Brady Beach, a stretch of brown sand protected by outcroppings that drip foam from surging waves. Shore pines, shaped and bowed by ocean winds, struggle for purchase on the rocks. The Cotters' rental cabin can be got at from the road or from the beach, and it is the latter route they take, by tidal pools in which orange and purple starfish nestle.

A stunning setting. This is what Margaret is missing. Had she been available, he would have brought her along. Her loss.

The Cotters' lot is surrounded by a picket fence, and is well cared for, with fruit trees in blossom, pink and white, rhododendrons in heavy bud. Three main windows face the sea, a smaller one above serves the loft. Inez Cotter, a spindly but agile woman of seventy-nine, interrupts her dusting to show them in.

The interior offers worn but comfortable furniture. Full kitchen, bedroom, a loft, a staircase built into the wall. An airtight stove provides heat, though there's also a fireplace, and, outside, stacked wood. Stained glass in the door and windows. The word *cozy* would come to mind had not a murder happened here.

Mrs. Cotter looks weary, as if she has been cleaning all day. It cannot be an easy property to manage, she lives across the inlet.

"Police had it closed down for two weeks, they were tromping through here like goats. We weren't sure we were going to rent it out after that, but it isn't easy getting by on pensions alone."

Arthur pays in advance for the night. He will try to cancel the Breakers, though he'll keep his dinner reservation.

Mrs. Cotter has no guest register, just a book in which tenants are asked to comment on their stay. Only two notations for March: "Much enjoyed by all, saw a bear." "Totally groovy." None from Eve Winters or her companions.

Mrs. Cotter recalls her as easy to talk to – she had tea with her twice, saw no indication she felt in danger. "Not a concern in the world. She just wanted to escape for a while."

"Tell him what you overheard," says Claudette.

"Well, her girlfriends stayed over the first night, dog-tired from the trail, but not so tired they didn't have a loud argument in the morning. I was standing at the door with extra linen. One of them was ranting. 'It's over, Ruth,' and then, 'Repeat, it's over. Do you receive?' And then, Ruth, I guess, pardon my language, she says, 'Ef you, your effing highness.'"

"Did you tell this to the police?"

"Sergeant Flynn thought it was funny, he laughed."

Arthur is left alone to unpack. He is gratified to see an oilskin hanging by the door – rain is promised this evening, a storm. From the wall, a mountain lion stares coldly at the camera, red reflections in its eyes.

In the bedroom, a double bed, rustic wooden table – as in the police photographs, but lacking Eve Winters's sprawled corpse. It's a good thing after all that Margaret couldn't come – spending a night here might not fit her concept of romance.

"Well, Beauchamp, are you going to be able to sleep here tonight?" The only answer is a moaning of the wind in the trees.

◆

A vigorous stroll, working off the beef stew, takes him up a hill to the Breakers Inn, a handsome log structure with a majestic overlook. The

Galloways charge half-price for a late cancellation, which seems fair, but they're sour and standoffish; despite that, he'll return here for dinner.

By mid-afternoon, word has swept through town that Nick Faloon's lawyer is sampling its delights – locals stare and fall silent as he walks by, treating him as they might a visiting gunslinger. He overhears two women giggling. One says, "He wants to hook up with Holly." He turns to her, and she quickly puts her hand to her mouth. The entire village knows he seeks Hoover, courtesan of the lumber camps. She must know that too, and is in hiding.

He finds Meredith Broadfeather at the Clayoquot, a hefty woman whose jean jacket sports a large, defiant button: "Whose Home and Native Land?"

Since it is still a pleasant day, the sun burning away the mist, they choose a quiet table outside. He is quickly put at his ease – Broadfeather, a sociologist with the Huu-ay-aht Band Council, has no quarrels with Faloon. "I always liked him, poor old Nick. I just can't imagine him raping or killing that woman. If he did, why would he wait for the cops to show up before he ran?"

She occasionally had coffee here with him, a polite, considerate man who often put up band elders for free. She shares in the suspicion – which seems locally held – that Holly Hoover was not frank with the police about her doings on the eve of April Fool's Day.

"You can't get across the inlet on foot – it's pretty well impossible unless you're a bear, it's all swamp and bush. I bet Holly took Dr. Winters across. She uses her canoe a lot, to keep in shape. The next morning, Lennie Joe, he's a fisher, saw it tied up this side." She gestures toward a dock: a blue canoe is tied astern of a cabin cruiser. The *Holly Golly*. Small boat, big power, a pair of 225 Mercury engines.

"This woman seems to ply her trade very openly. I assume the RCMP feel she provides a necessary service."

"Yeah, you'll see Jasper Flynn over here occasionally, pretending to work her over, but real friendly – he pretty well gives her licence, like a kind of silent pimp."

Holly Hoover, unemployed, single, a local, said Sergeant Flynn in his report. The entire biography. If Broadfeather is right, Hoover has been well protected: she has no convictions for prostitution, or for anything, according to the criminal records office.

He's intrigued by Broadfeather's second-hand account of a high-powered boat running without lights in dangerous reef-strewn waters. Two young volunteers had been occupying an islet as part of a Huu-ay-aht land claim. At around 3 a.m. on April 1, they were roused from their tent by the sound of a vessel racing north, though they couldn't see it.

Arthur brings out an area map, and she points to the islet, one of the Deer Group. Deep-water channels converge there. Northwest lie the tourist towns of Ucluelet and Tofino, a paved highway. Northeast, up the long ribbon of an inlet, is an even more substantial community, Port Alberni.

"Did these fellows tell the police?"

"John Wayne over there?"

Arthur sees an RCMP boat at the coast guard dock, Jasper Flynn tying up. The sergeant has learned that the perpetrator's lawyer is in town, up to no good. He intends to keep an eye on him.

"Our people don't talk to him unless they have to. Anyway, he's not asking. He's got it sewed up."

Arthur puts on glasses and studies the map again. The Deer Group, the Chain Group, the Broken Islands. Narrow channels, reefs, and dead-end inlets. A boater would need intimate local knowledge at night, radar, sonar. Flat out, it would be two hours to Alberni or Ucluelet.

He tries without much success to envision Angella racing through dark unknown waters in a high-powered cruiser.

◆

Before returning to his cottage to clean up for dinner, he finds a pay phone and calls Kim Lee.

"All good at farm?"

"Good. Happy. Not worry."

"Stoney?"

"Every day work hard. Take truck."

"Margaret?"

"Happy."

A wind has come up by the time he reaches Brady Beach, and he can see angry clouds rolling in. Mrs. Cotter has not locked up, but he finds the key under the mat as promised. He has to tug the door to open it. The interior is spotless, but the place still confounds him with dread.

He must shower, though he feels unnerved at the prospect – Dr. Winters's nakedness, the bath towel on the bed, are clues that she was attacked after taking a shower. Avoiding the bedroom, he undresses under the cougar's glare. He talks to it, needing sound: "Maybe she's innocent after all." Angella. "Or did she have a local confederate with a fast boat? Unlikely. Just can't see that silly woman murdering anyone."

Other possibilities are emerging, like mushrooms in the fall. He must take written statements from the two young braves. Inez Cotter, as well. It seems likely that the quarrel she overheard involved Eve Winters. The other person, Ruth – her surname escapes – is single, a UBC graduate student. The remaining two are paired.

He must not forget about the condo builder from Topeka, with his late-night rambles. Who knows, maybe he carries a vial of roofies in case opportunity presents itself. More important, what about Holly Hoover, who may well be familiar with street drugs? Could it have been the *Holly Golly* that the Native boys heard speeding away? Or was it just a beer-fuelled weekend jaunt, a couple of locals . . .

✦

From the trail that takes him to the Breakers Inn, he passes by Hoover's home – Claudette pointed it out to him, a renovated construction trailer. No lights within, but the evening hasn't fully set in. He doubts that she will answer her door.

A couple of men with shovels are poking around in the bushes by the path to the inn. They follow him with their eyes, as if hoping he will lead them to the treasure. It has begun to rain as he climbs an outer staircase to the roofed deck. There he takes in the black western sky, sees the Deer Islands, the hazardous channels that separate them.

Within, a long table is set for seven, Mr. and Mrs. Galloway toting trays of seafood to it. Arthur engages a pair of German hikers. As they're describing their close encounter with a black bear, he turns to see Jasper Flynn come up the stairs, bearlike himself in a bulky RCMP jacket.

He pretends surprise on seeing Arthur. "Now there's a likely suspect," he says. He declines the Galloways' offer of a drink. "I'm on duty, just paying a courtesy visit."

The owners seem anxious – a man in uniform is not good for business – so Arthur beckons Flynn to join him outside.

"Returning to the scene of the crime, Mr. Beauchamp?"

"I generally make it a rule to do so."

"Always a good idea, sir. Especially if you lead us to the dough your client ripped off from this joint. Just kidding." He tweaks his large, overgroomed moustache. "Glad you're staying here. They're good folk, the Galloways."

"As it happens, I'm not staying here." Flynn came up by the lobby stairs, so Arthur assumes he peeked at the guest registry.

"Oh, right, Nick's lodge. I hear his girlfriend's running it. Nice lady. Anything I can do to help you out?"

Mrs. Galloway beckons: dinner is served. "I hope you'll have a chance to talk to this fine lady," Flynn says as he turns Arthur over to her. "She heard them talking that evening – Faloon and Dr. Winters."

Mrs. Galloway nods. "She told him exactly where she was staying, at Brady Beach."

"Got to scoot. Try the butter clams, they're always good."

◆

As Arthur trudges back down the road in soaking rain, his stomach starts to protest the butter clams. The way is tricky in the darkness – he has, of course, forgotten to pack a flashlight. He makes out that Holly's trailer is still unlit. Twice, he wanders into dense foliage.

When he finally fumbles his way to the cottage gate, he again strays, collides with an apple tree, then follows the fence to the seaward side of the house and the front door. There is dim light here, an eerie fluorescence in the ocean. The door swings open with a tug. He'd forgotten to lock it – yet another memory lapse. "Arthur Beauchamp, meet Dr. Alzheimer. Bloody God, I'll be in diapers soon."

As he fumbles for the light switch, he becomes aware, from the scent of patchouli, that he is not alone. Pale light through the windows glimmers on a mass of curls, a woman on the floor. Then the room is starkly lit by lightning, and he can see she is propped up on her elbows, looking out at the storm.

A soft, drawling voice: "Power went out."

"Holly Hoover, I presume?"

"It's okay, I talk to myself too."

"Actually I was talking to the door. It doesn't seem to be behaving." It is warped. It takes a hard pull to lock it. No mention of *that* in the police report.

Hoover flicks on a cigarette lighter, holds it until Arthur finds a kerosene lamp and lights it. A well-proportioned woman in sweater and jeans, a tanned, youthful face framed by, as Claudette promised, an explosion hairdo.

"I don't want anyone to know I'm here, Mr. Beauchamp." Arthur turns down the lamp to a glimmer. "Mind if I smoke?"

"Not at all. I don't have anything but instant coffee."

She rolls a cigarette with practised fingers. "I brought a couple of cider. You want?" Two bottles on the floor beside her.

"I'll have coffee."

As he gets a kettle going, he ponders the reason for this clandestine visit. He wonders if she's on drugs, with her slow, husky voice.

"This has been eating at me. I've got nothing against Nick. He's a famous underworld figure, I respect him. He gave me a room." A resigned sigh. "That caused him hassle."

"Claudette suspects you slept with him."

"Yeah, I did. I guess it went all over town."

Arthur returns with his coffee, sets kindling aflame in the fireplace. The sky flickers, a rumble of thunder. Or was it his stomach? One ought not to eat clams in April. Holly has a cider in one hand, a cigarette in the other, an ashtray on her midriff. She has kicked off her shoes; her feet are on the window ledge. Arthur asks her how she came by her current occupation.

"I quit college two years ago for a life of fun, but found I couldn't make a living off shell necklaces and homemade bath oils. Had to find something that would pay. I had a bad habit of fucking anything on two legs anyway, so the transition from sleazy amateur to skilled professional actually gave me a sense of self-worth. Things were going fine, I could afford trips to the city, top-shelf bud, I was saving up to scuba in Cuba. Now this shit. I'd like some legal advice, Mr. Beauchamp."

He adds logs to the fire, and stands close to warm himself. "Will you answer some questions first?"

"Shoot."

"Do you always use a condom during sex?"

"Except with women." She turns on her stomach and blows him a smoke ring.

What's she stoned on? Patchouli easily trumps the odour of marijuana. "What happened to the condom Nick wore?"

"Hanging off his dick the last time I saw it." A few moments. "Am I expected to remember? It got trashed, I guess."

Arthur wonders if a prostitute would keep the occasional used safe, an excellent blackmail tool. But Hoover seems candid. Arthur is feeling queasy but must soldier on. He extends Angella's photo. "Ever see this face around town?"

She studies it, looks up. "When?"

"March 31."

"Looks vaguely like a dorky dame who came hurrying out of the pub as I was going in."

Arthur wishes he had other shots of her. Hoover hands it back, shrugs. "I'm not good at faces."

"Was Eve Winters in the bar as this woman was leaving?"

"Sitting on a stool. Her, I recognized. Doctor Eve. I knew she was staying in town, Inez Cotter mentioned it. Went up to shake her hand, I'm a fan. We got to gabbing, she started coming on, she's *très* gay. I was impressed, she was famous. I didn't want her to know I was low-life, I told her I made jewellery. Which I used to when I was a Zen chick. I didn't want a scene, some drunken bozo coming up to the bar and blowing my cover, so I just finished my drink and split."

"But that's not totally true, is it? That's what you told the investigating officer."

"Right. That's not the whole story."

"Go on."

"Okay, let's say something else happened. Let's say these two ladies actually decide they want to get it on. Let's say they arrange to leave the bar separately, to avoid gossip."

"Tell it to me straight, Holly."

She drains her cider, takes a breath, and tells him she took Winters across the inlet in her canoe, unobserved. A misty, romantic evening, a tingle in the air. Some hand-holding on the dock, an invitation from Winters to share a bottle of wine.

"I was conning her into bed, it didn't feel right. Money wouldn't be involved, I wanted to assure her of that. So I found the balls to tell her how I made a living."

"And how did Dr. Winters react?"

"Cooled her right out. I got the impression she was disgusted at herself, stooping so low. She thanked me for the company and took off for Brady Beach. I stood there feeling stupid, had a cigarette, and went home."

"And you didn't mention this to Jasper Flynn?"

"I was freaking, I didn't want to be dragged into this. He wasn't much interested, anyway. Then I got to feeling nervous about it, and a week ago I went to Alberni to tell Jasper the corrected version. That I paddled her across. Not the making out, the hand-holding stuff, out of respect to Dr. Winters, but I mentioned she asked me up for a drink."

"And what did he have to say?"

"He was like, don't complicate matters, I don't have time right now, I'm late for my son's hockey game, I don't want to see you charged."

And without bothering to solicit a written statement, he sent her on her way. She has told no one else. Her confidences are disarming on her face, but it's unclear why she hadn't told the truth in the first place. If it's the truth. The partly consumed bottle of Chablis, the two glasses in the sink, suggest Winters was entertaining someone: If not Hoover, who was her guest?

When the sky lights up again, Arthur thinks he sees movement outside, a dark form by the window. But he's skittish, it's the shadow of a bush moving in the wind. His discomfort has now progressed to his lower intestines.

"Am I in any kind of trouble?"

"None, I should think. You made amends with Sergeant Flynn. You'll tell the truth in court."

She slips on her shoes. "Jasper will yank my licence. If he even knows I talked to you, he's going to be pissed purple."

"Why?"

She merely shrugs.

"You seem to have a special relationship with him."

"People talk, but it's nothing like they think. I don't pay him off in money or in kind. Jasper's not corrupt, but he's lazy, he figures I save him a load of work keeping the boys happy in the camps. Not as many brawls, guys fighting over the girls, of which there's a shortage. I'm doing a public service, I cut down on sexual crime. So, yeah, he tells me not to be obvious about it." She rises. "I've got to go."

He follows Hoover to the door, torn between obeying the demands of his bowels and wanting to talk more with her – does she know anything about date-rape drugs?

"You will be subpoenaed, Holly. You will be sworn. You will risk perjury if you don't tell the truth."

"I intend to tell the truth. I know Nick's getting a raw deal, but I don't want to become a suspect. I'm here because I want it on record I told you the whole story early on. I don't want to be accused of making this up."

Arthur takes her rain slicker from a peg. He'll be a gentleman, hold it for her. She turns, pinches his bearded cheek. He steps back, startled.

"You know what – someone told me you were a vicious son of a bitch in court. But you don't seem so bad. I like you, you're cute."

Arthur is all business. "I'll need your statement in writing." He puts his shoulder to the door to open it. He can still feel that light pinch. Somehow it aroused him, a little sample of pain to tempt him, she reads him rightly as a masochist. "Do you have a flashlight?"

She shakes her head. "I don't want to see anybody. Can't have people thinking you invited me over and we rode out the storm in the dark." She smiles, seductive in the yellow lamplight. Suddenly, she is pressed to him, and he is momentarily overcome by patchouli and hot breath and buoyant breasts pooling against his ribs.

He backs up, and she stays in step with him, like a dancing partner. She stabs her tongue into his ear, an electrifying sensation, then whispers, "How do you want me to pay for the advice?"

"No charge." A strangled sound, it barely escapes.

"Thanks, counsellor." Her hand goes between his legs, hefting the baggage there, her fingers tracing along the stiffening spine of his penis.

Then she is gone.

◆

At 3 a.m. he is still awake, tossing and farting. He has given a wide berth to the murder bed, is on a foam mattress in the loft. Outside his small window, the wind groans in the trees, and a swollen sea lashes the beach. He ought to test the door again, to ensure the lock clicked shut.

The byplay with Hoover, the exchange of advice for a crotch caress, keeps returning like a dirty joke. Did you hear the one about the hooker and the lawyer? A subtle joke, because who knows who's screwing whom? Arthur feels used by her, but isn't sure why. Had he somehow invited that intimate au revoir?

That he had fantasies involving her is disgusting. A young prostitute . . . Her lick and fondle, her offer of more, her warning about nasty rumours: a shot across the bows? A threat to embarrass him in court if his questions are too probing?

"'More is meant than meets the ear.' Who said that? Milton?"

This vocalizing to the void has got to stop, it's a habit from the garden, talking to his beets. He tries not to think of the farm (he shouldn't have allowed Stoney loose with the backhoe), it only keeps him awake. But two cups of instant coffee are doing that anyway.

The kids must still be arriving. He closes his eyes and counts goats, but the image of them springing over a broken fence makes him more fretful. His thoughts finally find their bumpy way to Margaret. He is in dire need of her comfort, her confidence, her ability to keep her amateur farmer husband from tripping over his feet. He must devise a face-saving plan to bring her down from that tree.

He backs up, that's wrong. He must think in new ways if he's to grapple with the ineffable inexplicableness of the female psyche. Margaret wants no face-saving plan. She wants to be rescued. *You're going to perform like Cyrano or else.*

The storm abates for a while, and there is an eerie silence but for the murmur of trees shedding rain, then the winds start anew. He finally surrenders to sleep and agitating dreams of looking on while Margaret hugs a fleshy, muscular tree.

15

After his fitful sleep, Arthur is anxious to put a gruesome night behind him, and, as Syd's Beaver coasts into Blunder Bay, he entertains thoughts of a nap. But he is suddenly wary because Stoney is waiting at the dock, effusive in welcome, eager to be the porter of Arthur's bag.

As if trying to shield Arthur's view, Stoney walks backwards in front of him. "While you were gone, I must've put in fifty hours, I wanted to surprise you. Struck a spring, it looks like, it's filling fast. We weren't expecting that rainstorm last night, she kind of caved in on the sides, but not a problem."

When Stoney steps aside, Arthur sees a berm has been cast up beside the pond, a clay mound on which Lotis Rudnicki and Shiftless and Underfoot and two geese are standing, watching events unfold. Nearby, Dog is hitching a chain to the backhoe, which is running, but with a slight cough.

"Had to make an emergency run for diesel yesterday, missed the gas station by five minutes. I would of siphoned the Toyota, but the tank was locked, and I couldn't find where you hid the key." An accusatory tone. "Anyway, when I got back, I parked the old girl by the edge there. Must have slipped out of gear overnight, and started rolling. It was one of them chance events you can't predict."

Arthur manoeuvres past him to the pond, where he observes the cab of his Fargo, or that part of it that shows above the water.

"We'll have her flushed out, carb cleaned, the fuel lines, everything, and she'll be ready to roll when the roosters crow."

Arthur watches in an exhausted daze as Dog uncoils the chain and wades into the water fully clothed. While fastening the chain to the undercarriage, Dog slips, submerges. Finally, to Lotis's applause, he rises. He waves to Stoney, who climbs aboard his backhoe and puts it in gear. Predictably, it utters a final cough and dies.

Stoney taps at the fuel dial for several moments, as if that might correct the problem. "There's always something, eh, Arthur? Maybe I can use the tractor to pull it out?"

Arthur shakes his head. His little tractor would end up joining the Fargo.

"Okay if I borrow the Toyota then? I'll be back in five minutes with some diesel."

Margaret's truck is clean, undented, he'd bought it last year for her birthday. But Arthur is too enervated to resist, and he yields up the keys.

He stares at the submerged truck for a while, a meditative time disturbed only by the chattering of Dog's teeth. Lotis sends him in to warm up. "You're still my hero," she calls after him.

◆

In the Woofer kitchen, Arthur hovers over Kim Lee as she slices a warm whole-wheat loaf. "Lotis make." Lotis, the baker, wonders never cease. Kim rewards him with the crust for his sad-faced pantomime of hunger.

Retrieving peanut butter from the fridge, he glances down the hall at Lotis leaving the bathroom, topless, pulling up her jeans, hurrying to answer the phone. He averts his eyes from this casually immodest performance.

"Yeah, we're packing a lunch for them. I'll get a ride with Arthur. Ciao." She strolls into the kitchen tugging down a new T-shirt: I'm a Friend of Gwendolyn. "We've ordered three hundred." She hands him one. "Thirty bucks. Who was Gwendolyn, anyway?"

"A corruption of a Salishan name – G'win d'lin, a maiden of the forest who joined her lover in the Salish sea, and who lives there now, and whose long hair can be seen drifting like kelp with the tides."

This causes Lotis an odd moment. She seems speechless. There's a shine to her wide oval eyes as she says, "That is fucking beautiful." She turns spirited, theatrical. "I want Gwendolyn's *role*. For every tragedy, there must be a balcony scene. 'O, swear not by the moon, the inconstant moon, that monthly changes in her circled orb.' East Pasadena Rep, I was fifteen, it ran two weeks."

A creditable Juliet. "'How silver-sweet sound lovers' tongues by night.'"

"I'm beyond impressed."

He's too modest to boast about his heralded performance with the Garibaldi Players: Sir Toby Belch in *Twelfth Night*.

Lotis hands him a thick file: Dr. Winter's entire output of published columns, three years' worth, magically secured from the vast tangle of information that floats about in the World Wide Web.

He idly leafs through them as he relates his adventures in Bamfield, capped off by Holly Hoover's nocturnal visit. "She made a rather bold sexual advance before she left. Awkward. For me, at least."

She wrenches the details from him, how Hoover offered sex as payment for advice.

"Were you tempted?"

He responds huffily: "Of course not." It will be a task confessing to Margaret. Confessing? He's guilty of nothing.

"And you don't think Jasper Flynn is humping her?"

"She says not."

"And what? You believe her? You think Flynn turned her down when she grabbed *his* dick?"

Arthur can find no delicate way to respond.

Lotis is intrigued by the spat overheard in Cotters' Cottage between Ruth and, presumably, Eve Winters. "'It's over, Ruth'? Whoa, I should've figured they were keeping something from me."

She lunched Saturday at the home of Dr. Glynis Bloom, an anaesthetist, and Wilma Quong, an accountant, who were co-operative but subdued. Dr. Bloom was the more outgoing, and talked fondly of Winters, a friend of a dozen years. Also there was the graduate student, Ruth Delvechio, closed and apprehensive. She and Eve Winters had been romantically interested, but no mention was made of an affair-ending quarrel.

"A few bitching sessions – you expect that on a tough six-day hike – but 'Fuck you, your fucking highness' never came up. I can see why Winters wanted to shed her, she's chronically gushy. 'It's lovely that you're working for the environment, that's just *so* important.'"

The unofficial reason Winters stayed on in Bamfield might have been to escape Ruth Delvechio, but Winters told them she wanted to spin out her holiday. She'd written two columns in advance, and was charmed by the village. The others had to return to their work and studies.

The name Adeline Angella meant nothing to them, but they recalled Winters's display of temper about a threatened court action. "Apparently Eve could let fly, which makes for a different image of the cool-headed shrink."

Lotis also met with Dr. Winters's secretary, who was of little help. "Didn't recall Angella's name, only vaguely recognized her photo. Doctor Eve keyed all the patient interviews into the computer herself, all except the clerical odds and sods, appointments, accounts."

Arthur is missing some of this. He's sitting, absorbed in one of Winters's columns, "The Man Who Thinks He's a Masochist," advice to Mr. J: "It is not unnatural to be attracted to strong women. In fact, it is a healthy sign. Through antiquity, women have sought strong males, now in this more liberated age there is a greater balance of attraction. Unconsciously we seek healthy partners to improve the species." She tells Mr. J he must rid himself of any notion he suffers masochistic tendencies.

"Quite right," he says aloud. He reddens, covers the page.

"Earth to Arthur Beauchamp."

"Sorry, there's too much traffic in my head . . . You've done some good work, Lotis." For some reason those were difficult words. Why does it rankle him that she's so unexpectedly competent? "I hope I'm not pressing you into service too severely."

"Shit no, I'm pumped."

He can't remember, even as a young lawyer, having such bumptious energy. Or idealism, however flawed. He had no passion to change the world. The law was based on centuries of common sense. The law was his god, the courtroom his universe. He was born stuffy.

"I dragged Buddy Svabo from his backyard barbecue to ask if he'll release Dr. Winters's files. 'Not,' he said. He wants to argue it tomorrow." The disclosure hearing. "Also, he's hinting he has a jailhouse informant. A fink, I don't know who. He says he doesn't have to identify him."

Arthur sits up, startled. "That's preposterous. If Buddy Svabo has engaged a lying informer, it will rebound on him." Would Nick Faloon be so careless with his words in prison?

"I had a quick visit with Nick, he looks like shit, depressed, unshaven, and out of shape. He thinks he burdened you with a case you can't win. Also, he wonders when you're coming to visit him."

"I haven't found the time yet." But he must, and soon. Faloon has to be persuaded to come clean about his night with Holly Hoover. Claudette has a forgiving nature.

◆

Arthur is naked, lumbering through the woods with gluey slowness, fleeing a pursuing grizzly. He reaches the safety of the road only to find his truck gone . . .

"Dream bad." As Kim Lee nudges him awake, he is partly on a sofa, partly on the floor, running from the bear. "Stoney come. Late go now." This means Stoney is back with the Toyota and Arthur has overslept. She is extending the basket of out-take.

Hurrying out to impound the keys, he sees that Lotis has already commandeered the truck, is in the driver's seat. Stoney has brought not just diesel fuel but a wetsuit for Dog, who is looking forlorn and froglike in flippers, mask, and snorkel. Arthur can't bear to watch this drama play out, climbs in beside Lotis, who turns on the ignition.

"I thought you didn't drive."

"I'm from southern California. We late, go feed."

◆

A quick stop at the General Store, where Aloysius Noggins, still in clerical collar after Sunday service, is enjoying his reward, a steaming rum coffee. He's waiting for the ferry – he'll be meeting Selwyn Loo, escorting him to the Gap.

Reverend Al studies Lotis's rump as she picks through a bin of oranges. "Blessed is the man who endureth temptation."

"Speak for yourself."

"I am."

He has just come from a meeting of the Save Gwendolyn Society. A bake sale has brought in $324. A bingo at the hall tonight might double that – if enough event-exhausted Garibaldians show up. Against these microscopic amounts, some donations from afar have been sizable, $500,000 from a U.S. philanthropist, $200,000 from a wildlife fund.

The key is to keep Gwendolyn Valley in the news. The protesters are alive to that. Lotis has been brainstorming with them, scripting ceremonies to amuse the reporters, keep them happy.

"DAY ELEVEN!" cries the Sunday newspaper. Twenty-one days, Margaret promised, ten to go. She could reneg, and try for the Guinness record. She's become unpredictable in her middle years. It's not menopause, she's over that. Some other womanly thing.

"Any eagle sightings?" Arthur asks Reverend Al.

"I'm about ready to admit to the futility of prayer."

"Can't stop progress." Ernie Priposki, over-refreshed, staring with glazed eyes into space, somewhere beyond the canned soups.

On the Gap Trail, Arthur is met by Flim and Flam, as locals have taken to calling the filmmakers, and their cameras dog him silently all the way up the trail. At the Holy Tree, he finds Lotis fastening the lunch basket to the rope, Slappy overseeing. Cud Brown hangs over the railing, fixed upon Lotis.

Margaret appears, bundled in sweater, jacket, and toque.

"Are you feeling all right, my dear?"

"A bit of a sore throat."

Arthur barely heard that, she's hoarse. Cud speaks for her. "Your lady's got a cold. We're trying not to get too close." His facetious grin.

Arthur's worry level ratchets up another half-dozen notches. "Is she running a temperature?"

"Yeah, she's kind of hot."

Margaret finds her voice. "It's minor. Over tomorrow." A switch of topic. "You look like you've been putting on weight."

"I'm fit as a fiddle."

"A bass fiddle."

Cud hauls up the basket, calls down to Lotis. "Man, this smells like it came out of the ovens of Arcady." Arcady, as if the poseur has studied the Greek myths. (Has he ever read Tennyson? A Shakespeare sonnet? Blake? Housman?) "Who baked this?"

"The person you are speaking to."

"You don't look like a home-baking type."

"You don't look like a sexist." Tossing her hair.

"I wasn't until I met you, my lovely."

"Yeah, I have this power to bring out the inner jerk in people."

There is tension in this scene, entertainment for the cameras. It galls Arthur that Cud is loafing around up there, living off the community dole. These sandwiches came from the kitchens not of Arcady but Bungle Bay. It's the Garibaldi Writer-in-Residence grant.

Arthur makes sure that Margaret has cold medications, and urges her to rest. That's not all he wants to say, he has a host of concerns and questions. Insistent but with misgiving, he calls upon Cud to watch over her, ensure she drinks water, stays covered.

A few minutes later, Selwyn Loo comes into view, walking slowly, his cane ticking against rock and root. Reverend Al is beside him, offering no aid but his voice. "Straight ahead."

The media part as if for Moses, affording Selwyn clear passage to the tree. A wholesale sucking-in of breath as he nearly trips on a buttress root. A collective exhalation as his hands go to the gnarled, knobbed bark of the ancient fir.

His fingers find a teardrop of sticky sap, which he puts to nose and tongue. He cocks his head, seems to be listening to the tree, as if to hear it breathe. The moment is shattered beautifully by a piercing note, a flicker flying by. He kneels and finds a newly fallen cone, thick with seed, which he spends a moment fondling, then pockets. "Good afternoon, everyone," he says.

This is an almost transcendental moment for Arthur. He feels something powerful welling from him, like love. For Selwyn, for Gwendolyn, for the primal splendour of this forest. For the mystery of life itself. He resists an urge to join Selwyn at that tree, to put his arms around it, to hear it breathe, find its cone, its seed, its offering.

✦

Arthur denies himself a second helping of stew – unless he gets a grip on his appetite, he will soon resemble Barney, the farting horse. An alcoholic may occasionally cut a romantic figure, but nobody loves a glutton.

Selwyn begged off staying the night, but enjoyed – in his manner, ever dour and long of face – a Blunder Bay walkabout. As they wandered along the paths, a solitary eagle flew in slow, grave circles above them. "They mate for life," Selwyn said. He continues to suspect Garlinc shot one of the pair. He apologized for his gloom. "Depressive episode."

Lotis took him to the ferry. Despite her frequent chiding of this morose fellow, her feelings for him, Arthur suspects, go beyond simple friendship. Beyond affection, maybe even to the barren wastelands of love not returned.

"Scene five, how she spent her summer holidays." Lotis hoists a tray with bowls of stew for Stoney and Dog, who are in the barn, celebrating – the Fargo has been pulled from the pond. "Call 911 if I'm not back in five."

He follows her out. A nippy evening, with stars and a burgeoning moon. In less difficult times, he and Margaret would be strolling to Blunder Point under that moon, their after-dinner ritual, with Slappy, his diligent inspection of every rock and bush and turd.

Lotis emerges from the barn waving away smoke. "Whoa, I got a contact high just walking in there. We're going for a walk, want to come?" *We* includes Slappy, who came home today, charmed by Lotis. Maybe there's a smell that she and Margaret share, something brave and rebellious, a smell that tells the old dog he'll have adventures with them.

On the way, Lotis doesn't try to break Arthur's silence, and the only sounds are footfalls and snapping twigs, and Slappy behind them, sniffing and snorting.

Where the trail takes a short, steep upturn, Arthur absently takes Lotis's hand. "Let's not twist any ankles this time, my dear."

"What?"

His mind has become a wandering fool. "Mental slip, sorry."

"You're totally hopeless without her, aren't you?"

16

Because all the rooms in the Victoria courthouse are taken, the disclosure hearing takes place in a study area of the law library. Arthur has Lotis at his side; Buddy Svabo sits alone, looking pugnacious. Judge Iris Takahashi is here to arbitrate, Arthur's former student, dimly remembered. On the other side of a glass partition, wandering around the stacks with a briefcase, is Staff Sergeant Jasper Flynn.

Arthur is cross, depressed – Munni Sidhoo, the biotechnology professor, worked all weekend on the semen sample, and her result, no surprise, has Faloon's DNA floating about in the biochemical mix. A long shot that didn't pay off.

"We seek to examine," Arthur says, "the dirty underwear my learned friend has been loath to disclose. He claims to enjoy the services of a jailhouse snitch."

"My witness is a Crown informant. By long-standing rule, I don't have to divulge his name."

"Nonsense," says Arthur. "He will be called to give evidence. He won't be wearing a bag over his head."

"This person is in jail awaiting sentence, he's at risk if he's exposed."

"You'll have to make safe arrangements for him," says Takahashi. "Counsel is entitled to know who he is and what he intends to say."

"How is it the defence gets everything and gives nothing?" Buddy's exasperation is poorly feigned. "Okay, you've got me on the ropes.

Father Yvon Réchard of the Holy Roman Church – more of a saintly soul than you expected, eh, Artie?"

"And how does he find himself behind bars?"

Buddy shrugs. "One of those Indian residential school things. Thirty years later, a bunch of guys decide to complain. They're grown up now, you'd think they'd want to put this behind them."

"Put what behind them?"

"Well, Father Réchard . . ." To give him credit, Buddy reddens as he grapples for a safe way to answer. "He's up for seven counts of sexual assault."

"Which you intend to prosecute with faint heart." Arthur wonders how strong his own heart is, he shouldn't get riled. But he finds his voice rising. "Or maybe not at all – is that the deal you made? You'd swap the ruined lives of seven men for perjured testimony?" As Arthur slaps the table, lawyers in the library turn from their studies. Jasper Flynn, standing among the legal texts, glances up, stiffens, as if ready to go into action. Lotis looks surprised to see that the icon has a temper.

Buddy has raised his hands defensively, as if protecting his head. "Hey, hold on, Artie, if he gets a cheaper sentence for co-operating, that's up to the judge, I'm neutral."

Doubtless a deal not made on paper, but with winks and nudges between Svabo and counsel for the priest: a suspended sentence, probation. Arthur must sit down with his client, must garner information on this pedophiliac.

Buddy hands out copies of Réchard's statement. A mere three paragraphs, in a neat hand on lined paper. He occupied a cell adjacent to Nick's. They often shared a table at mealtime. They talked about religion and philosophy. The priest believed Faloon was a Catholic – "fallen, like myself, so far from grace."

Arthur picks up a hint of Milton in that line. The final paragraph, the nub of this jailhouse confession, is less poetic, just as pious: "I felt something was bothering poor Nick because he had been sleepwalking in his cell. I asked him if he wished to relieve himself of any troubles. He shook his head, and I didn't press it. But that night I heard him whispering to me from the next cell. He said, 'I couldn't help it. She was beautiful. I just couldn't help myself, I couldn't help myself.' His voice trailed off as he repeated that. I felt it my duty to come forward."

"Short and sweet," says Buddy, trying to look virtuous.

"He felt it his duty to come *forward*?" Arthur raises his voice again. "The very forward Reverend Réchard, is it? If the man has no compunction about betraying the confessional, why should we assume he's honest at all? I can hardly wait, Buddy. I am champing at the bit. I want the jury to see how desperate you are."

"I have to call whatever evidence comes my way, Artie, that's my job."

"Whom did he come forward *to*? I want every word of every interview that led to this. I want every piece of paper you've got on this fellow."

"Not. Can someone tell me why we're even here?" A testy, aggrieved tone. "The case is tight – we've got DNA, you guys are looking at a ten-billion-to-one shot. Faloon is going to do it all, the freaking *book*, and he can forget parole." His temperature is up, his face red. "How are you doing with those new tests, Artie? What about *our* rights to disclosure? I'll eat my shirt if the results don't spell Faloon in neon."

"The presence of the defendant's DNA has been confirmed."

"Bam. Case closed." Buddy punches the air, causing Takahashi to jump. "Cop a plea, Artie, let's get this stinker buried. You've got no idea the pressure I'm under from some lobby groups."

Feminist groups, he might have said, were he not aware of Takahashi giving him a cold eye. "Let's get on with this," she says. "I have a continuation."

Arthur moves to the issue of Dr. Winters's files. He doesn't mention Adeline Angella. The defence, he explains, merely seeks to know if any patients harboured a murderous delusion or grudge. "Why is the prosecution balking at producing her records? It causes suspicion to bloom like the flowers of spring."

Buddy acts offended. "These are peoples' emotional lives we're talking about, they came to her expecting she would keep their secrets."

"And carry them to the grave?"

"You want the moon – Dr. Winters practised a dozen years, we're talking several hundred people with painful traumas." Buddy turns to Takahashi. "It's a fishing expedition, and he's looking for a red herring."

"What do you say to that, Arthur?"

"We have a particular fish in mind."

"Yeah, who?" says Buddy.

Arthur can't believe he's pretending ignorance – doesn't he know Doctor Eve was consulted by Lorelei, the temptress? *A desperate need to examine her sexuality.*

"You should produce the files, Buddy," Takahashi says.

Buddy had hoped to win at least a draw. He looks at Sergeant Flynn, raises his arms in supplication. Flynn puts down a text, picks up his briefcase, and walks ponderously to their room.

"This shark is beating me to a pulp, Jasper. Give him the files."

Flynn hands Arthur a disc. "This is everything, sir. What Dr. Winters didn't keyboard in, our techies scanned."

Arthur is distrustful of the wizardry that supplanted copiers. Does information remain errorless when it has passed through the innards of a computer, digested, digitized, shat out? He asks for a printed list of patients. Buddy greets that with a sigh of such anguish you'd think he'd been ordered to strip naked. He lifts a weary hand toward Flynn, who produces a computer printout, about forty pages.

Arthur looks at the second page – between a G. Anfield and a P. Annhauser, there's an A. Angella. He leafs through the remaining pages with no change of expression.

"This was compiled how?"

"From the deceased's index cards," Flynn says.

"I'm sorry, people," says Takahashi, packing her notes away. "I can't keep my courtroom waiting."

Buddy rises. "Anything else you need, Artie, I'm always happy to oblige."

As the others pack up, Lotis gives Arthur an exaggerated look of dumb surprise. The name Angella has been overlooked by the techies in the course of their scanning and keyboarding. Maybe computers have made cops lazy. Unless Svabo's blustering hides a dramatic talent, he has no clue that Angella is holding back critical information.

Lotis sums it up. "Angella doesn't want the bulls to know she screamed blue murder at Dr. Winters."

Brian Pomeroy picked up her anxiety about testifying – unusual given her enjoyment of the spotlight. But the searchlight of suspicion glares fiercely too, and she must have hoped Flynn's team lacked the patience to read Winters's files. They have their killer; why put in the extra hours?

Arthur says, "I take it you are adept with a computer." Why would he think otherwise? – this young smarty knows everything else about the modern world.

Predictably, Lotis pulls a notebook computer from her pack, flicks it open, slides in the disc. After a few moments and a few cascading screens, she types "Angella." The computer tells her, "Not found." Lotis sweeps hair from her forehead, puzzled.

Here is Jonas Anfield, who doesn't know how to tell his wife to stop having affairs behind his back. The next file isn't Adeline Angella but Penny Annhauser, whose boyfriend hates dogs and she loves them.

Arthur has underestimated Svabo's duplicity. "We have caught them red-handed, concealing information from us. They have spirited away the Angella file but forgot her name was also in the card index. It explains why our lightweight friend seemed a little jittery."

"That may not be the actual scenario." Her impish smile.

"What other possibility is there?"

"The other possibility is that we already have that file. Dr. Winters left it with her lawyer, your misogynist pal Cleaver. He gave it to us at El Beau Room, remember?" Apologetic, as if embarrassed to witness the deterioration of the icon's mental faculties.

He harrumphs. "Yes, of course. I have it at home. Yes, that helps explain why Svabo hasn't twigged."

But how telling it is that Angella didn't share with Buddy her history with Winters, her furious demands for redress. As for Père Réchard, Lotis will run out to the jail with a copy of his statement, and will ask Faloon for his version.

They pause by the table where Jasper Flynn was reading a text. Lotis picks it up: the current edition of *Canadian Divorce Law*.

"Troubles on the home front," she says.

That takes Arthur where he doesn't want to go, his own prosaic, snapless marriage. The worms of paranoia keep finding new places to dig at him. This morning, over coffee, he was haunted by an unsavory vignette: Margaret and Cud sharing confidences, intimacies. He's not simply a lout with a Hogarthian appetite. He turns out to have a coarse, homespun charm. When one pokes hard, one finds little tender areas, he's sensitive beneath his baboonish exterior. A decade younger than her, virile, needy. *You're not going to tell your old man, I hope? No, of course not.*

What is the matter with him, what causes all these improbable imaginings? It's the Annabelle Syndrome. She twisted his psyche with her constant scavenging of handsome men, caused a permanent warp, something complex and crippling. Acute jealous anxiety disorder, little understood.

He reminds himself to call a casualty of another troubled home front, Brian Pomeroy, who has been leaving fulminating messages, his marital crisis worsened by his evening with Angella. The untimely call from Caroline, who overheard Angella's chiding tones and her "Ouch, your knee," has slammed shut the door of reconciliation.

Now comes Arthur's first use of the evil cellphone as Lotis steps him through his call to Brian, who receives the news of the day with grunts of interest, then begins to rail.

"I'm suing for access if she doesn't cough them up this weekend. *Easter* is coming up, for Christ's sake. I want to take them camping. Caroline would prefer to keep them at home in front of the tube, scarfing junk food while she marks her students' puerile essays on Benét and Auden and Spender."

Arthur waits until this eruption is done. He has learned it's never wise to offer family advice, especially to friends. Nor does he intend to plead Brian's case to Caroline, who is as bright and brittle as her husband. He suspects Brian savours being wronged, the nobility of it – a spy on the rack, refusing to confess his clandestine role on behalf of an innocent man. (Yet there is intensity in his marriage. It breaks, it mends; over many separations and reunions, it stays alive. If there's romance in conflict, Arthur's a drab lover.)

"Adeline Angella, at least, *is* talking to me. She phoned last night, offended – why hadn't I held to my breathless departing promise to call her? I told her she was very much on my mind. When I see her next, it's in public, with witnesses."

Brian will find a pretext to ask where she was on April 1 – if she has an alibi, it's best to know early. If it's a false alibi, the defence must prepare to counter it. If it's honest, the defence must shift targets.

◆

After helping Edna Sproule with a breech birth, Arthur runs to the house to clean up, then rushes to the ferry to pick up Lotis, fresh from her visit to Faloon. She heaves her packsack over the tailgate, lights a cigarette, and they head off. She has finally got a haircut, now she can see.

"I thought you were quitting."

"Tomorrow. Cold turkey Tuesday. Last time I quit, it was the headless scene from *Scream Seven*. Be happy I won't be in your hair."

"In whose hair will you be?"

"Not sure how to answer that." She flips through a notepad, quick to change topics. "I told Nick he'd better fess up to Claudette about screwing Holly. It's important, I said. You used a safe, what happened to it? He can't remember, thinks Holly trashed it."

"The sleepwalking?"

"He downplayed it." Imitating his soft voice: "'I'm dreaming I'm in the cage like a animal, I wake up and I been wearing out the carpet, it ain't nothing to bother Mr. Beauchamp about.'"

One suppresses the truth one fears – another reason for Arthur to see him soon. He once ran a sleepwalking defence after learning, from his expert, that people can do complex tasks when disconnected from reality. But he has no taste for arguing his client acted unconsciously; it implies a savage murderer hides within.

"I phoned Claudette to confirm he paced up and down in his sleep, and she said, yeah, it was like he was locked in a cell. He also talked in his sleep." Examining her notes. "Things like: 'Let me out of here. What's your badge number? I'm clean, ask Corporal Johnson, he handles me.'"

He interrupts. "Ah, so let us assume Réchard *isn't* lying." She is getting a little too overweening with her brilliant deductions. He's not too senile to see the logical premise. "Nick was trying to justify his night with Holly Hoover. 'I couldn't help myself. She was beautiful.' He'd suppressed it and it came out in his dreams."

"Good for you," she says, wetting an index finger and awarding Arthur an invisible check mark.

He drops her at the Woofer house, watches as she shouts a greeting to Kim Lee, retrieves her pack, kneels to shake Slappy's paw. *Lotis the nymph, if rural tales be true, as from Priapus' lawless lust she flew . . .*

Adding to the Owl's misery, he's been expelled from Protective Custody and is back in the main monkey cage. He can't be in PCU at the same time as Father Yvon Réchard, according to prison regulations, because the aggrieved party might cause injury to what in police lingo is a co-operating individual.

Not that Faloon would be capable of such unprofessional behaviour, but others in the main wing definitely are, for instance the burly person he's talking to in the yard, Greg McDeadly they call him, though it's really McDade. You don't want to call him McDud, which a loudmouth did years ago and has the knife scars on his ass to prove it.

McDeadly is a connected guy who works for the d'Anglio family and can get you favours. When he's on the street, which isn't often, his job for Tony d'Anglio is to put the rub on competing crime czars and traitors and rats. He recently got collared for an attempt on Twelve-Fingers Watson, which is why he's here.

McDeadly insists he can get transferred easy to PCU, with his connections, it's in his field of expertise to take down Father Réchard. "I will do you justice. Pay me when you get out, Nick, I know you're good for it. For me it's a matter of principle when it comes to squealers. The practice should be discouraged."

"It's very kind of you to offer, but Mr. Beauchamp isn't worried about this fish, he'll serve him up to the jury with pickles on the side." Which is a load of bravado, because Faloon isn't sure that will happen, not at all. Not with him having flunked the DNA retest, according to Beauchamp's new student, who came out here yesterday with a sackful of bad news.

She asked him if he'd ever slipped anyone what they call rochies or roofies, for instance to immobilize the mark before putting on a snatch, and he was offended. He has ethical standards when it comes to drugs, like guns.

Claudette is due this afternoon, and he's tense with wanting to see her big smiling face. He has to be cheerful for her, he doesn't want her to know how hopeless things feel.

"What was you supposed to have told this songbird?" McDeadly asks.

"'She was beautiful, I just couldn't help myself.'" Phrases that feel foreign to his tongue, yet why that distant niggle of memory that he spoke them?

"That don't sound too bad, you could've been asking the father for forgiveness over jacking off."

"It's bad enough." Faloon looks like a schemer, playing along with Réchard that he was Catholic – how is that going to look to a jury? The Arab infiltrator. Maybe that's the whole deal, it's why the government has zeroed in on him like a laser-guided missile, he's Lebanese, an Arab, a terrorist.

What makes him worry that he used those words is that at breakfast the next day Father Réchard came up to him with a knowing look and a lowered voice: "I know exactly what you mean." After that the priest's counsellor came visiting, a dumptruck with a reputation for pulling off deals so he can go skiing.

Faloon has finally got round to facing the possibility of himself as the perpetrator. He walks in his sleep, talks in his sleep, so maybe he stalks in his sleep, kills in his sleep. Compelled by a force outside him. *I just couldn't help myself.*

He didn't go that far when talking to Lotis Rudnicki, who's street-smart and too much of a knockout to be doing the ugly work of a lawyer. She must have seen he was dejected – the Father Réchard business, the ironclad DNA evidence. On top of it all, Mr. Beauchamp never coming to visit. Obviously, that's because he doesn't believe in Faloon and can't look him in the eye. Out of loyalty to his most faithful client, Mr. Beauchamp has put aside his blissful life to take on a hopeless loser. Faloon owes it to him not to let his career end with such a dull thud.

McDeadly pulls out a packet of tobacco and papers. Smoking is illegal in the joint these days, even outside, but it isn't enforced to the hilt. He halves the rollie, one for Faloon, and they light up, the Owl going along even though he doesn't normally smoke.

"I want to get a private letter out," Faloon says. He chokes, it's pipe tobacco.

"That can be done."

"You have a reliable source for this fine product, McDeadly?"

"Yeah, one of the screws is my ex-brother-in-law, he kites it in. You want a lid?"

"Please."

✦

Waiting for the visiting hour, for Claudette, he washes his armpits, drags a comb through his receding hair, tries on a smile: the cool, confident, innocent look while inside all is torment. The killer who strikes in his sleep, will that be the headline? How does he share his terrible thoughts with the woman he loves – if that's what it is, love.

He's going to clear the air. For at least one brilliant holy moment of your life you have to be totally honest with the one lady who gives a shit about you. Who's prepared to make the great sacrifice of marrying you, even though he can't remember proposing.

He's been rehearsing the right words to tell Claudette about Holly, and even as he waits outside the visitors' room, he practises under his breath. "In case something happens to me, I don't want an event from the past to rear its ugly head between us." Too formal. "She took advantage in my drunken state." Not true. The fact is

Holly looked hot and she was offering, and he . . . well, he's human.

He is marched in, and there she is, the bountiful hostess of the Nitinat Lodge. Soon to be owner.

They both want to touch but can only put hands to the glass. "I sorely miss you, darlin'," she says with her lovely Maritime accent.

He asks how she's doing, and she's doing fine, the lodge is doing great, wait till he sees the flowerbeds she planted. She runs on about that, how they're going to have a great time running the Nitinat, a husband-and-wife team, she'll do the cooking and he'll clean the eaves and paint the decks.

He puts on a happy face. "Yeah, we'll be sitting fat." Enjoying the idea of being in love is one thing, with marriage come chores . . .

"So how're *you* feelin'?"

"I'm tops. I'm going to be out of this coop soon. I always look on the sunny side." She studies him dubiously. He asks if she had the papers notarized yet about putting the lodge in her name.

"I will, honey, what's the rush? You ain't going to die in the next couple of days."

"I want the legalities done, I'll feel better if you're secure."

She carries on about Bamfield, about the search for the loot, how one guy dug his way into an underground vault that had fifty gallons of stilled hooch, all of Bamfield partied. Faloon isn't sure if he even remembers where the treasure is. Sixty paces northeast of where the path breaks off for Brady Beach — or is it northwest?

Claudette also tells him there's a story going around about how Holly Hoover came calling on Mr. Beauchamp in the night. She doesn't believe there was an improper outcome to that, because he seemed really straight and proper.

The mention of Hoover releases a spring latch in Faloon, and his mouth pops open. "I fucked her." No preparatory text, nothing, just the blunt admission, and when he tries to explain and apologize in a low, scared voice, she puts up a hand to stop him.

"I kind of knew you did." Her weary sigh means he could've saved a lot of misery by being honest from the start.

"Thank God it's off my chest. I'm sorry, things have been piling up, they . . ." He brakes. "No, that's crazy, why am I saying that? You're here, I'm happy, this is the high point of the week."

He's not going to tell her about Père Réchard, or about how there may be a monster inside him, the sleepwalking killer. He can't handle it, doing the book, forever looking at bars. It would destroy her too, visiting every week, then once a month, five times a year, growing older, sadder, lonelier . . .

"You okay, Nick?"

"Absolutely."

"You sure?" Looking at him penetrating, maybe seeing the evil. "Don't do nothing stupid, okay?"

17

"Goway bigpack," Kim Lee says inscrutably, as Arthur spoons up granola in skim milk. She pantomimes a woman walking, followed by a four-legged creature: Lotis has gone off somewhere with Slappy. Arthur stuffs a basket with hot muffins and jam and a Thermos of vegetable soup, and pours a coffee for the drive.

A mile up Potter's Road, he comes upon Slappy waddling behind Lotis's big pack – strapped to it are a rolled foamy, sleeping bag, rain jacket, sweaters. She hoists this freightage over the tailgate, helps Slappy in, climbs in beside Arthur, and as he pulls away, she says gaily, "Hauling supplies to the front line." She has dyed her hair green and painted her lips green. Green fingernails.

"Supplies for whom?"

"Well . . . me. I'm quitting smoking, it's my cold-turkey project. I'm going to have a dialogue with your life partner. I'm going to try a prisoner exchange."

Arthur is torn: however much he longs for Margaret's return, he can't afford to lose his articling student to a tree. Or, as could well happen, to the Women's Correctional Centre. He reminds her that Corporal Al has been ordered to limit occupancy up there to two persons.

"I can handle Corporal Al. If Margaret wants an excuse to come down with head held high, I'm that excuse. I'll stay just long enough to get over the nic fits. Three, four days at the outset."

She appears not to understand that a proper barrister doesn't dye her hair green and run off to join a forest sit-in. "Santorini's vanity is of the sensitive kind, he'll see it as a personal slap that a lawyer defies his order so deliberately."

"Am I missing something? The Appeal Court voided his order."

"I know this fellow. He will take pleasure in finding my articling student guilty of contempt. You will be made an example. You will be jailed. Denied admittance to the bar. You must not do this."

"Yeah, well, having a law degree doesn't exempt you from the picket line. I'll handle Santorini. He *likes* me. I say that because he can't stop undressing me in court. This is my baby, this project. Spartacus didn't lead from behind. Nor did Joan of Arc. Or Ghandi."

Arthur picks up a hint of grandiosity, a martyr complex, a disability that has been the downfall of revolutionaries throughout history. He plays to her vanity: a splendid career is at risk because of a flip and ill-considered decision.

A lazy shrug of unconcern. "'Too rash, too unadvised, too sudden.'" Another of Juliet's lines. That riles him, her mocking tone of smug superiority, her lack of deference to a wise elder. His initial impression, the hippie schemer in the Rise Up T-shirt, may not be that far amiss.

"Sorry, I'm cranky, I'm on withdrawal. I am going to *do* this."

He imagines it was like this with Saint Joan: one is arguing with a wall. He'll try not to appear self-righteous as they're handcuffing her; he'll try to ignore the roars of laughter in the Confederation Club: poor old Beauchamp, he had to go bail out his student.

He lets her off at Stump Town. More tents, more activists, more banners. Scantily dressed young people, some in green face paint, are performing a slow, ritualistic tableau. A modern dance company? A theatre group?

"You won't find a place to park," says Baldy Johansson, at his car window. "There's gonna be a pagan ritual. Or something."

"Snug yourself in here, Arthur." It's Todd Clearihue, pulling out from Garlinc's reserved space. He's in an old Ford pickup and wearing a Budweiser cap.

Lotis has been busy with her pack, but now is looking icily at Clearihue. His unsubtle approach, after he picked her up hitchhiking, has quickly become a part of island lore.

"You want to be careful with that one," Clearihue says as their trucks pause abreast. "We had her checked out. B-movie teen actress, flamed out at twenty-five. Divorced parents, drugs, sex, abortion, total crack-up, can't deal with her life, runs away to Canada. Professional shit-disturber, way out in left field. Commies in the family tree."

He isn't telling Arthur much he hasn't already heard or guessed.

Clearihue squints at the painted dancers. "This is starting to look like a bazaar in Kathmandu. You should move those kids out, Arthur, they don't enhance the image for the fundraising."

Clearihue isn't aware Lotis is at his open passenger window until she says, "What did you do to *your* image, Todd? You were always so clear-cut. Sorry, I mean clean-cut. What's with this old beat-up truck?"

He makes no effort to turn toward her, says wearily, "Good morning, Lotis."

"The new you just doesn't work for me. Local yokel with a beer commercial on his head. When you're trying to fake your way into the community, you don't wear five-hundred-dollar boots."

Clearihue strenuously ignores her. "How's the fundraising coming, Arthur? I'm concerned, I mean it. I must've put in nine hundred myself, all told. Sunk at least sixty into the bingo last night."

He alights from the cab. "A private word," he says, finally glancing at Lotis in her bold maquillage, the Green Avenger, then moving nose to nose with Arthur. "Between you and me and our tax accountant, I could persuade my associates to go as low as fourteen if we get the right charitable concessions. And here's the kicker: we may even be willing to carry mortgages for half of it. A monthly payment plan. We'd try to enlist the major landholders. Like yourself, Arthur."

Arthur shivers, plays with the unspeakable concept of Garlinc foreclosing on the entire island, owning Blunder Bay. He contents himself with, "More foundations will offer more grants if the price is reasonable."

"Can't do." Clearihue steps back from Slappy, who is sniffing at his shiny cowboy boots. The green-face troupe is going single file up the Gap Trail. "Guess there'll be a lot more when university's over. I'm hip to it. I marched for peace, I was pretty radical back then."

"Whoa, baby, I can see why *that* image had to go." Lotis again. "Marching for peace at the wheel of a fifty-thousand-dollar topless Audi?"

"You keep coming from behind, don't you?" Clearihue says.

"I heard that's the way you like it."

Clearihue returns to his Ford, his smile unwavering. "Okay, buddy, good luck. See you in court tomorrow."

Lotis isn't through. "By the way, whatever happened to our little sail?"

Clearihue seems unfamiliar with his stick shift, can't find low gear. "You don't want to get too close to this one, Arthur. She's a bit of a tart. You wouldn't believe how much she was willing to extend herself for a ride in a fast car." A glare at Lotis. "Quit stalking me."

"You lying self-admiring sociopathic *freak!*" Lotis starts after him, but he is finally in gear and down the road. Arthur can see why her film career "tanked," as she'd told Arthur, after too many scraps with directors and producers.

Glowering, Lotis hoists her pack and goes up the path with Slappy. Arthur follows with his food basket, joins a gathering by the Holy Tree. "What's happening?" he asks a wild-haired teenager.

"They're tryna get the tree to vibe with love, or some hokey shit like that."

News cameras are aimed at a circle of performers – some green-faced and clad in garments adorned with leaves, others wearing animal masks, all holding hands around the tree. Somehow they have coaxed Reverend Al into joining the circle, and he's flushed with embarrassment. The women holding his hands are protected from the elements only by sprays of leaves.

The vibes are more Vedic than pagan, if Arthur correctly interprets the chant. Hands go up. "O-mm," intones the leader, who leaves the circle, flapping her arms. The others join her in a choreographed dance of birds flying, all chanting "O-mm." Corporal Al, standing to the side, looks on approvingly.

Watching from above are Margaret, standing, wrapped in a blanket, and Cud, swinging in a hammock. Life is sweet for the poet laureate of Garibaldi. One of his short works has been quoted in the *New York Times*. *Liquor Balls* has gone into a second printing. Single women are writing letters to him.

The omming continues for several minutes, bystanders joining in, until even Arthur, enveloped in the hum, finds himself giving voice. A hush follows, broken by Cud. "What kind of horseshit was that?" Not loud, but carrying well in the silence. Margaret looks at him severely.

The circle breaks up, and Corporal Al says, "Real interesting. Now I want everyone to kindly leave, except those with business." The performers and onlookers go, but the press stays on, alert to human interest when Margaret's husband is mooning around.

Lotis sets her gear down beneath the platform's overhang, relieves Arthur of the basket, calls for the supply line. Cud, sensing food, maybe smelling the biscuits Arthur baked by hand, bounds from the hammock, lowers the rope.

Arthur asks Margaret about her health. She is focused on the green-haired, green-lipped waif below her. "What? Oh, I'm loads better. Temperature normal." She says this with clogged nose. "The farm?"

"Hovering at the brink of disaster. I'll write the details."

Lotis affixes both the basket and her heavy pack to the line, and Cud must work up a sweat hauling them up.

"Beam me up next," Lotis says. Hearing this, Corporal Al walks smartly up to her, and they engage in a low, intense debate.

As Lotis pleads her case, Corporal Al glances at Arthur. Finally, he joins him, away from eavesdroppers. "Sorry, Arthur, I didn't realize you were falling apart that bad." He bows, Tai Chi style, and leaves.

The rope ladder flutters down, followed by a safety line. Lotis hooks up to it, and climbs, hamming it up, waving to the cameras, falling into Cud's arms as he helps her over the railing. After hurriedly unravelling herself from his grip, she dares Margaret's germs, whispers words that, astonishingly, cause her to laugh. The two of them disappear from view. Cud pulls up the ladder with a broad, swaggering smile. Now he has a harem.

Lotis's ascent has reporters talking into satellite phones. Activist-lawyer defies courts. Arthur can only wonder what Santorini's reaction will be to this nose-thumbing by another agitator from the Blunder Bay farm team. It might take not much more than a stalled vehicle on the causeway to inspire another exponential sentence.

Vowing to return to his hike-a-day regimen, he trudges up the hill-side. Slappy, twice deserted, scrambles behind. He pauses often to catch his breath and enjoy the panoramic views above the Sproules' pastures. "Splendid," he pants. "Majestic."

He wonders if the Sanskrit *om*, that spoken essence of the universe, has found its winged target, but he sees no eagles. He's still put out at Lotis, but supposes that was her idea of a noble gesture. Her mess, but he'll try to pull her out of it.

Near the top of the switchback, not far from the bluffs, he makes his way to a mossy granite ledge, and lies on his back to regain his wind. Slappy finishes a tour of the area, and settles beside him. The day is warm, the sun high, and doves moan in the trees. The moss is warm and soft, and his body tired, and he allows sleep to come.

On awakening, he is disoriented by many things. First, by a remembered dream of Promethean death: he was bound to a cliff-face, an eagle flying off with his innards to Margaret and Cud in the nest, mouths wide, demanding to be fed.

An awareness even more morbid: Doc Dooley is kneeling beside him, taking his pulse.

Add to that a distant, disturbing shout: "There's a good shot from here."

Arthur becomes aware that evening is nearly upon them, a crepus-cular light. Another call from afar, a woman: "A better shot over here."

"What are they shooting at?" Arthur asks, rising to his elbows.

"How many fingers?" Dooley's bony hand is in front of Arthur's face.

"Five. I'm in fine fettle."

"How is he, Doc?" Corporal Al's voice, from a radio on Dooley's belt.

"Rumours of his death are greatly exaggerated. The bugger was asleep."

"Sorry if I'm a worrywart," says Corporal Al, "but he's been having an emotional crisis."

Dooley frowns. "What were you doing out here, Beauchamp? Spread-eagled on the moss, you were, like a human sacrifice."

Arthur sits up. "I stretched myself a bit, took a nap. What's all that shouting?"

Now it's Reverend Al on the radio: "Doc, a television crew is heading your way."

"What's happening?" Arthur asks.

"What's happening is . . ." A pause to build suspense. Arthur takes pleasure in watching the doctor's face crease into a rare smile: so rare that he wishes he had a camera. "We have an eagle pair. The mate has returned to the nest." Arthur is astonished to see him take a few light steps, as if from a long-remembered Irish jig.

Dooley is pleased with his place in history – he was the first to sight the returning male, talons clutching a love offering: a large, overripe fish for the female, who has taken to the nest. Other witnesses include members of an Oregon birding club who pause on the way down to show Arthur digital images: two fiercely frowning eagles perched by the nest.

The television crew appears, straining under the weight of equipment. Puffing along behind, as if drawn by the magnet of their camera, is Kurt Zoller, with a squawking walkie-talkie, Corporal Al issuing commands: "I want no more than half a dozen folks up here at a time, and I want them quiet."

"Roger, copy that, over." Because he has an authoritarian bent, Zoller is regularly deputized for traffic control. He takes up position to guard the pass.

Arthur decides not to tarry, Kim has made dinner. He'll return this evening for the changing of the guard ceremony. On his way down, he comes upon Nelson Forbish panting against a tree, looking as if he might explode. "How far, how . . . am I almost there?" Arthur knows he's not going to make it, and leads him back to the Gap. "I was the first one to hear, I could've had a scoop."

At Stump Town, a guitar-banjo-bongo trio is warming up for a celebration. Reverend Al pours Arthur a hot toddy from his Thermos, and they click cups. "I have to admit the pagan ceremony brought faster results than mine. Little twinge of doubt there." He has just returned from the Holy Tree, whose tenants are celebrating too. "They're having a gay old time scripting a set-piece for this evening, though God knows what. They want you there. I'll pick you up."

Though still smarting from Lotis's defection, Arthur is buoyed by the hope of reuniting tonight with Margaret. Tomorrow, he will make a vigorous pitch for Lotis – Santorini may not slap her in irons now that the eagles are nesting. He can hardly allow cutting to begin now anyway.

Reverend Al pulls into the driveway, beaming. "I'm thinking of incorporating a few Vedic ceremonies into my next service. One must borrow the best from other creeds."

"What brings this heresy on?"

"We have eggs, Arthur, two of them. Enjoy this."

A glossy photo: two frowning eagles perched by the nest, surveying their realm, the Kingdom of Gwendolyn Valley. Partly obscured by the lip of the nest are two grey oval shapes.

"Leif Thorson came out of retirement, fused vertebrae and all, put on his spurs, went up the rigging of the tallest fir on the bluffs, and rappelled to a tree overhanging the Gap. Two healthy-looking eggs, Arthur. Thirty-five days of incubation, eighty days before the juveniles leave the nest. Have we bought the summer?"

"I'm not sure." Who knows what could happen with Santorini the Unpredictable. Never mind, if today's rustic ceremony plays out as he expects, Margaret will be home tonight. He has baked a lemon pie. A little scorched on top, but a respectable effort.

Musicians are playing again at Stump Town, the band swollen to six, augmented by fiddle, flute, and ukulele. Young people are dancing. Corporal Al is standing by his bicycle, panting in sweat-soaked regimentals but grinning with the accomplishment of his steep haul to the Gap.

"This is getting too noisy," he says. "I'm shutting it down before Vern comes by with his trombone. Can't use the hall, it's got a spring flower fundraiser, so I'll ask the Rosekeepers if they mind moving the party to their picnic grounds. It'll probably go all night, in case you boys feel overcome by the need to dance."

Nearing the Holy Tree, Arthur hears two female voices, joined in a chant. In their aerie, Margaret and Lotis have their arms around each other, and are reciting a banal oft-quoted poem: "Woodman, spare that tree." They're hamming it up, a vaudeville routine.

Cud Brown leans scornfully against the trunk, arms folded, refusing to add to some lesser poet's celebrity. The performance draws a sardonic cheer from a couple of reporters.

The rope ladder flutters down. Arthur wonders if he's expected to climb it, to participate in this revue, join them in a soft-shoe, or perhaps the grand quartet from *Rigoletto*. But clearly his role will be to receive Margaret in his arms as she descends from her throne. He should have brought flowers. He must think of bon mots for the intruding microphones.

Arthur settles under the ladder, holding it steady. She'll not forget the safety line, he hopes. Slappy knows what's up, he's wagging his tail fiercely. It's a beautiful scene, lit by a spike of sunlight through the trail. What descends, directly above, is a floppy pair of large boots below knobby knees and hairy thighs. Arthur steps back to widen the angle, confirms that the scruffy shape coming down is Cud Brown, with his old army rucksack. His sour face hints that this is not his finest hour.

Margaret launches one of her paper gliders. It takes a wide circle toward Cud, then catches a breeze and dips several feet down, and is finally hooked in the claws of a dead branch within Cud's reach.

He has the gall to open and read it. He shouts to its author: "Oh, real sensitive. I got feelings." Cud resumes his descent and drops the now formless airplane. Arthur sticks it in a pocket. And now he's assailed by a miasmic stench. It's a whiff of Cud, now only a body length above him. The loosely booted feet, when level to Arthur's nose, have a peculiarly rich tang.

"Whew," says a young man helping hold the ladder. A flashbulb blinds Cud as he releases his rucksack. This fifty-pound object lands on Arthur's chest as he cranes to look up, and sends him hard on his rear, missing Slappy by a hair. An excruciating pain in the tailbone tells Arthur he won't be sitting for a while.

◆

Arthur didn't want to look foolish by bringing a pillow, so this morning he stands at the back of a half-lit courtroom, watching a video on an eighty-inch screen, footage spliced together from newscasts. Denied his hope of breezing to victory, Paul Prudhomme is trying to persuade Santorini he's being mocked.

Selwyn seems in deep concentration, creating images from sound. Then a smile as Lotis says on screen, "Beam me up."

"You might recall Ms. Rudnicki from this courtroom, milord," says Prudhomme, "but without the green hair. Flouting, in front of the press, your order prohibiting anyone else going up that tree."

Santorini lets loose a chuckle, but smothers it. Arthur cannot fathom the mood of this mercurial judge – he's watching intently, particularly the beaming-up, a camera focused on Lotis's buttocks. Her ascent, her backward glance, her fist of triumph, made it onto U.S. newscasts: the ex-Hollywood starlet who risks arrest for defending an American emblem.

Prudhomme does not inflict on them the bathos of *Woodman, spare that tree*, but does linger on Margaret waving at Arthur, launching her bad-news glider. It had a demoralizing effect on Arthur: a glum evening, sharing his lemon pie with Kim Lee.

Margaret's note was annoyingly upbeat. She's on the homestretch, nine days to go. (*We're winning, Arthur! We have eggs!*) Having survived a week and a half with Cud Brown (*A mop, a scrubber, and two pails of water – would you mind, Arthur?*), she'll come down proudly when her term is up. As to the malodorous poet, she wrote: *What an animal — I was always picking up his greasy socks. Thank God for Lotis.* While Cyrano stalled at the starting gate, the Green Avenger raced to triumph, rescuing the fair damsel from the poet-in-exile's gamy consanguinity.

The courtroom gasps as the rucksack fells Arthur, his mouth open in clownish astonishment, Slappy darting away. This has Santorini in another struggle against laughter, his face going red.

"Meanwhile," says Prudhomme, "the defendant Blake remains up that tree in defiance of your Lordship's strictures." Prudhomme is carrying on stoutly, though rattled by Santorini's sniggers.

"Weren't you in the Appeal Court when they quashed my order? Never mind, play that last part again."

Fast rewind, Arthur rising, looking goofy, Slappy scampering backwards. Again, the rucksack drops and Arthur sits down hard.

"Ho! That dog got out of there just in time."

The usually sanguine Prudhomme is exasperated. "Milord, this travesty has been going on for two weeks now. Surely the plaintiff is entitled to some relief."

"Whole different state of affairs. A pair of eagles, that's what we have, and two in the shell. You claimed that nest was abandoned, and now you've got yourself in a pickle."

"Milord," says Prudhomme, "may I have a few moments?"

"I'll wait." Santorini can't help grinning as he looks at the standee in the back. "Would you be more comfortable if you sat, Mr. Beauchamp?" The room erupts in laughter.

The plaintiff's team caucuses: Prudhomme, two helpmates, and Todd Clearihue, whose smile is fixed and looks surreal. Selwyn's antennae may be picking up stray words — he fiddles in his briefcase, pulls out a file.

Prudhomme leaves the huddle. "The plaintiff wishes to inform the court it shares a concern about these majestic birds, and will consider the more costly option of bringing in equipment by barge."

"It is not an option." Selwyn passes up a thick affidavit. "A sea otter habitat would be under threat."

"That may be so, Mr. Loo, and we'll get to it when we get to it. Meantime, I'm granting a temporary restraining order against cutting within two kilometres of that tree. We'll put this over for one week. Counsel, will you join me in chambers?"

Santorini is shrugging his robe off as they enter, snapping his collar button loose. "Just going to make the last nine at Langara. It's a fundraiser, kids' hockey, I have to show up. Damn it, I almost split a gut in there. That Lotis Rudnicki – I finally figured out where I'd seen her, a TV commercial. 'Did you use enough soap, dear?' I always laugh at that, the way she's so deadpan."

Selwyn is smiling broadly, a sight rarely seen. Prudhomme smiles too, but with the weariness of defeat.

"Looks like your lady got the better of both of us, Beauchamp." Santorini takes off his striped pants. "You poor bugger, I could tell you were expecting her to come down. I saw how your expression changed, your jowls sagged. And when you fell . . ." He can't complete, his belly is shaking with laughter.

Loser of five straight murder trials, his manhood under test, Santorini has finally forced Arthur to the ground. Arthur is piqued at this razing. He didn't realize he had jowls. At least he has hair on his head.

But he accepts the ribbing. "The injury is confined to the area lyrically described by Shakespeare as the afternoon of the body. Otherwise, only my ego smarts."

"Hey, I'm not laughing at you, I had that happen to me, some blind idiot caught me in his backswing with a five iron."

Selwyn is expressionless. Santorini zips up a light jacket. "I'm off, but stay, relax, I'll have my clerk bring in coffee. Doughnuts in the fridge. You want to discuss reaching some kind of accommodation, gentlemen. Talk. Make love, not war."

After the judge leaves, Prudhomme fetches Clearihue, who says, "We may have to appeal this and harvest some timber off the shore to pay the legal costs."

"*Harvest?*" Selwyn says. "We're not talking about potatoes."

"We can tough it out until the fall," Clearihue says. "I'm not going lower than thirteen, twelve and a half bottom, plus our outlays have to be covered. Christ, we paid eight for it, where's our profit? And you know what? With the international attention this property is getting, the price may be going up."

Arthur takes that as a bluff. Time is on Gwendolyn's side. The legal costs must be bleeding Garlinc.

Clearihue glances at Prudhomme, then adds, "We can give you maybe a month, then it's half down, the rest secured. I think the folks of Garibaldi – I'm including myself, I'll chip in my share – can probably raise a few million on their land, and we'll absorb all legal fees, how's that?"

Arthur packs his briefcase, rises. "I don't want to be late for the ferry." He doesn't think he'll bother with tonight's AA meeting. The school, those hard wooden benches.

18

Arthur puts on a suit for the Save Gwendolyn meeting – he would prefer clean country clothes but he can't decode the dials on the washer. He's still unable, a week after his fall, to sit comfortably in a vehicle, so he'll walk to the hall. There's no urgent cause to drive anywhere, though a visit to Nick Faloon is long overdue – he might worry that Arthur is defending him with faint heart.

It's April 25. Day Nineteen! ("THE EAGLE HAS LANDED!" cries this week's *Bleat*. "OUR LOVEBIRDS REUNITE!") Not, however, the love-birds of Bungle Bay, though Margaret, if she holds to her vow, has only two tree-sitting days left. The punk-haired sprite must return too. Or else. They've won, take a bow. There is peace in the forest. The threatened appeal hasn't materialized, but Garlinc won't come to the table, so they must return to court.

Edna Sproule waves from behind the barn – she is a saviour, attending births of eleven kids. A relief column of Japanese Woofers is on its way. Meanwhile, his waterlogged Fargo has been missing for a week and a half. So has Stoney, whose backhoe is still sitting by the lip of the non-pond. Margaret will not be pleased.

But she'll find the girls from Mop'n'Chop have cleaned the house from roof to basement. He has paid the bills, has stocked up. There will be daffodils in the parlour, hyacinths in the dining room, a sprig of lilac on her pillow.

He'll try to impress her with his key role in the struggle. Had he not landed so hard on his ass, Santorini might not have been so generous with his restraining order. And did he not lead a team of botanists to that tiny patch of Phantom Orchids? Was he not treated to a chorus of their hurrahs? He will regale her about the murder case, show her another Beauchamp, the hard-driving lawyer. She's a mystery addict, she'll love this whodunit. She'll love Arthur.

And what to do about hooky-playing Rudnicki? *Three, four days*, she said, now it's a week. Arthur was forgiving to a point. She had good intentions: quit smoking, reunite him with Margaret. She read Santorini accurately – no arrest warrants went out for the leading lady of his favourite commercial.

However, if she doesn't come down by tomorrow she'll be seeking new employment. He said as much in his last post to this act-on-a-whim wannabe lawyer.

Duties are piling up for her. Witnesses' memories could go stale if their words are not recorded soon, so Arthur has arranged a weekend trip for her, a cruise to Bamfield on the *Lady Rose*, an overnight stay at the Nitinat Lodge. She is to take signed statements from Claudette, from the Cotters, from Meredith Broadfeather, and the two Huu-ay-aht braves, and from Holly Hoover if she can cajole her.

Arthur has received assurances from high officials of the Save Gwendolyn Society that Lotis's bubble is about to burst. Several complaints have been made about her jumping the line. Reverend Al will argue the case for Arthur at the meeting this afternoon.

"You've sacrificed enough," he told him. "First your wife, then your Woofer, or whatever she is."

◆

"'Laurel is green for a season, and love is sweet for a day; but love grows bitter with treason, and laurel outlives not May.'" Sung aloud to a forest glen, Swinburne's "Hymn to Proserpine." Yes, she has laboured well this spring, the goddess of vegetation. Grass thick in the fields, apple trees pinking, skunk cabbage bursting from the swales with yellow spikes in yellow cups.

He must stop to catch his breath on Breadloaf Hill, at a plateau overlooking Garibaldi's first land-use mistake: a fifty-lot subdivision, Evergreen Estates. Septic problems in a rain catchment area. A smell comes from the taps of the community hall.

Inside the creaky wooden building, sixty locals and a dozen off-islanders are in noisy debate. Cud Brown is on his feet. Tabatha Jones is glowering at him, the debaucher of her only child.

Presiding is Leif Thorson, a repentant former logger, lost in a forest of points of order. Arthur has walked into a procedural quagmire, and follows Reverend Al outside before being called upon to untangle it.

"We have some excellent candidates," Al says, "high-riggers, canopy experience, to replace those two recalcitrant women, so we're bringing them in from the cold."

"What is Cud carrying on about?"

"He's off on a wild tangent."

They look in again. Leif Thorson is saying, "The way I figure it, Cud, if you're gonna nominate someone to go up that tree, they got to consent. Who do you want to nominate, anyway?"

"Tabatha Jones."

Leif turns to her. "Tabatha, you consent?"

"I certainly do *not*." Furious, she stands, marches over to Cud, wags a finger at his nose. "You're not getting close to her, she's with her dad in the city."

Reverend Al moves quickly to avert violence, leads Tabatha out. She turns and shouts, "You're *my* age, you pedophile!"

That prods Cud to rise in pursuit. "She's eighteen, she's ready for life!" He stops at the doorway, calls. "Hey, Tabatha, Felicity says you stifle her artistic growth."

As Reverend Al leads her down the hill, she shouts, "Your poetry stinks, according to what I read before I flushed your book."

The meeting is far more sober when it reconvenes. The society hears a presentation from three strapping lads, Reverend Al's high-riggers. They will haul up climbing gear, tools, two-by-fours, coils of cable, for an emergency supply route by zip line. After their bid is accepted, they head off in a van packed with supplies. Handsome fellows, Pyramus, Leander, and Adonis.

A discussion ensues about how to entice Lotis from her lair: there's concern that the deposed rebel leader – she's in her element, centre stage – won't bow to the diktat of the Central Committee. Arthur can't sit, tires of standing, sneaks off.

He's still muttering about Lotis an hour later as he puffs past his farm gate. "There's no room for an immature prima donna on the Nick Faloon defence team. You can't run a murder trial this way. It's not a film set where you can replay the scene a hundred times to get it right."

A pleasant rhythmic sound from behind a big-leaf maple pulls him up. Squirt, splash. He carries on around the tree to the goat-milking parlour and sees Lotis milking a nanny. The lens-loving schismatic returned in a flash, she's back without a struggle, she's a Woofer again. He wonders how much of his rambling she heard. He steps forward, pretending he was reciting verse. "'The nymphs in twilight shade of tangled thickets.'"

"What's that?"

"Milton."

"Didn't sound like Milton earlier." Squirt, splash.

"Very well, I was musing about how a fine career would have been nipped in the bud if you hadn't materialized."

"I like this last bit, where you spank the udder to get the last few pulls of milk." She slaps Annabelle on the rump and sends her away. She has milked other nannies, has a full pail. She looks tested and tough. A tangle of faded green hair. A pack of Nicorettes in her shirt pocket.

"And how *did* you materialize?"

She takes off her rubber apron, washes her hands. "Actually I sneaked down before dawn. I wanted to meet with my Greenpeace team, go over their presentation."

"*Your* Greenpeace team."

"Yeah, I put in an order for some of their top climbers." The three high-riggers.

"How did you place this order? Through telepathy?"

"Satellite phone. We must use the weapons of the counter-revolutionary pigs to our advantage." A fairy smile, her flower-petal lips. Teasing him, knowing such jargon rankles him. "These guys are running a zip line up to the bluffs, just below Gwendolyn Pond. Though maybe I shouldn't tell Arthur Beauchamp, he talks to himself *very* loudly."

"And what about Margaret? Is she on her way down?"

"After she does her full stint – two more days, that's her goal. She's a stick-to-it gal, give her a break."

Arthur is silent as he totes the pail to his house. After they pour the milk in the cooler, he says, "Am I to understand that these . . . these eco-acrobats are going to be sharing the tree with her for two nights?"

"Jealous much? Come on, Arthur, they're not planning an orgy."

"I'm only worried about arrangements," he says sharply. "All those cables and tools and two-by-fours, how can there be any room for people? How can the platform hold the weight?"

"It's all being hauled up into canopy, Arthur. As we speak."

He hopes Margaret's new roommates, unlike Cud, do their armpits. "So what brings you scurrying back? The guilt, I suppose, now that the theatrical urge has been satisfied."

"The Faloon case was bugging me. I kept thinking about how his semen ended up in Eve Winters. The theory that Angella kept it keeps dialling a wrong number."

This ruse will not succeed. She wants him to think that while he was fuming, she was pondering, working.

"Something Claudette said kept niggling at me," she says. "The bear or raccoon or whatever was getting into the garbage at Nitinat Lodge. I'd never thought to ask if she and Nick were using birth control, or what kind, so I got on the horn to her today. She's not on the pill. Sometimes they played Vatican roulette. Otherwise, condoms. They're on a septic field, so they don't flush them. They go into the trash."

According to Claudette's best recollection, the last time the marauding pest showed up was three nights before Eve Winters's murder. Unseen, in the blackness of the night. Though garbage was strewn, the culprit left no proof of identity, no bear-pies.

Arthur has a hard time seeing obsessively neat Adeline Angella rooting about the garbage for a discarded condom. On the other hand, the theory expands the list of perps who could have concocted an ingenious plan to murder Dr. Winters and leave Nick grasping at one chance in ten billion.

"What do you think?" Lotis asks. "It'll float?"

Odd question – there are the makings of a reasonable doubt here, with some intensive digging and prepping the soil. "Why shouldn't it float – isn't it the truth?"

Her cocky smile.

"I'm going to presume this isn't something made up between you and Claudette," he says. "She volunteered this information?"

She looks shocked. "Of *course*, Arthur. Please." She pulls out the Nicorettes.

✦

On this, Day Twenty, the prospect of Margaret's imminent return home is causing Arthur butterflies. He's not eager to be in a court-room today, he should be at home creating another lemon pie. Champagne is in the fridge – Margaret has every right to get a little tiddly tomorrow.

He was ribbed ferociously this morning at the General Store. "Hope your wife don't find it too crowded up there with all them young studs." "I bet *she's* gonna come down smiling." Arthur took it like a man.

The injunction hearing was put over to the afternoon, and it's nearing two as he and Lotis make their way into the Great Hall of the Vancouver Law Courts. Themes, goddess of justice, greets them, proudly blindfolded. There are other sculptures, Inuit, on display where Selwyn Loo is waiting, his fingers lightly caressing a soapstone bear. "We don't have Santorini today."

Their judge has run off to the dry hills of the Okanagan, a pro-am charity event – he's teamed with a guest celebrity, a Masters winner.

There's media coverage. Santorini has let it be known that nothing short of a terrorist attack — certainly not an environmental crisis on Garibaldi Island — will dislodge him from those fairways and greens.

"Fine, we'll adjourn the matter until he gets back." None of the other judges will stand in. This case has already bounced to the Appeal Court and back, and is likely regarded as in the same category as dogs' breakfasts and cans of worms. Unless forced to by rare circumstance — such as Santorini drowning in a water hazard — no judge of sound mind will want to pinch-hit. But why is Selwyn looking more dismal than usual today?

"The Chief Justice himself insists on stepping in, Arthur."

Arthur feels his jaw drop. Wilbur Kroop? Surely Selwyn is joking. Arthur looks up and locates Garlinc's legal team at level four, in amiable conversation. It's no joke, they're enjoying their good fortune.

"I hear he can be difficult," Selwyn says.

"He's an irascible fathead."

The wars are legendary. Twenty years ago, Arthur spent three nights in jail before surrendering to him, apologizing in court. Three nights withdrawing from alcohol were more than he could take.

"He won't be pleased to see me," Arthur says. "I'd best stay hidden."

Despondent, he watches Court 41 fill with lawyers, public, and press. The door closes on them. He paces. There had been hope with Santorini, at bottom a fair-minded man. Wilbur Kroop sees protestors as outlaws bent on challenging the sacred institutions of capital and state. Society's imminent collapse into anarchy is a theme that garnishes many of his judgments.

Half an hour passes. When the door opens for traffic in and out, he hears Prudhomme arguing the Wildlife Act, Selwyn talking about Phantom Orchids. He hears Kroop ask a question, so at least he's listening. Maybe he's changed, mellowed with age, like fine whisky. The analogy isn't apt: Kroop is the worst kind of non-drinker, someone who never did, a teetotaller all his life.

Finally, after another twenty minutes, Arthur surrenders to curiosity, slipping in as the door opens to release a few bored spectators. He perches painfully in the last row. Wilbur Kroop looks well at seventy-three, a great bald walnut-shaped head, eyes that seem to emit black light as they roam about the room, finally pausing at Arthur, squinting, moving on. Selwyn is still on his feet, the going rough.

"No, no, Mr. Loo." A squeaky unnatural voice from a heavy person, accented by the clacking sound of poorly fitted false teeth. "Surely it's not your position that the courts should stand idly by while a gang of squatters – who seem to have no jobs to work at or classes to attend – occupy someone's titled property, and – if I rightly read the affidavits of the plaintiff corporation – roast hot dogs and smoke cannabis and engage in naked displays for the titillation of television news audiences."

Arthur dismisses the fancy of the mellowed judge.

"Are you asking me a question, Chief Justice?"

Kroop glowers at impudent Selwyn. "What I seek to know, Mr. Loo, is how you might feel if a legion of trespassers set up camp in your backyard."

"I live in an apartment."

"Come, come, I think you have my point. The plaintiff bought this property for $8 million in anticipation of fair profit through development and harvesting of timber, and their plans have been held up for over three weeks by this sit-in business – yet they are willing to compromise. They will go in by barge. They will not touch the so-called Holy Tree. They will cordon off and protect that little meadow with the rare orchid species. And the chocolate lilies . . ."

He squeaks to a stop, ponders, detours: "What I can't understand is why the police are doing nothing. This fellow in charge, Corporal Ivanchuk, seems a bit of a layabout, people are going up and down that tree like yoyos. And here's another concern: Where's the Attorney General in all this? Removing these protestors should be the state's work. The company must not be burdened with these costs. Mr. Prudhomme, please give my regards to the Attorney General, and tell him he would oblige me by enforcing, with appropriate manpower, the rule of law on Garibaldi Island."

Selwyn subsides into his chair, mouthing a sibilance that younger ears than Kroop's might hear as "shit." The Chief Justice glares at him, does another sweep of the room with his cold black eyes, again settling for a moment on Arthur. He works a pair of wire-rimmed spectacles over his nose, and scrutinizes him out once more, as if to be sure, then returns to Prudhomme.

"You have your restraining order. All these people, including the four who are up that tree, will leave immediately. Those who refuse are to be arrested and brought before me on charges of criminal contempt. This entire farce has to be brought to an end. We cannot have anarchy in the forests."

Arthur bolts from the room.

19

Twilight nears as Syd-Air drops Arthur at the wharf of the General Store in Hopeless Bay. He left Lotis on the mainland with the Toyota, so he must somehow cadge a ride to the Gap. Margaret now has no choice but to come down voluntarily or face jail. Let the three Greenpeacers defy Kroop if they wish, let them take the brunt of his wrath, but she should not, she has served honourably.

The store's only customer is Winnie Gillicuddy, hectoring Abraham Makepeace with questions and complaint. "How old are these carrots, they feel like rubber." "Where in heaven's name is the Cream of Wheat?" Arthur reaches up to retrieve it for her. "Thank you, young man." She doesn't recognize Arthur in his suit, with briefcase.

"Can't lend you my car, it's broke," Makepeace says. "I'll call this new taxi service for you." A flyer on the bulletin board: *Tour the island in one of our vintage vehicles, $7.50 to anywhere.* He dials a cellphone number. "They're on the way."

While Arthur paces and frets, Winnie cashes her pension cheque and Makepeace totes up her month's bill. "Put the rest on Scratch and Win," she says, "and don't forget my pint."

Makepeace tells Arthur, "She always has a few drops on pension day."

"Don't you talk about me as if I'm not here."

"You better not get pie-eyed again, Winnie."

"Thank you for minding my business."

A few minutes later, Bob Stonewell is at the door, dark aviator glasses, a half-smoked rollie stowed over his ear, a cellphone hooked to his belt. "Who wants a taxi here?"

"I'm your fare, Stoney, and I'm in a hurry."

A blank look is quickly replaced by an overabundant smile, hinting Stoney was hoping not to bump into him. "Arthur Beauchamp, the town tonsil, just the man I wanted to see. Here, let me get that briefcase."

Stoney wrestles it from him. Arthur steps out and sees his Fargo, a worn chesterfield in the back. Stoney slips the joint from behind his ear and lights it, seeking the courage to contend, once again, with the rightful owner and occasional user of this vehicle.

Arthur considers climbing onto the chesterfield, stretching out, resting his throbbing rear. But he gets in front, and Stoney pulls away, stubbing the joint, releasing a cloud of smoke from his lungs, and a gust of words. "Yeah, we finally got the old girl flushed out and back on her feet after that accidental drowning. This trip's on me, Arthur, no obligation, never mind what it says on the sign."

The sign, which obstructs the view through the windshield, advertises the $7.50-fare-to-anywhere and the cellphone number.

"I'm wondering as a favour in return if there's any chance I can incorporate the Fargo into the fleet for a couple of days. Hey, man, you'll be helping me in an economic crisis. I got two other machines that just suddenly broke down, so I'm kind of living on borrowed time until maybe Monday, Tuesday at the latest, when I'm getting delivery of a mint '58 canary-yellow shark-finned Chrysler, I'm trading with Honk Gilmore for it, giving him back the backhoe, a machine that caused me more misery than made money. I'm going to finish the pond first though, I got a reputation."

"I don't care about the damn pond! The Fargo's not important! Margaret's important!" Stoney looks shaken at this outburst. "Tell me what's happening at the Gap."

"I heard a bunch of cops rolled in."

"Have there been arrests?"

"Hey, man, relax, that fort is impregnable. Only one way to get up there, and that's by a rope ladder they ain't gonna let down."

Arthur twigs to an unforeseen problem. If Margaret comes down that ladder, the police could take control of it, storm the redoubt, seize the tools and cable. She would never allow that to happen. He's dismayed.

Early-evening shadows creep upon Stump Town as Arthur alights. Several reporters are sitting by their vans, grumbling, though Arthur isn't sure why. He joins the two Als at the Save Gwendolyn information booth. Corporal Al looks depressed. Reverend Al remains plucky. The few dozen young folks remaining are dismantling their tents.

Corporal Al says, "The inspector's hauling me in, Arthur, because of that judicial rebuke. He's sent a crew to enforce the injunction, and I'm out of the picture."

"They're reading the injunction to our tree-sitters as we speak," Reverend Al says.

"Well, why aren't we there?"

"We've got orders to quarantine the area," Corporal Al says. "No press even."

Arthur sees this as a strategic error on the part of the authorities. The media may be fickle friends, but are far more influential than most judges want to admit. By and large, the Save Gwendolyn Society has been winning the war of images.

He strides off to the trail head, where he comes upon a uniformed woman standing sentry.

"Sorry, sir, we're not allowing the public . . ."

"I'm not the public." He steps by her, marches ahead, pausing only when he sees Flim and Flam – they've snuck through the forest, are behind a fallen tree, aiming cameras at five uniformed men. They, in turn, are looking up at the heavy-bolted fortress. At the railing, Margaret is dwarfed by three young men with the sinewy physiques of basketball players. She looks frail beside them, defiant nonetheless – Arthur knows that arms-folded look, understands there'll be no early homecoming.

The commanding officer is a sergeant of stern military bearing. He waves his handcuffs, shouts up to them: "I have orders to take you in unless you leave immediately."

"We forgot our parachutes," a blond ponytailed leviathan says.

It is then that Arthur sees the rope ladder in a twisted heap at the officers' feet. The sergeant looks mistrustful, as if assuming they're withholding a solution. He may be right – the *matériel* for the zip line isn't in view, most of it has been hauled high into the canopy. "I call on you to identify yourselves . . ."

Arthur breaks in. "I instruct my clients to remain silent." A commanding voice that has the sergeant almost snapping to attention before he turns. A quick spate of introductions, then Arthur engages him in a testy debate about the press ban. Their uncaring attitude about the niceties about fundamental freedoms has him enraged, and his dressing-down has them stalking off.

A thick silence ensues. Then all four above applaud. So do Flim and Flam. Margaret blows him a kiss.

✦

The next morning, half an hour after gulping his granola, Arthur is back in Vancouver. He's gratified that Tragger Inglis is footing his sky-high account with Syd-Air. Indeed, Roy Bullingham has gone solidly to bat for the Gwendolyn team, has donated old Riley to the cause, and they've come up with twelve grounds of appeal. There will be a price to be paid by the sweat of Arthur's brow.

He leads Selwyn and Lotis into a courtroom filled with reporters, many of whom smile at the lawyer who stood up for them yesterday. Today's application, before a single judge, is to stay proceedings until a full-dress appeal can be scheduled.

The gods are with Arthur: the judge is Bill Webb, a fellow reformed drunk, founder of the Trial Lawyers' AA chapter. His chances buoyed, Arthur argues vigorously that Kroop showed bias. Prudhomme responds with the hoary argument about the cost of these many delays of the inevitable, but His Lordship lets him know that justice will not be rushed.

Gwendolyn wins a one-week reprieve. Bill Webb looks poker-faced at Arthur. "By the way, welcome back. We'll adjourn."

"Whoa, have you been sleeping with that judge?" Lotis looks at Arthur with awe, perhaps sensing unrevealed powers. But there's a bond between alcoholics who've shared pain and confession; it's worth an occasional seven-day adjournment.

"The appeal won't be so easy," Selwyn says. The pessimist is right. Kroop took a few wide bends but never went off the road. Rhetoric isn't appealable.

At the other end of the table, Todd Clearihue has a waxy smile as he confers with his legal team. Prudhomme smiles too, clinking the coins in his pocket.

◆

Faloon pulls a soggy tobacco pouch from his sink, squeezes its juice, dark and brackish, into his tin cup. It's the right time to do this. He's alone, it's after six, the quiet time, the doors unracked, the occasional guy listening to a radio or reading.

Faloon is on last grub call and he's going to try to make it as far as the lineup even if it means doing a swan dive into his mashed potatoes. He puts the pouch under the tap, gives it another soaking. He read somewhere once how just a few drops of pure nicotine on your tongue can kill you in thirty seconds.

He hopes Claudette got around to putting the Nitinat in her name. Also that she got word in time so she doesn't come out to see him tomorrow, her regular day, Friday. He didn't plan this too well, they could've had one more visit. He keeps telling himself he's doing this because she truly loves him, and he wants to give her a better life. Because if Faloon ends up doing a back-gate parole in a coffin she may spend the rest of her life in her own prison, the prison they call heartbreak, like the song goes.

Even Arthur Beauchamp couldn't beat every rap, sometimes you get a dozen people in a jewellery store all picking you out of the lineup, you got to cop a plea. It's a risk-filled line of work, if you're caught behind the display cases, all you can do is act indignant, you go,

Hey, I was only looking for the bathroom, and you hope you brazen it out the door, but sometimes you can't.

And he isn't going to brazen this one out, either, this murder beef, not with having confessed it to Father Réchard, even if it was in his sleep. Not with the DNA. Not with his dumb moves, his stupid plan to get the hell out of Dodge City dressed as Gertrude, it was like admitting guilt to the world.

The Sleepwalking Killer. *I couldn't help myself.*

He's now collected half a cup of tobacco juice with this latest squeeze, which is about what the recipe says. If you picture a full ashtray left out in the rain, you get a rough idea of what it looks like, but worse. It smells like cat shit.

He raises the cup, close his eyes, and does a little prayer just in case. He thinks of how Eve Winters had small talk with him that night at the Breakers, finding him more interesting than the condo guy. How they shared confidences, and her poetic way of talking. *The wild relentless surf.*

He gulps the juice, swallowing, gagging, swallowing again, the sludge burning its way down to his stomach, prickling like a thousand tiny biting spiders. Bleat goes the sound system, it's last call for chow. The thought of food is suddenly a very alien concept, he feels himself already turning green, but he's not going to die unnoticed in his cell if he can help it.

His body has started to race as he moves out, gets into line, staggers, makes it almost to the cafeteria, staggers again, some guys laughing, thinking he's drunk. But when he's in the banquet hall, steadying himself against the stacks of plastic trays, suddenly his weakness and nausea are gone.

He's strong, a fierce power is racing through him, he could actually tear the heart out of the guy serving the boiled cabbage.

But this is nothing compared to when the nicotine really hits, because now he's in costume with a cape, he is Super Kangaroo, he can spring over everyone's heads, spring to freedom, he's out of this joint.

With a roar, he jumps. He makes it high into the night sky, where there are only stars and sound, distorted familiar commands, "Inmates return to units!" "Count up!"

◆

Emerging from his crowded house, Arthur bows as his Tai Chi master dismounts from his bicycle. "Sorry," says Corporal Al, "I couldn't get through by phone. I didn't know you were having a meeting." He is looking at a rusty VW bus festooned with stickers urging inhabitants of the planet to save it.

"Lessons in civil disobedience." In the event that the appeal fails, Lotis has recruited an instructor for a brigade of civilly disobedient youths. "We'll take tea on the porch so as not to disturb them."

It's evening now, and Arthur has spent much of this day haggling with the stiff-necked sergeant. But finally reporters are free to roam where they want, and the tents are returning to Stump Town. An eighty-foot ladder, a type used by firefighters, lies athwart the stumps. The police weren't able to wiggle it through the thickly wooded forest surrounding the Holy Tree.

The law is aware a zip line is being strung – climbers were spotted in the canopy working with bolts and a hand drill. Arthur worries about how Margaret will get down. With spurs, pulleys, and a rappel line? It sounds fearfully dangerous. She blew him an extra kiss today, a two-hander. A reward for his small victory in court.

Over tea and gingersnaps, Corporal Al explains he's being transferred to northern Manitoba. He harbours no ill will toward those banishing him, his superiors, the judge who denounced him. "My time on Garibaldi was pretty well up. Headquarters claims you get too friendly with the natives if you stay longer. Flin Flon will be interesting. Brisk climate, good fishing."

But the reason for this visit, it appears, is not merely to say farewell. "A client of yours, that fellow Nick Faloon, fell ill. They rushed him to hospital."

"When was this?"

"Maybe an hour ago. Head office asked me to pass the word on to you."

"It's serious?"

"He was in the food lineup, and leaped over a railing and collapsed, clutching his chest."

A heart attack? Arthur is stunned. He can't help feeling some blame, he should have visited him. Depressed, said Lotis, out of shape. *He thinks he's burdened you with a case you can't win.*

Faloon connects only though flashes, glimpses of the living world: he's in leg irons, he's being trussed to a gurney, the ambulance is screeching out the gate, a rubbery scent from the oxygen mask. A hand on his chest, words coming like thunderclaps: "Heart's jumping all over the place." Going out again, jerking awake, another voice, morose: "I hate to see guys die right in front of me."

A flash of Claudette again. Solemn, in black. No, no, she's happy, an angel. Only snippets of memory are left. Eve Winters, smiling down at the Owl, so beautiful. A last sensation of circling the drain. Then oblivion.

Tension spices the tea and gingersnaps at Blunder Bay. Arthur, Lotis, and Corporal Al are listening to a news station. An excited voice: "We have a live report from hospital. Are you there, Clarice?"

"Yes, I am, Dale."

A squawk from the radio on Corporal Al's belt. "Garibaldi, Staff wants to talk to you."

". . . in one door and out the other, to a waiting van," Clarice is saying. "They wedged the door shut, so the jail escort couldn't pursue."

Corporal Al, in Arthur's left ear: "Well, isn't that the darndest thing . . . On a gurney? Holy mackerel, Staff, that's pretty wild."

"You're saying, Clarice, that we have an escaped killer somewhere out there."

"Here's what I was told: he was foaming at the mouth when the ambulance pulled in. Two men came running from Emergency in surgical gowns and masks. They told the prison escort they'd take charge of the gurney, and somehow in the confusion they were allowed to wheel it through the ward and out another exit. Police gave this description of the van: a black early 1990s Econoline, B.C. plates, possibly stolen, fresh vomit spattering the right side. The men are considered dangerous. Back to you . . ."

Dazed and dismayed, Arthur nearly steps on Underfoot as he turns down the sound. Corporal Al clicks off, scratches his head. "Real embarrassing debacle, must have been something to see. No ID on any of the accomplices. Nicotine poisoning, they're guessing, makes the heart buck like a crazed horse."

"Glad I quit," Lotis says.

This is not something one ad libs, so Nick must have despaired of his chances some time ago. It's Arthur's fault, denying hope with his broken promises to show up.

Abiit, excessit, evasit, erupit, Cicero cried. *He has departed, withdrawn, gone away, broken out.* The master of disguise has donned the winged sandals and cap of Mercury, patron of travellers, shepherds, cheats, and thieves.

PART TWO

Rough winds do shake the darling buds of May.

— Sonnet 18, Shakespeare

20

Without planning to, but drawn by the morbid curiosity felt by a witness to a train wreck, Arthur finds himself taking Slappy up the Sproules's grasslands, the shortcut to the Gwendolyn Bluffs. He dreads what he is to see, a carnage of fallen trees.

He'd argued the appeal well, had those judges working. Five of them sat, as is common when judicial bias is claimed. They had reserved, and Arthur was optimistic. The ruling came two days ago. Arthur won just a single dissent. The majority opinion: Property rights prevail.

Then at dawn yesterday, through sound-muffling rain, came the vibrations of a falling giant, then another, birds in screaming flight. The Greenpeace climbers sped to the canopy, high enough to gain a pocket view of treetops disappearing.

The crew from Sustainable Logging had come on a landing craft, with saws and jerry cans of fuel. An ambush of the forest, site-clearing for Gwendolyn Village – as the mall is styled in Garlinc's brochure, "In Harmony with Nature."

As Arthur scrambles up a mossy abutment, he zips up his rain slick – lowering clouds have begun to shed their burden. He looks at the eagles' nest, at one of the great birds taking flight. Then he wills himself to view the torn land below, splintered firs and cedars, tangles of boughs, uplifted to the sky as if in prayer.

Some twenty acres of old-growth were felled along the beach before protestors poured in, some through the Gap, others by sea, a convoy. There was a standoff, the crew foreman red-faced and sullen. The loggers retreated but the protest armada remains – Arthur counts thirty boats sitting at anchor or beached. Tents amid the driftwood, small figures milling about. No arrests yet, but warnings issued. And making its way toward the beach: an RCMP cruiser, officers with batons, guns, handcuffs.

Margaret is still in the tree in this unmerry month of May. Day Thirty-five! Emergency rations are sustaining its occupiers, three of whom are adept with pulleys, cable, and rappel line, one of whom raises goats and geese. She was to have rappelled down in a safety harness, but now she is staying, determined to defy capture.

That's what she declared in a note she floated to him. *Unable to talk without crying. That psychopath is holding Gwendolyn for ransom. He cut off one of her ears and mailed it as a warning. If we don't pay up, it'll be an arm or a leg.*

Her savage metaphor rings true. The ransom fund is slow to build. Four million dollars has been raised from nature and philanthropic societies and corporate grants. A few hundred thousand from individuals, wealthy and poor. More is pledged but not enough. Clearihue continues to hint the price may go up: he has inquiries from investors in the States, from Germany, from Hong Kong.

The national government still refuses to chip in, offering a myriad excuses: money is tight; elected officials must be accountable; Garlinc's inflated price will have the Auditor General screaming for blood; it's political suicide if the state is seen as bowing to illegal demonstrators. Underlying all: Clearihue is a contributor to the Liberal party, the Opposition will say it's payback time.

The RCMP cruiser anchors. Officers pile into a Zodiac, and it casts off and heads to shore.

Arthur can smell the powerful odour of destruction. May, nesting time, a time for birth not death. A smell too pungent for Slappy, who turns, urges Arthur home.

The eagle swoops down the valley, screaming.

Arthur remains in a cantankerous mood that afternoon as Syd's Beaver lifts from Bungle Bay, wipers flapping, rain sheeting by. A misty glimpse of the mess at Gwendolyn Beach adds to his choler. As he was returning from his hike, ten young people were arrested – the maximum the police could handle on their Zodiac.

Lotis and Selwyn are in Victoria, where this first batch of accused are to be hauled before Wilbur Kroop. As part of his crusade against anarchy, he will punish them by setting an example, that's his style.

Arthur knows that he must compose himself, focus on the case of his truant client. Nick Faloon may have disappeared, but the case won't go away. Upset that a high-profile prosecution is sifting through his fingers, Buddy Svabo proposes to bypass a preliminary and go to trial next month by direct indictment. With or without the accused.

Arthur was given notice a week ago of Svabo's motion, which collides with the enshrined rule that a defendant must be present at his trial. His first reaction was to scoff. So might the presiding judge, Larry Mewhort, a former defence counsel, though not the brightest star in the firmament.

Arthur's second reaction was an inspired flip-flop. A quick trial could be to Nick's benefit. Especially were he to return suddenly – a surprise witness at his own trial. Buddy would be caught off guard, ill prepared to cross-examine.

The condom-in-the-trash defence may lack substance, but if combined with a clear motive and a vigorous confrontation with the siren of the Rhine . . . Arthur has earned reasonable doubts with less. Faloon may attract only a minimal sentence for his escape if the defence can show he was wrongly accused, wrongly jailed. There is nothing but suspicion to tie him to the thefts at the Breakers Inn. But is Arthur thinking coolly, or is his mind too aflame over the logging at Gwendolyn Bay?

And how to locate this species at risk, this threatened Owl? Surely he hasn't flown the coop merely to hide in a dank hole somewhere nearby. A migration to more distant climes seems likely. To more profitable climes.

The Beaver descends low over the Fraser Delta and its swirl-patterned tidewaters to the river's south arm, brown and swollen with spring runoff. It's raining hard as they pull into the Fraser River seaplane dock.

Umbrella unfurled, he slogs up the road to a waterfront pub. She's sitting in a corner nook, eyes half-hidden by dark bangs. A wig, or she dyed her hair. Perrier in front of her, a packed suitcase beside her. She offers no sign of recognition as he approaches.

"Cat?"

She rises, gives him a perfumed, overfriendly embrace. "We kind of figured you'd call, Mr. Beauchamp. And just in time." She beckons to an older gentleman finely dressed, who joins them from the bar, bringing his pint and a flight bag. Willy the Hook.

"And where are you two off to?"

"Le tour de France," says Cat, patting his cheek and returning his wallet.

◆

The Owl is playing poolside behind a *Herald-Tribune* and a coffee that costs a sawsky with tip while he waits for Willy and Cat, who are flying in first class thanks to Harold W. Stein over there, the lawyer from Boston, who is out here sweating away the kilos. Faloon weeded out a gold Visa from this gentleman's wallet a few days ago, the pants hanging on a peg while Stein was getting a rubdown. You've got to respect this fine Cannes hotel, the Belvedere, its pool, steam room, changing room, big bath towels that hide a busy hand.

This has always been the Owl's forté, the play for the blooper, the plastic. In his system, you never lift cash, you don't touch the six other credit cards – Harold W. Stein might not notice one is missing or he might wonder if he left it in Boston, or maybe it'll be a few weeks before he gets around to calling the friendly folks at Visa. Or maybe he'll only notice when he gets his statement and suddenly loses his newly tanned complexion.

Faloon did a tester on the Visa two days ago, Wednesday, it held up, a $3,000 diamond from a *bijouterie*, a bauble. Then yesterday he went back and scored a sapphire-inlay ladies watch he said was for Mrs. Stein. Thirty-five K.

Sitting across the pool from him is a lemon-haired looker by the name of Gina de Carlo – the "starlet," people around here call her, but no one can put a finger on what film. She's leafing through a glossy called *Shape*, which she has in spades, a beautiful tall young creature, in a way she reminds him of Dr. Eve Winters, or what she would've looked like at nineteen or twenty. (Images keep returning of her dead body, and they bother him, like something is coming back that he doesn't want to remember. Something he doesn't want to think about at all.)

Ms. de Carlo has no visible means of support except from Sierra Leone's ambassador to France, who stops here, according to Popov the Russian, every other weekend, diplomatic pouch in hand, to visit her at the Belvedere. The pouch – a briefcase – will be full of the kind of ice that doesn't melt.

Popov is among the top five in the world, just ahead of the Owl. He was in his regular café in Marseilles, and planned to do the Belvedere himself until he got recognized by the desk. "I turn you onto nice wrinkle," he said. Thus inspired, Faloon checked into the Belvedere five days ago, and he plans to skip out in the traditional way tomorrow. In the lexicon of the trade, no insult intended to the great man, this is called taking it on the Arthur.

Meanwhile, Stein, who bears an unnatural resemblance to Faloon, short and bald on top though pudgier, sits happy with one of his clients at poolside, not missing his Visa, billing everything to his room. He's pretending not to be looking at Gina de Carlo's tits as she dives topless into the water.

Maybe it's the image of breasts, it doesn't take much, and zap, Faloon is feeling pangs about Claudette. The tour Côte d'Azure is in honour of her, the Owl has vowed to get her a stake, in case he has to rot for the rest of his life in the crossbar hotel. It's the Love Tour, maybe the Last Tour, the Terminal Tour. The Reckless Tour.

Nick the Goods, the town booster – he's back in business, coming out of retirement after a miraculous flight to freedom. Faloon never escaped before, never skipped, he was an honest thief who always paid his bills, but he had no recourse, because this time they were going to nail him.

He doesn't remember much about his journey on a gurney from ambulance to hospital to side exit to waiting van, except the throwing up. He got the basic details on re-entry, while the guys took a hacksaw to his irons as he was throwing up in a motel room toilet. Three co-workers of Greg McDeadly from the d'Anglio family, whooping it up, ecstatic, everything went as planned, with their doctors' smocks and caps and surgical masks, and their calm, "Okay, fellas, we'll take over."

Still peering over his *Herald-Tribune* at Gina de Carlo, he jerks when a hand tickles his thigh, and it's Cat McAllister, who has stolen up and sat down. When he folds his paper closed, Willy the Hook Houston is across from him.

He's happy to see them, but he has to restrain enthusiasm, which he restricts to a continental kiss for Cat and a handshake with Willy, followed by a sharing of how everyone looks great, and a funny anecdote from Cat about how she almost forgot the name on her passport at customs. But the three of them keeping it low-key, not drawing attention away from topless Gina.

He lets them know that the beer belly who's about to walrus into the pool after her is Harold Stein, whose generosity is helping fund this tour. He explains about how Gina is concubine to an ambassador of a land where diamonds flow like milk, who will be entertaining a dubious broker from Antwerp tomorrow at 3 p.m., when millions of euros could change hands, money that should be diverted to a nobler cause.

But Faloon starts getting obstacles to this brilliant plan. The Hook has a problem with blood diamonds, part ethical, part fear. "In such countries, they amputate arms and feet, old boy. And . . . and there's other concerns, right, Cat?"

Faloon realizes they have shown up with their own agenda when Cat opts for a massive change of subject. "Honey, we been asked by Mr. Beauchamp to persuade you to drop in for your trial."

Willy hands him a note signed by the great man. *La situation est plus encourageante.* "It means you got a real good hope." As if the Owl can't read French. "He says your presence in court would be very helpful, so you can tell the jury your side. Maybe you want to talk to Mr. Beauchamp, who is waiting by his phone."

Going back there, sitting in the dock, waiting for them to convict him, it would be like a slow death. The Owl isn't going anywhere near that trial. He's broken out, he doesn't want to break back in. But he feels sorry about Beauchamp, it's like he let him down. "Is he mad at me?"

"He was philosophical. He was hoping to have a big win to end his career in a blaze of glory."

Cat adds, "Call him. That's what pay phones are for, Nick."

He doesn't want to talk to Mr. Beauchamp out of fear the silver-tongued orator will have him turning himself into the local gendarmerie for immediate transport to Canada. *Yes, sir, that makes absolute sense, sir, I'm on the next flight back.* He has better places to go, Brazil, Indonesia, some corrupt land.

A waiter hovers, so Faloon orders drinks, in English. Second-language ability is best not broadcast. Talk is suspended because here is a black guy in a white suit strolling around the bar to the pool, skin shoes, skin belt, Leonard tie, tooled black leather briefcase, a flashy Pepsodent smile for Gina. His Excellency Omar Lansana. Handsome, well built, young for an ambassador, maybe thirty-five.

"To keep Gina installed here, I figure it costs a yard a night, and presumably it ain't the taxpayers of Sierra Leone who are footing the bill."

"How does it work?" says Cat, seeing the potential, observing that Lansana's case has weight, it's not just full of papers.

Faloon explains Popov's wrinkle, how the maids hand in their computerized key cards to the desk clerk each morning, and how their cards get wiped and recoded. A careful observer can actually make out the master code being punched in by the desk clerk. The gizmo that issues this code is accessible to a guest who drapes a coat, a newspaper, whatever, over what he's doing. While two highly professional stalls give him shade, keep the clerk busy.

Cat smiles. Faloon knows he can count on her, her attitude is life is a dare, she'll go along with anything.

They watch Ambassador Lansana kneel at the rim of the pool, share a laugh with his mermaid. He picks up her key card from beside her Veuve Clicquot, gives her a thumbs-up sign: he'll be up there, waiting, have a nice swim.

If routine holds, Popov said, Lansana will put his dip bag in the hotel safe, until his meet on Saturday with the middler from Antwerp, Émile Van Doork.

✦

While Cat's out shopping for clothes, Faloon and Willy have tea outside at the Carlton, watching the girls strut by the beach, showing off their bejewelled belly buttons. Willy continues to throw cold water on Operation Lansana, he thinks he saw coppers hanging around the Belvedere, thinks there's heat, thinks maybe Faloon has been using too many stolen credit cards.

"Come on, I spent a whole week working this up. He could have half a billion in rocks in that dip bag, look how he lives."

"Maybe he has piss all in it. Maybe there's nothing in it but documents. Or drugs. If it's narcotics, I don't want any part of it."

"It ain't dope, you seen how heavy Lansana's bag is, if not raw diamonds, gold ingots." Though it would be Faloon's luck to find three years' worth of *Hustler*, or parts for a guided missile system.

"Okay, chum, he's carrying this fortune, where's his bodyguards?"

"Omar's doing an illegal, he don't want attention drawn to him. All I'm asking is give me shade."

Willy sips his tea, a long, crafty look, and quietly sets his cup down. "I'll make you a deal. After we do this job you will telephone Mr. Beauchamp. You will listen to his advice about beating this wrong rap. You will give him a chance to say if you can come home with confidence. You do that, and I am behind you all the way on this caper."

The Owl is over a barrel. He agrees.

✦

Faloon goes to his room to shower and change, wondering about the — what was the phrase? — "encouraging situation," careful phrasing from the great Beauchamp, but what did it mean? Something to do with Adeline Angella? He keeps revisiting that evening in her apartment, the cognac, the come-on, her movie. She was Audrey Hepburn, he was Cary Grant. *You're not supposed to ask. Pretend you're a masked intruder.* And after the kiss, hoarsely, low, *Now I pretend to resist.*

There wasn't much resistance there, or much of anything to tell the truth, the task interrupted when she went to get the condom, and Angella faking it, he thinks, faking that her resistance was overcome, faking enjoyment, orgasm. It was a long time since his last release, and maybe as he was pumping and dumping a mother lode, that's when the Trojan slipped off. As he lay aboard her panting, his peter shrinking, she said, "What's the true story about the Kashmir Sapphire?"

She already asked him that a dozen times, he sensed he was being conned. It was like she gave him a favour, and now it was his turn. He pulled his pants on, not bothering to puzzle what happened to the skin, deciding to extricate fast from an unstable situation. Looking at his watch, patting his pockets. "Jeez, I must've left my heart medicine at home."

He ended up looking like Wam Bam Sam. The eight lady jurors didn't like him for that, and when you add in his long record of stealing earrings and necklaces, they probably said what the hell and gave the benefit of the doubt to the wrong party, decided not to believe that Angella threw a bowl of plastic flowers at him as he bounded to the elevator.

Does she then call 911 in a fit of pique? Or does a plan of revenge grow more slowly in her mind, as her perceived wound festers? Mr. Beauchamp's brilliant speech just didn't find enough buyers that day in Courtroom 67.

21

Arthur is surprised to find the parking lot empty at Nouveau Chez Forget and a sign saying "Closed. *Fermé.*" It's Friday noon, a restaurateur's busiest lunchtime. "So let's grab a bite downtown," says Brian. They're en route to the Victoria courthouse, where Buddy's application to try Faloon in absentia is on the docket.

Arthur bangs at the door. Through the glass, Pierre is seen emerging from the kitchen, tucking in his shirt. An impatient look as he opens up. "Anyone else, I put a bullet in their head." In a lowered voice: "I 'ave something going on."

"Arthur, there's a really good Italian place on Wharf Street."

Pierre looks disgusted, pulls each of them in by the elbows. "Something simple and quick. The sole, a bit of salad."

They take a table. He returns to his kitchen. They hear a tinkling of female laughter.

Brian taps out a number on his cellphone, waits impatiently for an answer. "To talk to Caroline about the kids, I have to go through Lila, who doesn't have a cellphone and only occasionally turns her machine on."

Ultimately, he says, "Bitch!" hangs up, and lights a cigarette. "How is it someone who claims to be a marriage counsellor is never by her phone? They'll pee in their pants when they learn I have proof of my innocence – 'you're not supposed to smo-oke.' When they finally hear that tape, they'll be falling all over each other in grovelling apology."

Brian has avoided Angella since that evening – because of domestic strife, because Faloon is no longer in the court system, but mostly in fear of her. She has continued to stalk by phone.

"You get, 'Just phoning to say hi,' and then she runs on about something so insubstantial I lose the thread. Finally cornered me yesterday at the Ritz. For your listening pleasure . . ." Out comes the computer, but his phone interrupts. Brian answers with a robotic voice. "You have reached the suicide hotline. Please leave a number . . . Lila? Don't hang up, please I beg you, I just called you two minutes ago . . . You *did* pick up? Sorry, didn't hear that. Anyway, it's about Gabriella . . . I said what? I called you a bitch?" A pinking complexion, a man hearing harsh words. "No, no, I swore because I dropped a cigarette ember on my crotch. Lila, I can't tell you how delightful it is to hear your non-recorded voice."

Brian wins her ear with a teary tale of how Gabriella came to his law office, wanted him to play hooky with her. Lunch, a movie, a stone-faced reception when he returned her to Caroline. The denouement, his lonely return to his hotel, is vaguely poetic in its telling, and seems to raise a reasonable doubt in Ms. Chow-Thomas's mind. "That's great, Lila. I'll come by when I get back from Victoria." The cellphone clicks shut. "I think it's starting to dawn who's really to blame."

Arthur imagines it is no easy task to be a relationship counsellor, an occupation inherently risky. Eve Winters must have known that, a lesson reinforced moments before her death.

"I'm getting a deal at the Ritz because I beat a beef for the owner for running a book in the back. The pub is done up with old movie posters and attracts the upper underworld, chisellers, top-of-the-line hookers. Internet scammers and spammers – you see them with their laptops, comparing notes. I am not friendless in this place, many are free to continue their crooked lifestyles thanks to me. The attention whore is all atwitter as she plops beside me."

So this is where you're staying. I must say I was a little nervous coming into the rough part of town. It seems a little bohemian – is it an artists' hangout?

You're very perceptive.

You look so sad. Poor Brian.

He fast-forwards. "She orders a gimlet, a drink that causes confusion at the bar, the last time a gimlet was ordered in this joint, Jack Kennedy was boffing Marilyn Monroe. I deliver a stunning critique of 'You Don't Have to Ask' – I'd grasped her brilliantly understated message about illicit love, it thrives on secrecy, grows with danger. This sets her heart aflutter, she carries on about how it must be lonely living in this hotel, and how is the current situation between poor me and poor . . ."

Caroline is her name, isn't it?

Yes.

Still pretty rough going?

I've seen better days. Taking them one at a time.

"This is how to reach her, you fire the clichés with both barrels. I told her how on April Fool's morning, as we were about to go for a family romp in the park, I reached in my pockets for my gloves, and out popped the unmentionables." A sigh. "The cruellest memory is Amelia saying, 'Oh-oh,' as she looked at Caroline's livid face. Anyway, the segué: I casually ask Adeline where she was at ten o'clock that morning."

Why would you want to know?

This may sound silly, but I want to see if our signs were, ah, conjoined at that moment. I'm into that sort of thing.

That doesn't sound silly at all. That was a Saturday? Oh, I was probably at bingo, the Holy Rosary Hall. Or was that the VOSA wine-tasting? Victims of Sexual Abuse. We share, we celebrate each other.

But what were we sharing at that moment, the lawyer and the writer? I, in the vestibule of a house in North Vancouver, you . . . where? There's a spiritual reason I ask – well, there I go again, you probably think it's one of those silly New Age things . . .

You goose, not at all. I hope that wasn't the weekend I celebrated too much – my story in Tales of Passion *came out on a Friday, and I had a teeny, teeny bit too much at the Wanderlust. I was probably still in bed at ten in the morning . . . Or was that the previous weekend?*

Brian closes the computer as Pierre brings the matelot de sole. "Enjoy your lunch." He hurries off.

"Enjoy yours," Brian calls. "I'd pushed as far as I dared the concept of our two souls conjoining in an April Fool's spiritual fuck. So we're left with an array of possibilities, bingo, wine-tasting, getting pie-eyed in the Wanderlust, or – this is where I put my money – none of the above. The Wanderlust is a hokey bar in Whalley – I popped in last night. Four guys were on the stage. I thought they were doing a parody of a barbershop quartet. They turned out in fact to *be* a barbershop quartet. The Whalley Wanderers, who sing for their beer. The song that brings the house down is 'I Love to Go A-Wandering.' Valderee, valdera. Hiking and climbing gear all over the walls, pictures of the Alps. I didn't figure Angella for outdoorsy. Maybe she followed Eve to Bamfield, the silent stalker of the West Coast Trail."

None of her alibis are likely to prove ironclad, though they must be delved into. But Arthur wonders how she might have known Eve Winters would be in Bamfield, in Cotters' Cottage, and that Faloon lived nearby, a handy local scapegoat. Did she do the deed herself, or hire an agent, a contract killer? But Angella is meagrely off, and hit men don't come cheap.

◆

Buddy Svabo bobs and weaves outside the courtroom to let Arthur know he's feisty, up for another battle of wits, then cracks open the door, to show him Larry Mewhort within – he is yawning, listening to a lawyer's catalogue of spousal sins.

Buddy closes the door. "He's yours for the taking. He has a big hole next month, he was supposed to do the last trial of the Vancouver assize, a two-weeker, it blew up. He doesn't want to get stuck in divorce court cleaning out the backlist."

Arthur isn't sure how Mewhort, with his legendary slowness of mind, ever got raised to the bench. But accidents happen. As a criminal lawyer, he often stumbled into legal potholes, and leaned heavily on Arthur for advice.

"You don't have to sell me on Larry. You have to sell me on going to trial without a client."

"What've you got to lose, Artie? You're not going to put Faloon on the stand anyway, because with his record I'll freaking tear him apart." Buddy's afraid this file will drag out and be pulled from him – a missed chance at a sure winner, a chance to better Beauchamp, spoil his return. "We together on this? I've got a solid argument, section 475, an absconding accused waives his right to be present."

Mewhort, a small, puffy man with a shock of white hair that resembles a fright wig, looks on with dread as Svabo rolls a trolley of casebooks into court and lines them up on counsel table. Arthur isn't similarly armed, and wins a hesitant smile of gratitude.

They wait until an uncontested divorce wends tediously to its foregone conclusion, then Buddy files his direct indictment and passes ten pounds of photocopied cases up to the bench. Mewhort blanches. "Do we need all that law, Mr. Svabo? Tell me in simple words what this is all about."

Buddy begins with a recitation of intended proofs so indisputable, he implies, that obtaining a murder conviction is akin to filling out an order form. The Crown will allege Faloon knew Winters was staying in Cotters' Cottage. The murder came on the heels of four burglaries. Faloon is a notorious professional thief with a rape conviction. An underworld figure with easy access to Rohypnol. He avoided detection and arrest by disguising himself and stealing a truck. He escaped from jail, further proof of a guilty mind. A priest will recount his solemn confession: *She was beautiful. I just couldn't help myself.*

But it is the DNA, ah, the DNA, that Buddy revels in, splashing about in its perfumed waters. "And when the semen was tested by my learned friend's very own scientific expert, whose profile did she find? My goodness, it's Nicholas Faloon. Surprise, surprise."

This florid display is for the press. Arthur is still feeling leakages of anger over the sneak attack at Gwendolyn Bay, and it's puddling at Svabo's feet. Let this overconfident peacock rush the trial ahead, then Arthur will unmask Angella as Lorelei, who swore vengeance against Doctor Eve. Faloon will be sitting there looking innocent as a cherub. Surprise, surprise.

Buddy makes an issue of the advanced ages of the Cotters, they may not be available in five, ten years, whenever Faloon is hauled back into the system. There are cost factors, witnesses are subpoenaed for the third Monday of June, the Hyatt has been booked for the out-of-towners, if the trial doesn't go ahead a jury panel of seventy will be sitting around twiddling their thumbs.

The final incantation, the burdened-taxpayer theme, is again for the press. Their presence in such numbers seems to cause Mewhort anxiety. His gaffes have been frequently reported.

When Buddy spreads open a thick volume of the *Chancery Reports*, the judge raises his hands protectively. "Just a minute here, I don't get this, doesn't section 475 only apply when an accused absconds in the middle of the trial? He's out on bail, sees his trial going badly, and walks out in the middle of it. I think I had a case like that."

Buddy argues that the word *trial* needs a liberal interpretation, it begins when an accused is charged. He picks up the thick casebook.

"Hang on, before we get into that, what's your position, Mr. Beauchamp?"

"I am prepared to choose a jury on June 19 and go to trial."

"Without the accused?"

"Let's hope he'll show up."

A sigh of relief. "Problem solved. Well, that wasn't so bad. And we do it in Vancouver, right? Victoria's too tea, tweeds, and tourists for me." An offhand civic insult that will doubtless make the news columns. "Okay, there are no more pre-trial issues?"

Buddy looks at Arthur, expecting him to make robust complaint about Adeline Angella being called, but Arthur feigns a lapse, frowning. "No, I can't think of any."

"Call the next divorce."

✦

Faloon is up before seven, without his regular sleep, coming down from nightmares, but he has to keep up his routine, today especially. The overnight clerk, Gaston, knows he shows up early for a newspaper and a coffee, reads it standing up at his favourite spot by the potted palm, the shady end of the burnished walnut check-in counter.

Gaston's final task before he goes off shift is to sign in the cleaning staff and activate their master-key cards, punching in the magic number that opens all doors. This process is underway as Faloon settles in under his palm tree, coffee and *Herald-Tribune* at hand. He engages Gaston with his standard opening, "How're you doing today, partner?" as he watches Gaston's pudgy index finger peck out today's master code.

One big score, that's all Faloon wants, then take it on the Arthur before the town heats up. But Cat and Willy have got to lay off him about that murder beef, he doesn't want to explain for the umpteenth time they'll be going home without him, he's heading in the opposite direction, to the exotic lands of the East.

But he has to honour his deal, phone Mr. Beauchamp, if only to apologize. He'll be respectful but firm about his decision. He'll explain about the sleepwalking, the monster that hides inside his skin. *Small man but strong like a cougar.* That phrase comes back, but from where?

"I 'ave migraine," says Gaston. Yesterday it was a pain in the bowels.

Faloon tries for a light subject, his plans for the day, a boat cruise that's supposed to stop at some great nude beaches. This is interrupted from down the counter by, "I wonder if it's possible to get some service here." Willy, impeccable in a five-thousand-euro suit he clouted yesterday from a men's store. And then Cat, at the far end of the crescent, in her new finery, indignant: "I believe *I* was next."

Gaston is frozen for a moment in mid-stride, he doesn't know who to attend on first. But somehow he pulls it off, asking if the gentleman would mind if he first met the needs of the lady. Cat wants tourist information, Willy wants directions to a complex destination. It's a little scene, just enough to distract the attention of the few early-birds by the coffee urn.

Less interesting to everyone is that Faloon has accidentally dropped the sports section over the counter, and has to reach way over it for twelve excruciating fumbling seconds, hitting a digit too few, having to insert his key card again to get it right.

He heads up to his room, 516, just down from 508, where Omar Lansana and Gina de Carlo share a bed. The master key card works fine. He worries about having to brace Ambassador Lansana, an athlete, the legs of a racer, fiercely protective of his jewels.

◆

It's three o'clock. Cat is hanging by the pool, in a bikini under a sarong. The Hook is near the pool elevator, with a view into the lobby, where Faloon planned to nest behind a newspaper. But his choice spot is gone, a stuffed Louis Quinze in an alcove. A casually dressed young man is occupying it, studying photographs under a lamp. Strips of photos, like from a surveillance camera. Faloon sees another husky man, leaning against a pillar, equally obvious. With him is the manager of the jewellery store where he poached those watches off Harold Stein's card. Something has gone kerflooey, maybe Visa put out an alert on that transaction.

Before the Owl can change his mind about Project Lansana, Willy strolls from the pool area, giving the office, two arms crossed, a go, which means Omar and Gina are poolside. Faloon flashes him that bulls are on the scene, three middle fingers down, thumb and little finger up, like horns. Willy hesitates, takes a turn into the can to give Faloon a minute to make up his mind.

He puffs himself up with courage, he's going to do this, he's going to take the elevator to the fifth floor, and if there's a cop waiting outside his room, he's going to nod and smile and unlock Lansana's suite down the hall, 508, and he's going to walk in like he's Jacques Chirac. And he's going to hide under the bed. And he's going to wait.

At this point, something happens to make this gamble better than a sheer impossibility. Harold W. Stein walks from the street with his client. They're in a jokey mood, this is their tax write-off holiday on the Riviera, Faloon overheard them, some kind of commodities deal.

Before they reach the elevators, the two dicks in the lobby converge followed by two more from outside. Badges come out, and identification is demanded. You can tell Stein and his friend are put out, with their stressed speech patterns. Stein makes a point of *not* showing his passport, affronted, do they know exactly *whom* they are addressing?

As Willy leaves the gent's room, he almost walks into Stein, swearing retribution as he's being led out to the bun wagon for an interview in quieter surroundings. This is the right time to go to the fifth floor. Willy sees him heading that way, then sidles out to the pool area.

There's no action on the fifth, no cops. A Do Not Disturb on the knob of 508, they don't want the maid poking around while they're at the pool. The door answers easy to the key card, and he is in. A canopy bed, king-sized, for which Faloon is thankful, he'll be under it. It shows hard loving, sheets mussed, the spread hanging to the floor. No black *portefeuille* in obvious view.

The balcony door is locked, windows curtained but with a strip of sunlight through a gap. Taking an angle through it, he spots Lansana and de Carlo rising like a handsome god and goddess from the pool, him muscled and dusky, her lithe and golden. Puffing up to greet them is a man with less healthy colour, his face like a slice of rare beef. Émile Van Doork has arrived with an attaché case. It's a quality item, red leather with metal studs.

A few lounge chairs down, there's Cat, smearing on lotion between sips of a martini, casually watching.

A tiny flash of sunlight bounces off the key card Lansana gives Van Doork. The diamond expert is trusted to come up to 508 to evaluate the shipment before they bicker over price. Which means two things – Van Doork is on his way, and Lansana's dip bag should be somewhere in the room.

He looks behind the desk, under it, the closet, under the extra linen. Pauses to look out again, Van Doork heading for the outside elevator, it's enclosed in glass so you can see out. Cat trying not to be obvious about following him. No briefcase in the dresser drawers. Nothing in the bathroom. Another look outside, and there's the elevator smoothing to a stop, Van Doork in it, Cat too, it looks like she's flirting with him.

Faloon squiggles under the bed, a ten-inch clearance, just enough for this burrowing Owl. That's where he finds the thick black *portefeuille*.

The door opens, and Faloon can see Van Doork's feet, and soon expects to see his startled eyes. But Cat is out there stalling. "Left my key at the pool. Mind if I use your bathroom?"

She's picked up the Owl is in trouble, she's slick, doing the bit where she holds her legs tight with the need to pee. No gentleman would refuse such a request, especially from a beautiful woman, but maybe Van Doork being a crooked diamond dealer is too paranoid to bite. Cat goes past him, rushing inside, Faloon can see the hem of her sarong sweeping by.

The bathroom door gets yanked open, Cat going, "Oh, God. Thank you. Had too much to drink." To the trained ear the sound is more like running the tap than a whiz.

Now it's truth or consequences, because here is Émile kneeling beside the bed. Faloon gently nudges the briefcase in the direction of his reaching fingers, which almost graze Faloon's hand as they touch leather. Van Doork slides his attaché case beside it, and sits on the bed with a grunt. You can tell he's out of shape, wheezing, though maybe he's panting over this lovely snockered creature.

From the can, the door a little ajar, Cat keeps up a torrent of distracting words: "God, what a way to meet. You on holiday, too? I'm celebrating my divorce. I'm a Libra, by the way, what are you, Aries, I'll bet."

The first spoken word from Van Doork: "Aquarius."

"I had a little accident . . . now this is *really* embarrassing, I think I'm stuck in the bidet."

The mattress bounces as Van Doork stands. In the few seconds it takes for him to reach the bathroom, Faloon is out from under, and in the few seconds more it takes for Van Doork to still his heart while looking at Cat naked on the bidet, Faloon has wrestled out both cases, brief and attaché, and in two more seconds the door to 508 silently closes and the Owl is gone.

The handoff to Willy doesn't happen, it's faster to take the stairs. Faloon signals him a three, meet on the third floor, then totes the two cases toward a stairwell.

Almost predictably comes the ultimate fuddle of the day. Cat steps out of 508 looking white and wide-eyed, her sarong fluttering as she races to the pool elevator.

Because he's puzzled and concerned for her, Faloon hangs back when he should be humping it down the stairs. Then he's frozen there when Van Doork staggers from the room clutching his chest and slumps bug-eyed onto the hallway carpet.

As Cat enters the elevator, Omar Lansana exits, lavishing a blazing smile on her, losing it when he sees Van Doork keeling over, and, at the far end of the hall, a stairwell door closing behind an attaché case, a briefcase, and two owlish eyes. These eyes see Lansana charging like a maddened bull. Faloon figures he has maybe twenty seconds on him, twenty seconds to live.

22

"I hear them boys like to do it with their spurs on," says Gomer Goulet, a comment timed for Arthur's arrival at the General Store, and made the more odious by a wink that crimps half his face.

"Lay off him," Emily Lemay says. "Poor Arthur, poor baby. I'm gonna come over and do your laundry, sugarpants." The word is out that he is washer-challenged. The girls from Mop'n'Chop did the clothes last week – acting out of pity despite their no-laundry policy.

"The door of Blunder Bay is always open, Emily."

"So is hers," says Priposki, several sheets to the wind and it's only 11 a.m.

Emily scrapes back her chair and charges. Juggling his rum-laced coffee, Priposki struggles up to defend himself. She bats him in the eye and he sits back in his chair with a thud, though without a drop spilled. She returns to her seat, cracking her knuckles, while he stares at her with dazed, creeping awareness that there are limits to bad taste.

"You're barred," Abraham Makepeace tells the loser of this one-sided scuffle. Arthur helps the wretch to his feet, walks him outside, and he lurches mumbling up the road to his shack.

Arthur remains on the steps, coffee and pipe at hand, watching an RCMP launch rip past the buoy at Hopeless Point, on its way to chalk up today's quota of arrests, kids who will later wave from the stern, showing off their handcuffs.

On the weekend, Sustainable Logging brought heavy equipment to the beach by tug and barge, intending to tow the timber to a booming grounds. But protesters chained themselves to trees and machines, and police spent yesterday cutting them free, the loggers forced to stand idly by. A similar process should be underway presently.

Lotis is still in Victoria, helping Selwyn defend the arrestees. The appeal process is moving ahead, but slowly, the Supreme Court calendar clogged by a constitutional issue.

Many more young folk trooped to Garibaldi on the weekend: students, teenagers. *Guess there'll be a lot more when university's over. I'm hip to it.* The former peace marcher won't drop his price, plays the victim role – he's just a guy trying to make a buck, he's pitted against the green hordes.

Stump Town has moved to Gwendolyn Bay: motley boats, tents on the public beach. The press too have deserted Margaret and her three musketeers. Margaret won't have to endure all that manly sweat for long. They'll soon have gravity-fed water for their makeshift shower, by PVC pipe from Gwendolyn Pond. The comforts of home, plus testosterone. Why bother coming down at all?

In the store, Makepeace is sorting Arthur's mail. "Book-club selection. Some personal letters, sealed, I can't help you with those. A video, Lotis must've ordered it from the States, there's customs owing. Also . . . where'd I put that fax?" Presumably he'd placed it somewhere for his further study and enjoyment.

He returns from his office. "Sitting right beside my coffee, couldn't see it for looking. From France. Maybe you can figure it out, I can't."

Cat McAllister's scrawl: "The Owl pulled a real doozie. He was supposed to phone you, but I got no idea where he's at. We'll be back tomorrow." Bringing clarification, he hopes.

By the time he gets home, depression has settled over him like a fine mist. It stays the night, percolates through his dreams, one of which has him burrowing into a pile of laundry to escape Emily Lemay.

✦

While Arthur doddles in the garden, a civil disobedience instructor demonstrates the art of chaining oneself to the back axle of Bungle Bay's old John Deere. (Are courses for this offered in colleges today, Arthur wonders.) A dozen high-energy youngsters watch and compare notes. Reverend Al, who has sequestered Bungle Bay as resistance headquarters, looks on approvingly.

Here come more guests, rolling up the driveway: Freddy Jacoby in his fin-tailed Cadillac, Brian Pomeroy asleep in the front seat, Cat McAllister and Willy the Hook barely awake in the back.

When Jacoby alights, Brian stretches out. A mickey of vodka falls from his pocket. Plotzed already, at mid-day.

The others stare confusedly at a girl being chained by ankles and wrists to the underside of the tractor. "We apologize if we have come at an importunate time," says Jacoby.

"A school for the resistance. They hope to be arrested and jailed."

"Gorblimey," says Willy.

They settle on the deck, and Kim Lee brings appetizers and teacups. "Flesh pot coming."

Cat and Willy look as if they've had their fill of fleshpots. They came by way of Nassau, Willy in tangerine shorts that clash with his red, knobby knees; palm trees on Cat's shirt.

She hands Arthur a three-day-old *Le Parisien*, a tabloid. The head-line story, SCANDALE ET MEURTRE À CANNES, is about a love nest in a posh hotel, with photos of the late Émile Van Doork, a diamond merchant; Omar Lansana, Sierra Leone's ambassador to France; and a former Paris call girl named Gina de Carlo. No photo of Nick Faloon, who fits the description of a middle-aged man police are seeking.

Arthur puts on his glasses for the smaller print. Calling into ques-tion the headline, the author of this enthusiastic account admits, in reluctant afterthought, that Van Doork may have succumbed to a heart attack. Lansana has disappeared, perhaps to his embassy, perhaps to Sierra Leone. Ms. De Carlo, in whose name the alleged love nest was registered, said only, "Ne sais pas, ne parle pas."

"I don't know if Nick made it, Mr. Beauchamp," says Willy, "or if he got nobbled." When he last saw Faloon, the ambassador was bounding down a stairwell after him.

As his guests stir and sip, Arthur cross-examines them. In sum, it appears Faloon vanished after a dodgy climax to a thieving spree, along with, possibly, a fortune in diamonds and euros. That he hasn't phoned Arthur, as promised, bodes ill.

A loud noise, a thud, and a splintering. A yell: "Shit!" It's Brian, stumbling from the Cadillac. Somehow – in the throes of a nightmare? – he nudged the gear lever, and the car rolled down a slope into a corner post of the garden fence. Brian stands for a moment, looking bewildered.

On close examination: a smashed headlight, a twisted fender that rubs against a tire. Jacoby shrugs. "A minor catastrophe in the universal scheme of things, except we may have to indulge you, Mr. Beauchamp, for a taxi."

Arthur has the number handy. Stoney promises to send "one of our fleet."

"You will stay the night," Arthur informs Brian. "You will dry out for at least the next twelve hours." Arthur will recommend he take leave from work, go into intensive treatment.

Brian nods, uninterested, dials his cellphone. Further evidence that he has fallen apart comes as he snaps it shut. "She won't let me talk to the kids, claims they're in school. What school? Sunday school?"

"It's Tuesday, Brian."

"That can't be right." He fumbles with his phone. "Operator? Operator, what day is this?"

Arthur plucks it away, pockets it. "I am seizing this device."

"Wait, no, you can't." Frantic.

He leads the cellaholic to the house, puts him in the spare bedroom. Kim is to guard against escape attempts.

Outside, Stoney has parked the Fargo and is voraciously eyeing the gleaming classic Caddie, running a finger along the chrome behind the fins.

"Can you recommend a bodywork specialist on this here island?" Jacoby says.

Stoney smiles grandly. "No problem."

✦

Todd Clearihue holds the courtroom door open for Arthur, who walks past him without a word – he can't bear to look at his unwearying smile, fears he will give in to violent impulse.

Again, Arthur parks himself in the last row, and again Wilbur Kroop, on mounting the bench, hunts him down with his steely eyes. But this time he smiles, as if pleased to have drawn him to his lair.

Prudhomme is also here, he's but a spectator too. This is a criminal matter now, and the Crown is represented by Jennifer Tann, a good-hearted woman of middle years who seems uncomfortable with her assignment. Selwyn, Lotis, and a few other lawyers line the defence table.

"How many new guests will be joining our company today, Madam Prosecutor?" A kind of chuckle issues from Kroop's small, pursed mouth: "Himf, himf." The jailing of protestors has put him in a good mood. He has set the next six weeks aside, to the end of June, for bail hearings and speedy trials and all the other detritus that follows in the wake of a contentious injunction.

"Only eight today," Tann says.

"And why is that? I understand there's been a mass migration to the logging site."

"The police had to unshackle all these people from machines. It was a day-long process, milord."

"Let's bring them out in one group, I don't want to spend the rest of the day at this."

Earlier, Selwyn, desperate to disqualify Kroop, slowed proceedings with argument: his Lordship has prejudged matters; a judge innocent of the issues should sit; the presumption of innocence was withheld from these jobless roasters of hot dogs. Kroop listened patiently, thanked him, and dismissed the motion without reasons.

243

The clerk calls out the list, and into the prisoner's dock crowd five men and three women, none over twenty-five. Most wear Save Gwendolyn T-shirts. A young black man has a slogan embossed on his: "We've upped our profits, up yours."

Selwyn and the other lawyers urge reasonable bail. Kroop stares at the wall clock, as if timing these exercises in futility. The Chief Justice has issued a diktat: bail will be ten thousand a head, cash down, no exceptions. It will be forfeited by anyone returning to Garibaldi Island.

One of the lawyers pleads that his client could lose her job as nurse's aide if she languishes in jail.

"That ought to have been uppermost in her mind as she was chaining herself to an excavator. Call the next case."

"Bill Watters," says the clerk. The fellow in the message T-shirt shuffles to his feet. No counsel rises with him.

"Where's your lawyer?" Kroop asks.

"Don't have one. What good would it do me?"

Kroop glowers, here's another upstart. "A lawyer will help you to understand the charge and the consequences that could follow."

"Okay, well, what exactly am I charged with?"

"Being in criminal contempt of a Supreme Court order to stay off private property."

"Who issued that order?"

"I did, as it happens."

"If you already ruled we're in contempt, what more is there for you to decide at our trial? You called us lawless dope-smoking squatters and . . ."

Kroop cuts him off. "Young man, such reckless ignorance convinces me you're in dire need of legal counselling, and some lessons in manners. You would do well not to make utterances that could be construed as adding to your contempt . . ." He stalls, backs up. "Of which, of course, you're innocent until proven guilty." The judge is enduring a rare moment of fluster. "Beyond a reasonable doubt."

"The way you're setting punitive bail for everyone, it's obvious you don't have any doubt at all. That's not bail, it's a jail sentence. I don't have a nickel, let alone ten thousand dollars."

Lotis turns, locates Arthur, winks. The message: This mini-protest has been scripted to bring home the folly of Kroop's bad snap judgments. "Call it punitive bail," Selwyn would have told Bill Watters.

Kroop's black eyes almost disappear behind drooping folds of skin – he's fighting his fury, wants to explode at this riff-raff rebel. "The court will not be provoked by a show of petty insolence." Tight and reedy. "I shall disregard your comments as having been made out of simple-minded naïveté." He shouts, "Get a lawyer!"

The young man shows undue courage: "Why? You've already decided I'm guilty." A grumbling of approval comes from the back, where the protestors' allies have gathered.

As if searching for support elsewhere, Kroop reviews the press table, sees a few disgusted looks. He doesn't have an ally on the Crown side either – Jennifer Tann proposed the defendants be released on good behaviour bonds. She too is displeased at Kroop's teach-them-a-lesson, assembly-line justice.

Kroop glances at Arthur, who's smiling, enjoying his discomfort. The Chief Justice looks quickly down, in the manner of one realizing his fly's open, exposing his prejudice. He doesn't want all his hard work to be reversed on appeal.

"Check the calendar, Mr. Gilbert. Who's available to sit this week?"

"On this case, my Lord?"

"Yes! This case! I'm not talking about someone sitting on the moon. Anyone standing idly by?" Chief Justice Kroop has power to delegate which judge sits where, and is clearly about to use it. Goodbye Wilbur Kroop. No one could be worse.

Paul Prudhomme and Todd Clearihue, who'd been enjoying this pageant until now, have sunk in their chairs. Another judge. More delay.

"All defendants will be remanded in custody until tomorrow at ten o'clock." A dark look about the room: "I cannot preside at a forum in which the air is thick with distrust." "Ad hominem," he challenges credulity, "I have never had my fairness doubted in thirty years of meting out justice."

The clerk studies the rotas for the week. All Supreme Court judges are on trial assignments, reserved judgment days, or ill.

"Who's doing divorces in Vancouver?"

"We have, ah . . . Mr. Justice Mewhort sitting all month."

"And next month?"

"He's on Assize for the last two weeks, *Regina versus Faloon.*"

The sensation in the pit of Arthur's stomach brings back the night of the bad clams.

"Faloon, yes, I think that crossed my desk. That's the one involving the young lady who was, ah, allegedly raped and murdered. Remind me, who's counsel on that?"

"I have Mr. Svabo for the Crown and Mr. Beauchamp for the defence."

Those burning black eyes track down Arthur again. "Yes. Yes. That will work. Please inform Mr. Justice Mewhort that his presence is requested in our lovely capital city for the next six weeks. I shall personally attend to his divorce trials and to the little matter involving Mr. Faloon. Himf, himf."

His bulky frame rises, giant Polyphemus, the Cyclopean, returning to his cave after devouring a Greek for dessert.

PART THREE

He was but as the cuckoo is in June,
Heard, not regarded.

– Henry IV, Part I

23

On Garibaldi Island, Arthur had been in the habit of rising with the sun, but when he does so this morning he's disoriented, lost in the vastness of a voluptuous bed. Perhaps it's a rest home, everything clean and colour-bright. But no, the four erotic Japanese prints on the wall, lovers entwined gymnastically, suggest a clinic for the sexually disabled, or perhaps a stylish bordello.

He forgot to draw the curtains last night, so it is well that his room doesn't face east – the sun reflects harshly enough off a nearby high-rise. That, he realizes, accounts for the garish orange of the wall beside him.

Though the city sleeps on – it is only 5:30, two days shy of summer solstice – Arthur is now sharply awake, aware of why he's here: *Regina versus Faloon* opens at 10 a.m. for a two-week run in the Vancouver Law Courts before Chief Justice Wilbur Kroop.

And where he is, he apprehends, is 807 Elysian Tower, a condominium newly bought by his friend and partner, Hubbell Meyerson. For the remainder of the month, if he cannot wheedle his way out of Kroop's court, this will be Arthur's home: a luxury two-bedroom on the eighth floor, just opened, smelling of fresh carpet and wallboard and oiled wood. Next month, Hubbell will have renters for this swank waterfront investment.

Arthur supposes there are modern people – successful in life, liberal in outlook – who would find those Japanese pen drawings boldly risqué, innovative. Even appropriate for what is, after all, a bedroom.

"Fun," is how the designer would have put it, but the prints make Arthur uncomfortable. A curve of thigh leading to a junction of parted legs and half-submerged penis causes him a familiar distress, reminds him he's old-fashioned, a square.

"One ought 'not to add the disgrace of wickedness to old age,'" he recites as he rises from bed. Why does he remember the words of Cato and Plutarch and forget so much else?

In the kitchen, as promised by Hubbell, is an instrument of glistening chrome that makes cappuccinos, lattes. Somewhere there's an instruction book. Brian Pomeroy is coming by with bagels – he likes gadgets, and will know what to do.

He studies his hoary, hairy image in the bathroom mirror. He can't go into court like a hayseed, so he's reserved a chair at Roberto's for a trim. "A bloody tonsorial overhaul in fact, you look like the ancient mariner." He talks to fill the silence, missing the farmyard cluck and clatter. Missing Margaret.

Day seventy-four! Two and a half months, she's closing in on the world record. Some fellow in California redwood country holds it, and a Tasmanian pair are close behind. Those two came down because the woman got pregnant. Margaret is beyond the age.

She has vowed to stay until the arrests end. Her companions go up and down the trees as if on escalators, though they're careful not to disturb the eagles. The two hatchlings have survived, the mother brooding them, the male scavenging the beaches and stealing from ospreys.

More climbers have been recruited, bronzed and lithe men and women moving through the forest like spider monkeys, extending zip lines into the valley, metal lianas in the canopy. The media liken them to the outlaws of Sherwood Forest.

Arthur pulls on sweatpants and his Save Gwendolyn T-shirt, slides open the balcony door, looks out over the floating gas stations, over Ferguson Point and the forest, the cables and stanchions of Lions Gate, stretching like a web between the park and the North Shore. Eight floors below, on the seawall path, a lone man trots by – intrepid like Arthur, daring the dawn, firing himself up, the work week has begun.

Then he deflates with the prospect of writhing under the spurs of Wilbur Kroop. Arthur could apply to adjourn the matter out of his court, but would have to eat crow for having agreed to defend an absent accused. Faloon, he assumes, remains somewhere on the wrong side of the Atlantic Ocean.

He tries to puff himself up. He has won more trials before Kroop than he lost, and most of his defeats were reversed on appeal. He is not afraid of him. It is the jury, not the judge, who decides guilt, and if he is forced to go ahead, he still retains his trump card, Adeline Angella with a motive for murder.

The strategy will be to bait the line with red herrings: Hoover and the late-night wanderer, Harvey Coolidge, and even Ruth Delvechio, Winters's jilted lover. The prosecution mustn't suspect Arthur has a different fish in mind.

Brian Pomeroy's efforts to track Angella's movements on April Fool's Day haven't borne fruit, though one of her alibis is blown. Brian found a past-event calendar on the Web site of Victims of Sexual Abuse: its wine-tasting event was the previous weekend. But it remains uncomfortably possible that on the evening of March 31 she was at her favourite bar, the Wanderlust, and the next day at the Holy Rosary bingo.

Brian recently finished a month of rest and therapy, but won't be in court today – Angella must remain ignorant of his spying. At any rate, it's doubtful whether he's recovered from what his partners decided was a full-blown nervous breakdown – they packed him off to Arizona, to a clinic.

Nor will Lotis Rudnicki be present. She has been called to the bar – not without some gripes from a few stuffy benchers – and is a full-fledged lawyer now. But she's needed in Victoria to counsel arrestees, take statements, arrange for legal aid and bail. Larry Mewhort has been predictably lenient, releasing all on their promise to appear for trial.

Unhappily, the Appeal Court upheld Kroop's order restraining trespassers, though it vacated his bail conditions and varied Mewhort's. All arrestees must wear electronic monitors on ankle bracelets. Somewhere, presumably, sirens sound and lights flash if they return to Garibaldi.

As colleges empty, recruits flood to the West Coast. So far, 188 people, mostly young but some seniors too, have been equipped with monitors – which they flaunt like badges of honour. A game is being played, with rituals, the loggers boating in each morning, then watching an RCMP sergeant read the injunction to the presumptive arrestees, after which constables strain with hacksaws and bolt cutters and pry bars. By the time the last protestor is unchained and arrested, the working day is over, and everyone leaves. They take weekends off.

Arthur's elevator stops for a pair in cycling gear. "Yay, Gwendolyn," one says, admiring his T-shirt. When he steps outside into the crisp morning, he finds the seawall busy with runners, joggers, walkers – simultaneously disgorged from their buildings at 6 a.m., a clockwork emigration. He will not be at ease in the city, with its spurts of energy, an unnatural place where all that grows has been planted by man.

Nor does he expect to feel relaxed in the courtroom, Kroop or no Kroop. Again, he worries that his craft has corroded beyond repair. But Doc Dooley was encouraging. "The well-exercised mind doesn't cease to work at sixty-eight. Your skills will return as if they never went away."

Mens sana in corpore sano. He pictures Émile Van Doork stumbling from a hotel room after successive jolts: seeing Cat naked and helpless, finding he was duped. His own heart must stay combat-ready. He has a trial to win.

He attacks the seawall promenade.

✦

"I bear bagels," says Brian Pomeroy. He has caught Arthur fresh from the shower, swaddled in a towel. "Though you are wet, I am dry. I have taken the cure." He is chipper and tanned. He sweeps into the kitchen, surveying with approval its aesthetics, its gadgetry.

He has brought orange juice, and pours a glass for Arthur, then vigorously sets to mastering the coffee machine.

"That Arizona clinic has performed a miracle," Arthur says.

"The Tough Love Health Club. Middle of the desert. Nowhere to escape, nowhere to run to, you stick it out or die." He finds a bagel slicer. "Ever been in a dry-out centre, Arthur?"

"I lasted three days."

"Tough Love comes with brutal therapy. The screwing around with other women, the guilt, that's what led me to drink. The resident panic mechanic decided I have some kind of overactive testicular drive complicated by hedonistic impulses. Or some shit like that. I have to control it, it's that simple. Easy to do if I stay off the behaviour-altering chemicals."

"Splendid. Come with me to an AA meeting. A booster shot, best taken at least twice a week to start with."

"Sorry, I'm not religious. Call me when they set up a chapter for the godless. I can stay off the gargle on my own, Arthur, I don't need help from a higher power − you've got to find the strength within, that's what they teach at Tough Love. And I can feel it, brother, I can feel the *power*."

Arthur won't nag him. Maybe he is one of the rare ones and has the strength. Maybe the boozing was a response to stress. That also seems to be lessening.

"No more secrets. I told Caroline the whole story, my secret agent role. I'm back in the neighbourhood, house-sitting for friends down the street. Next stop, a workshop on Cortes Island. Caroline and I will be with five other couples, under the baton of a relationship guru recommended by Lila. *Intensive* is the word for this sort of circle jerk. We're expected to pour out everything, our bottled feelings."

Arthur can't imagine confessing his traumas and failings to strangers. He wouldn't know where to start. He imagines himself listening with a sick grin as Margaret advertises his plodding ways, his oppressive formality. ("He wasn't such a drag when I married him," she says tearfully.)

The coffee machine bubbles merrily, hisses steam, produces frothy coffees. They take their mugs and bagels to the living room, which has a Japanese motif, like the bedroom but without the touch of Eros.

Brian sits on a tatami rug and asks, rhetorically, "How in hell have we managed to get to day one of a murder trial without a client?"

Not a call or postcard. Claudette hasn't heard from him either. The French police seem not to be trying hard to find him. The death of Émile Van Doork has been written off as due to natural causes, and fraud and theft aren't a top priority.

"If Nick promised to call, he will. He hasn't because he's lying low." But Arthur's optimism feels strained.

"What if he's dead? Ever heard of a stiff being convicted of a crime?"

"If he's dead, a body would have been found. He's scared and on the run."

"Maybe he should stay on it. How did Captain Bligh crash the party?"

"Somehow I must have offended the gods."

"Any chance of bypassing the old bugger?"

"Minuscule." By now, Arthur is almost costumed for work, a three-piece suit. He picks up his briefcase.

"Don't forget your phone." Brian is looking into the bedroom, the cellphone on the night table, with its confusing instruction booklet. Arthur has been powering it up.

He succumbed to the importuning of friends. The phone promises him easier access to Garibaldi, to the defenders of Gwendolyn Valley, even to Faloon when he attempts contact. It can't be that difficult to master. He has broadcast the number on the island.

"Is Hubbell kinky?" Brian is studying the Kama Sutraesque prints.

"I suspect he's trying to be hip." Hubbell is of an age with Arthur, and about as lacking in libertine leanings. Bullingham would have a fit.

✦

It is Bully himself he encounters as he and Brian ford the fountains and pools of the piazza outside the tower housing Tragger Inglis Bullingham. Every morning at nine the old man trundles off for scones and coffee at the Confederation Club, where he and his cronies complain about the state of the world.

"Glad to see you still know how to knot a tie, Arthur." He acknowledges Brian, shakes his hand hastily, avoiding prolonged contact with such rabble. "You won't have much fun with Wilbur Kroop and his ill-fitting dentures, but good luck anyway. I have made Riley available should you need case law. When you have time, pop in and we'll talk about the Wilson case. Chairman of Brunswick Trust, dispatched his wife – allegedly of course. Set to go this fall, Cleaver's maintaining a holding pattern until you're available."

"Don't hold your breath, Bully."

"Nonsense, you've had a long-enough vacation."

Bully has never been known to take one, and holds with suspicion anyone who does. He won't listen to further protest, and sets off for the club.

Arthur and Brian carry on to the mezzanine, to Roberto's hair salon. Arthur has entrusted his hair to Roberto since he was a barber named Bob with a striped pole outside a homely two-chair shop. Now he's a stylist and operates from a parlour of elegant yet restrained taste.

There is much tsk-tsk'ing as he examines the tangle of whiskers and hair. "We must do away with the beard. It detracts from the commanding nose. It is such a power symbol."

"Cyrano," says Brian, not looking up, studying the models in an Italian fashion magazine.

"The Cyrano look, si, perfecto. Swordsman of the courts. The moustache can stay, it gives accent to the nose." Arthur bows to his will, and tufts begin to fly.

"You on top of the jury roll?" Brian asks. A panel of sixty will be showing up, homemakers and plumbers and shoe sellers culled at random from voters' lists. They've been well picked over, most having served on at least one jury during this assize. Arthur would have preferred them fresh and innocent – experience breeds cynicism, distrust of the system.

"Watch out for three, eighteen, thirty, and fifty-one. They were on the Michaelson jury." A contentious conviction last month. One ought not forget Shakespeare's counsel: *The jury, passing on the prisoner's life, may in the sworn twelve have a thief or two guiltier than him they try.* It is not thieves, however, whom Arthur will worry about, but the overly righteous and stern.

Brian's phone rings. "You have reached the Sixth Sense Law Office. We know who you are and what you want, so at the sound of the tone, please hang up . . . Of course, Lila, I knew it was you . . . By your laugh, I'm reminded of the bells of St. Mary's . . . No, not a drop . . . Yes, it's been suggested, but I'm not AA material, not clubby enough . . . Sure, if you have some ideas . . . Always willing to listen . . ." He takes his phone outside, lights a cigarette.

Here is a marriage under repair. The new improved Brian Pomeroy. New life, relenting wife. There's glue in the shared love of children – Margaret has never known the joy. Ah, but she has a nest of them now.

"The swordsman takes shape," says Roberto, flourishing his scissors like an épée. "You will look twenty years younger."

◆

In the locker room, the makeover from humble farmer continues as Arthur dons starched shirt and dickey, striped pants with suspenders, drycleaned gown. In this uniform, he feels transformed, a different man, competent, assured, his self-doubt dissipating like mist. Bring on Wilbur Kroop. He is Arthur Ramsgate Beauchamp, Queen's Counsel, standing tall, freshly shorn, and of imposing nasal eminence.

He strides up the stairs to level six, to the largest of the assize courts, 67, scene of many of his famous duels. From a vine-draped terrace, one can gaze down to the Great Hall, or up to the massive skylight. Young lawyers mill about the terrace, waiting for the doors to open, eager to watch the return of Cyrano, along with reporters and curious citizenry: fans of the courtroom who shun the daytime soaps, preferring their drama live.

Nearby, in a crowded witness room, Buddy Svabo and his errand runner, Jasper Flynn, are readying witnesses: crime scene officers, analysts, technicians. Not the key people, Holly Hoover, Adeline Angella, who are to be served up like dessert at the end of Buddy's menu.

Deputy Sheriff Willit opens Court 67. It's wider than long, the jury box to the right; in the middle, the prisoner's dock, glassed in on three sides, and the witness stand to the left. In ascending levels are counsel table, clerk's station, judge's bench. At the back, behind a shiny brass bar, the public gallery, behind that, wall-to-wall windows looking out upon the glass towers of midtown Vancouver.

The room fills to half-capacity. Attendance will grow as the public becomes aware the trial is in progress, presuming Arthur isn't able to abort it. He'll have a full house for his scene of exoneration with Adeline Angella, whose lies put Faloon behind bars. This chance to reverse Arthur's one great failure has helped energize him.

Buddy has a junior, Charles Stubb, known as Ears, a tribute to a pair of pennantlike flappers. He rises from counsel table, thrusts both hands, imprisoning Arthur's one. "Honoured to be opposite you, Mr. Beauchamp, can't wait to watch you in action."

"You'll be watching an old dog who hasn't learned a new trick in years."

"It'll be something for my memoirs." Stubb intends a political career but is entirely lacking in charisma, though a voracious glad-hander.

"Order in court," says Gilbert the clerk, a pitiable Bob Cratchit type. All rise as Kroop shambles from chambers and parks his ample form with a complacent grunt, as one might sit down to a tasty dinner. It's 10 a.m. exactly – Kroop, a stickler for time, has fined lawyers for being as little as ten minutes late.

A brusque nod to Buddy, a thin, sinister smile for Arthur. "I have before me a transcript of proceedings before Justice Mewhort in which he ordered trial of the accused *in absentia* – I daresay he is more profitably engaged elsewhere – a ruling that learned counsel for the defence seems to have heartily endorsed." He quotes Arthur's words, now regretted: *I am prepared to choose a jury on June 19 and go to trial.* "Gentlemen, are we ready to proceed?"

"Ready, milord," says Buddy.

A glitter in Kroop's anthracite eyes as he gazes down at Arthur. He's inviting him to crawl, to grovel for an adjournment. Before brushing him off, Kroop will scold him like a child who soiled his pants, express shock and dismay at his late repentance while jury and witnesses wait eagerly to do their duty to their country. Arthur will look like a fuddled, irresolute fool.

"I am content," he says.

Kroop has a reputation for eating clerks alive, and his favourite meal is Gilbert F. Gilbert, whose name has caused him to be mocked, making him timorous, easy meat for the Chief Justice. But he starts off fine with his proclamation that all witnesses must leave the courtroom until called upon to give evidence.

Perhaps fearing Ears will be of limited use at counsel table, Buddy seeks an exception for the case officer, asks if Jasper Flynn may sit up front to help with exhibits. Since the sergeant is to be the Crown's first witness, Arthur has no objection, and the officer ambles ponderously to the table. That leaves it overbalanced, a crowd at one end, Arthur friendless.

As Sheriff Willit leads the jury panel into court, Arthur watches for smiles, signals of benign temperament. Brian has crossed off names of those to be peremptorily challenged, one of them shown in the city directory to be a police officer's wife. But little else is known of this Vancouver hoi polloi. He has always preferred the U.S. system, where prospective jurors face friendly questioning.

"Read the charge," says Kroop.

Gilbert reads out the single count of murder. The burglary offences are to be tried later.

"Well, Mr. Gilbert?" says Kroop.

"Yes, sir?"

"Are you ready with the plea?"

"The plea, sir?" Gilbert may wonder if he's been mistaken for the accused.

"The plea. Where the accused does not answer, the court shall order the clerk to enter a plea. Section 602. Get on top of it, Mr. Gilbert, enter your plea."

"Not guilty, milord." He's flustered.

The process of empanelling the jury takes half the morning, Arthur exhausting all his challenges, eliminating one jeweller and two store managers, and using caution with anyone with expensive watches or decorations of gold, silver, or pearl.

He is satisfied with the final crop of seven women, five men, of age twenty-five to sixty-five, devoid of sourpusses. But not ethically balanced, Buddy seeming intent on standing aside anyone with a dark complexion or a suspect name such as Abdullah or Singh.

Buddy launches into his opening address, a workmanlike job, portraying the crime scene with sad-eyed solemnity, tracing with triumphant sarcasm the culprit's attempt to flee the scene, his pretence of being a Dutchwoman, his flight from justice and jail. He promises devastating evidence from Father Réchard but avoids mention of Adeline Angella, keeping her in his pocket, hoping the aging opponent in the other corner has overlooked this crucial aspect of his case.

The jury listens intently until Buddy picks up a sheaf of notes and begins a confusing explication of DNA profiling, and they lose all attention when tinny music sounds, two bars of "You Are My Sunshine." Arthur turns around, seeking its source, and sees smiles being stifled. The refrain repeats. Buddy stops midway through an exposition of vaginal smears.

"What is that infernal sound?" Kroop rasps.

Arthur is suddenly, abundantly aware that these incessant, simple chords are coming from his open briefcase on the floor. He pulls out a tangle of adapter cord, reeling in the phone as he might a fish, fumbles among the myriad buttons. A known voice speaks: "Yo, Arthur, what's happening, man?"

For a metaphysical few seconds, Arthur is transported to Blunder Bay. He knows a crisis is occurring. "Stoney? What the hell have you done now?" He shouts this, as if fearing the little device may not pick up his words.

"Hey, man, cool. I'm backhoeing your pond, okay, and suddenly there's this, like, stink coming from the septic field."

Arthur blinks, he's back in Court 67, goggling at this impertinent contrivance, trying to find a button that will take him off the air. Kroop seems rendered speechless, as if an affront has been committed that is beyond words of reproach, but there's loud laughter from the young lawyers in the pews.

"You at some kind of party? Sounds like a real donkey roast . . ." Ears comes to the rescue; Stoney is disconnected.

"Because of your hiatus from these courts, Mr. Beauchamp," says Kroop, "you might not have heard how I normally deal with cell-phone offenders. Repeaters are not given suspended sentences."

"My only defence, milord, is that I am telephonically challenged."

Kroop cranes his neck in a vain search for the person snickering. Arthur can only hope there is an upside to his inept display – hearts could go out to the outgunned old fellow at the end of the table; all the world loves one who flounders at skills they've mastered.

Kroop waves a hand in dismissal, as if flicking away a mosquito. "You have been warned." Arthur is surprised the judge didn't take off an inch of his skin.

Buddy tries to pick up where he left off, but loses his way when a page of his notes slips free and flutters to the floor. The remainder of his opening is a monotonic medley of the science of identifying deoxyribonucleic acid and the benzodiazepine called Rohypnol – it has the jury stirring in discomfort or staring at walls or, in a couple of cases, offering Arthur timid smiles. One of them is the foreperson, Ellen Sueda: a teacher, warm, intelligent eyes. Another is Martin Samples, third from the right in the back, who runs a Web site devoted to obscure noir films, which he rates on a five-star system. Maybe he will see Faloon as immersed in a Kafkaesque quagmire. Four and a half stars.

"We'll take the noon break," Kroop says.

Buddy follows Arthur out like a grouchy dog, snorting at his heels. "Don't tell me it wasn't set up, that freaking phone call. While I'm up there sweating." He continues on down the stairs. Stubb trots along behind him, with his pointless unabating smile.

✦

On the way to the El Beau Room, Arthur fiddles with his phone, determined to master it, dialling, holding it to his ear in imitation of several passersby, hearing it ring, feeling accomplished, modern.

One of the new Japanese Woofers answers and turns him over to Reverend Al, who has volunteered to run Bungle Bay for the next two weeks. Yes, Stoney is out there, at the controls of the backhoe, calling encouragement to Dog, who is replacing the shattered outflow pipes, up to his knees in fecal matter. It is a scene so evocative of the picaresque carnival of his island that Arthur feels a tickle of nostalgia.

Reverend Al tells him arrests have slowed in Gwendolyn Valley. Agile protestors have taken to climbing trees during predawn hours, and the RCMP are loath to pursue them. The tactic is to wait them out until they give themselves up at day's end. The Mounties have begun to see their endeavours as untypical of their many noble causes, and are showing signs of frustration – especially as the public mood is against them. This morning they busted Flim and Flam for getting in their faces with their cameras.

"Have there been any calls from, ah, overseas?"

"Nope."

Gaining confidence with the cellphone, Arthur rings Doris Isbister. No long-distance calls to his office either, a number Faloon committed to heart long ago.

Brian is waiting for him in the restaurant, drinking a potion called near-beer, which Arthur has always avoided: too near for him. Brian looks through the jurors' names. "I wonder if you want so many women, they sank you at Faloon's last trial." Eight women in that case, but the result was surely an aberration.

Brian has been on the line to Adeline Angella's priest – a flimsy ruse, an anonymous client seeking to remember the parish in his will. While chatting, he dropped the name of an acquaintance. Ms. Angella is one of his faithful, said the priest. He recalled that she won a prize at the April 1 bingo, a gift certificate from a flower shop.

"'How lovely,' I said as my heart was sinking into the mud. But let us pray. The bingo started at noon, and she owns a car, a little Chev. After doing the dirty, she could have caught a morning ferry to Vancouver."

Assuming she found a way to cross the Bamfield Inlet at two o'clock in the morning. How might she have done that?

As Arthur returns to the Law Courts, "You Are My Sunshine" burbles merrily from his suit jacket pocket.

"Reporting in." Lotis Rudnicki in Victoria, taking a breather from court. Mewhort released Flim and Flam without conditions after a lawyer for the Civil Liberties Association carried on about irresponsible and baseless arrests of journalists. "Only three other new cases, the cops are pooping out."

At the Law Courts, he remembers to turn his phone off.

✦

Buddy stands by the jury box, shifting on his toes, peppier than when last seen, ready to parry more low blows. "The Crown calls Staff Sergeant Jasper Flynn."

The officer takes the oath, standing tall and square-jawed. Arthur hopes to make some hay with his sloppiness at the crime scene. A dumb cop, Buddy said, yet he seems disposed to lean on him for help.

The witness establishes his credentials: on the force for nineteen years, a staff sergeant for three, based in Port Alberni for the last eight months.

"And before that?"

"Here at Thirty-third and Heather, General Investigation Section, Serious Crime Unit. I liaised with some of the outlying detachments, co-ordinating evidence."

"You have a family?"

"Two strapping boys, fourteen and sixteen."

"And you're a kids' hockey coach?"

"Yes, sir."

"And you've done volunteer work in schools?"

"I've done about fifty school visits, talking to kids in class."

This is to arm Flynn against what's to come, his sheltering of Holly Hoover. Arthur dares not object, but Kroop saves him from having to. "We have only two weeks, Mr. Svabo."

"I note a couple of commendations on your . . ."

"*Please*, Mr. Prosecutor. We all accept that he's a sterling fellow."

Pleased with that gift, Buddy desists. "All right, is the Village of Bamfield within your jurisdiction?"

"Yes."

Area maps are produced, showing the long bent finger of Alberni Inlet, the web of logging roads that lead to Bamfield. Photographs of the Breakers Inn, Nitinat Lodge, Cotters' Cottage, the crime scene: Dr. Winters's body, supine, a puff of cotton extruding from her mouth, the undergarment that blocked her airway. Most jurors glance quickly at these photos, distressed, but Martin Samples, the film noir buff, studies them with narrow-eyed concentration.

Close-ups of the Chablis bottle, uncorked, about ten ounces remaining. A grey smear of fingerprint dust, suggesting the surface was wiped by a cloth. Two clean glasses in the sink. Near the fireplace, a chair with bra, jeans, an outdoors shirt. A bath towel lying loosely on the bed. In background, from the wall, the cougar stares malevolently.

The murder weapon is passed among the jurors in a zip-lock bag. Serums and blood samples will be identified later, but are given exhibit numbers. The swab with the suspect semen is 52.

Kroop makes no attempt to alter the flow, rarely seeking clarification. Ears remains an unnoticed fixture at counsel table. With his handsome ears and his habit of chewing the ends of pencils, he brings to mind a rabbit.

Flynn is prompted to describe his doings on April 1, arriving by launch with two officers, first stopping at the Breakers Inn to investigate the thefts, then trudging up the rutted road to the cottage.

Arthur can see why Buddy wanted Flynn at counsel table despite his missteps: he is well rehearsed, organized, relaxed, even amiable. This notorious trial is the highlight of the officer's career, and he's giving it his best.

After sealing the cottage and calling in the Ident Section, Flynn went to the Nitinat Lodge, missing Faloon but finding a makeup kit and, in a trunk, garments of disguise. When he finally returned to Alberni, Faloon was in the lockup, in women's garb. Efforts to take a statement were fruitless, the suspect staring close-mouthed at him.

Buddy shows photos of Faloon, staring moronically, pretending illness. "You'd met him before?"

"I introduced myself when I was posted to the area. Paid him a visit."

"Why?"

Arthur is on his feet. "Before the witness responds, may I suggest we give the jury time off for good behaviour? A break until tomorrow, it's been a long and tiring day." It is almost half past four, and Arthur is weary himself.

Kroop cautions the jury, sends them to their homes, then says, "What answer do you expect to your last question, Mr. Svabo?"

"Sergeant Flynn knew the accused had a horrific criminal record, including a previous brutal rape and scores of thefts and break-ins. So he was checking him out. Like any responsible officer." Almost imperceptibly, Flynn nods.

"I have often doubted the wisdom of the rule, Mr. Svabo, but evidence of previous misdeeds remains beyond the pale."

"This isn't just bad character. It's a lifestyle. Faloon has shown up on police blotters around the world. Banned from at least half a dozen hotels in this very city. It all points to him being the person who did a nighttime foray through the Breakers just before the murder."

"He's being prosecuted for a murder, not a lifestyle," says Arthur, but with only half a heart. The jury has heard about Faloon's disguises, they will hear about the gangland-style jail breakout. They will not think he is a paragon. Especially after Adeline Angella tells why she sought him out for an interview.

"The objection is sustained."

"Okay, I've run out of questions." Buddy isn't unhappy, he was merely hoping to prejudice the judge against Faloon, paint him in villainous colours.

After court breaks, Arthur watches Buddy and Ears give kudos to Flynn for his fault-free performance – and probably encouragement for tomorrow, when he'll undergo Arthur's first cross-examination in six years.

24

Again, on this grey morning, Arthur does his health walk, along the seawall to Brockton Point, where totems rise above the mist of dawn. He's more at ease now that he's wet his toes, got that first day behind him.

Back at Elysian Tower, he spends several minutes hunting for his reading glasses – they're under Plutarch, where he ought to have looked in the first place. He put down the essays last night upon finding new and distressing meaning in the famous proverb: *When the candles are out, all women are fair.*

Candles are the illuminators of choice for Margaret and her band of merry Robin Hoods, that's how they light their way to bed. He shivers with disgust at his insistent, ridiculous suspicions. *You're too young, darling, we have to stop doing this . . .* He's appalled at himself. The Annabelle Syndrome.

Margaret could have come home weeks ago, they smuggled the rope ladder back up. It's hubris and stubbornness that keep her in that tree. But now she must compete with Arthur Beauchamp for the rave reviews. Day Two!

✦

As the judge is summoned, Buddy Svabo leans to Arthur's ear. "After you're through with Flynn, I'd like to do the folks from Topeka. They're in the Hyatt, costing us a freaking fortune."

"Anything to help the struggling taxpayer." For whom Buddy isn't showing that much concern. He doesn't need half those witnesses.

Kroop enters, fluffs his robe, and settles like a contented hen on a nest. He'll grow more cantankerous as the trial progresses, but today he shows the jury a small puckered smile.

Buddy tells Flynn to retake the stand, and bows to Arthur. Be my guest.

"We'll be a few minutes," Arthur says, "so you may want to sit."

"Thanks, but I'll stand." Flynn, who was on his feet all yesterday afternoon, reacts by standing taller. The jury seems to have taken to the handsome, burly officer: forthright, easygoing, the sort of fellow who'll sit down with your teenager and straighten him out.

"Officer, the last time we saw each other was in Bamfield."

"That's right, sir, a couple of months ago."

"You had business there?"

"Routine patrol, as I recall. Some of the boys in the bar get boisterous on a Saturday night."

"Did you have a little chat that day with Holly Hoover?"

He purses his lips, and his generous moustache moves in concert. "I think I said hello to her."

"Is she the young lady who was sharing barstools with Dr. Winters only a few hours before she was murdered?" This is the first mention of Hoover to the jury; Arthur wants to put her in the picture quickly.

"That's right."

"In your report, you describe her as 'unemployed, single, a local.' The fact is, she's vigorously employed, is she not?"

Another twitch of moustache. "Not in a legitimate sense, I guess. She does a lot of entertaining of men."

"Less timidly put, she's a prostitute."

"I don't think she's ever been arrested for it. It seemed fairer to call her unemployed." The officer is showing decency, letting the jury know he's not one to add to a woman's soiled reputation.

"Surely you know she hires herself out to loggers up and down the coast from a boat called the *Holly Golly*?"

"Never had a complaint."

"Who would you expect to complain?"

Again Kroop fails to locate the perpetrator of a poorly smothered laugh. Buddy is in close, deep conference with Ears – can it be that Hoover's career as *demi-mondaine* comes as a surprise to them?

"Mr. Beauchamp, I cover a huge jurisdiction, I don't have a lot of manpower." A helpless face. "We have to concentrate on what bothers people most – property theft, assaults, domestic violence."

Arthur confronts Flynn with his snippet of a report about Hoover and Winters chatting about music, hiking, and the weather. "These pages don't offer the slightest hint Ms. Hoover operates a motorized bawdy house up and down the coast. Did you not think that may be of interest to this court?"

Buddy pops up. "He's trying to smear a witness we haven't even heard from."

"Is this going anywhere, Mr. Beauchamp, or is it merely a titillating digression?"

"The doings of this woman on the night of the murder are of considerable moment, milord. As is her relationship with this witness." He snaps his suspenders, a habit when he's about to zero in. He moves closer to Flynn, softens his voice. "Many of the good people of Bamfield believe she has an unofficial licence to carry on her business."

"I don't issue such licences, Mr. Beauchamp."

"They say you're often seen talking to her."

"I talk to a lot of people."

"In fact, you look her up every time you come to Bamfield."

"We bump into each other."

"Yes, at her home and on the *Holly Golly*."

Flynn may not know Arthur is merely surmising, and he looks at Buddy, finds no help. "Once in a while. Just to talk."

Arthur pauses, letting the jury play with their speculations. A woman in the back looks offended, either at Flynn for being chummy with this Magdalene or at Arthur for his lewd insinuation.

"I'm in a tough spot here," says Flynn.

He looks pleadingly at Buddy, who bounces up, too eagerly, to make rescue. "All right, I didn't want it to come out, but after these snide innuendos, I can't see any way around it. If this puts Miss Hoover in danger, it's on Mr. Beauchamp's head. Sergeant Flynn will have to explain the true nature of the relationship."

"Holly Hoover is a police informant," Flynn says.

Arthur has underestimated Buddy's wile, he ought to have known this was coming. An innocent explanation for their many meetings, for Flynn's mollycoddling, his house calls.

Buddy presses his advantage. "Sergeant Flynn meets regularly with her in Bamfield, sometimes privately, sometimes in public. It looks like he's cautioning or hassling her. Not. He's receiving vital crime-stopping information."

Instead of objecting, Arthur wades into battle. "Nonsense. This case aside, there's hardly been a crime worth stopping in Bamfield for the last twenty years. Are we to believe this woman earns the officer's generous leniency by snitching on hunters who bag deer out of season? Everyone in town knows about the cozy arrangement between him and his so-called informant, and she's under no threat whatsoever."

"You are flagrantly out of order," Kroop says. "Let's get back on track, Mr. Beauchamp."

Arthur is chafing at having the rug pulled out from under him. Hoover probably does feed information to Flynn in exchange for his winks and nods, it's smart police work. The jury may well resent Arthur for portraying this dutiful family man as a lecher on the take. Buddy had prepared Flynn well, advised him to take a few blows, bob and weave, then land a haymaker.

"Officer, how many times have you met with Ms. Hoover since the murder?"

"Two, three times. I took an initial statement from her that day."

"From which you learned she was the last person to see Dr. Winters alive?"

"Except the killer." He's confident now.

Arthur flutters a page of Flynn's evidence summary. "And this is all she had to say? A bit of inconsequential chat at the bar of a public house."

"Yes, but she told me only half the story. About a week later she gave me the long version. About how she met Dr. Winters outside the bar, and they went by canoe to West Bamfield."

Hearsay by the carload. But it's Arthur's fault, he has opened it up. He must stay on the attack. "I put it to you, officer, that you sought to dissuade her from admitting to this."

"I certainly did not."

"You told her to stick to the short version and not complicate matters."

"I told her just the opposite. The conversation's in my notes, and I copied them to Mr. Svabo."

Arthur struggles not to show his distress, turns to Buddy.

"Don't look at me," Buddy says. "I sent a letter of further particulars, let's see . . ." He bends, whispering to Ears, who shuffles through a file and hands him a memo. "On April 7, to Mr. Brian Pomeroy, when he was still acting for the accused."

This cross-examination is turning into a disaster. Pomeroy, the inattentive ex-dissolute, is to blame, too engaged in marital strife to read his mail.

Kroop has enjoyed watching Arthur squirm, but reluctantly orders a break. Arthur needs it, a chance to retool. As the jury is led out, he sees disappointed looks from the counsel who came to watch the storied barrister in action.

Buddy hands Arthur a photocopy of Flynn's handwritten notes. "I thought you had all this stuff."

The notes back up the witness's account: "Hoover attended Alberni h.q. 14:15 hours to see undersigned having 'remembered' she took deceased by canoe across inlet around 22:00 on prior 31 March. Because of rain, 'we didn't dawdle' and not much conversation except deceased couldn't wait to get out of wet clothes. Undersigned warned Hoover re withholding material evidence. She refused to sign statement until talked to lawyer."

A version sketchier than the one she confided on that stormy night the lights went out at Brady Beach. No mention of Winters's invitation to extend the evening over a glass of wine.

Again he reminds himself that this will matter little in the end. He's merely spreading manure across the field, an odour for Buddy and Ears to sniff at, to distract them from Adeline Angella's pungent Fantaisie.

Bolstered by that thought, he sticks it out, hoping to pick up the pieces of his cross-examination. When Flynn resumes the stand, he prods him about his threat to charge Hoover with obstructing justice.

"Why did you stay your hand?"

"I guess I figured no harm was done. Anyway, she had a right to see a lawyer and get advice on her situation, and I assume she did that."

"She talked to a lawyer?"

"On Saturday, April 15, I saw her leaving the licensed premises with a six-pack of cider. I asked her where she was going. She said she was on her way to talk to you, Mr. Beauchamp."

Her tongue in his ear, her hand between his legs, the clams roiling in his gut. Flustered, he can only ask, "Did you have any other dealings with her?"

"Just to serve a subpoena on her."

Arthur shuffles through notes, unsure where to pick up. "Ms. Hoover claimed to *remember* paddling across the inlet with Dr. Winters?"

"*Remember* was the word she used."

"And didn't she also remember Dr. Winters invited her to join her at the cottage for some wine?"

The question causes a stir among the press and brings Buddy bouncing on his toes. "Mr. Beauchamp's trying to sneak in a wild theory by the back door. It's all hearsay."

"It's hearsay, Mr. Svabo, but we should give Mr. Beauchamp leeway, don't you think, given the obstacles he's encountering?" A patronizing knife. "What's the answer, officer?"

"She didn't say anything like that. But she tends to remember things when she wants to."

This is going nowhere. Arthur must find a less-travelled road, where the potholes aren't as treacherous. "Whatever she might have said, someone was being entertained in Dr. Winters's cabin that night.

The bottle of Chablis and the glasses in the sink might suggest she had a guest, do you agree?"

"It's possible."

"Hardly likely that she would be sharing wine with an intruder."

"I couldn't say, sir."

"Who might very easily have slipped a few tablets of Rohypnol into her wine."

"Yes, but someone could also have sneaked in and done that."

"A garment stuffed down the victim's throat – an odd means of suffocating someone, do you agree?"

"I guess so." Flynn twiddles that moustache.

"Ever heard of anything similar in a murder investigation?"

A shrug. "I can't bring anything to mind."

"You've told us you found no fingerprints of interest. None of the accused."

"That's right, but the glasses had been washed, and the bottle wiped, it looked like."

"You have a knack for answering questions I haven't asked."

"Oh, come now, Mr. Beauchamp," Kroop says, "he's doing his best."

"Then he doesn't need any help from the court."

"This court does not take sides."

Arthur wants to have it out with him, make the jury aware that behind a facade of fairness lurks a partisan for the prosecution, with a bias showing like poorly tucked-in underwear. But he must not let his temper get the best of him, for now he'll take his licks.

"All but two prints came from known individuals, as you put it. From whom, precisely?"

"The deceased, of course. There were quite a few of hers. Inez Cotter, the owner of the cottage. And two of the women who had been hiking the trail with Dr. Winters."

"And who else?"

"Well, Constable Beasely and I were the first into the cottage – that's after we looked through the window – and we rushed straight to the bedroom, and I guess we didn't put gloves on right away. So there's a few of mine, and a couple of Beasely's."

Arthur can't make headway even on this trifling irrelevancy. An accusation of careless police work would be seen as a cheap shot from an exasperated lawyer – the sergeant is human, he'd just seen a shocking sight.

"No prints from Holly Hoover?"

"I'm afraid not, sir." The condescending smile grates.

"What about the third woman hiker?"

Flynn consults his notes. "That would be Ruth Delvechio. No prints from her."

Finally, a point for the defence. The embittered Ruth Delvechio, graduate student, tossed away like a worn toy by the imperious Doctor Eve. *It's over, Ruth. Ef you, your effing highness.* A last sharing of wine. Afterwards, the glasses washed, her prints wiped. A plausible script?

"Officer, I understand Ruth Delvechio was in a relationship with Dr. Winters." The deceased's homosexuality has been well reported by now. She hadn't hid it, hadn't advertised it.

"Yes, from what I've learned."

"In your report you refer to the other two women as, quote, admitted lesbians." Buddy winces, and Ears's smile sits marooned on his face.

"That was a tasteless choice of words, Mr. Beauchamp. I guess what I meant to say is they were open about it."

"They've lived together for several years, correct? Dr. Glynis Bloom and Wilma Quong."

"They said that."

"And Dr. Winters and Ruth Delvechio made up another pairing."

"I guess so."

"And you received a report that those two had a brouhaha in the cottage."

"I heard something from Mrs. Cotter about a quarrel. I didn't think it unusual. Lots of people fight. Friends and couples fight."

"Though both the victim and accused dined at the Breakers Inn, you went first to Cotters' Cottage."

"Yes, I found out where Dr. Winters was staying, and myself and two members went there on foot."

"Much closer, though, was the small lodge where the accused lived, the Nitinat."

"That's true."

"And it's fair to say that Mr. Faloon was high on your list of suspects?" Arthur may as well put Faloon's past on the table. *Vir prudens non contra ventum mingit.* A wise man does not piss against the wind.

"He was the number-one suspect, yes."

"So why didn't you dispatch either of your officers to the Nitinat?"

"There was a thief in town. We didn't know if he was dangerous. Our first concern was Dr. Winters."

An unresponsive answer, but a good one. Arthur has rarely encountered such a well-prepared witness. A dumb cop, said Buddy. Not.

"You couldn't send one of the constables there?"

"That would go against procedure. He wouldn't have backup."

"An officer needs backup for puny Nicholas Faloon? He can't weigh more than – what do you have him at, about a hundred and thirty pounds?"

"About that. A little over fifty-eight kilograms."

"Five and a half feet in height?"

"Yes."

"And Dr. Winters was at least four inches taller?"

"She was about five-ten, yes."

"And extremely fit? An athletic woman?"

"I wouldn't argue."

"There were no signs that the victim suffered any debilitating blows to the head or body? Nothing to render her helpless or unconscious?"

Kroop interjects. "Mr. Beauchamp, you're forgetting about the date-rape drug. What's the name . . . Rohypnol."

"Thank you, milord, for your invaluable assistance." Arthur's icy stare is returned in kind.

Arthur is tempted to needle Flynn about his negligence in skipping past Angella's name in Winters's records. But the urge comes from a childish wish to pay him back, and he quickly suppresses it. "No more questions."

"We'll break for lunch," Kroop says.

✦

Arthur takes a long walk up Burrard Street to the art deco bridge that straddles False Creek. He's not hungry, and he wants to avoid pitying eyes in the El Beau Room – all will have heard about the debacle in Court 67. He should consult Brian Pomeroy, but doesn't want to deal with his blunt wit. Nor can he bring himself to call Lotis.

He can't remember when a cross-examination so backfired. His earlier doubts are verified, his courtroom skills have rusted up and seized, his one great talent has gone stale, frittered away on songbirds and roadside poppies and daily hikes to the General Store.

Only the prospect of returning, even in shame, to his island retirement stays him from total wretchedness. It's not that Flynn blunted the secret weapon, Angella, but that Arthur's pride has been bruised – he was outduelled in the arena where once he was king. He ought not to have taken on Flynn at such length, should have shied away from the profitless wrangle about Hoover.

He looks down at the tide-bloated inlet. "Shit!" This brings a flurry of pigeons flapping from under the bridge.

✦

Before court resumes, Buddy sidles up to Arthur again. "Change of plan. I'm going to do some forensics this afternoon."

"What about the Topekans and their huge bills at the Hyatt?"

"A few administrative problems have cropped up." That is so vague as to be meaningless, but Buddy doesn't clarify and Arthur doesn't ask.

The day is taken up by experts in DNA, serum, and blood analysis, who seem unready, resentful at having been moved up the list. The jury labours hard, trying to follow the biochemical jargon, the mixing solutions and reactive agents, extraction and precipitation, swabs and smears and stains, the chain of custody from crime scene to lab. Ears, assigned the task of leading these witnesses, is having trouble coping with the complexities of DNA.

Arthur has declined to make things simple by admitting any of these facts — he's stalling for time in the fast-fading hope that Nick Faloon will burst on the scene in all his owlish glory.

✦

For some reason — his loneliness, his dull, dispirited performance — Arthur feels his alcoholism acting up as he waits for an elevator at Tragger Inglis Bullingham. He has been avoiding his old office, hiding from Bully and his crusade to drag the deserter back to the front lines. He must also avoid the partners' lounge, where Messrs. Schenley, Seagram, and Walker wait in ambush behind the bar.

He sneaks into the library, where wizened Ed Riley is burrowed into a hill of case law. "Something on continuity of forensic exhibits, please, Riley." The analysts had problems identifying a few of the zippered plastic exhibit bags. The jury might be persuaded some were mixed up, a desperation defence.

His old office is used by visiting rainmakers, lawyers, business leaders, but otherwise the firm has kept it empty, like a mausoleum. Which, as Bullingham frequently reminds him, is yearning for his presence. Doris Isbister maintains it as is, the Lismer on the wall, the Etruscan prints, degrees academic and honorary, the cabinet with his clippings, the immaculate desk with legal pad, ready jar of pens and pencils . . . and now a computer.

They tried to set him up with one years ago, but after several trials he demanded they remove the ugly mechanism — a TV with keyboard. The complexities seemed designed in hell. Keats didn't need a computer. Nor did Beethoven. Nor, for that, did Clarence Darrow.

He calls Doris in, a mistake has been made. She gives him a peck on the cheek and tells him he's being silly, everyone works with a computer today. Documents are transferred this way. Firms and friends e-mail each other. He is no longer simple Arthur Beauchamp, he is Beauchamp at TraggerInglis dot com.

She passes him a book, *The Idiot's Guide to Computing*. "This is a mouse. Click it here and see what happens."

The screen goes white. A list of messages appears on it. Doris shows him how to open the first one, from the computer company congratulating him on his purchase. She lets him open another – it's from the entire staff of Tragger Inglis, welcoming him back. Suspicion fastens on Bullingham.

"I'll leave you to it, dear." Forcing him to swim on his own. She pauses at the door, speaks meaningless garble. "Dual 64 G5, two point five gigs."

Arthur moves the mouse, and arcane symbols appear at the bottom of the screen. He has heard of computers hanging up at the mere touch of a key, viruses, massive erasure of files, he must be careful. The next message is from Pomeroy and Company. "I am sick at heart, maestro, I just found this hiding in the bowels of my computer." A copy of Sergeant Flynn's missing addendum about Holly Hoover ferrying Winters across the inlet.

Lotis too has learned he's computerized. "I've been Googling DNA. The science is advancing exponentially, all they need is a flake of dandruff, a bead of sweat, a partial fingerprint." There follows a line lifted from a forensics text: *Vaginal swabs or stain from post-coital drainage will typically contain sperm cells mixed with vaginal cells.*

She concludes: "Just in case Angella did keep Nick's discharge in her sperm bank, we should ask Dr. Sidhoo to have another look at the sample. I'll call tonight and we'll kick it through."

Maybe computers have their uses after all – Arthur had almost given up on that theory. The Case of the Loosely Fitted Condom. Or it may have broken, as Lotis suggested. Probably a dead end. Arthur prefers the looter-in-the-trash idea.

Here's a final message, from one Richard Stiffe. Does Arthur know a Richard Stiffe? He reads with alarm: "Your credit card will be billed at $22.95 weekly. A free CD three-pack of *Sultry Sexteens* is shipping to your billing address. Please confirm . . ."

A hideous case of mistaken identity? Was this intended for a different, shameless Beauchamp? He is halfway across the room to summon Doris when he stops, feeling foolish. Junk mail. It floods the computer-driven society. This is the brave new world.

◆

That evening, he watches the news hour on Hubbell Meyerson's wall-mounted, flat-screen television. The trial's coverage leans to the lurid, quoting Arthur's lines: "floating bordello," "the cozy arrangement" between hooker and cop. Viewers may get the false impression Arthur came out unscathed.

Lotis phones to say Dr. Sidhoo has actually found a trace of an unknown third person in the semen sample, and will try to build a DNA profile. Ruth Delvechio? Someone else with whom Eve may have been intimate? Or Adeline Angella? The tissues Brian pocketed during her crying jag will provide a control sample.

Arthur has only a scant knowledge of microbiology, and can't imagine how an analyst might find a sprinkling of vaginal cells in a bit of swab. But he supposes there may be tens of thousands of the little beasties there. Lotis has assured him an expert can build a profile from the most minute specimens.

"Hey, according to the news, you shot out the lights today."

Not.

25

Exhaustion imprisons Arthur in his bed until half past seven — he's rising later each day, adjusting to the rhythm of the city. He squints at the pen drawings, a man's head buried between a woman's splayed legs, then rolls awkwardly from bed.

Bagels, tea, and morning paper. He refuses to read about his disaster in Court 67. Gwendolyn is buried in the middle pages, six more arrests. Trial dates for the protestors are clogging the court calendars. The authorities are fast running out of leg bracelets for their electric monitoring program. Something is going to have to give.

As spied upon last week through powerful binoculars, Margaret looked thin, wasted, ragged. His badgering note about her physical and emotional health, her state of comfort and cleanliness, got this airmail response: *Arthur, you must stop worrying about me. I'm better off than hundreds of millions of women on this planet.* She's keeping in shape, she's equipped, harnessed, she's been in the canopy, it's exhilarating.

He's too late for his morning safari to Lord Stanley's park, but has time to stride briskly to the Law Courts through the dense checkerboard of the West End. The day of summer solstice blooms warm under filaments of fading mist, a day when he ought to be picking asparagus, not enduring the bitter harvest of the courtroom.

A news camera follows him up the courthouse steps. He smiles, waves, assumes a guise of confidence.

Before court sits, Buddy, his manifest of witnesses already in disarray, announces another schedule change. "The pathologist asked if I'd move her ahead. Not, I said, I have some heavy-hitters due up. But it turns out she's got a trial conflict. So I guess we'll have to get to the good folks from Kansas when we get to them."

This procrastination argues something has gone askew. Yesterday these good folks were costing a freaking fortune, now they'll bide their time.

Dr. Rosa Sanchez has added grey to her hair since Arthur last met her. A senior forensic pathologist, competent and casual, she lacks the stiff mannerism of many professional witnesses. She's helpful to juries, translating medical jargon into recognizable English.

Buddy Svabo rushes her through the autopsy, as if finding it morbid or tasteless, then asks her opinion on the cause of death.

"Asphyxia due to occlusion of the trachea. In simple terms, her airway was blocked and she expired for lack of oxygen."

The indicia included heart congestion and cyanosis: blue discolouring of the lips, which were also marked by slight contusions. Not severe enough to be caused by a blow to the mouth, nor bearing any relation to the chipped front tooth. Both wrists had minor abrasions, as if pressure had been applied. No other soft tissue injury other than light bruising around the lower abdomen.

"Given that her blood alcohol reading was .04 at the time of death and that she'd been consuming wine, what conclusions do you draw?"

"That reading would be consistent with her having had three or four glasses of wine within the previous two hours."

"But on top of that, we have . . ." Buddy struggles with a word from her report. "Flunitrazepam . . . I'll use the trade name, Rohypnol. Tell us about that."

This potent sedative, she explains, is on the banned list here but used in Europe and in Latin America, most often as a sleeping pill, but occasionally as an anaesthetic. Its use as a date-rape drug is widely known. It may cause impaired judgment and motor skills, short-term memory loss, blackouts, and even coma. "The intensity of effect depends on dosage, elapsed time after ingestion, and varies with the individual."

"Okay, given that this drug was found in Dr. Winters's bloodstream, what can you tell us about how much she ingested?"

"That's a hard one. Flunitrazepam metabolizes rapidly. We don't know when she ingested it."

"Okay, let's say Mr. Stubb here – he's about Dr. Winters's height – let's say he popped a couple of . . . what are they, a milligram each?"

"They come in one or two milligrams."

"Will he black out if he takes, say, more than three milligrams?" Perhaps concerned that Buddy will pull out a packet of rochies and employ him as lab rat, Ears drops a half-chewed pencil and becomes comalike himself, a smiling upright cadaver.

Dr. Sanchez studies Ears for a moment. "Yes, he might. But the deceased may have been semi-conscious and putting up at least token resistance. The abrasions to the wrists and chipped tooth suggest that."

"Excuse me." Buddy huddles with his coach, Jasper Flynn, who sends in a new play. "Okay, the light bruising around the lower abdomen. Could she have received a blow to the stomach?"

"It is possible."

"A blow that could have incapacitated her?" Buddy boldly demonstrates, a low, sweeping uppercut.

"At least temporarily."

"Especially when her senses were already dulled by this powerful drug?"

"Yes."

"And she could have been gasping, out of breath?"

"The resulting trauma could have been that severe, it is difficult to say."

"And the bruising to the wrists, is that consistent with an assailant seizing and gripping them tightly?"

"Possibly but not likely. The bruising was solely on the interior aspect of her wrists, near her palms."

"Well, let's say she's on her back, and he's straddling her, kneeling on her wrists, and she's struggling to free herself." Buddy illustrates with another visual graphic, turning again to his junior counsel with an apelike posture, knees bent. Ears makes himself small, fearing he will be called upon to play the role of Eve Winters. "And her horrible nightmare ends when he stuffs the panties down her throat."

Making objection to these dramatics would only signal Arthur's concern and give this theory added stress. Martin Samples is awed by Buddy's shtick, a *coup de théâtre* transcending anything seen on film. However clownish and gruesome, the mime will indelibly remain with the jury: a credible reason why Winters, already woozy with Rohypnol, was unable to resist, to push or scratch or flail or kick. It explains the lack of defensive wounds, of fingernail scrapings, of blood stains, of hair pulled out by the roots.

Could Adeline Angella have delivered such an incapacitating blow to the solar plexus? A picture of this uptight, tidy woman performing with such violence refuses to take on definition. The chipped tooth bothers Arthur. It's as if she had bitten not a finger but something hard, metallic.

In cross-examination, Arthur stresses the minimal nature of the injuries. Dr. Sanchez agrees they could have been sustained on the trail, from slips and falls on roots and creekbed rocks.

"No trauma to the vaginal area?"

"No, there wasn't."

"In fact there was no bruising anywhere on her body that might normally be associated with a violent sexual assault, isn't that so?" The point is vital to his case that Eve Winters wasn't raped.

"I would agree, Mr. Beauchamp."

"Thank you."

Kroop, sensing a possible hole in the Crown's case, moves to plug it: "Clarify for me, doctor – would you expect bruising to the deceased's private parts if, during copulation, she was beyond all mortal capacity to resist her assailant?"

Dr. Sanchez looks around as if for help. "I'm . . . sorry, my lord, I didn't follow that very well."

"If she were dead."

Behind Arthur, someone sucks in air. Sanchez responds with a shrug. "With all the variables, I couldn't say."

A telling reminder of why judges ought to stay out of the fray. Some jurors look slightly irritated by his Lordship's crude intervention. Martin Samples, however, enjoys this black moment, a barely hidden smile.

"May I be allowed to continue, milord?" Arthur's faux politeness causes someone in the gallery to snort.

"Do so, and don't make a major issue of it." Kroop is hunched back, scowling at Arthur with his ferrite eyes, blaming him, as if he engineered the awkward moment.

Arthur establishes Rohypnol's notoriety as a tool of sexual predators, and asks Dr. Sanchez if it can lead to death.

"Yes. Particularly when mixed with alcohol, Rohypnol may cause respiratory depression, aspiration, or even death."

"And certainly coma."

"Yes."

"And there is no way to be certain that Dr. Winters was conscious when she was asphyxiated."

"I can't dispute that."

"It's a uniquely powerful sleeping pill?"

"Yes, used mainly for sleep disorders."

"Such as?"

"Insomnia, recurrent sleepwalking."

The one question too many. *You're not supposed to ask.* Arthur spins out his examination for a few minutes in an effort to bury the last answer, then packs it in. Nick Faloon wasn't using medication for sleepwalking . . . Or was he? Did anyone bother to ask him?

Still avoiding the Topekans, Buddy brings in Constable Beasely, Flynn's sidekick. He adds little but an echo of evidence heard. Beasely at the Breakers Inn, Beasely at the crime scene, Beasely at the Nitinat Lodge. Beasely finding nothing. Certainly no Rohypnol.

After Buddy's store of questions is exhausted, he looks pleadingly at Arthur to take up the slack with cross-examination. "No questions," Arthur says.

Buddy must clear his throat before addressing the judge. "I'm afraid that's all I have for this morning."

"Mr. Svabo, are you saying you have run out of witnesses?"

"At this point in time."

"Mr. Prosecutor, at this point in time we are about to take the morning break. When we return in fifteen minutes I expect the stand to be occupied by a person prepared to give relevant testimony."

He leaves, shaking his head. Kroop detests incompetence, abhors clumsy prosecutions, and might be incited to start sniping at the Crown. *Carpe diem.*

While the prosecution joins in frantic, three-headed debate, Arthur slips out to crack open the door of the witness room. It's full of Topekans.

◆

Still buying time for some unstated reason, the Crown has dredged the holding cells in the bowels of the Law Courts, where Father Yvon Réchard has been awaiting his call to duty. This bald, lugubrious penitent lacks the collar, but has been permitted a black suit. He has a haunted expression – as if knowing he's hellbound. *Fallen, like myself, so far from grace.* He takes the oath with the Bible in both hands.

Buddy lightly touches on Réchard's sinning ways – the jury learns only that he's awaiting sentence on morals offences. Ellen Sueda, who is Catholic and instructs grade fivers, is already looking at him coldly, perhaps guessing the worst. Jasper Flynn is bent over a pad, doodling, fretful about this unsavoury witness.

As Réchard recounts talking to Faloon about faith and philosophy, his lawyer makes clamorous entry, still knotting his tie, face muscles bunched with indignation. Howie Solyshn, known as the Dealmaker, a large, loud, and windy rascal. He steams past the bar of the court, roaring at Réchard. "Don't say another word!" The witness recoils.

"What are you doing here, Mr. Solyshn?" Kroop's eyes have sunk into their sockets.

"I represent Father Réchard, who I was assured was not on today's witness list."

"You have no standing at this trial."

"I have every right to advise my client about self-incrimination."

"You would interrupt the proceedings of this court and have the jury twiddling their thumbs while you finally instruct a client who has been ten weeks under subpoena. Ample opportunity, Mr. Solyshn."

"I'm making a motion to adjourn."

"I cannot hear your motion. I cannot hear *you*." With each syllable, Kroop's voice rises. "You do not have standing. So sit down!" A screech.

Resigned to his fate, the rambunctious Dealmaker plumps down on the bench behind Arthur.

Buddy must now go into bullying mode with Réchard, who's been so cowed that his voice has dropped, his words less intelligible, his French accent more pronounced. Haltingly, he tells of finding Faloon in a pensive mood one day, inviting him to unburden himself, then taking confession several hours later. Réchard glances at Arthur, at Solyshn, a silent plea for mercy.

Arthur has a perfectly valid explanation for Faloon's words: *She was beautiful, I just couldn't help myself.* He was sleepwalking, sleeptalking, his unconscious mind on his guilty night with Holly Hoover. But Arthur won't rely on that. More profit lies elsewhere.

To Buddy's final question, Réchard repeats a phrase from his statement: "I felt it was my duty to come forward."

A tap on Arthur's shoulder, the smell of Solyshn's salty breath. "Help me here, pal, ask for a recess."

Arthur stares him back into his seat, rises to face Réchard. Shallow breathing. A repeated grimace, like a tic. Staring at his hands.

"You felt it your duty to come forward. Pity you didn't feel such a citizen's duty about your own crimes. Look at me!" Réchard does so with difficulty. Arthur snaps his suspenders. "Witness, one of the reasons you're in jail is that eighteen years ago you sodomized an eleven-year-old boy who was in your care."

"That's one of the . . . yes."

"This occurred at a Native school where, among other subjects, you taught religion. The words of Jesus Christ."

"Yes."

"As well, you're charged with forcibly using a nine-year-old the following year."

"I face that charge too, yes."

"You're *guilty* of it."

"Yes. I am. Yes."

In this manner, occasionally seeking elaboration, Arthur takes him through each of his seven counts. Still sour at the priest's presumptuous lawyer, Kroop lets Arthur run unleashed. Jurors are looking askance at the witness. The press is busy, but the gallery still. Neither Buddy, the pencil beaver, or the doodler dares look up.

"And you pleaded guilty to these seven charges?"

"I did."

"There was a plea bargain? The Crown dropped another eight charges?"

"I would not say a bargain . . . Okay, yes." This after a furtive look at his lawyer.

"When did you enter these guilty pleas?"

"I think maybe late in March."

"Three months ago. Some in this room may be wondering why it's taken so long to get you properly put away." A low rumble of assent from the public area. "If you perform for the Crown here today in Court 67, you'll earn a recommendation of leniency. Am I not correct?" His voice has been rising.

He doesn't catch Réchard's full response, only the words, "He told me to . . ."

"With the coin of perjured testimony, you expect to buy early freedom from your crimes against innocent children, is that not the deal?"

Arthur is building to a crescendo, but already there's surprising impact: the witness has turned white, is rising from his chair. He extends a shaky arm, points to the Dealmaker. "He told me to do it." Réchard looks pleadingly at Arthur, at Kroop, like a friendless begging dog. "I didn't want to."

"Hold on there, partner." Howie Solyshn is back on his feet, fingers of both hands curled tightly, as if around a neck.

"Mr. Sheriff, please escort Mr. Solyshn from this courtroom."

Solyshn glares at the judge, waves off Barney Willit, and strides angrily away.

"You made me do it," the ex-priest calls.

"No more questions." One of the great skills of cross-examination is knowing when to stop.

"Take him away," says Kroop. He has the politeness to wait until Réchard is removed before saying, "Disgusting, Mr. Svabo. Disgusting."

Arthur feels much recovered from yesterday's debacle. The jury must be wondering why Buddy would be so desperate as to call that fellow.

Buddy is fixed on the clock, as if willing the hands to move. Kroop has his pencil poised, ready to fill more pages of his journal. "Mr. Svabo, please get on with your case, we have twenty minutes of precious time left."

"I thought Mr. Beauchamp would take up the rest of the morning."

"Well, he didn't, did he? May I be so bold as to ask why you keep running out of witnesses?"

Arthur rises. "If I can be of help, I saw several of them in the witness room. U.S. citizens whom the Canadian taxpayer is lavishly hosting in the Hyatt Hotel."

Buddy is boxed in. "Okay, call Mr. Karlsen." He gives Ears a wag of the head, tells him to fetch. Kroop continues to glower at Buddy through the ensuing minute of silence before Ears leads in the first of the Topekans, a meaty businessman who keeps looking at his watch as if he has a plane to catch.

Arthur must concentrate, he is almost too buoyed up to focus on Karlsen's fishing holiday. He and his group booked five days of trolling in Barkley Sound and lounging at the Breakers Inn. They didn't otherwise bestir themselves except to explore the boardwalk shops and visit Brady Beach. On Friday, two strangers joined them for dinner. From photographs, Karlsen identifies the nondescript little man in the owlish glasses and the comely blond therapist.

Karlsen noticed Faloon wasn't drinking and Winters was only sipping wine, though it otherwise flowed freely. He and his wife retired at about ten o'clock. He can't remember hearing anything that night but crashing surf. The thefts were discovered just before breakfast, the men comparing half-empty billfolds, initially blaming the owners and staff, demanding action, complaining about slow police response.

The thief didn't touch Mrs. Karlsen's five-thousand-dollar necklace, and Karlsen lost only two of the six thousand in his wallet. "Heck, I probably wouldn't even have noticed the money was gone if Harvey hadn't asked me to check my wallet."

Harvey Coolidge, who plunked himself beside Winters at dinner. Who likely asked where she was staying. Harvey Coolidge, who went out for a walk in the middle of the night. Arthur has no questions of Karlsen, he will wait for Coolidge.

✦

At lunch break, while walking to the Confederation Club, Arthur feels the old craving, a memory of martinis at noon, a tradition with his cronies. He can hear the shaker even before he enters the lounge, like music, a tambourine.

He's no longer a member but is welcomed as one. Indeed the maître d' almost weeps to see him. "We thought you'd given up on us, sir." Arthur is settled like an invalid into a plush chair beside his landlord, Hubbell Meyerson, just back from a trademark dispute in Shanghai. He raises his martini. "L'chayim." Arthur orders a Virgin Mary.

Hubbell expresses greeting-card sympathy over Arthur's wifeless ordeal, but can't smother a smile. Arthur supposes it's quite a joke among the profession, this spectacular uncoupling that extended through the lush, fertile spring. *Day Seventy-six! Read all about it! Tune in tomorrow!*

"Everything's all right with you and Margaret?"

"Yes, of course." Blurted.

"She's having the adventure of her life. People need to do that. At least one adventure."

What is he babbling about? Arthur regales him with Howie Solyshn's bad day. He imitates Réchard's pointed, shaking, bony finger. *You told me to say it.*

"Couldn't happen to a nicer shyster. Enjoying the apartment?"

"Better if I didn't wake every morning to the sight of engorged penises. I'm reminded of age and incapacity."

"Speak for yourself." Hubbell is a year older than Arthur, no fitter, but apparently lustier. "Early nineteenth-century art that inspires and instructs in the act of love. Pillow pictures, that's the term Anika uses. My designer, amazing woman." He waits until Arthur receives his bloodless Mary, lowers his voice. "Hope you won't need the apartment for the weekend."

"I shall be on Garibaldi Island."

"Good. Your lips are sealed. I have a little thing going on the side."

"Not with this Anika?"

"Mm-hmm."

"How ridiculous, Hubbell. You're a happily married man. A grandfather thrice over."

"She doesn't have a problem with that. She's married too. Very ... hormonal woman. Hasn't been getting enough of the you-know-what."

Arthur knows what. He's having another Annabelle moment. She had a voracious appetite too, but for young men. She was about Margaret's age when she married her conductor, fourteen years her junior ...

He has little appetite for lunch and less for listening to Hubbell's *elogium* to his reinvigorated manhood, aided by Viagra. Only ten bucks a pop. There's some in the medicine cabinet of 807 Elysian Tower. Arthur is encouraged to try one. A tester. Guaranteed to get a bone on. Take a couple. Arm himself for his reunion with Margaret. She won't be climbing any trees after that.

Arthur is shocked speechless. Viagra has turned his friend into a lecherous fool. Or is Arthur the fool for lagging behind the times when a marriage might be saved for ten bucks a pop?

◆

The parade of Topekans resumes at 2 p.m., portly middle-aged men and their thinner weight-watching wives, all dressed up for the occasion and anxious to please. Arthur senses their affront that Eve Winters ignored them at dinner in favour of Faloon, who in turn was ignored by all but a former insurance executive who recalls Faloon saying he was retired from the jewellery business.

His sharp-eared wife overheard snatches of conversation between Faloon and Winters. "Not that I was trying to listen, they were talking quite low. But she was going on about her hike, and the cabin where she was staying, funky, she called it. And she asked him if she could find any fun in Bamfield – that's the word she used, fun – and I heard him give directions to some kind of place with music. She gave him her card."

"Dinner was very jolly," another woman testifies. "When I learned what happened to that poor thing I was . . . well, I'm still in a state of shock. She was so . . . regal."

Harvey Coolidge has yet to take his turn, and Arthur has few questions for the others, who seem disappointed, snubbed again. Ingrid Coolidge is the seventh Topekan to take the stand: attractive, mid-thirties, a trophy wife of the wealthy developer, her senior by two decades.

After retiring to bed, her husband became restless – too much wine, an acid stomach – and went out for a walk. She stirred awake when he returned. She can't say how long he was gone. Nothing else disturbed her in the night. In the morning, he pulled his moneybelt from under his pillow and, upon discovering a "considerable sum" was missing, raised a hue and cry.

"How much was this considerable sum?" Buddy asks.

"I . . . can't be sure. Harvey handled all our financial matters."

Forty thousand dollars, by his account. Twenty-five by Faloon's. A hint of cozenage. Arthur will ask if he had theft insurance – he may have hoped to cover a hefty deductible. One who is dishonest in small matters may be unscrupulously venal when larger issues are at risk. *Falsus in uno, falsus in omnibus.*

In cross, Arthur hones in on the amount lost: "I expect your husband will say he was out of pocket by forty thousand U.S. dollars. Does that sound right?"

"That's what he said."

"Do you doubt it?"

"I don't know."

She doesn't always trust his word. "Some twenty-five thousand remained in his moneybelt the next morning?"

"Yes, he counted it out."

"So altogether he was carrying sixty-five thousand. Where in this tiny village could anyone expect to spend that much?"

"I think he just closed a deal on a condo unit."

"A down payment in cash?"

"He never bothered me with the money aspects of business."

"One assumes he keeps a bank account."

"I don't know much about it, I'm sorry."

Arthur shares the suspicion that shows on many jurors' faces. The conclusion seems unavoidable that Coolidge treats the IRS with jaunty disregard.

"At dinner, your husband was seated to the right of Dr. Winters?"
"Yes."

"He talked with her?"

"Oh, he always has a lot to say."

"Witty and engaging fellow, is he?"

"Well, he . . . likes to entertain. Tell jokes."

"He's about sixty?"

"Sixty-one."

"Big rangy fellow?"

"He's a big man. He keeps in shape."

"If you are an example, madam, he obviously has an eye for a good-looking woman."

She seems flustered. "Well, I suppose, I don't know."

"And he was giving Eve Winters quite the once-over, wasn't he?"

Kroop tires of waiting for Buddy to object. "Mr. Beauchamp, I would suggest that you take care not to overstep the bounds of decency."

"Thank you, milord. I'll reword that. He was ogling her all through dinner, wasn't he?"

"Don't answer that question," Kroop says, his dentures clicking.

Arthur ploughs ahead. "And later, in bed, he was restless, sleep wasn't coming."

"I guess so."

"He often has difficulty sleeping?"

"When he overdoes it."

"Occasionally takes a sleeping pill?"

"Yes, but . . . I don't know if he brought them."

Fine. Arthur will let the matter rest there. "And he went out for his walk?"

"Yes."

"In the rain."

"I'm not sure if it was still raining."

"And he disappeared into the small hours of the night?"

"I . . . suppose."

"Did he shower before returning to bed?"

"I don't . . ." A hesitation. "Yes, he must have."

Because he'd been rooting in the Nitinat's garbage for a discarded safe? Arthur will shelve that farfetched possibility, Coolidge is not his real target.

Kroop sighs impatiently. "These questions are much better asked of her husband, Mr. Beauchamp."

Buddy, who has been stirring restlessly, winces. "On that matter, milord, there's a slight problem. Mr. Coolidge suddenly had to return home to attend to some financial matters."

Arthur exclaims, "He *what?*" This is the glitch the Crown has been trying to conceal.

"He's coming back in a few days, after he straightens out his problem."

"A problem?" says Arthur. "What problem?"

"Some tax matter," Buddy says.

Arthur cocks his ear. "Taskmaster?"

"A *tax* problem."

"We can only hope Internal Revenue will allow this ogling under-taxed Topekan to come back. And I'll bet he had a far graver reason to flee the jurisdiction." Full and roundly said. Nobody has thought to send away the jury. They're smiling, enjoying him – he's on a roll today.

As he sits, Kroop looks at him like he would at a dog who'd fouled the rug. Buddy rises to re-examine: "You told Mr. Beauchamp your husband took sleeping pills – do you know what brand?"

"I don't, I'm sorry."

The one question too many.

"Okay, but were they legally prescribed?"

"Well, I assume . . . I honestly can't say."

Two questions too many. Kroop snaps his daybook shut with such force that Ears breaks the pencil he was chewing. "We will adjourn until tomorrow, ten o'clock."

Arthur has ended the day on an encouraging note. In truth, he will be happy if the joke-telling developer never returns. Better to have him run off like a fugitive than swear on oath he left the Breakers for twenty minutes to walk off his burps and farts. In making a late break for the border he has helped direct a fat red herring to Arthur's hook.

26

I n court this morning, among the young lawyers here to watch and learn, is Brian Pomeroy – curiosity has got the best of him. The prisoner's dock remains starkly empty, a glassed-in vault without a body. Buddy looks grumpy – the Crown's case is being forced onto detours. Despite a rocky start, Arthur has piqued the jury's interest in other culprits. Doctor Eve's hiking companions comprise today's list, and he has a few questions for Ruth Delvechio, her ex-lover.

First up is the anaesthetist, Glynis Bloom – early forties, a prematurely greying soldier's haircut. Her manner is poised, her answers flavoured with a breezy turn of phrase, as she describes six days of tramping on sand and sandstone, up muddy trails, over waterways, their packs heavy with tents, clothes, and "enough granola to feed a herd of cattle." In the evenings, they would explore the beach for shells, write letters and postcards by candlelight, play cards, read.

"Okay, and you finished this hike?"

"Yes, we actually did."

That generates the fabled titter that runs through courtrooms, stilled by Kroop's searching spotlights. Buddy might not have pulled this boner if Flynn hadn't been tugging at his sleeve, reminding him of some overlooked morsel of evidence.

"I meant . . . Let me go back. When the four of you started off on March 21, you signed in at the trailhead?"

"Yes."

"And then you signed out at Pachena Bay?"

"Yes."

She identifies their signatures on a register for March 26. Beside hers, Doctor Eve wrote, *Magic*.

"And what did you do after that?"

"We persuaded our sore feet to carry us the last mile to Bamfield."

All four bunked in Cotters' Cottage that night. Dr. Bloom and her partner, Wilma Quong, had to leave the next day, but Eve Winters had another week of holiday. "She was knocked out by the place."

"Knocked out?" A small, pursed smile from Kroop. "I regret, madam, that my ear is not trained in the nuances of modern speech."

"What a jerk." The scornful whisper of Brian Pomeroy. Kroop could not have heard, though his ears picked up something, causing him to lose the stub of his smile.

"I meant she was captivated by the ambience of the village, the lovely little beach, everything. 'I'm never leaving this place,' she said." Dr. Bloom bites her lip – as if she only now appreciates the irony.

Buddy spoils the soft moment with rude bluntness. "Well, she was sure right about that." An embarrassed silence has him shuffling through papers, seeking some better note on which to conclude. Again Flynn tugs at him, and they confer, then Buddy asks if Winters suffered any injuries on the trail.

"Just the usual bumps and thumps."

"Any injury to her teeth?"

"No, nothing like that."

Buddy sits. "Your witness."

On rising, Arthur expresses condolences for her loss of a friend.

"Thank you, she was special."

"A fascinating woman, by all accounts."

"Intuitive. She could see through your skin."

"I would often come upon her column. There was help there for even a used-up old fellow like me." *The Man Who Thinks He's a Masochist.*

"I think there's probably a lot of use there yet, Mr. Beauchamp." She is smiling. Kroop isn't, and seems poised to shut down this cocktail-party colloquy.

"She was entertaining?"

"Usually."

"Occasionally volatile? She had a temper?"

"She had a temper and could use it."

"And what might cause it to show?"

"Frustration if things weren't going her way. Impatience with some of her clients."

"You gave an example to my assistant, Ms. Rudnicki."

"Yes, Eve was in a rage over a threatened lawsuit by a woman who claimed to see herself in one of her columns."

Lorelei. Arthur glances at Brian, who gives a little shake of his head. Quite right, Arthur shouldn't risk pursuing this now. Dr. Bloom can be recalled later. He asks about Winters's mood during the hike.

"Usually carefree, but there was an underlying strain."

"That had to do with the relationship between Dr. Winters and Ruth Delvechio?"

"It was faltering."

Winters and Delvechio were together for six months. Lotis surmised it started as a fling – Delvechio moved in after staying a night, then stuck like glue.

"In fact, they had a very serious quarrel, did they not? At the cottage?"

The witness hesitates. They hadn't mentioned this to Lotis when they met because Delvechio was present. "Yes, I think that's fair to say. Ruth wanted to stay on in Bamfield with Eve. Eve wanted to be alone."

Arthur has a sense Bloom isn't fond of the young student. "This had been simmering?"

"Well, Eve once told me she felt like a leaning post . . ."

"Nope," says Buddy. "This is pure hearsay." He's disgruntled by the relaxed rapport between counsel and witness. Though he has kept his temper well, he can be counted on to blow his top at least once per trial.

A lecture from the bench: "Madam, you were poised to jump into the troubled waters of the rule against hearsay. It is offended when we are asked to believe the words of one who is not a witness."

"Let me just say I sensed a dependency that made Eve uncomfortable."

"Angry words were used on the morning of your departure?" Arthur asks.

"It was no love duet."

"I understand Dr. Winters told Ruth, 'It's over.'"

"Exactly, yes."

"And Ruth Delvechio's response was what?"

"She told Eve to fuck herself." Kroop looks up sharply, displeased at this woman's bold use of taboo language. "Then the landlady came by and Eve went out for a walk. The rest of us packed to leave."

"For the *Lady Rose*."

"Yes, we'd left our car in Port Alberni."

"Ms. Delvechio was in a dark mood on the journey home?"

"She wasn't a barrel of laughs."

Arthur draws from Bloom that Delvechio spoke little during the drive to Vancouver, stared morosely out the car window. She asked to be dropped off at her mother's house. Bloom and her partner had no contact with Delvechio between then and April 1. They've seen her infrequently since.

Arthur is satisfied with this sketch of a heartsick vassal of her royal highness, curtly uncoupled and shamed. Motive enough for murder? Likely not, but another red herring for the bouillabaisse he's stirring.

Arthur is about to sit, then remembers to ask about the balky door of Cotters' Cottage.

"I almost put my back out tugging it closed."

"And the lock would then click shut?"

"Correct."

Something else is niggling at him. Buddy hadn't asked how this hike came about.

"It was Eve's idea," the witness explains. "We first talked about it almost a year ago, but left it too late to make reservations for the summer, so we chose the end of March and prayed for sun."

"Reservations are required?" This is news to Arthur.

"Parks Canada restricts the numbers who can enter. For summer, you have to book a year ahead."

"And when did you book?"

"Four months earlier, in November."

"They check you off as you enter the park?"

"And lecture you about bears."

"Did you see any?"

"We were trying hard not to."

Arthur thinks he's done, but again something is bothering him. He fiddles with papers, buying time.

"Are you through, Mr. Beauchamp? The jury might prefer enjoying their mid-morning coffee than watching you stand there ruminating. Himf, himf."

"A final question. How did you learn there was a cottage for rent on Brady Beach?"

"The Internet, a list of places to stay in Bamfield."

"And when did you make reservations with the Cotters?"

"In November. At the same time we booked for the trail."

Here is food for thought. A magazine writer capable of basic research could have tracked Winters's movements, learned she reserved for the trail, for Cotters' Cottage.

"Can I assume that's your last final question, Mr. Beauchamp?"

Wilma Quong, a timid, bespectacled accountant, must be prodded through her testimony. She isn't as forthright as Bloom about the spat, and blushes even to use the inane euphemism "f-word." She is so apprehensive and soft of voice that Arthur makes her ordeal brief – she is blunting the force of Bloom's more candid testimony.

Quong squeezes beside her partner, a few rows back, as Ruth Delvechio takes the stand. Auburn-haired with wide pale eyes, pretty if her face weren't so stretched and tense. This tautness is only slightly relieved as she catches the eye of Glynis Bloom, and she frowns again as she looks upon Arthur, the defender of her lover's murderer, the enemy.

Buddy draws from her that she met Winters in September while researching for her master's thesis, a history of sexual misbehaviour in an isolated farm community. Their meetings grew more intimate and, Delvechio says with a flourish, "We fell desperately in love."

She moved into Winters's upscale condo and lived, according to Delvechio, in sweet harmony. "We were so happy, so, so much in love." At another point, she says, "It was so fairy tale." Cloying, Lotis warned, but the sugar is coated with a bitter shell. "And despite what some people may say, we shared that love till the end."

The Crowns must have taken Delvechio aside during the break, prepared her for Arthur, filled her in on his cross of Glynis Bloom. He asks if there was strife during the hike.

"There's always a little friction in close quarters like a two-person tent. I don't think we had many cross words. We were too tired in the evenings even to *talk*."

"We heard something this morning about an exchange in the cottage . . ."

She blurts: "That was *so* tempest in a teapot. You have to know Eve, she didn't mean it."

"She didn't mean what?"

"She didn't mean it was over. It was just a silly little thing. We would have had a good laugh about it when she came back home from her . . . whatever, her meditative holiday."

Buddy assesses the pros and cons of punctuating those last few words. Finally he can't resist. "But she never did come back home, did she?"

"I think I'm going to throw up." Again, it's Brian, directly behind Arthur.

Kroop glances up so quickly that he may have pulled a neck muscle, because he winces. "Who said that?"

No one responds.

Kneading his neck, Kroop looks about for a likely culprit, sees only a sea of innocent, sheeplike faces. He pins his fierce eyes on Arthur, his preferred suspect, then turns to the clerk. "Mr. Gilbert, did you hear someone say something about being sick?" He will wheedle the truth from the spineless clerk.

"I heard . . ." Gilbert clears his throat. "Something to that effect, sir, but I was looking down."

"You must keep a better eye on the courtroom. Was he close by?"

"Near the front, I believe," Gilbert says faintly. Almost everyone in the front benches heard Brian clearly, but none wants Gilbert's role as conscripted fink. Now the judge inspects the row of young lawyers. A long study of Brian Pomeroy, who, with magnificent gall, turns and looks behind him, redirecting the search.

"There will be an order of detention for the next person who attempts to mock the proceedings of this court."

Behind her hand, the forewoman, Ellen Sueda, is stifling either shock or amusement. A progressive teacher, no doubt, whose students aren't sent off regularly to the principal's office.

The episode causes Buddy to lose his way. He bends to Jasper Flynn to confer about the roadmap. Lazy, maybe overconfident, Buddy has relied on Flynn to do the tedious tasks of assembling this prosecution.

"Okay, Ms. Delvechio, when did you leave Bamfield?"

"It was a Monday. I'd already lost a day of classes, and had to get back."

"And where were you the rest of the week?"

"I had a full schedule on Tuesday and Wednesday, then an off day, and I had a seminar on Friday."

"And on that night, Friday, March 31?"

"I was at the UBC library until late, and after that I was at my mother's. You can ask her. I was there that entire weekend." Though accused of nothing, she's asserting her innocence.

"You were staying at your mother's because . . . ?"

"Eve forgot to leave me a key."

Buddy consults again with Flynn, then says, "No more questions."

Arthur takes a while to think about that last answer. He looks at his watch.

"Are you interested in joining us, Mr. Beauchamp?"

"Milord, I would prefer my cross-examination not be interrupted by the lunch break."

"Time flies, Mr. Beauchamp." Kroop puts his glasses on, sees the wall clock reads five minutes to the half-hour. "Oh, very well."

✦

In the El Beau Room, Brian astonishes Samson by ordering a grapefruit juice. "You on the wagon too, Mr. Pomeroy?"

"I have become a rabid teetotalitarian, Samson." The waiter walks off, shaking his head. "I've started seeing Lila two evenings a week – she's putting in extra hours, she sees hope for me. I'm getting a ton of insight. For instance: the bikini incident. I've been focused on that one wrongful conviction, the case of the planted panties, and have been blind to my other offences."

Arthur listens patiently but with his mind on Ruth Delvechio. He waits until Brian's mouth is busy with his club sandwich, then turns the conversation to her evidence, its unexpected gifts. "The chip on her shoulder suggests this self-obsessed woman has something to hide."

"Yeah, she's *so* agony of lost love," Brian says. "Fragile. Handle with care."

"I think not. I'll storm her defences. The jury isn't buying the twaddle about Winter's enduring love for her."

"I'm out of there. The chief has my number, he'll be onto me like a pack of dogs on a three-legged cat. I like what you've done, Arthur, you've got suspects popping up right, left, and centre. Buddy is ducking and dodging, they're coming at him from everywhere. He's distracted, he can't see the danger lurking in the bushes, the bingo queen."

Brian plays with an unlit cigarette. "Caroline stopped lecturing me about smoking months ago, but Lila said that's because she gave up, complaining was hopeless. I was hopeless, the marriage was hopeless." He breaks the cigarette and kneads the tobacco into a saucer. "You can see how reborn I am, Arturo. I am the new version of me, booze-free, drug-free, charter member of Adulterers Anonymous."

Arthur is booze-free and drug-free, smokes only the occasional pipe, and is only theoretically capable of adultery. Maybe he should forget being drug-free and add a little Viagra to his life. Hubbell would have Arthur believe a pharmaceutically triggered erection is the key to ultimate happiness.

Something is missing from Brian's list of resolutions. Women want more than easy vows of abstinence, but Arthur's not sure exactly what. Clearly, Brian and Hubbell have no idea either. He suspects it has something to do with listening. Tuning in. Not reading the newspaper while she's venting about imbecilic trustees.

"Can you find out if Delvechio's mother backs her up?"

"I'd get on it, but this is a make-or-break weekend. Caroline and I have that couples workshop on Cortes Island. You'll have to use your scary student."

"You find Lotis scary?"

"You don't? She's an idealist and therefore dangerous. She doesn't know the legal game, thinks it's politics." He represents several of the Gwendolyn protestors, and has got to know her. "Don't let her loose in the courtroom, she's a monkey with a buzzsaw. Also, her vibes of godlike infallibility piss me off. She has a Napoleonic complex, she's a borderline personality. She doesn't attract me, I prefer the sane."

Arthur picked up where Buddy left off: "You say Eve Winters *forgot* to leave you a key to her apartment?"

"That's right." Delvechio tosses back her hair defiantly with a glance at Bloom and Quong.

"Isn't it a fact, Ms. Delvechio, that Eve Winters refused to give you the key?"

"She forgot."

"Did you ever go back there?"

"Yes, I had all my books and notes at Eve's, my computer, everything. The caretaker let me in so I could collect them."

"And you moved into your mother's home."

"Yes, in Shaughnessy." A bastion of the well-to-do.

"Who else resides there?"

"No one now. She's recently divorced and my sister is away at a private school."

"And what does your mother do?"

"Dr. Delvechio is the assistant director of a pharmaceutical company."

"Which is named?"

"Advance Biotechnics Inc. It's listed."

"She's obviously a busy, hard-working woman."

"Yes, very demanding of herself."

"Works late? Sometimes on weekends?"

"She was home on Friday, March 31, if that's what you're getting at."

"You confirmed that with her?"

"Of course."

"Did you ask her to say you were home that Friday night?"

Buddy leaps to the rescue. "That's below the belt."

"I am cross-examining!" Arthur thunders.

That even restrains Wilbur Kroop, who seemed on the verge of upholding the objection. But he lets Arthur carry on; he will pick his spots to tangle with him.

Arthur retreats from this dicey area, not wanting to reinforce her alibi. "Truthfully, Ms. Delvechio, you weren't at all eager to leave Bamfield and get back to classes, were you? You wanted to stay with Eve."

"Did Glynis Bloom say that?"

"Just this morning." He quotes her answer: "'Ruth wanted to stay on in Bamfield with Eve. Eve wanted to be alone.'"

"Glynis must've been confused."

"I regret to tell you she was forthright and plain. The fact is Eve wanted a holiday away from you. She found you clinging, cloying, and self-absorbed. She announced your severance so loudly it could be heard outside the cottage walls. 'It's over, Ruth. Repeat, it's over. Do you receive?'"

"She had one of her little outbursts. It was about . . . nothing." That tattletale phrase flutters like a flag at a country fair.

"*Nothing*, Ms. Delvechio?"

"Her emotions were so close to the surface . . ."

"We accept that, Ms. Delvechio. Tell us what caused her to blow up." Cyrano's sniffer has picked up a scent. He snaps his suspenders. "What was the quarrel about?"

Delvechio clears her throat, can't answer. She is labouring so hard that Buddy chooses unwisely to interrupt. "Milord, this is totally . . ." But he too must struggle, unsure what he should complain about.

"Totally what, Mr. Svabo?" Kroop says.

"I object to how much time this is taking. I have a raft of witnesses, and I'd appreciate knowing how long he's going to be with this one."

Arthur coldly stares Buddy back into his chair. "We'll move along faster if my learned friend stops playing jack-in-the-box and lets me go about my business in peace." Arthur is on familiar ground at last, doing well what he does best.

"For the third time, Ms. Delvechio, what was the quarrel about?"

"Nothing," she repeats with lowered voice. "A silly thing."

Arthur waits.

"Over a letter."

"What letter, Ms. Delvechio?"

"She'd been writing a letter to a . . . well, I suppose, a friend. A former friend. I happened to come upon it."

"How?"

"It was in a compartment of her pack. Something she'd been scribbling while we were on the trail."

Arthur waits once more, prying out answers with silence.

"We'd just settled in. The others were walking the beach or somewhere, and Eve's pack was lying there and I decided to clean it out for her, all the sand and dirt and whatever. And there was this writing pad, and I happened to be glancing at it when Eve walked in, and she grabbed it and gave me a bad time over it, and that's it. And then Glynis and Wilma came in, and Eve said we'd talk later, the two of us. But we never did, until there was that little eruption the next morning."

"To whom was she writing?"

"I really don't know."

"Come now, Ms. Delvechio."

"I honestly don't know the woman. Dear . . . Dear Daisy, that's all I saw."

"Dear Daisy or Dearest Daisy?"

"Dearest or . . . I don't know."

"Darling Daisy?"

"I don't know!" She seems on the verge of tears, but Arthur presses on.

"Daisy who?"

"Daisy whatever, Eve never told me. Anyway it was over. Long ago." Now comes a tissue to her eyes.

Glynis Bloom is looking at Delvechio with a skeptic's arched eyebrows; Wilma Quong seems puzzled.

"Bring her a glass of water," Kroop orders. When the sheriff moves to the pitcher, Kroop says, "Mr. Gilbert will do it." The whipped dog rises. Flynn looks very tense for some reason, his neck muscles bunched as he crouches over his pad.

Arthur waits out her long, shaky sip. "Are we to understand, Ms. Delvechio, that Dr. Winters and Daisy were lovers?"

"A fleeting affair. It ended just before I met Eve. It was never going anywhere." Another sip. "Daisy was very, totally married."

"To whom?"

"Some . . . I don't know, rough trade, Eve called him. A jerk."

"What kind of jerk?"

"Abusive husband, Eve said. I don't know anything more about Daisy, except Eve called her a diamond in the rough. I assumed she was your basic trailer trash. The affair was *so* dead in the water."

The pour of metaphors ceases, and she dabs her eyes again.

Buddy says, "If we could have a brief recess, milord, so the witness can compose herself . . ."

"We will take our break at the usual time."

Arthur must be as hard of heart as the judge, must resist sympathy: these are the tears of self-pity. "Dead in the water? Yet she was writing Daisy a love letter?"

"To announce it was all was over, to persuade her not to write any more."

"Is that what her letter said?"

"I *assume*. I told you I didn't read it."

"How many pages was it?"

"I don't know. Maybe three. Four."

"A four-page rejection slip? Come now."

"Believe what you want."

"Six months after you took up with Eve Winters, they were still writing to each other?"

"Whatever."

"The truth, Ms. Delvechio, is that Eve was writing to say she was sorry she rejected Daisy for you. It was *your* relationship that was dead in the water."

"That is so totally . . . not *true!*"

"What did Eve do with this letter after she snatched it from you?"

"She stuck it in her pocket."

"You don't know if she mailed it?"

"I assume so, since it wasn't found."

"How do you know it wasn't found?"

"I . . . I think someone would have mentioned that." She looks at the troika of Crowns. No help forthcoming. Buddy has his arms folded, Flynn is busily doodling, and Ears chewing.

"Did Eve keep an address book?"

"Yes, but . . . I'm not sure if she had it with her."

"What kind of address book?"

"A little ring binder, stiff grey cover."

"Was Daisy's address in it?"

"I never bothered to look." Another sip of water, but she's recovering.

"Ms. Delvechio, did you ever mention this letter to the investigating officers?"

"I don't think I was ever asked." That may seem evasive even to her, because she adds, "It wasn't my business to mention Daisy to anyone. Especially if she was in a bad marriage situation."

"Daisy's husband was physically violent?"

"Eve said something about him being jealous and abusive."

"Did he beat her?"

"Eve didn't say exactly. I assumed. I didn't ask."

"How did she and Daisy meet?"

"I don't know."

"How did Eve happen to mention her friend Daisy to you?"

Delvechio slumps a little, crumbling. A deep breath. "Okay. This was back in the fall, October maybe. Eve was being all moody. She had had a couple of drinks and . . . She just started talking about this Daisy person, this totally ridiculous affair. How Daisy was so refreshing and original even though she wasn't awfully bright or educated. Never went to college. She had a family, a couple of boys. I didn't get it, it was so *not* Eve Winters: I had this picture of Daisy Mae in a tattered skirt living in some runty home in Dogpatch, struggling with her sexual identity and a horrible marriage."

"And what else did Eve say?"

Delvechio shrugs. "I think she surprised herself running on like that, and she looked up kind of startled, as if she forgot I was present. And she put on the brakes. I gave her a hug, and she smiled and shook off her little blue funk, and that was it, and she never mentioned Daisy again. It was like she just disappeared from the map." She straightens, returns to an earlier theme. "And then . . . well, it was like magic the way it happened – Eve and I fell in love."

"Please tell us what was in the letter that Eve caught you reading."

"I hardly *looked* at it!"

"Come now, what was in that letter that was so upsetting?"

"I didn't!"

The tears return, but no one on the jury seems to share her sorrow. Martin Samples has seen bad actresses cry before. One and a half stars out of five.

"No more questions."

✦

That exchange has Arthur in a contemplative mood during the break, as he stands by the vine-draped terrace of level six, staring down at three scurrying figures in the Great Hall, a sheriff leading two lawyers with gowns flapping. A jury has rendered its verdict. He shivers at the thought of that intense, taut moment, the jurors shuffling into court, red-faced from battle, the last holdout grim-faced and sour.

Delvechio's imagery sticks in his mind: Daisy Mae Yokum in her ragged skirt and polka-dot blouse, pretty and bouncy and refreshing and real. As portrayed in the funnies, read furtively when he was a boy, his father frowning upon the practice. Who is the abusive Li'l Abner?

Could Ruth Delvechio have dreamed up this complex murder? Yes, this clinging creature has a jealous, conniving mind. She has become an admirable suspect. Her mother holds high office in a drug company. Does Advance Biotechnics do DNA testing? Manufacture Rohypnol for export?

Bloom and Quong are in intense conversation near the stairs. Arthur approaches, asks if he may speak with them.

◆

When court resumes, Arthur asks to have Dr. Bloom recalled. Buddy has become increasingly fidgety through the afternoon, and says, "He's had his one kick at the cat, that's what he's allowed."

Kroop may be tiring of these spurious objections. "I trust you will keep it brief, Mr. Beauchamp."

"Thank you, milord." Courtesy reigns.

Bloom is sworn again, and Arthur draws from her that she knows nothing about a woman named Daisy, never heard Winters speak the name.

"Were you aware she was writing a letter while you camped on the trail?"

"She was constantly writing. Letters, notes for her column."

"And at any time did you see her with an address book?"

"Yes. She had a schedule for the *Lady Rose* folded into it, and we checked it to make sure we had the correct sailing time."

"That was the day you departed Bamfield?"

"Yes."

"You heard Ms. Delvechio describe Eve's address book."

"A small ring binder with a stiff grey cardboard cover. That's what I saw."

"Thank you. I would now like to recall Sergeant Flynn."

This generates yet another huddle at the Crown end of the table, three bent heads. Buddy rises, but Kroop says, "Same objection, Mr. Svabo?"

"Yes, he . . ."

"Same ruling."

His Lordship finally seems interested in the whodunit Arthur has been spinning, maybe he's a fan of the genre. Buddy hasn't helped his cause with his slapdash style and inelegant tongue – the Chief is a stickler for the Queen's English.

Flynn abandons his doodle pad and takes the stand, holding himself with the stiffness of a prairie dog sniffing the air for danger.

"Did you find Dr. Winters's address book anywhere in the cottage?"

"No, sir."

"Or any address book?"

"No."

"Or a letter written by the deceased?"

"Nothing like that."

"A writing pad?"

A hesitation. "No, sir." Working at his moustache.

Arthur shares a moment of silent speculation with the jury, then sits.

In the old days, Arthur would start celebrating a good day by raising two fingers to the bartender. In the sober present, he will rejoice with a double latte – one doesn't celebrate with tea.

As he tackles Hubbell's complex machine, he tries to put aside Daisy Whatever – *Eve never told me* – but she clings. She kept wandering into his head this afternoon while unimportant witnesses, owners and staff of the Breakers Inn, were on the stand.

Maybe Daisy is a nickname or pseudonym – Doctor Eve's column used them frequently. Her advice to abuse victims was always blunt. To one beaten wife it was simply, "Flee, flee." Daisy may not have been a patient, of course, but it seems a fair guess she was – how else would Winters have met someone so out of her milieu?

Behold: designer-coffee issues from a spout. From another comes a frothy topping. Feet up, latte at hand, he probes the multichannel universe as he waits for the six o'clock news. Here, incredibly, is a channel devoted solely to reruns of *Star Trek*. Eerily, here is one for book lovers. And something called Court TV.

Back comes Daisy, Eve's true love. Delvechio had reason to spirit away an incriminating love letter to her rival, an address book with Daisy's name. But why would Adeline Angella do so, why would she filch so much as a writing pad? Angella is beginning to seem an inconvenience. Harvey Coolidge is barely in the running.

Yes, Arthur has cultivated a garden of reasonable doubts, any of which may win an acquittal – but is that enough? Nothing would satisfy him more than to bring the real killer to justice, to play Perry Mason, point the stern finger of retribution at a quavering figure in the pews: *You, madam, callously slew this fine young lady!*

On the supper news (*We take you to Garibaldi Island*), he's treated to the spectacle of Winnie Gillicuddy linking arms with her mates beneath a banner: "We are the Raging Grannies." When it's her turn to be arrested, the officer has to duck a sweeping handbag.

An exasperated RCMP spokesman carries on about the "thankless task of upholding the law in this difficult situation," regrets the arrest of a woman of such years, and stakes a claim to magnanimity for not charging her with attempted assault.

Here's Kurt Zoller, complete with lifejacket, finally earning his chance for fame. "As elected trustee, I want to express our whole-hearted outrage at this treatment of a gentle old lady . . ." His rhetoric seems about to take flight, like a kite catching the wind, but is snipped, and viewers are treated to Winnie being escorted from the hoosegow by a squad of Raging Grannies. She raises a fist of triumph.

"Ma'am, what are your plans?" a reporter asks.

"I'm going to go home and feed the chickens."

Arthur is into his second latte when Lotis calls, elated. While remarking on Winnie's bravura, Justice Mewhort mused, *obiter dictum*, about his own wonderful bossy grandma. After that, he ordered the release of today's catch of protestors and directed there be a one-week détente. No logging, no arrests while everyone talks turkey. Arthur's hope for Margaret's return soars. She vowed to come down when the arrests end, now she can claim victory.

He sets Lotis a task: she is to search in her computer for the name Daisy, who may show up in the CD that Svabo reluctantly delivered up. If Winter's clinical records are Daisy-free, the computer will be asked – somewhat like a genie, Arthur supposes – to locate accounts of abused wives raising two boys in mean surroundings.

Lotis and Selwyn are cleaning up the flotsam left in the wake of the contempt hearings, but she'll try to join him tomorrow.

The chiming clock has long ago counted out its monotonic midnight, and Arthur is still wide awake. The day's adrenalin has been slow to burn off, and he overloaded on the lattes. He's been reading fitfully, putting Doctor Eve's columns aside, picking up *Medea (The streams flow with ambrosia by Zeus's bed of love)*, finally turning off the light.

Anticipation of Margaret's homecoming. so often felt and so often denied, has added to his insomnia. How is he to react to her? How will *she* react? There's an awful chance she'll be closed to his embrace, rigid. The more pleasant imagining has her melting into his arms, but what then? A long hot shower, of course, a decent meal, her own bed, where she waits for the great swordsman to slip into the sheets beside her . . .

A distant siren. A car alarm and its raucous sonata of whoops and wails. The thrum of a ship heading out to sea. He ought to have closed the window but can no longer abide unfresh air.

The moon glows through his undraped windows, and he can make out the pillow pictures, feels a disturbance, a roiling below. He squirms, shifts. He rises. He goes to the bathroom, reads the label on the Viagra.

27

It is only as his taxi is hurtling down Georgia Street that Arthur realizes he's forgotten his briefcase. He has his cellphone, though, and is still trying to get word to the Chief Justice through the clerks' office. But what can he say? It was a hard night, milord. In my stiffly discomfited state I set my alarm for the wrong hour.

Finally a response, someone in the registry: "Mr. Beauchamp, I don't know how to say this, but the Chief has started without you."

Time-obsessive Wilbur Kroop must have gone off the rails. A murder trial is chugging along in Court 67, and neither accused nor counsel are anywhere near the building. However exhausted, Arthur will find the strength to demand a mistrial.

Who was on today's list? Several denizens of Bamfield. The Cotters of Cotters' Cottage. Holly Hoover, the seafaring hooker.

The taxi gets jammed in a one-way street, so Arthur jogs the last block, through the Great Hall and into the barristers' room. He fumbles with his locker combination. Shirt, dickey, gown. What a tragedy – he'd been getting on with Kroop, and now must face his wrath. Privileges will be withdrawn, objections overruled.

He takes a deep breath, then enters 67, and stands for a moment in a fog of weariness, getting his bearings. Elderly, spindly Inez Cotter is in the witness stand. Buddy is by the far wall, shouting at her.

"Sorry, ma'am, but you'll have to speak even louder. I want to be able to hear from across the room."

"Is this better?" Her tiny, piping voice. "Three o'clock on Friday was the last time I ever seen or talked to her."

"This was when you brought Dr. Winters her laundry?"

She nods.

"Get your lungs into it, Mrs. Cotter, we all want to hear."

"Yes, sir." She would not be more intimidated were she facing a bully at a bus stop. Arthur is fascinated, perplexed, and immobile.

"Describe her demeanour on that tragic day, the last of her life."

"Looked like she didn't have no worries, like she was free of all burdens, that was the impression I got."

"And how much time did you spend with her?"

"She made tea, and she paid me for the laundry and something extra, and we had a little chat about this and that . . ."

Buddy cuts her off. "I want to thank you for coming all this way to help us, ma'am. That's all the questions."

Arthur decides, for a lark, to join this travesty. As he advances past the bar, Kroop glances his way with little interest, the merest nod of recognition. Jurors, for some reason, offer looks of sympathy. He'd not had time to shave, he must appear a mess, a ghoul in a gown.

"Cross-examination," says Kroop.

A tousle-haired shorty rises from behind the cover of bulky Sheriff Willett. Lotis Morningstar Rudnicki. "You're, um, seventy-nine years old, Ms. Cotter?"

"Yes."

"And you still manage to maintain that beautiful cottage for rent. That's wonderful."

"Kind of you to say, dear."

Arthur sits beside Lotis, who starts, then her face floods with relief. "Can I . . . may I please have a few seconds, your Lordship?"

"Welcome Mr. Beauchamp back for me. I trust he's feeling better." Adding to the surreal atmosphere is this display of good humour by Wilbur Kroop. Lotis looks absurdly formal in her black barrister's gown. No makeup – she eschews it except as an occasional art form. A silver ornament in her lower lip, small and fine, discreet enough. She's cut her hair.

An angry hiss: "Where have you fucking *been*? Act like you've had gastroenteritis. You told me to carry on till you got here."

Lotis has pulled his pants from the fire, but his gratitude is slightly soured by resentment. Something else for the whippersnapper to crow about. Let's see how she handles the heat of the courtroom. She can't do much damage with Inez Cotter.

"Carry on, my dear." Arthur winces for the judge, as if fighting off another attack.

Lotis looks at him pleadingly, is denied. He'll be damned if he'll mention the Viagra, the long, unsettling night. She takes a deep breath. "Okay, Ms. Cotter, your chat with Dr. Winters – what was that about?"

"Objection. Hearsay."

His Lordship, still aggrieved at Buddy for his lumpish prosecution, says, "I didn't hear you objecting when Mr. Beauchamp went on a hearsay rampage yesterday."

Lotis looks uncertain. "Have I won that one?"

"Having already heard you on the subject of hearsay, Miss Rudnicki, and having been thereby persuaded that the rules of evidence are no longer taught in our law schools, I rule that Mrs. Cotter's chat with the deceased comes, as you put it, somewhere within the zillion exceptions to the hearsay rule."

Arthur cannot help but laugh. The pixie has been getting her come-uppance from a master of the art. It is just as well for her that Kroop is in a sanguine mood, content to throw light barbs. He probably admires her gumption. He dislikes weakness in lawyers. In anyone.

Lotis resumes. "Okay, what did Dr. Winters say to you?"

"She asked how long mail takes to reach the mainland."

"What did she want to mail?"

"She had a few postcards and a letter."

Which were never found and, one assumes, never sent – none of Winters's friends mentioned receiving a card from her.

Though Lotis has trouble framing her questions, she brings out Sergeant Flynn's lackadaisical reaction to the squabble between Ruth and Eve. "He had a little chuckle over it," says Mrs. Cotter.

◆

The morning break finds Lotis hectoring Arthur. "A *murder* case! Half past nine, I phoned, no answer. I'm thinking, What if he's had an accident? An illness, an attack? Then it's five to, and everyone, Gilbert Gilbert, Buddy Svabo, his nerdy junior, are giving me horror stories about how the Chief Justice is going to rip your face off if I don't come up with something. I *lied* for you! In open *court*."

He sits. "Well done."

A theatrical, gasping look of amazement. "What *happened* to you?"

"Far too complex to explain." A quick shift of topic: kudos for her cool head in a crisis, her admirable relief pitching. Excellent rapport with Mrs. Cotter. A few rough edges that will rub smooth with the years.

"Don't give me that bullshit. They were trying to make a fool of me."

Buddy probably seized every chance to do so, but the patronizing tones of the judge would rile her most. In her arena, the street, she is queen. In court, uniformed, she has to abide by the rules and rigorous formality she despises. She can adjust or chuck the job. But she is mollified by his compliments, and her temper subsides.

"What have I missed?"

She reviews her notes. "Bill Links, the whale-watching guy, asked Nick if he heard about the robbery last night, and they sat over cappuccinos speculating that it was an inside job. In front of the jury, Buddy went, 'Cool as a cucumber.' The prick."

"You have to fire back, Lotis."

"You kidding? I'm scared shitless. It's a murder charge! I'm not defending some teenager who climbed a tree!"

"Easy, my dear." Arthur mustn't take pleasure from Ms. Know-it-all's discomfort. No one is born a trial lawyer. The dues of sweat and fear and error must be paid. Maybe by your fifties you get it right.

"Mr. Cotter was next. He's hearing impaired, that's how Buddy got into the habit of shouting. Came by to see if Eve had enough firewood, stayed for granola. 'Damn fine young lady,' he said. She asked to be invited to their fifty-fifth anniversary next year. Gave him a peck on the forehead as he left."

Lotis slumps into a seat beside him. "It's all about Eve, isn't it? Everyone loves Eve. Flighty young students, eighty-five-year-old codgers. *I* love her. I even like that she sometimes acts the queen and sleeps with married women." She's talkative, peppy, she got through it. "What I don't understand is, Why am I talking about her in the present tense?"

Maybe because Eve is somehow floating around, a frustrated spirit demanding their ear, calling, like Buddy, from across the courtroom.

"I'd like you to remain at the helm for the rest of the morning." The next witness is Meredith Broadfeather, the Huu-ay-aht sociologist. She'll do the defence no harm. "I will save my strength for this afternoon." Holly Hoover.

"Whoa, I filled in, it was an emergency, you overslept after doing God knows what last night. I'm not *prepared*."

"It's a test you'll face many times. Cross-examining on the fly against surprise testimony. Ninety per cent of good cross-examination is knowing when *not* to ask a question. The rest involves good instincts. Let's see how yours work." He sits back, closes his eyes.

"The judge thinks I'm dumb as cowflop. I don't understand the hearsay rule."

"No one does."

"I expected to watch and learn. I don't do impromptu . . . Arthur?"

He's back in Dogpatch, daisies growing everywhere, faceless, beckoning. Find me. Find me. Lotis squeezes his knee and he blinks awake.

"We're being called to court. You're not ill?"

"No." He gains his feet.

"What were you up to last night?"

"Nothing really. Thinking, reading. Problem with the alarm clock." He turns his face from her. Without a beard, it's harder to hide his blush.

"You're not having an affair, are you?"

Gilbert pokes his head out, flustered. "Get *in* here, for goodness sake. We're *late.*"

When court is called, Kroop charges in like an impatient bull. His first order of business is to ride his clerk. "That took nearly seventeen minutes. I said ten minutes, Mr. Gilbert. Ten minutes, not ten *hours.*"

"I'm sorry, milord."

The clerk must be looking forward to the weekend with more alacrity than even Arthur. Apparently he had a breakdown some years back, due to some form of neurological imbalance of which Kroop seems either heedless or uncaring.

The judge snaps at Meredith Broadfeather as well, tells her to remove her polemical button from her fringed, deerskin jacket. *Whose Home and Native Land?* "Advertising is not allowed, madam." Broadfeather obeys but gives Lotis a look. Two militants here, a risky setup.

She describes following Sergeant Flynn and two constables to the Brady Beach cottage. They called out, pounded on the door, struggled with it. She slipped around to the bedroom window, and almost fainted on seeing Winters naked in death.

Broadfeather saw the officers examine the body for vital signs. They were radioing for support when one of them noticed her at the window. "They told me to skedaddle."

"Why had you followed them there in the first place?" Buddy asks.

"Because when the police are in town on a weekend they're usually looking to bust an Indian. I like to witness. I don't like my people getting beat up."

That is more than Buddy bargained for – it reflects poorly on his seatmate that a leading figure of the Huu-ay-aht community so distrusts him. Jasper Flynn shows bland unconcern, doodles. The prosecutor can see no good in tangling with this witness, and ends his examination with muttered thanks.

Lotis may have forgotten she isn't watching a skit, and sits smiling. Arthur has to nudge her. "Oh, my turn?" She jumps up and, to Arthur's delight, goes on the attack. "So when Jasper Flynn's in town, you have to play a kind of witness protection role?"

Buddy makes a grand display of being irked. "I object, that's offensive, that's real low."

"She's entitled to explore an issue you raised, Mr. Svabo. Perhaps you asked the one question too many." Sardonic. Buddy continues to annoy Kroop, the showy style.

"You've had lots of contact with Sergeant Flynn?" Lotis asks.

"Many consultations."

"Confrontations too, Ms. Broadfeather?" *She doesn't know the game, thinks it's politics.*

"That's right."

"Much racism out your way?"

Flynn is seething. Buddy's indignant. "Aw now, that's too much. What's she trying to imply, that Sergeant Flynn harbours prejudice?"

"Whoa, why would you infer that?" Lotis firing back. Jurors are getting an inkling there are other facets to the gruff, friendly cop.

Flynn can take no more of these outrageous slanders. He stands, bows to the judge, and strides smartly to the door. Either taunting or pretending naïveté, Lotis calls, "Wait. Come back. I withdraw the question." But he leaves to nurse his wounds.

"Is this going anywhere, Miss Rudnicki? Ms., I suppose, that's what the young ladies demand. It sounds so harsh. Miz." This is followed by himfs. Is the old fellow *flirting* with Lotis? The only likely answer: he's seen the detergent commercial, has joined the numberless throng under her spell.

"I want to bring out that Nick Faloon gave free rooms to the Native elders when the weather kept them from home."

Svabo takes so long to object that Kroop upbraids him. "Of course it's irrelevant, but now it's in, isn't it? We may as well hear it from its source."

Broadfeather not only complies but adds, "He's a minority person himself, he's not racist."

This would be a good point to end on, but Lotis whittles away the winnings of a good cross by dragging it out, going back to the crime scene. "You saw the police checking the deceased for vital signs?"

"Officers Flynn and Beasely."

"Did they have gloves on when they were, like, looking for a pulse?"

"No, they put gloves on after. Not regular ones, latex gloves."

"Okay, thanks." Lotis looks questioningly at Arthur. Just sit down, his eyes implore, and she does.

Buddy is up to re-examine. "What did you mean, the accused is a minority person?"

"He was born in Lebanon," Broadfeather says.

"He's an Arab. Okay."

Lotis jumps up. "Are you trying to suggest that's bad? And you give us that load of cheese about *my* making racist insinuations?"

"Yeah, well, you hurt a veteran RCMP member's feelings . . ."

"That phony exhibition of walking out . . ."

"We will have *ord-er!*" Kroop gets his lungs into it. Scream Seven.

Arthur must tug Lotis back to her seat. She could get the defence into trouble yet. But she's gritty and quick. (And why is it so hard to concede that? It's her new-generation style, her in-your-faceness. He feels creaky in her company.)

Buddy squeezes in another witness before noon, grey-bearded Roger Kapoor, yard supervisor for Crown Zellerbach. Grizzly he's called, for good reason – at sixty he looks able to bring down a caribou barehanded. He's an entertaining talker with an entertaining tale: how he picked up Gertrude, warned her in pidgin English about a psychotic murderer, and subsequently observed her taking a standup pee. That prompts laughter among the jury, and is even awarded a single himf from the bench. Kapoor's wild ride in the back of his hijacked truck elicits more jollity.

The gruesome evidence is behind the jury now. The phantom of the courtroom is coming across more as a careless clown than a swash-buckling jewel thief, but it isn't a harsh image. Arthur hopes he'll find the energy for Holly Hoover, who licked his ear and fondled his groin, a memory, he sourly remembers, that arose last night.

He looks forward to getting past the afternoon, into the soul-healing weekend. His forgotten garden, his injured septic field, his soon-to-be-shared bed . . . He awakes to a gentle nudge. "Uh, Margaret?"

Lotis, tossing her hair, her condescending smile. "You were asleep. Which is okay, court has adjourned."

Arthur blinks, looks about, disoriented. Sheriff Willit is patiently waiting to lock up. "Was it obvious?"

"Well, your eyes were closed, but . . . Don't you remember rising for the adjournment?"

"I stood?"

"The clerk said, 'Order in court,' and yes, you stood."

It's what forty years of conditioning does to one.

They leave for the barristers' lounge, where Arthur nestles into a corner sofa on which he slept off many hangovers. Conversation turns to Margaret, to the truce in the forest. "She's won an admirable victory, so I expect we'll see her coming down presently."

"Keep your pants on, Arthur."

The insolent tramp. She could be more supportive.

She hands him a few printouts from Eve Winters's files. "No Daisies, no hillbillies, no mother living rough with two sons, no gorgeous diamonds in the rough. Doctor Eve specialized in the bourgeoisie."

He studies a profile of a woman who thought herself unattractive and was so afraid of losing her husband that she abided his adultery, shouts, and slaps. "Doris is actually lovely. Beautiful within too. She won't know that until she leaves him. She won't suffer financially, he does well as an investment counsellor . . ."

This isn't Dogpatch. Bamfield is Dogpatch. It is where one might meet a Daisy. Maybe she lived nearby, a logging town, and after getting rid of Ruth, Eve sought an assignation by mail. Maybe she did indeed send that letter, and the abusive husband opened it . . . Enough. He has too many suspects.

◆

Gulping coffee after an hour's nap, Arthur follows Lotis to 67, feeling less like a sleepwalking ghoul, he'll survive to the day's end. Holly Hoover – the same explosion hairdo, a smart outfit – is getting a final drill from Ears, who seems bothered. Maybe it's the smell of patchouli oil. Jasper Flynn is back in court and studiously avoiding eye contact with her.

Lotis at Arthur's ear: "What's under her left eye isn't all mascara." A camouflaged bruise, maybe a gift from one of her regulars, feeling betrayed. Having branded Hoover an informer, Jasper Flynn has probably put the *Holly Golly* out of business.

Buddy asks, "Your occupation is . . . ?"

"I'm a sex worker."

"Can you expand on that?"

She stares at him for a moment. "I'll expand on that by saying I'm a recently retired sex worker." A casual, stoned way of talking.

"Okay, but tell us something about how you do it."

"I usually do it on my back."

This has Kroop bawling for order. Giggles continue to escape from the gallery as Buddy reorganizes. "I meant the nature of your . . . your area of operations. You have a boat, I understand."

She makes no bones about having been hostess of the *Holly Golly*. One of the jurors, a business writer, is making notes, intrigued by such entrepreneurship. "By the way, I'm trying to sell her, if anyone's interested."

A rebuke from the judge. "Must I remind everyone that a trial is a commercial-free medium?"

"Let's go to March 31, Ms. Hoover, in Bamfield. You were in the bar that night."

"I didn't have a date, decided to go straight. Almost didn't. Should've kept my mouth shut."

"Let's back up here."

"Okay, backing up. There was a band at the pub. That's why I went." Arthur can't get a handle on her. Is she scornful of the prosecutor, the judge, the process? What kind of high is she on? Stoned yet aware. Flynn still won't meet her eye, though she occasionally looks his way. He's doing a lot of moustache twirling.

Hoover recognized Eve Winters, told her she was a fan. "I should've stuck with that, should've settled for an autograph."

"What you should've done doesn't matter, okay?"

"Yeah, okay. So we picked up we were on the same length."

Buddy sends a hard look to Ears, who presumably messed up the pre-trial interview. "I'm a little lost here, Ms. Hoover."

Kroop's piping whine: "If you're lost, Mr. Svabo, how do you expect the jury not to be? Please find yourself."

"You were on the same length – what's that mean?"

"She was coming on. I was coming back at her."

"Wait. You mean sexually?"

"Totally."

A tale known to Arthur, but not to Buddy. Flynn whispers something to him. The jury seems uncertain how to take Hoover, her unexpected frankness.

"Move it along, Mr. Prosecutor."

"Ms. Hoover, did you give a different version of this to Sergeant Flynn?"

"No, I gave him a shorter version."

"Why is that?"

"He told me not to complicate my story, it would only get me tangled up in this. And there's another reason I didn't say much."

Buddy is getting the kind of answers one expects from blind questions. He's too afraid of Kroop to ask for a recess, has no choice but to tough it out. "What's the other reason?"

"I didn't want to malign Dr. Winters's name, she's an honourable lady. She has a reputation and I have none."

"Continue with your story," says Buddy, sweating because he doesn't know where it will go.

"I knew she was staying over in West Bam, so I asked if I could give her a lift in my canoe. I didn't want her suspecting I was a tramp, and said I made beads and bangles and bath oils. Which I used to. Guess I'll go back to it."

"Just stick to what you did that night."

"Right. So we agreed to leave separately and meet on the pier. I figured her as fairly straight for gay, careful socially, but she'd just done the West Coast Trail, she was hyped for a new adventure. A kind of shipboard romance, not knowing the *Titanic* is going to sink."

"Mr. Svabo, please control your witness."

"Ms. Hoover, I'd ask you not to ramble. Please, *please*, just answer my questions."

"You said, 'Continue.' That's what I was doing. Continuing."

Arthur goes to Lotis's ear. "What is she on?"

"I bet she ate a bunch of pot. Slow-acting fudge pot."

The rest of her tale, embellished by detours Buddy can't reroute, is as was told to Arthur while the elements warred outside Cotters' Cottage.

"So what made you think she was inviting you over?"

"She said, 'I have a bottle of wine, two glasses, and a corkscrew.'"

Buddy huddles with his advisers. Who knows what comes next — maybe a casual admission that after asphyxiating the Rohypnotized Eve Winters, she doctored the body with Faloon's semen. Buddy looks up at the clock, then to the bench.

"Too early for the afternoon adjournment, Mr. Svabo. You haven't earned an adjournment. You have not properly prepared this witness. You will have to slog on."

"Then what, Ms. Hoover?"

"She said, 'I don't know what your situation is, I'm just out of a relationship.' I felt I had to be up front, I told her I was a sex worker but this wasn't business. She was nice about it, asked a lot of questions, but the romance deflated like a flat tire. I should've kept my mouth shut." She's wandering again, and no one is trying to stop her. "I wouldn't be in this courtroom if I'd stayed with her that night. She'd probably be alive."

That comes to Arthur's ears with such credibility that he shelves the possibility she is the murderer. His cross will be difficult, he won't have his heart in it. But why had she kept the truth from the prosecutors until now?

Buddy shows visible relief, fear of the unknown dissipating, as his witness explains how, after several awkward minutes, they took leave of each other, Winters to her cottage, Hoover to her trailer.

Arthur is moved by this rainy, misty parting. Hoover is torn with guilt that she was honest with Doctor Eve when a lie might have saved her life. A conundrum of truth and consequences.

"Okay, so you went directly home?"

"I stood there doing a slow burn with a cigarette, feeling like an idiot. Went up the hill. Unlocked the door. Showered, painted my toenails, and went to bed."

"And to sleep?"

"Eventually. Played some music. Smoked some grass. Cried a little."

"You were there all night?"

"By myself."

"No more questions."

"Okay, but I have something else to say. I don't appreciate being falsely outed by Jasper Flynn as an informer . . ."

"I said, no more questions!" Buddy, drowning her out.

"*Order!* Cross-examination will begin after the recess."

◆

So as not to overhear Buddy's tirade against his helpmates, Arthur spirits Lotis to an empty interview room, chortling. "She had Buddy practically standing on his head. Flynn's hold on her is broken, he's sabotaged her, ruined her, driven her from Bamfield. She's in no mood to help the Crown, has nothing to lose by telling the truth. I hate to say it, but we have an honest witness on our hands."

Lotis looks horrified. "You *bought* that . . . that show-and-tell?"

Arthur is taken aback. "I beg your pardon?"

"Whoa, Arthur, you're too exhausted to see through her smoke." She sits him carefully in a chair. "She's an actor doing a stock character, the prostitute with a heart of gold." Mimicking: "'I didn't want to malign her name, she's an honourable lady.' Hey, man, this stoner has given three or four different stories about how she met Eve, she's a chronic liar."

"Her account is entirely the same as that I heard two months ago."

323

"She's a world-class manipulator. Told you how cute you were, and gave your cock a rub to seal the deal." Grinning. "It's awesome that you can blush on command. Damn it, Arthur, she'll have you buying the *Holly Golly* before she's through."

Arthur almost hears a clank, the rusty gate of his mind swinging open to a different view. The bossy nymph (and how he hates to admit this) could be right again. What if Hoover's the assailant? What if her whole thrust is to disarm the notorious Arthur Beauchamp? *Someone told me you were a vicious son of a bitch in court.*

My God, had six years of potting about in his garden done this to him, made him a romantic trusting fool? Arthur is the only foe Hoover fears. She has Jasper Flynn duped, as well as Buddy and Ears, and here comes Beauchamp stumbling along behind them, zombies under her power. *I've got nothing against Nick.* He believed that.

Back to Plan A. This involves Faloon's night with her, and a condom he never saw again.

Gilbert bursts into the room, frantic. "*There* you are. *Please!*"

Kroop nods to Arthur, who rises, willing away the weariness. "Ms. Hoover, let us clarify for the jury that in mid-April you and I met in Bamfield in the very cottage where the murder occurred."

"I heard you were staying there, interviewing people, looking for me."

"When I returned from dinner you were in the cottage, uninvited."

"It was raining pretty bad, didn't think you'd mind."

"I found you sitting on the floor with two bottles of cider. I made coffee for myself, and you gave me an account of your role in this case."

"The same as I just gave in court."

"You were there for an hour before going on your way?"

"About that, yeah."

"Nothing untoward happened?"

She hesitates. "You were a gentleman, if that's what you're asking." She's not about to mention her low-grade sexual assault.

"Well, that's what I want my wife to hear." Laughter from the pews.

"I'm sure no one here thinks you're capable of doing such a thing, Mr. Beauchamp." Kroop squirms with pleasure, relishing his mean-spirited double entendre, winning the bigger laugh. Occasionally he likes to show he's human.

This affords a segué into Hoover's sex barter with Nick Faloon. On the morning after, she recalls, Faloon begged her not to mention it. That didn't stop the gossip – it was known she'd stayed at the lodge.

"Just to be clear, my client found sexual satisfaction?"

"That's what it felt like to me."

"Who provided the condom?"

"Me. Always."

"And was it disposed of?"

"I assume. He lived there, he knew where the garbage was."

Arthur has ventured down that path as far as he dares. Martin Samples may be musing about used condoms: collected, boxed, filed, frozen, could they be weapons of blackmail? Two and a half stars.

"It has escaped no one's attention, Ms. Hoover, that my learned friends for the Crown were gulping air as you were recounting your unconsummated date with the deceased. Why do you suppose that is?"

"Probably because Jasper didn't file it in his report."

"You told him about Dr. Winters's invitation to share a glass of wine?"

"Right to his face."

Arthur makes his way along the counsel table, returns Flynn's collegial, square-chinned grin – they share dismay at the audacity of this pathological liar. "Does he have a problem with deafness, do you think?"

"Kind of doubt it, because he threatened to lay a charge on me for obstruction."

Arthur will divide and conquer. Though the jury remains impressed with Hoover, their primary affection is for Jasper Flynn. They remember his formidable performance against Arthur.

Kroop has been strangely inactive, his eyes settled into their fleshy nests. Like Arthur, he may have mastered the art of dozing sitting up. It's been a long week for the old fellow.

"The problem we have, madam, is that Sergeant Flynn denies you mentioned any invitation to spend time with Doctor Eve in her cottage."

"Then he's lying, isn't he?"

"Perhaps we can let these twelve honest citizens decide who's lying. Against you, Ms. Hoover, with your busy life as a sex provider and your habit of withholding vital information from the law, we have Staff Sergeant Jasper Flynn." Arthur is behind the officer, a hand on his shoulder. "A nineteen-year veteran of the Royal Canadian Mounted Police, a family man, a proud hockey father."

"A liar who accused me of being a rat." Her marijuana fudge, or whatever it might be, is wearing off; her bitterness shows a sharper edge.

"You claim you're not an informer, madam, but who in your position wouldn't? Do not pretend to us that you weren't trying to stay on Jasper's side by feeding him tidbits. Your clientele doesn't buy your denials, if I read the bruised eye correctly."

"I'm out of it as soon as I sell my boat. And you know what, I feel totally used. If I'm a fink, why can't I get on witness protection? You know why? Because Jasper says I'm too small a player. Small enough to be thrown to the wolves." She finally goes eye to eye with Flynn, who has been emboldened by Arthur's comradeship, has been staring defiantly at her. "I could say a few things, you bastard." Flynn starts.

A general holding of breath as the room watches Kroop for a reaction. There is none. It is impossible to tell if he's sleeping or scowling.

Flynn recovers, ruefully shakes his head, expressing pity for her. Arthur pats his shoulder. "Against the resolute testimony of an officer who gives up his spare time to lecture to kids in classrooms, and whose only fault is his overmanicured moustache, we have the word of a vengeful *fille de joie*."

Hoover gives him a cold and hurt look – she thought she'd blunted his attack two months ago with her caress. *You're cute.*

Arthur flips through his notes. "You knew Dr. Winters was staying over in West Bam. How did you come by that information?"

A hesitation. "It was all around town. Inez Cotter, she would have talked about it. It was a big deal. Doctor Eve."

"Do you know much about roofies, Ms. Hoover? Mexican Valium?" Kroop isn't stirring, Arthur's enjoying his freedom from judicial overview.

"Yeah, I had a guy try that on me a few years ago. Date rape, Roche rape, why pay a hooker? You wouldn't believe how common those club drugs are, Rohypnol, GHB."

"Easily obtained?"

"Over the Internet, under the counter."

Why can't she be evasive? Arthur moves near the jury; Flynn returns to his doodles.

"How much are you asking for the *Holly Golly*?"

She glances at the judge, sees no vital signs. Arthur wonders if it's possible he has simply died.

"Given she's got a few years, forty thousand dollars. That includes state-of-the-art directionals, all new lounge fittings, and an entertainment system that set me back nearly ten. Two 225 Mercs, plus auxiliary engine and canoe. P.O. Box 98, Bamfield. Or HollyGollyCruises, one word, at Hotmail dot com."

The entire room is now satisfied the Chief has drifted off. A problem arises in that it is nearly four-thirty, quitting time. There is not one soul in this courtroom brave enough to arouse him, including former amateur fighter Buddy Svabo. He is letting Arthur get away with murder.

"Were you out on the *Holly Golly* on Friday, March 31?"

"No, I was taking the day off, plugging some leaks in the trailer."

"What about that night – did you go out for a spin?" The two young Huu-ay-aht heard a fast boat going full out, no lights; its skipper knew the waters. But Arthur doesn't want to share these details yet.

"Why would I do that?" Evasion, finally.

"To flee from the scene of a crime." The room stirs, slowly stills.

She blinks, speaks three low but emphatic words. "No ... fucking ... way."

"It has already been established, madam, that you have an unsettling habit of making unannounced visits to Cotters' Cottage."

No response.

Arthur remains by the jury, keeps his voice level and low, content to let justice slumber. "Do you have a single witness who will say you went home, stayed home, didn't go out later that night?"

Again no response, a melancholy look, as if resigning herself to being browbeaten by the lawyer whose ear she tongued. She's a serial victim, scorned by Eve Winters, Jasper Flynn, now Beauchamp.

"Tell me if you find anything wrong with this picture, Ms. Hoover: spurned by the regal Doctor Eve, perceived as the town slut, condescended to, the humiliation rankling, growing . . ."

"Excuse me, Mr. Beauchamp." It is Gilbert, who has stolen up behind him and is pulling at the tassel of his robe. "Union regulations."

Arthur is vastly offended – his cross-examination was reaching a crescendo, he had the jurors with him. He looks up to see Wilbur Kroop's head is tilted sideways – he looks in danger of toppling over entirely.

Gilbert carries on up to the bench, finding untapped wells of courage. "Sir?" He is about to nudge Kroop to consciousness when eyelids slide open and lips move.

"Well, Mr. Beauchamp? Do you have any more questions? Otherwise we'll call it a day."

Either the silence woke him or he was never truly asleep. Before Arthur can respond, Kroop, sensing movement behind him, or the smell of fear, turns to find Gilbert frozen in position, his hand an inch from his shoulder. "What are you doing?"

"Ah, regulations, sir."

"*Regulations*? What regulations?"

"Union regulations, sir."

"What are you talking about, man? What are you doing behind me?"

"I thought you might have slipped away from us for a few minutes, sir."

"Because I was resting my eyes, you thought I slipped away? *Slipped away*? You utterly incompetent, snivelling, pusillanimous *idiot*! Get down where you belong!"

As Gilbert makes his way ferretlike to his place, Arthur can think only about absconding to the relatively sane domain of Garibaldi Island. "If your lordship pleases, I'll continue with Ms. Hoover on Monday."

Kroop nods, massages a neck muscle. "Witness, you are under cross-examination. You will return to this court at 10 a.m. on Monday, and until then you will not talk to any person about your evidence. You *will* not. Do you understand?"

"Yes, sir." Hoover is finally cowed. It took Kroop.

"Mr. Gilbert?" The judge looks darkly down at him like a vulture eyeing carrion.

"Sir?" He jumps, he'd been staring into space.

"Adjourn this court, Mr. Gilbert." Kroop shakes his head. "Union regulations. It's come to that." He rises and walks off, wrathful as God, tempted to send the flood.

28

fter calling ahead, Arthur and Lotis are met at the ferry by Fargo taxi. Lotis takes a chance on the open-air chesterfield while Arthur goes coach-class with Stoney. He ought to have chosen the chesterfield. Bad night, long week.

"How's the trial going, eh? Everyone's proud of the way you went from ordinary farmer to make a comeback as a famous lawyer. Hey, I would've showed up in a '58 Caddie Series 62 V8 convertible, but that ain't to be. A couple of goons stole it right off of my lot."

Arthur has the picture. Stoney did minimal repairs, test-drove the vehicle to ensure its road-readiness – earning fares along the way – until Freddy Jacoby repossessed it.

When reminded where the car came from, Stoney pulls a joint from behind the visor. "Right. How'd I forget that? I must've been in trauma, it's not every day a mint '58 luxomobile lands in your lap. Yeah, Mr. Jacoby, a straight shooter, he paid in advance after I faxed my estimate. I was gonna have the Fargo sitting on your doorstep bright and shiny, but as a result of this setback, I'm down to one vehicle again."

"Stoney, I intend to redeem this truck when the trial ends. You will deliver it up and there will be no excuses."

"I promise." He lights up, and they continue in silence toward Potter's Road. There's no time to detour to the Holy Tree. Bungle Bay's caretakers, Reverend Al and Zoë, are expecting him. They'll know Margaret's plans.

Behind a curtain of canary-yellow broom and purple spikes of foxgloves lies St. Mary's Church, beyond it the graveyard, a haphazard array of leaning markers. Pastured horses bowed as if in prayer. No breeze stirs bush or bough – Garibaldi seems apprehensive, an island in suspense while the truce holds.

Stoney turns into Arthur's driveway. "If you pick up a kind of tang in the air, it's temporary until I do one more patch on the pipes. Monster job getting your field back on line."

As they pass the backhoe, a whiff of excrement. But they are quickly beyond it, through the gate past the garage. Here the air is more flavourful, lamb shish kebabs grilling on the stone barbecue. The two Japanese Woofers are tending it under Zoë's direction. Reverend Al is sitting on the grass with a jug of homemade wine, celebrating the truce.

"Happening scene, man," Stoney says. Not expecting an invitation for dinner, he declines anyway. "I'd join you, ordinary I would, but I don't have time to sit on my ass, I got a thousand things."

Lotis hops off, and Arthur is about to follow when Stoney says, "You ain't forgetting something?"

Arthur looks around for what he might have dropped, sees Stoney's palm out for the seven-fifty-to-anywhere fare. Predictably, he can't make change for a ten.

Kim Lee comes from the Woofer house with a salad.

"Lookin' good," Stoney says.

She pauses. "Lookin' good you too." Arthur must warn her not to flirt with the scallywag.

He makes directly for Reverend Al, who is blessed by a ray of setting sun and well into a bottle of his excellent red plonk, blue-ribbon winner at the last Fall Fair.

"Because you have taken the pledge, old boy, you're unable to celebrate by partaking of the blood of Christ. Since someone must rejoice for you, I'll do double duty."

Arthur sees Al's big smile. Margaret is coming home.

◆

After dinner, they lounge by the outdoor fire, enjoying the long, languid evening. The sun has met the horizon, splinters of gold and flecks of rose. Al is well into his cups, and Lotis heading that way, raucous and theatrical. Arthur is invigorated by caffeine, spiced by Margaret's pledge to hug her tree goodbye on Sunday. (Not Saturday, a poor media day, so he has tomorrow to prepare. A third lemon pie, he's mastering the art.)

He must gird himself for another corny publicity event. He prefers not to be adorned in leaves, like an elephantine forest elf, or be called upon to recite the *Desiderata* or some such treacle. The only thing worse would be the Garibaldi Highland Pipers, who are demanding their turn, getting antsy. Bagpipes. Arthur shudders.

"It's Cyrano versus the fluffhead." Lotis wags a finger at Kim Lee in parody of Arthur's cross examination. "Against a low-life tramp like yourself, madam, we have Sergeant Jasper Flynn, a standup family man." Though the Woofers may not understand the script, they applaud the performance.

"Arthur's such a ham." Lotis snaps imaginary suspenders, puffs herself up, affects an unflattering swollen belly. "I ask you, madam, if there's anything wrong with this picture – spurned by Doctor Eve, treated like the town slut, humiliation biting at her ass until she can't stand it, she . . . What *were* you going to say, Arthur, before Gilbert stole the show?"

He meets the challenge. "Sitting in her leaky trailer, painting her toenails to the fierce tuneless beat of modern rock and roll, she continued to nurse her grievance over a six-pack of cider . . ."

"Whoa. She's a garbage head. She's doing crank, crystal, cartwheels, and in this totally gonged state she magnifies Eve's brush-off. The snob, she'll pay for that insult. Who does the bitch think she is anyway, I'm gonna march over there and . . . and what?"

"I am the resurrection and the life." Reverend Al slurring. Zoë has put a blanket over him.

Arthur tamps his pipe. "With no plan in her drug-addled mind except to retrieve the tatters of her honour, Hoover remembers the Rohypnol, which she keeps handy in case a john threatens to become difficult." This scenario is making sense. Hoover's rival evildoers are fading into the gloom: no-show Harvey Coolidge, bitter Ruth Delvechio, and Arthur's old favourite, Adeline Angella. And where has Daisy gone, who recently haunted his thoughts and dreams?

The confused Woofers take their leave, but Arthur and Lotis continue their skit. There's no one to watch but Zoë. Al is snoring.

"She spies through the window," Lotis says. "Fire in the fireplace, bottle of wine, half-filled glass. Eve is in the shower. Holly opens the sticky door with a gloved hand, mickey-finns the drink, and hides in the loft."

"Or she merely announces she's come for that promised glass of wine. Eve accommodates her." Arthur has his second wind. He sends a billow of pipe smoke to scatter the hovering mosquitoes. "After her wine is doped, she goes woozily to bed, and enters deep sleep. Now Holly will enjoy the vengeance of a vulgar joke – when Eve awakes her mouth will be full of her own underwear." He nods emphatically. "She washes both glasses, wipes the bottle, and is about to leave when she notices Eve is unnaturally still. Intoxicated to the point of gross misjudgment, Hoover has blocked her airway."

Here he stalls. What about the semen in her vagina?

Inspiration. "In panic, Hoover hastens to the *Holly Golly*, races off, no clear destination in view, no plan, just mindless fear. But as the amphetamines lose their grip, her capacities return. A substitute suspect is locally available. She and Winters even shared a laugh about the droll little fellow, he'd been Eve's dining companion. Hoover happens to be in possession of a little rubber sac containing his semen. She returns to port, retrieves the prophylactic, creates a plausible look of rape and murder, and goes home to bed."

"Why would she keep an old slimy safe?" Zoë says, finding the gaping hole in this hastily built structure.

"She's the eco-hooker," Lotis says. "She doesn't throw used rubbers in the drink. She zip-locks them, labels them. Keeps them with the frozen salmon in case something bounces back at her. Somebody's messy divorce. Maybe she's got a couple of Jasper Flynn's used tires too. It's obvious he's been boffing her. She hinted as much." *I could say a few things, you bastard*. Arthur saw Flynn go red and rigid.

Though Zoë looks dubious, Arthur feels he has the makings of a reasonable doubt. He has subpoenaed Claudette, she'll tell the jury about the animal rooting in the garbage. Hoover could be that animal. Yes, she's become a highly qualified perp. Clear opportunity, no alibi – the elements missing against Angella and Delvechio.

"And to think that only a few hours ago you were buying Holly's beeswax." Lotis, with her well-honed knack for puncturing the windbag, turns to Zoë. "He's been doting on her ever since she grabbed his nuts. Can't figure what he was up to last night. Got something going on the side, Arthur?"

Arthur coughs out smoke, averts his eyes from her favourite message T-shirt. *Rise up!* "I meant to ask you about those new tests Dr. Sidhoo is running. When are the results due?"

"She's working through the weekend. It's a long shot, she's not sure there's enough material left for a clear profile."

The tinny bars of "You Are My Sunshine" announce a call from Brian Pomeroy. "Caroline's a nervous passenger so I'm letting her drive. Thus we work out our differences in enlightened new ways. Say hello to Arthur, love."

Caroline's voice: "Hi, Arthur, we're about to get workshopped. I'll try any nutty thing once. How's Margaret?"

"Still at large, but a recoupling ceremony is planned for Sunday. Good luck with your own relationship."

"You're the one I truly love."

How alike are Brian and Caroline. Competitive, caustic, wry. How unalike are direct-action Margaret and slow-to-react Arthur. A different chemistry at work.

"Poop me up on the trial," Brian says.

Zoë and Lotis rouse Al and lead him to the house, while Arthur strolls to the beach, recounting his good day with Holly Hoover. "We're starting to put our energies in new directions. Angella may no longer be on the A-list."

"After all the work I put into that attention whore?"

"In the remote chance her DNA turns up in the remnants of Exhibit 52, she'll be back in favour."

"Interesting side note: Lila and Doctor Eve were casual friends from the Psych Association. She's been following the trial. Watch for the curve, honey. I gave her the lowdown on Angella, showed her Eve's column, the man-eater with skewed sexual preferences. Watch the centreline, love. Try this on, Arthur, Lila's theory: Angella is in extreme homosexual denial. She had a desperate need to stop Eve's mouth from speaking this impossible truth, to gag her, to choke her on her own underwear. Ciao." He disconnects.

Arthur mustn't discard Angella. He has a cornucopia of suspects, he must maintain them, groom them, march them around the ring, let the jury determine who is best in show. "How can you *not* have a reasonable doubt, ladies and gentlemen?" He orates to the ocean, punctuating his points with an index finger. "The flimsy vessel of the prosecutor's case has foundered on a sea of doubt. Wave after wave of doubt, ladies and gentlemen."

But doubt is not enough. Acquitting Faloon does not avenge Eve's death. He yearns to nail the case closed, to put the finger on the perp, to see her cuffed and led away, bemoaning her guilt.

He's in a fine mood. There's peace in the forest. He has a small stash of Viagra. The trial is turning in his favour, suspects galore. Too bad Faloon isn't around to enjoy exoneration. Probably hiding in some dank hole. But why can't he phone?

◆

Faloon wiggles his pinkie for another coconut, the kind with rum and a bent straw. He can finally lie under the sun again, after that burn last week. Time for a swim, but it's a Herculean task to decide between the pool and the ocean.

Nangeeah flashes him a big smile as he fixes the drink. He likes Faloon and his fifty-euro tips, has lined him up with some of the local fauna. One of whom is in a bikini in the adjoining beach chair, Hula-Hula, he calls her, because of the way she can shake it. Hula-Hula of Bora-Bora.

The Owl figures he's been forgiven by God for his past life of idleness and thievery, but isn't sure why. Maybe it's divine compensation for the ten-spot he drew because of Angella. Maybe it's God's way of saying there is a God. Maybe it's a little holiday before he burns in hell. Whatever, worrying about it is a mug's game.

He's especially not going to worry about assassins from Sierra Leone creeping out of the jungle at him, as they did in last night's featured dream. He gets nightmares like that, Lansana coming after him with murder in his eyes, the Owl frozen at the stairwell door, though in reality he went spinning down the stairs like one of those cartoon characters with propellers for legs. Using his master twirl, he lucked into an empty suite just before Lansana made it to the fourth floor. Lansana carried on down to the desk and the Owl walked out a side door with a laundry bag full of euros, jewels, and towels for bulk.

Farther down the list of things not to worry about is Vancouver, though he's not sure what's going on there, he assumes his trial got put off. He'll get around to calling Mr. Beauchamp one of these days to apologize. That's a promise.

Nangeeah delivers the rum, and a beer for Hula-Hula, who's a lot of a woman, sort of like Claudette but copper-toned and lazier. Which brings Faloon to someone else he isn't anxious to worry about. He'll send for Claudie. Definitely. When the time is ripe. He can't phone – no one's going to convince him her line isn't bugged.

He's not going to feel guilty about his Polynesian holiday: he earned it. He'll cut up the touches with Cat and Willy. In time. He'll be honest in telling them how much non-taxable income was sitting under the king-sized canopy bed – roughly thirty million in uncut diamonds and five million folding euros. He took enough cash for expenses, buried the rest three feet under the plastic flowers on the freshly dug grave of one Sebastien Plouffe. Then he bought a wardrobe for a cruise that Popov the Russian lined up for him. After this caper, Faloon has got to be seeded four or five, inching ahead of Popov, who himself had to admit that.

As his ship pulled out of Cadiz, there was a moment of panic that he forgot the name on the tombstone, but it came back. Sebastien

Plouffe of Cimitière Saint Pierre, Marseilles. It was a midnight dig, but there was enough glow to make out the stone – Sebastien bought it early, fifty-seven. Feeling connected to him, hungry to know him, Faloon has created a fiction. Jowly, beefy, taken in the prime because he wouldn't cut down the calories. A councillor, a ward heeler, corrupt in small ways. Worried about the Arabs and Turks. His daughter gone astray, on drugs. Problem with smelly feet.

Hula-Hula is up, pulling his arm, the pool beckoning. The dining-room manager sidles by. "Will the lady be sharing your regular table tonight, Monsieur Lapierre?"

"But of course. We'll start with the Sauvignon Supérieure."

Alfred Lapierre, that's who he is, down to his last passport, a French one, down to his last wig and moustache. He tells everyone he's living on an income, which is true. Maybe he should settle here, far away from those cold winter rains. Investing in the Nitinat Lodge was a loser's move, where was his head at?

◆

A warm slap of sun on Arthur's face brings him upright in bed. It's mid-morning, Bungle Bay has long been up and about, no one's waiting for the laggard. He has paid for his stolen hours with a week of toil and sweat. It's the last mate-less Saturday, tomorrow she descends.

At the window he takes a lungful of country air, but it's flavoured with a hint of methane, like a gassy fart. A hallucinogenic fart, either that or he is truly seeing Stoney work up a sweat, cutting a length of pipe. Dog holds a shovel.

To add to this pastoral yet industrial scene: the Japanese Woofers are repairing the fence, Kim Lee is feeding the chickens, and Zoë is in the goat pen, surrounded by prancing kids. Reverend Al is snoring in the next bedroom.

A note by the coffee maker demands Arthur's presence at the Woofer manor. His mood sours, he wants to leave business behind this weekend. Steaming mug in hand, he attends to find her highness at her computer. A *Criminal Code*. A text on criminal evidence. The Faloon files. Lotis has raided his house for them.

A curl of smoke from a cigarette in an ashtray. Arthur doesn't deny himself a soupçon of guilty pleasure at this evidence of wobbly willpower.

"The Blunder Bay chapter of Willing Workers on Organic Farms is now on-line. Munni Sidhoo transmitted some autoradiographic images. The comparison sample worked fine, Angella's snot and sniffles." She shows him a printout: "DNA ladders, they're called." Thin vertical lines, in segments. "This one is Adeline, say hello. Dr. Sidhoo is rooting through the semen for her twin."

If by some miracle this seeming time-waster works, Lotis will be unbearably smug. As it is, he has a sense of being patronized. He resents her unspoken disdain for his technological ineptness.

"Been on the horn to Claudette. She hasn't heard a squeak from Nick, she's worried sick. Holly's black eye came from a barroom scrap with a drunken log-truck driver. I gave up looking for Daisy. Eve probably shit-canned the file."

He praises her diligence. She shrugs, flicks her hair. *Nothing to it, Arthur.* He can't concentrate on these things. Tomorrow is Day Seventy-nine. He ventures out to inspect his woeful, weedy plot. The invaders must die.

◆

The afternoon of this sparkling day has Arthur manoeuvring his runabout toward Gwendolyn Beach, as his crew of Lotis, Al, and Slappy wave and bark at anchored locals. There's Clearihue's yacht. He and Arthur have an appointment in the war zone.

Stump Town has moved here, settling amidst the great firs and cedars spilled helter-skelter like God's matchsticks. Wilbur Kroop's worst nightmare has come true: naked hippies on the beach or swimming in the chilly saltchuck.

A medieval tapestry decorates the shore. "Qualified Reiki Therapist," a banner says. "Yoga Research Society," says another. Beside it, inconsonant with this mellow 1960s revival, a khaki military tent houses Kurt Zoller's tour business, Garibaldi Adventures.

Beyond is the twenty-acre clear-cut. Already an otter habitat has been lost. The confrontations must end before more of nature is tramped upon, despoiled. But there's hope. Almost $7 million has been raised or promised. The Gwendolyn Society's last-gasp strategy, fiercely debated, is to borrow the rest.

After discharging his live cargo, Arthur anchors out and takes the dinghy in. Zoller helps drag it up so Arthur can skip to shore without getting wet, then announces he's off to fetch a fare. "More tourists." Now Arthur must push Zoller's craft off the beach, and his shoes fill with water.

Flim and Flam, always silent, always observing, raise cameras as they spy Arthur on a slab of driftwood, emptying his shoes. Also grinning at him are two Mounties, a skeleton crew today, enjoying this week-long break from thankless duties.

Lotis has been sent to search for him, finds him squeezing his socks. "Clear-cut won't talk to any of the local peasants. You de man." Why does he want to meet here, amid the green ruins? Maybe he thinks the ugly backdrop will give him an edge.

He slips on his wet shoes, follows her through the maze of fallen trees, hears the honk and squeal of the Garibaldi Highland Pipers, practising for the ceremony tomorrow, when Margaret will descend by zip line. Three bagpipes, one drum, a rendition, however incongruous, of "Will Ye No Come Back Again."

Clearihue applauds the pipers vigorously. Boots and denim, a tooled leather hat. He's growing a beard, though with undetermined success on his boyish face.

Their tête-à-tête takes place by a stump, its juices oozing, sap rising to phantom branches. The corpse of this tree lies atop several others, still sending out growth.

"We're riveted on your trial, Arthur, the whole island, it's all we talk about." He claps Arthur on the shoulder. "Glad you're back, I didn't want to deal with the locals; frankly, I'd be taking advantage." One week off-island, and Arthur has lost his local status. "Be nice to get this timber out of here. Sure opens things up though, doesn't it? Stage Two is that ridge over there, incredible view lots, top dollar for them."

"Our figure was $12 million the last we talked?"

"Directors beat me up over that, Arthur, I have to jack it up. Fifteen, I can sell them on that." Though no one's nearby, he comes close enough for Arthur to smell his aftershave. "We have some strong outside interest, Americans, Europeans. An e-mail from a Saudi sheik, he wants his own wilderness retreat, God forbid. It's all the publicity, Arthur, the human-interest stuff, it may be backfiring."

"What are you trying to say?"

"I'm saying this has become such a headache we may have to unload fast to the highest bidder. We have an Arizona developer coming by, I don't know what to tell him."

"You might tell him he'd be insane to pay millions of dollars for endless years of problems."

"He owns half of Tucson, he's a billionaire, he's got time. A gated community, that's what his team is talking about, three hundred lots. He's promised to protect the environment, I got that out of him."

Twice the devastation Garlinc would have wreaked, the valley torn apart, the island's population tripling. Surely this is all bluff. No smart investor will touch land so deeply in dispute, occupied, besieged. Yet Arthur supposes the publicity has indeed sparked interest – an article in *Time* has made Gwendolyn a celebrity.

Arthur bites the bullet. "We can't go above your previous offer." The society can go to the bank for the rest, and pray donations will continue to flow.

"The expenses are eating us alive, Arthur."

"An astute negotiator such as yourself shouldn't be displeased with a fifty-per-cent profit over two years, particularly when the bulk of it can be written off as a charitable donation."

Clearihue contemplates, then sighs. "We'll go twelve and a half, and eat our costs."

"Twelve all in, Todd."

Slappy has emerged from among the broken boughs. He sniffs Clearihue's boots, accepts a pat from Arthur, pisses against the stump.

"Ah, what the hell. Twelve all in, but the society will have to sign an interim by Monday with at least a dozen guarantors."

"You're speaking for your board?"

"Of course. No problem."

Arthur tells him to draw up the agreement. He holds out his hand. Clearihue hesitates, then engages with him, a firm double pump.

Lotis, as is her habit, has snuck up on Todd, is standing above him on the jagged end of the weeping fir. "You want to stop taking those designer steroids, Todd, there's hair coming out of your face."

Without turning, he barks, "Get a job, Rudnicki. I hear there are some openings for suicide bombers."

"Yuppie scum."

Arthur interrupts sharply. "We have no time for this. Lotis, please pass along word that we have a deal for twelve million. We'll meet tomorrow to ratify it, and go to the bank on Monday."

He foresees few problems – the Bank of Montreal is a major client of Tragger Inglis, and Bully serves on its board. Now he must return home to make some calls. "How do we get out of here, Slappy?"

The old spaniel leads the way, around a slash pile. Clearihue calls, "Hey, good luck with your trial. I mean it."

Arthur casts off none too soon, avoiding Zoller's launch as it whips toward the beach and swerves hard to port, creating a surge that nearly swamps the departing pipe band. Riding the second swell, Zoller neatly brings his bow onto the sand.

Cutting a natty figure in his neon-orange life jacket, he's putting on a show, impressing his fares with his maritime skills. They have the look of generous tippers, several large men, one with a Stetson and a string tie. Maybe Clearihue wasn't joking about the Arizona developer. Arthur must move quickly to firm up the deal.

◆

He's relieved to find Bully by his phone in his home office. He's in an agreeable mood – Tragger Inglis is having a good month – and proposes no obstacles to Arthur's plan. But there's a catch.

"A sizable retainer is available on the Wilson murder, Arthur. Set to go mid-October. He doesn't want Cleaver, he doesn't want anyone but you. Strong defence, he wasn't aiming at his wife."

Arthur hedges, promises to consider it. He's as keen to take this case as ride a rocket to the moon.

Arthur must next contend with Brian Pomeroy's strident call-of-the-day. "You wouldn't believe all the New Age shit going on here. The guru, sorry, *relationship facilitator*, is so droll and cool and self-effacing I want to ralph. Caroline shares my cynicism. We're bonded in distaste for the banality of it all."

Like most of Brian's harangues, this seems to serve little purpose other than letting off steam.

"We're into confessing our naughty habits and moral shortcomings. Not sure if I like the way the facilitator is pressing me to open up my past. If he's New Age, I'm Old Age, I prefer the medieval system where you confess to God and priest. But I forgot the reason I called. Oh, yeah, I just heard on the news – Faloon's on his way back."

29

On the Owl's left, window seat, is a sour immigration official from Tahiti who never opens his mouth. On his right, aisle seat, is Corporal Johnson from Commercial Crime, Vancouver, who has handled Faloon for years, which is why they sent him.

They've been sharing memories, like the time Johnson strip-searched him, not even glancing at the Piaget on his wrist. "I was pretty green then," Johnson snorts. He's in his fifties now, a paunch, balding like Faloon.

The French guy is scandalized by this jesting with a prisoner. He and his henchmen caused a scene in front of everybody at Faloon's hotel yesterday afternoon. Coming at him with guns, as if he were John Dillinger. Faloon took it as a personal insult. It should be like tag football, you just touch a guy.

"Remember that stakeout on Broadway?" Faloon says. "You're at the peephole, and I'm tapping you on the shoulder, going, 'Looking for me, corporal?'"

Maybe Corporal Johnson doesn't like being the butt of these memories, because he stops laughing. But you've got to have a sense of humour about life's ups and downs. It doesn't pay to beat yourself up over what's not your fault. In this latest situation, Faloon got betrayed, is all. Despite all his backslapping, Popov the Russian resented being bumped from number five in the world. Popov had been in line for a piece of the buried treasure, but now he isn't going to get a dime.

Faloon isn't fond of the alternative theory that he made himself an object of suspicion by spending too large. It's the last thing a lucky thief should do, flipping a waiter a century here, half a yard there, like he did on Bora-Bora. His only excuse is he was exhausted from lying low, he had to come up for air.

"I'm real disappointed in you, Nick," is Corporal Johnson's attitude, asking how he could ever pull such an amateur stunt, going through fifty K in two weeks. The bulls found three hundred more in the Owl's suitcase plus the forty in the lining of his suit, which he made the mistake of asking if he could wear so he wouldn't look like some cheap hood in court.

Faloon acted hurt they wouldn't believe he had an amazing streak at Monte Carlo. The gendarmes tried to smoke him out about the jobs in Cannes, but Faloon saw no profit in helping them. With Lansana not talking, they didn't want the hassle of grinding him through the French courts, easier to let Canada have him.

Facing a murder beef is bad enough, facing Claudette will take nerves of steel. He swore he'd never lie to her again, and now this. He hopes the official reports don't mention Hula-Hula or any of the other girls. He was going to get word to Claudie, honest. He was marooned on a tropical island.

Corporal Johnson gets on him again. "You got to be ashamed, Nick, you were doing good, burned your parole papers. Now you got a bad streak going, you're wanted all over the joint. Canada, France, Africa."

"I'm a little guy, a shoplifter, why am I getting other peoples' heat? Corporal Johnson, be honest, you don't think I murdered that Winters lady."

But Johnson won't talk about the April Fool's murder, not a word, he's got strict orders. Faloon grows small as he pictures Mr. Beauchamp glowering at him, pissed because everything went off the rails after he'd set two weeks aside for the trial. A horrible thought: the great man refuses to act for him, turns him over to his off-the-wall female assistant.

He has to cling to hope. *La situation est plus encourageante.* But if things don't turn out so rosy, it's the big one, life in the attitude-adjustment centre. Goodbye, Claudette, forget me, have a happy future. Goodbye the good life on his newfound wealth. (Buried somewhere in that sea of gravestones in Cimitière Saint Pierre, guarded by the late Sebastien Plouffe. Bet he weighed three hundred pounds. Died of gluttony, traffic jam in the arteries. Voted *Front Populaire.* Made Arab jokes.)

✦

Arthur hears mutterings of discontent as he walks from St. Mary's to seek breeze and shade. This pocket-sized church holds only fifty souls and was sweltering within, and the faces of Reverend Al's grumpy flock are shiny with sweat.

"I was staring at my watch the whole way," says Ernie Sproule. "He went on for forty-seven minutes, nineteen seconds."

Reverend Al and Zoë are nearby, shaking hands with parishioners, chatty and gay. "Hope I didn't go on too long," Al says. "I had the spirit in me today."

Prompted by the settlement reached with Garlinc. No major celebrations yet — agreements must be drafted and signed, the funding campaign must push ahead. Arthur feels unburdened: he's able to concentrate on refurbishing a marriage and defending a thief newly arrived from Polynesia.

Faloon should be in the Richmond lockup by now, near the international airport. Arthur has arranged with the Crown to meet him there within the hour, via Syd-Air from Blunder Bay. The timetable is tight — he must shuttle back to Garibaldi for another reunion, Margaret's return to earth. Three p.m., no later.

There's a do at the hall later, a potluck, a relaxed occasion to honour Margaret. Then will come the delicate first moments of being alone with her. Then the night, and whatever God intends.

Driving home, he frets — she hasn't been emitting deafening signals that she misses him. The word *love* speckles her paper glider notes, but only in ways casual or dutiful. Such festering doubts have combined with eleven weeks of sleeping alone to create a suffocating shyness.

"Be attentive but do not smother." Down-under Deborah. "She'll need to talk, don't fall asleep on her. Make love to her like the sensitive New Age male you long to be."

He couldn't bring himself to mention the Viagra, it's not something one talks about with a daughter. The two tablets from Hubbell's stash will do for now, but he supposes an uncomfortable, throat-clearing session with Doc Dooley is a prerequisite to obtaining more.

Back to Vancouver in the morning, the trial must go on. He must finish his cross of Holly Hoover, then the Crown's case is almost in. A few minor witnesses and Adeline Angella.

Here comes Kim Lee, pedalling hard, waving urgently, pulling him over.

"Lo-tis prease hoary home." She throws her bike in the back.

"My God, what happened to her?" She fell off Barney. She stepped on a hive of yellow jackets.

"Happy, happy happen."

"Happy . . . happy, good?"

"She solve case."

✦

Lotis rises from her computer, stubs her cigarette. "Ultra low tar. One weakness isn't bad."

Arthur has learned to abide such intimations of near-perfection. He waits impatiently. She smiles, enjoying the moment, drawing out the suspense.

"Munni Sidhoo built a profile of Adeline Angella from Nick's semen. These are the autorad charts." The printer clicks and buzzes. "Angella dosed the corpse with Nick's ten-year-old seed. She's our perp."

Arthur stares dumbly at the DNA ladders. "No chance of a mistake?"

"Whoa, get with it. Dr. Sidhoo wrote the book on DNA."

He sags weakly to the couch, elated with a sense of impending triumph – yet there's a sense of loss. All those other suspects, wasted. He finds irony. Almost convicted by science, Nick Faloon finds salvation from it. In the end, not law but science determines who is innocent, who guilty.

It was Ms. Know-it-all's idea, this sifting through the semen sample for Angella's DNA. He will forgive her smugness, her truancy, her capriciousness, even her revolutionary jargon.

He has one more task for her – to check out Angella's alibi. *I think I may have had a teeny, teeny bit too much at the Wanderlust.* Lotis is to use utter discretion when talking to the staff. No stranger must know the defence armament holds such a powerful weapon as the DNA of troubled, obsessive Adeline Angella, who hadn't been candid with the Crown – Buddy would toss her away like a worm-eaten apple if he knew she'd been Doctor Eve's venomously unhappy patient.

Here comes Syd-Air. In half an hour, Arthur will be shaking his client's hand, telling him he has chosen a propitious time to come back. As of tomorrow, when Angella takes the stand, the defence becomes a prosecution, the greatest, most honourable of defences, turning the tables on the true murderer.

It's around noon, Faloon figures, as the wagon pulls up behind a typically square suburban RCMP detachment, in a town called Clearbrook. He feels fagged, slow, stupid. He wasn't able to collar a nod the whole time from Tahiti, he never could sleep well on a plane, especially between two honking big cops.

"First thing, I want to call my lawyer."

"Staff Flynn's in charge of that," says Corporal Johnson.

They go through the security door, and there he is, Jasper Flynn, in the booking room, a big salesman's smile under his bulky 'stache, as if he's meeting a wealthy customer. "Have a good flight, Nick?"

"Yes, thank you, and I want to talk to Mr. Beauchamp."

"He been warned?"

"Couple of times," Johnson says.

Jasper breezes through it anyway, after which Faloon says, "I want to commend you on your reading, Sergeant Flynn, especially the last part, where I have a right to a lawyer."

"Let's get the bureaucratic shit out of the way. We got to book you, do the prints and art." To Johnson: "You tell him how it's going?"

"No."

Jasper Flynn shakes his head, demonstrating sadness maybe. Tell him what? Faloon isn't going to ask. He's got one thing to say to this copper. "When I am I gonna call Mr. Beauchamp?"

"Hey, Nick, it's Sunday, let the man relax."

He's whisked through the system, Sergeant Flynn granting his right to a leak but not a phone call. Otherwise everything's a blur, and what Faloon wants right now, more than even a lawyer, is a few minutes kip. But Jasper won't even lock him up. "Let's go for a ride." Friendly, not like some gangster movie.

Out they go into the sweltering day, no bracelets, nothing, Faloon with his suitcase on rollers, trundling to Flynn's Explorer, which has windows you can't see into. Then Flynn opens the door, shows him this German shepherd in the back with cold eyes and a low growl. "Old Shep's harmless," Flynn says.

Faloon says, "Nice doggie," and sits up front. "Where you taking me, Officer Flynn?"

"Moving you away from the city. There's a lot of public feeling over this case, Nick, we want to avoid a media circus." He pulls away. "Buckle up."

So here's Nick, no constraints except a seat belt, perched in the cockpit of this bus, with its kids' sports equipment in the back and a dog that could possibly go for the throat, a very unofficial vehicle, which means the inside door handles should work. Maybe Flynn wants him to run when they get to a stop sign. Then he's going to shoot him. Roadkill.

The paranoia keeps him awake as they swing onto the freeway, the 99, heading east up the Fraser Valley. A media circus . . . Do they even know he's here? Does Mr. Beauchamp?

"I don't get it, Nick, you make a clean getaway, a big score on the Riviera, and you blow it all by wild living at a thousand-buck-a-day resort."

That's why he's a copper. Guys like Johnson and him don't understand. Thieves have a different nature. Different aspirations.

"How's that going to sound to the jury tomorrow?"

Faloon starts. "Would you repeat the question, sergeant?"

"It's going bad for you, Nick."

"What is?"

"Your trial. Jury's waiting for the lawyers to finish blowing wind so they can convict you and get back to their families."

"My trial . . ."

"I forgot, you been out of touch. You're an absconding accused, Nick, that means a jury can convict you in your absence. Last few witnesses are going in tomorrow. Your ex-girlfriend, Adeline Angella, will talk about how you put a knife to her throat. You're in the toilet, Nick."

Faloon sits back, relieved that the horseman turns out to have a sense of humour. "I'm calling you on that one, Sergeant Flynn."

At a cloverleaf, they pull over at a gas station. "Stay," says Flynn, getting out at a self-serve pump. The Owl's not clear if that's meant for him or the dog or both, but he stays. It's hot in here with the air conditioning off, even though Flynn left the driver's door open. That gives a view of newspaper boxes. A tabloid headline: "*Golly, Holly!*" A shot of Hoover walking from the courts, a sexy smirk, like it's all a big joke.

Though he barely touches the door handle, he hears a throaty rumble from harmless old Shep. Flynn has trained this dog to kill absconding suspects. Meanwhile he's out there pumping gas with his door wide open, like an invitation. The Owl wonders if the trial's really going that bad. Maybe it's the Crown's case that's in the toilet.

"Want anything?" Flynn, pulling out his wallet. "I'm getting an ice-cream bar."

"One of those newspapers would be good, Officer Flynn."

"Naw, it would only depress you."

Flynn doesn't want him to see beyond the headline. This is the confirmation Faloon wanted, this is a setup, this pit stop is staged. This is Flynn's career case, he's not going to let the perp walk, he wants him to run, his mauled body will be recovered in the high grass behind the Texaco station.

When Flynn flagrantly turns his back and walks to a convenience store for his ice-cream bar, Faloon doesn't budge. When Flynn returns chomping on it, he's unhappy to see that the Owl hadn't taken advantage of his leniency, and slams the door shut, and they take off.

◆

Dinner at the Clearbrook RCMP is a takeout double patty slid through the meal slot, which Faloon has almost polished off when a constable comes down the aisle for him, jingling keys. "Your lawyer's here."

Mr. Beauchamp's voice comes like rolling thunder down the hall. Then it's Flynn, his spiel about how he was hiding the Owl from the media. Then a thunderclap: "Don't give me that blather! You had me chasing all over God's kingdom!"

The Owl can't remember the great one being so riled. He hopes it doesn't have anything to do with his phone call to Garibaldi Island, after he finally got his rights under the Charter. Mr. Beauchamp's wife answered, weary and wiped, like she just got home from work. She didn't know where Mr. Beauchamp was. Sounded a little cheesed.

His counsellor is standing just outside the secure area, dressing down the Roadkill Warrior. "Why wasn't I *told*? I ought to have you up on charges for kidnapping."

"Sir, I can't believe the dispatcher didn't tell you. We move people all the time in high-profile cases, I got Buddy Svabo's okay . . ."

"If you've destroyed my marriage, Flynn, I hope you roast in hell!"

◆

Arthur stares out the window of 807 Elysian Tower at the lingering agony of the June sunset. Presumably this tangerine sky is glowing for Margaret too, at Blunder Bay or wherever she is. The potluck at the community hall must be long over. She'll be relaxing by the beach, on a driftwood log, watching her first sunset in thirteen weeks. That's why she's not answering the phone, she's enjoying herself. Maybe with friends, Al and Zoë.

Margaret will have a laugh when she finds her answering machine clogged, unable to absorb more of his alternating contrite and jocular apologies, his dreary twaddle about the mischievous designs of Sergeant Flynn, about how he missed the last ferry, how every air taxi service was booked.

The only human he reached was Lotis, and the connection was bad. She was on her way – by bicycle or bus, it was unclear – to the Wanderlust, Angella's suburban waterhole. "I love to go a-wandering," she sang, her words breaking up. Arthur persisted in the face of her lilting reassurances. Hey, boss, relax a little. Margaret came down safe, she's looking great. The ceremony was a hoot, the Garibaldi Pipers played "My Bonnie Lassie." The press loved it, it was beyond hokey.

He finally rouses Reverend Al. "She was having dreams of luxuriating in a bath and sleeping in a bed. Can't blame her for not answering the phone, this is her first private moment, she's probably enjoying being alone." He retracts that too late. "Prefer to have *you* there, of course, but that wasn't to be. Anyway, she sacked out half an hour ago."

"Did you explain why I wasn't there?"

"Told her you fled out of fear of the Highland Pipers."

"That I avoided them was the only amazing, saving grace."

"Arthur, please accept this from a friend. She's a little depressed. It was an important time for her, and you weren't there. She accepts that. She understands that this is a critical time for you too, for your trial. She wants you to concentrate on it. She doesn't want you to think about her or worry about her."

The warm, reassuring pastoral tone only makes Arthur more anxious.

30

Ruffled and sour after a restless night, Arthur arrives in court a minute before starting time. Faloon's already in the dock, in natty suit and silk tie and rimless spectacles. Nicholas is not a thug, that is the statement, he's a gentleman thief. (A successful one. "I got real lucky in France, Mr. Beauchamp.")

The jurors goggle at the returned exile. Photographs hadn't prepared them for his clerkish look, a small man dwarfed by the sheriffs. Forewoman Ellen Sueda frowns, as if struggling to see him as a killer. When Kroop shuffles in, he too spends a few moments contemplating this late arrival. Missing is Arthur's junior, still on the trail of Angella's alibi.

"For the record," says Buddy, "the accused has been taken into custody and is present."

"Do you confirm that, Mr. Beauchamp?"

"Indeed. Mr. Faloon invited arrest on becoming aware the Crown's case was falling apart."

That editorial has Buddy sputtering. Improper, low! Beyond the bounds! Sitting too close, Ears recoils from a light wet spray.

Kroop waits until Buddy peters out, then flourishes his water pitcher. "Mr. Gilbert, this is empty."

"I'm sorry, sir, I assumed the sheriff's staff . . ."

"Their role is to ensure order and security. Your tasks are less exalted, Mr. Clerk. While you set about getting the water I will see counsel in my chambers." There's a tautness to Gilbert – for a moment, Arthur has the impression he's a rubber band about to snap. As court adjourns Gilbert walks determinedly from the room.

Kroop rarely invites barristers to his sanctum, and Arthur has never been so favoured. On the way in, he brushes by Jasper Flynn. "Really sorry about yesterday, Mr. Beauchamp. I'm going to find who screwed up."

Arthur's too miffed to respond. The unreachable Margaret Blake will be on his mind all day, a crucial day, this trial is about to take an unexpected shift. *She doesn't want you to think about her.* (Means what? She wants you to forget about her?)

There's a sense of the nineteenth century about the Chief Justice's space – musty and murky, curtains closed to sunlight, a brass desk lamp. No computer. On the wall is a Gainsborough, a girl chasing a butterfly: unexpected lightness, therefore eerie. Framed nearby, a photo of a steely-eyed young man in a 1950s haircut on his call to the bar. No pictures of loved ones – Kroop married the law.

He motions them to chairs, then sits behind his desk and glowers at Buddy for a few moments, as if measuring his words.

"Mr. Svabo, I hesitated to interrupt in front of the jury, even as you were careering out of control. You have allowed Mr. Beauchamp to get under your skin. You may not be as used as I am to his grandstand gestures." He waves the subject away. "Gentlemen, there's no reason this should slow us up. The accused will be asked to confirm his plea of not guilty. Before we proceed with the rest of the case, I'll want his consent to be tried on such evidence as was heard in his absence."

Kroop wants to seal off any avenue to appeal. Arthur doesn't blame him, and assents, subject to Faloon being allowed to read the evidence taken so far. He can do that in his cell overnight – Arthur doesn't want this trial delayed.

"Excellent," Kroop says. "From the outset, I've had misgivings about trying an accused *in absentia*. Rich fodder for the Appeal Court.

But now he's here, and fit to be tried. Himf, himf. Please don't expect me to grant bail, Mr. Beauchamp." A sweet, small smile.

✦

During the break, Arthur waits on the vine-draped terrace, trying to keep his mind on the task ahead, the day's remaining witnesses. He's playing with his cellphone, and only realizes he's dialling home when Buddy joins him. He switches off before it rings.

Buddy is still rankled at Arthur's bold claim his case is falling apart, but he's rarely able to maintain his grudges, and they are soon talking timetables. "Next up, I got two exhibit guys and then the brain-dead screws who let Faloon escape."

"To save these fellows further humiliation I will admit their evidence. What about our disappearing friend Harvey Coolidge?"

"We're kissing Harvey off, Internal Revenue wants him to stick around Kansas. Don't pretend that doesn't make you happy – you got his statement, he was nowhere near Brady Beach that night. Sure, make a case. Harvey's running scared, Harvey's got no alibi for April 1. Only one more element is needed – a miracle. Like maybe Harvey's DNA is an exact match for Faloon's."

Arthur shrugs. Harvey doesn't matter any more. Angella matters, only Angella.

She appears below, as if conjured, frilly blouse, pleated skirt, looking lost, stopping by a potted ficus in the Great Hall, staring up at the angled roof, the blue-tinted skylight. Her eyes settle for a moment on the hawk-nosed barrister above, then she walks toward the stairs in her little penguin gait, arms held out like vestigial wings.

"She's a reluctant witness," Buddy says, "doesn't want to be dragged through this, you can't blame her. Jasper's trying to sell me on letting her go. My useless junior too. They say it's overkill – so we prove Nick has a habit of attacking women, why gild the lily? Until a few days ago, I was thinking about scrubbing her. But now you've got the jury so confused with side issues, I can't pull my punches."

Arthur seeks a neutral subject. "What's holding us up?"

"Problem with Gilbert, he's balking at returning to court. How many witnesses are you calling, big guy? Put Faloon on the stand, let me at him." He throws a one-two, perky again, a man who bounces back. "We sum up Thursday, maybe Friday, does that sound fairly ballpark?"

Arthur isn't ready to make commitments. He is obliged to give notice of Dr. Munni Sidhoo's evidence – her signed report is on its way by courier – but will wait until Angella is on the stand.

There is a stirring as Gilbert appears, stoop-shouldered and wan. With him is the Chief Registrar, who gives him a pat on the back, sends him into Court 67, and departs.

Kroop sits with his characteristic expression of stifled rage, his face made more fearsome by the mock cherubic smile he aims at his clerk. "Mr. Gilbert, do you have something you want to say to me?"

"Not really, sir." The tone is sullen, a hint of rebellion.

"I've been waiting nineteen minutes, Mr. Gilbert."

"I'm aware of that, sir."

"And what do you have to say about it?"

"Nothing, sir."

Kroop looks stumped by the unexpected pluck, asks sardonically, "Was it union business, Mr. Gilbert?"

"As a matter of fact, sir, yes. With respect, I would prefer to discuss it in your chambers, not in public." A transformation is happening, Gilbert standing taller, speaking firmly, drawing from the deepest wells of fortitude.

"Come, come, let's hear your grievance."

"It isn't written in the rules that the clerk must fetch water for anyone, sir, including the presiding justice."

During the frozen hush that follows, Gilbert begins to lose what little composure he'd mustered. Most jurors are ill at ease, but Martin Samples seems transfixed as he takes in this sadomasochistic standoff. Five stars.

Kroop's face convulses, his wattles flapping, as he rises several inches from his seat, as if about to swoop down on his clerk. Gilbert looks wildly about, picks up a stapler, raises it defensively.

"Why, you snivelling, spineless moron – put that down!"

Gilbert stares at his poor weapon, lets it fall, and stumbles from his station, unfurling a handkerchief. Strangers from the audience join him, help him to the door. In his utter misery, in his bleakest moment, he has stirred the hearts of even hardened courtroom habitués.

Kroop roars, "Bring me another clerk!"

◆

After a brief recess, a replacement is conscripted from the registry, an older woman, a veteran. As the room settles again, Arthur finds himself puzzling over why Holly Hoover, with her big hair and bruised eye, is back in the witness stand. He'd forgot about her in the recent excitement. When last seen, Holly was under a barrage, accused of being addled on uppers, arming herself with Rohypnol, marching off to Brady Beach to demand satisfaction for Eve's rebuff.

"Mr. Beauchamp, we've already thrown away half the morning with utter nonsense. Can we not pick up the pace?"

Hoover is looking immeasurably sad. How cruel of Arthur to have bullied this young woman, to have accused her of the worst of crimes.

"I doubt if I shall have more questions, but I'd like her available."

That causes murmurs and shuffling, disapproving looks from the press. Hoover shrugs, gives Jasper Flynn a cold stare. She tosses her curls and leaves without a look back.

"Good," Kroop says, "we're moving right along. Mr. Prosecutor?"

Buddy is confused by Arthur's sudden lack of interest in a key player. "Excuse me?"

"Next witness, please."

"Sorry, milord, I have to see who's ready." Buddy prods Ears to his feet, out to the witness room. Flynn follows.

"In my day, when I served Her Majesty in these courts, I had my witnesses primed and waiting. I don't see Mr. Beauchamp being unready."

This isn't a good development, this clubby affection for Arthur – it's liable to turn the jury against him. Few, except Samples, give any sign of liking the miserable fellow.

Ears brings in a young woman from the Ident Section who hand-delivered the semen swab to forensics, then to Dr. Sidhoo. No stranger had opportunity to contaminate it, that is the thrust of her testimony.

The final police witness, who dusted the fingerprints in Cotters' Cottage, is laboriously taken through photographs showing their locations. Known Individual EW, lower right bathroom sink. Known Individual JF, upper refrigerator door. Arthur is restless, it's not of interest, and his thoughts fly to Bungle Bay. There she is, in the laundry room. She's found the discoloured tablecloth, a yellow stain he couldn't get out. She's fed the lemon pie to the goats without tasting it.

He refocuses as Adeline Angella is ushered in by Flynn. As she takes the oath, she looks defiantly at Faloon, then Arthur. She is stiff at first, shoulders back, breasts taut against the fabric of her frou-frou blouse. But she soon achieves a rapport with Buddy, becomes less wooden, more confident, garnishing her answers with the weary smile of one doing a distasteful but necessary duty.

Her testimony is almost an echo from ten years ago: different venue, different jury, same script. "I was researching an article about the fascinating world of the jewel thief." "I realize now I was naïve, but I invited him up so we could continue our conversation."

Fearful of being crossed up by Arthur, this reluctant witness has laboured over the transcripts of ten years ago, when she stood up to him, brave and unbowed, winning the jury. Today, a little passion has been lost, as happens when a performer has lived with her lines too long. The jury seem confused about why they're hearing about these old events.

As her tale reaches its climax ("Suddenly there was a knife to my throat"), a student-at-law from Tragger Inglis approaches Arthur tentatively, as if he'll bite. He accepts her envelope: two copies of Munni Sidhoo's validated analysis.

When Buddy runs out of questions, Kroop asks, "Would you like to start now or this afternoon, Mr. Beauchamp?" A few days ago, before Kroop deserted the prosecution, he would have ordered him not to waste minutes of precious time.

"A few initial questions, milord." He will banish Angella to that state of judicial limbo known as being under cross-examination. "I understand, Ms. Angella, that you appear here reluctantly."

"I would have preferred not to do this again."

Arthur nods. "This is difficult for you?"

"Very. It means one more time reliving my . . . my experience . . ." The sentence dies, incomplete, as she watches Arthur leaf through a glossy magazine.

"Let us rewind the clock. Ten years ago, the version you just gave was accepted by a jury."

"Yes, I told the truth."

"It led to my client's conviction and a ten-year prison sentence."

"Yes, it did."

"Six months after he was convicted, *Real Women* published your explicit account of the events you've described." He holds up the magazine. "Your experience, as you put it."

"Yes. Well, I'm a writer."

Arthur asks about the cross-country lecture tours mentioned in her Web site, the many times she relived her experience before breakfast clubs, service clubs, women's groups.

"I want women to understand the trauma, what a victim has to go through, being bullied by lawyers."

Kroop interrupts. "Bullied, madam?" Presumably he finds the proposition ludicrous. "We will adjourn to two o'clock. Witness, you may not discuss your evidence with anyone while you are under cross-examination."

As court adjourns, Arthur passes to his client a few bound transcripts, the testimony from last week. "Some light reading for you, Nick."

"I will be glued to the pages. Also, I want to say I admire the way you got the judge in your pocket."

Arthur isn't quite as dazzled by that accomplishment. He must find a way to turn Kroop against him. He joins glum Buddy and his sanctimonious helpmates, who advised against calling similar-fact evidence from Angella. He lays Munni Sidhoo's report before them.

"What's this?" Buddy flips through the pages, the charts, the DNA ladders.

"Profile Three is Adeline Angella. Enjoy your lunch, gentlemen."

✦

On his way to the El Beau Room he again fiddles with his phone, almost loses courage but dials Blunder Bay. No answer. Margaret is likely at Gwendolyn Beach, preparing for another celebration. The papers are done, the financing in place, and Selwyn Loo is to meet Todd Clearihue on site to sign the deal. This will be Selwyn's first trip to Stump-Town-on-the-Beach – he's been too depressed to go near it. There are to be champagne and handshakes at this media event, and Kurt Zoller will be rendering some popular ditties on the accordion.

He connects with Lotis, on location at the Wanderlust. "The lunch crowd doesn't know Adeline, so I'll hang here a while. Manager showed me a past events calendar, an amateur barbershop quartet was gigging here March 31, regulars, they may know her. What's the score in 67?"

"It has the makings of a rout." But why does he hear the whispering hobgoblins of pessimism?

Someone at Gwendolyn Beach will have a cellphone. He dials Selwyn, who has been boated there. "Garlic's threatening to reneg, Arthur. That Tucson cowboy just offered them a huge whack of dough." A morose, end-of-the-earth tone.

Arthur tells him to relax. It's merely a ruse to sweeten the pot. Don't offer a cent more. Arthur shook hands with Clearihue, a deal is a deal.

The blind crepehanger is far less sanguine. "I have intimations of disaster." Have the gods endowed him, like Cassandra, another depressive, with the cruel gift of prophecy?

Selwyn is standing on a high bank overlooking the twenty-acre clear-cut. "I can smell it," he says. The smell of death and rot. It doesn't seem the right time to ask if Margaret is within hailing distance.

Brian meets him at the El Beau Room. Cranky, raw eyes, uneven shave. "Caroline has twice had affairs. Twice in the last five years! She *shared* this in front of ten strangers, eleven if you count the guru. She could have shared privately." A groan. "How I've come to despise that word."

"And how many such instances did you divulge during this ugly truth-telling?" Arthur has always assumed secrecy is part of the definition of an affair. Confessed openly, it loses its romantic lustre, it's merely adultery.

"I stopped at seven. The guru was goading Caroline with subversive shit like: 'Share with us your thoughts about Brian right now.' 'What do you want to say to him?' She started screaming at me. 'You're a self-centred asshole!' I told her I'm prepared to deal with that. She got more profane, mistaking my sincerity for sarcasm. She became lyrical. I was a sick, suppurating, secretary-humping whore. Everyone else looked relieved – their own fucked-up relationships paled in comparison. I'm seeing Lila this afternoon, I'm going to tie into her. Sending us off to do heavy encounter, it's like she *wants* the marriage to fail."

Arthur has little patience left for Brian's self-inflicted marital wounds. He has his own marriage to worry about. He has Gwendolyn to worry about. Would Clearihue dare to reneg?

Sandwiches arrive. Brian takes a deep breath. "Where's your spooky junior?"

"At the Wanderlust. The Whalley Wanderers are entertaining there tonight."

"*Entertaining*? I caught their act, bald heads, pot bellies, white shirts, and bow ties. The tenor has a squeak in the high range. So Angella's back in the running?"

"She leaped to the front." Arthur brings him up to date.

"Who came up with the brilliant idea to do this second analysis?"

"The spooky junior."

Brian shivers. "Omnipotent people freak me out."

"She's a nymph, a dryad. She was sent by Zeus to avenge Doctor Eve's death. Since nymphs are famous for their jests, I may end up being the April Fool."

The *Fourth Brandenburg*. "Hey, Frank, *como esta*? . . . No, Mommy and I had another little spat, that's all. No way, pal, we're defi-*notly* getting divorced."

This maudlin scene concludes with Brian wiping an eye. "Isn't that a great word? Little Frank discovered it. I asked him once, 'Who made that mess?' 'Definotly me.' I'll definotly be in court to watch your grudge match, I'm seeing Ms. Chow-Martin. Ask Adeline if she's got another contract with *Real Women*. Do you think it's possible, maestro, that she engineered this whole thing – murder, suspicion, accusation, confrontation – so she'd have something to write about?"

"She just walked in." Standing at the door, staring in. She followed them, Arthur assumes.

"Too late to get under the table?"

"Yes."

Brian turns, waves at her, smiles his ravaged, helpless smile. She looks coldly at her betrayer and his handler, returns outside.

✦

In court, Buddy is in intense dialogue with his DNA expert, who's frowning over Sidhoo's report. Ears stands by with his trademark ill-suited smile. Flynn is grim, muscles bunched in tension as he finger-combs his noble moustache. Faloon is sitting in the dock reading transcripts.

Arthur is no sooner seated than Buddy is upon him. "I don't get it. Goddamnit, what's the *point*?" He raises his voice. "What are you trying to *prove*?"

"That you've been barking up the wrong tree."

Buddy blows. "Okay, Artie, no more mister nice guy! I'm going to have my guys review Dr. Sidhoo's results, and I want her on the stand, and she better freaking be able to back this up!"

Not only does the entire gallery hear this, but the jury too – they are taking their seats. Buddy shuts up when he sees them, scurries to his seat as Kroop shuffles in. Angella mounts the stand, head high, chest out, like a robin about to serenade the spring. "May I say something?" she asks the judge.

"Madam, this is a solemn inquiry with ancient and respected rules. One of which forbids witnesses from making speeches. Otherwise trials might extend into the gloom of eternity. Please just answer counsel's questions."

Arthur doesn't want it thought he's afraid of what she'll say. "Ms. Angella, tell us what's on your mind."

"I want to correct any insinuation that I profited from my misfortune by writing articles and making speeches. The fact is, for the last ten years I've barely made enough to pay the rent. I am in debt. I am clinging to the poverty line."

Arthur nods. "Not much money in the writing game, I suppose."

"The magazine market is very tight."

"Maybe you'll profit better from your fiction." From his briefcase, he pulls out yet another magazine. "*Tales of Passion*, April edition. Your first published story?"

"Yes, as I told your colleague, Mr. Pomeroy, when he came sneaking around for information."

"This is the plot, as I apprehend it: Harry has locked himself out of his townhouse. He has to break in through a back window. In error, he enters a lookalike unit, and comes upon Tracy, a rookie policewoman, who is undressing for bed. Do I summarize fairly?"

"Thank you for reading it." Her tone distrustful.

"What interested me, as an amateur critic of the genre, was the pervading subtext of rape."

"I don't know what you saw in it, but most of my friends found it very comical and romantic."

Arthur opens the magazine to her story. "'Tracy felt her breath come quickly as he moved toward her, his shirt undone, revealing rippling muscles.' One would expect this cop to be running for her gun, not standing there panting in her undies."

"Well, he was also getting undressed, he thought he was in his own place."

An unresponsive answer, but Arthur merely says, "Let us see what the jury makes of it," and files the magazine as an exhibit. "Where did you get the catchy title from? 'You're Not Supposed to Ask.'"

"It came to me."

"It came to you because you spoke those words ten years ago when Nick Faloon asked permission to kiss you."

"That's not so."

"He wasn't supposed to ask. He was supposed to perform. A parlour game was enacted that night – you the playful maiden, he the pretend intruder. Ultimately you took him to your bed . . ."

"I object," Buddy says wearily.

"I uphold. This is not the time for windy speeches, Mr. Beauchamp."

Arthur strolls to the witness stand, close enough that she is forced to look straight at him. "Let me put to you, briefly and bluntly, a fair and reasonable version of what happened."

He does so in short sentences. She tried to wheedle the Kashmir Sapphire story from Faloon. Seduction was her final tactic. The condom failed its task. A fear of pregnancy, an unravelling, a call to 911. In panic she hid the condom where no one would think to look. It remained untouched, unseen, like a vice hiding in Pandora's box.

"That is absurd. That is so pathetic." This is the voice of ten years ago, more confident. "There *was* no condom."

"Yet you claim you begged him to use one."

"I . . . yes. I hoped he had one."

"You hoped he'd come prepared?"

"I don't know what I was hoping. Or thinking. I was hysterical! Afraid for my life!" She is persuasive in her passion. Forewoman Sueda is looking reprovingly at Arthur: he's compounding the assault.

This has sunk to being a replay of the first trial. How ill at ease he'd been with such intimate inquiries. The jury must have assumed his heart wasn't in it, that he was grasping at straws.

He must cut to the chase. He retrieves Exhibit 52. "Madam, in this zip-lock bag is the swab taken from the vagina of Eve Winters. I will be offering proof that it has your. DNA. How might you account for that?"

"*Impossible!*" Spoken with a vehemence that shakes Arthur a little. "It's a mistake! Take my blood!" She thrusts her arm at him, pulls back her sleeve, an offering to the black-robed vampire. The room is silent, Kroop alert as a hawk, expecting the Crown to object. Buddy sits there looking petulant.

"Ms. Angella, you were reluctant to come before this court . . ."

"Because of having to face this . . . this inquisition."

"Oh, there's a much more telling reason. You didn't want to risk exposing yourself as the killer of Eve Winters."

"Order." Kroop sends his lasers about the room, and the hubbub ceases. "Mr. Svabo, have you nothing to say?"

"I don't know what's going on here." He doesn't even rise, the fight has gone out of him.

"Mr. Beauchamp, that is a very bold accusation."

"Given a chance, I will back it up." Arthur bites that out.

Kroop gives him a much-welcomed cold eye. "Then get on with it."

Arthur opens his briefcase. "Three years ago, Ms. Angella, you engaged Dr. Winters's services."

She looks at him with alarm, then beseechingly at the three Crown heads, as if in disbelief that no one is objecting. Buddy looks like a motorist stalled at a rail crossing as the noon express rounds the bend. Ears's grin has turned gargoylelike. Flynn is playing with his moustache with both sets of fingers.

"You had a problem maintaining relationships with men. You sought Doctor Eve's advice."

Finally, she says, "This is irrelevant."

"Who told you this was irrelevant?"

"It has nothing to do with anything that ever happened anywhere."

A sweeping compendium of all that is under the sun. Arthur pulls the missing file from his briefcase, produces a patient consent form. "This is your signature?"

Angella goes white. "I only saw her a few times. I . . . I couldn't afford her, it turned out." Arthur glances at the jury, makes eye contact, wins smiles.

"And you didn't inform the Crown of this?"

"Because it's . . . it's nobody's business. It's privileged."

Kroop sighs. "Counsel, do you have copies of this material, so Her Majesty's envoys don't have to crowd around you?" Buddy is jostling Arthur's side, Ears breathing minty essences near his neck. "It is becoming apparent that Mr. Svabo is in the dark about certain matters. You may enlighten him during the afternoon break." He rises.

"I suppose it's too much to expect you would give the Crown notice."

"I assumed they'd done their homework."

The room empties of all but counsel, staff, and Angella. She is at

Buddy's ear, hectoring him. He disengages. "Can't talk, Adeline, you're under cross, can't talk." The sheriff takes her aside. Her careful hairdo is coming apart.

As the Crowns pore over a photocopy of Gowan Cleaver's file, Arthur enjoys a moment with Faloon. "How are you holding out?"

"Real excellent, Mr. Beauchamp, and better by the minute the way I see this is going."

"I've been ill mannered, I haven't asked about Claudette."

"She phoned, she's relieved to know I'm innocent. We want to have the pleasure of you and your wife to join a small group of friends next month, God willing, for our wedding."

"I shall definitely ask her." *I'm sorry, Arthur, weddings only make me sad. But thanks for calling.*

Outside the courtroom, Arthur toys with his cellphone. As soon as he turns it on, it rings. Reverend Al, frantic and panting, as if he's running. "It's chaos here. Selwyn has disappeared."

This is the information he gasps out: The celebration has become a shambles. Garlinc has reneged on the deal. The billionaire Arizona developer trumped the Save Gwendolyn offer by doubling it. There was an angry confrontation with Clearihue, almost a mob scene. No one was aware Selwyn had wandered off until Margaret raised the alarm. A group of kayakers spotted him disrobing at a deserted stretch of shoreline, letting out his ponytailed hair, wading out, swimming languidly. They thought he was enjoying himself, and they paddled on. That's what they told the search party a few minutes ago. Everyone is rushing to that area of beach.

Arthur is in shock twice over. The perfidy of Garlinc. If Selwyn drowns, they have driven him to it. "I'm being called to court. I feel helpless, but I'll pray."

He can barely digest this horrible information. A genius IQ, a boundless future, but a depressive condition. Arthur is overtaken by a powerful image of G'win d'lin drowning in the Salish sea, her hair pulled by the tides like strands of kelp.

◆

365

The Owl doesn't like the way Mr. Beauchamp comes back to court looking like his doctor told him he has a month to live. When he approaches Faloon, his eyes are damp and red. "Excuse me if I seem distressed. I may have lost a dear friend." He slumps into his chair.

Faloon isn't sure if he means the friend is dead or has run off, like an absconding wife. Given he was ready to paste Sergeant Flynn for sabotaging his marriage, it sounds like the latter.

You wouldn't believe from his defeated look that the trial's been coming up roses all day. A normal lawyer would be looking forward to finishing off Angella. There's *nobody* in here who looks happy. Mr. Svabo is smouldering, his dreams of besting the great Beauchamp burned to ashes. Sergeant Roadkill obviously wants to be somewhere else, anywhere, the South Pole in his Jockey shorts. Faloon's sharp eyes made out a cartoon on his writing pad, gross, a woman eating cock. Flynn caught himself, scribbled over it.

Everyone stands for the judge, who is feared widely and known as Father Time. The Owl is thankful that his fate is in the hands of twelve peers, ordinary, lowly citizens like himself.

Mr. Beauchamp takes a minute to compose himself, staring at Adeline Angella as if she's a picture in a museum. Maiden Turning on Tap, dabbing her eyes. He waits a bit more, then launches in, very controlled at first but you can tell he's furious inside, trying to keep the lid on.

She, on the other hand, looks like she's unravelling when Mr. Beauchamp gets on her about how she was living a fantasy life with her movie magazines and dreams of seduction. And how she had a sexual arousal disorder, as Doctor Eve called it. Flirting, then not making it to the end game. Faloon remembers how it was like making out with an air mattress, how she faked orgasm, though you can't ever tell.

The great barrister is getting into it now, he's on lockdown. He's put his wife worries aside, he has a trial to win. Now he's reading snatches from Doctor Eve's files. "Adeline appears to be in deep denial," "Adeline demonstrates little awareness of the source of her turmoil." The last note, "Adeline failed to show up for today's session." When Mr. Beauchamp asks why, he gets, "I didn't feel we were going anywhere."

A month later, Adeline got into Doctor Eve's column as Lorelei. Mr. Beauchamp reads it to her, her strict upbringing, her need "to discover inclinations which may be truer to her heart." Which seems a nice turn of phrase, reminding Faloon of Doctor Eve's poetic way of talking about the wind in the pines.

"I considered her a charlatan," Angella says at one point.

The *coup de grâce* is a recorded call, which Mr. Beauchamp manages to play on a cassette player after some fumbling. "You're an unprincipled, unethical bitch who pokes fun at her patients in print. You think you're so high and mighty and clever, wait till I see my lawyer, you bitch. I hate you." Very unbuttoned, and an extreme reaction considering nobody would have a clue who Lorelei was.

The jury is all ears. The judge is staying out of it, but maybe that's because he's having trouble with his false teeth, you can hear the clicking. You have to wonder what he's thinking behind his wide fleshy face and dark buried eyes.

Angella starts getting sniffy with her answers. If she felt this column was libellous, why didn't she hire a lawyer? "Unlike some people around here, I couldn't afford high-priced help. Anyway, I decided it was beneath me."

A magazine writer ought to be adept at research, does she agree? Surely she researched date-rape drugs? Weren't these drugs mentioned on her own Web site? She knew, didn't she, that Rohypnol was easy to get on the black market? She has to concede to most of this, but won't admit she knew Dr. Winters reserved for the West Coast Trail.

She denies knowing much about Bamfield, but then has to admit she knew Faloon was running a small lodge there. She had a right to know where her brutalizer was living on parole, so she consulted the police, who keep a sexual offender registry.

Mr. Beauchamp asks about her reaction to Faloon getting nailed for this bad beef.

"I wasn't surprised."

"And the reason for that is that you, madam, framed him for your own act of murder, an act as exquisitely planned as it was cold-hearted."

So far, Mr. Beauchamp is keeping his temper. He owns the courtroom, everyone else is a bit player, even Faloon, even the judge. It's his finest hour, it's got to be the cap to his noble career.

He wades right into it, the whole gruesome scene, right up to Angella closing down Eve's pipes. And maybe he's too relentless, maybe he's taking out his marriage crisis on her, this is becoming what's called badgering the witness. He begins shouting at her, accusing her of having sneaked into Bamfield on a mission of death, and she screams right back. "It's a lie, I didn't, I didn't! I wasn't anywhere near that place . . . I've *never* been there!"

"I put to you that on the night of March 31 and in the ensuing small hours you were indeed in the village of Bamfield."

"Help me!" She calls this out to the back.

A deep bass answers: "She was with us!"

The Owl swivels around, sees four suits, all balding and porky, all in bow ties, standing shoulder to shoulder, looking like they're about to belt out "Down by the Old Mill Stream."

"Sit down! One more eruption and I'll have you behind bars!"

They retreat to their seats, but Mr. Beauchamp looks like he was just hit by a truck.

"Your Lordship, please let me explain," Angella says. "These gentlemen escorted me home at one o'clock that morning. That's what they came here to say. I was a little tiddly, I'd been celebrating."

A while ago, Faloon was thinking about Sebastien Plouffe, buried underneath millions in the basement suite at the Cimitière Saint Pierre. Now he's thinking he might not be paying respects at his gravesite any time soon. Mr. Beauchamp isn't reining Angella in, he's still staring at the bow ties, it's like he's drifted somewhere. She's taking advantage. "They're the Whalley Wanderers, your Lordship. I have fifty other witnesses. My story had just come out, I was giving copies to my friends . . ."

Mr. Beauchamp takes a slow, heavy breath, braces himself. "Cease, madam! The question then arises, whom did you hire to murder Dr. Winters?" That's what he comes up with, his voice hoarse. To Faloon, it's a bad question, the jury's going to think he was B.S.'ing them earlier, it's a retreat to plan B, maybe C, maybe the end of the alphabet.

She gets him good. "I can barely afford to hire a cab, Mr. Beauchamp."

Faloon turns to see Lotis Rudnicki, the gorgeous sidekick, coming in, hair flying all over, shorts and flip-flops, a top which you can tell there's no bra under it. She runs past Faloon to Mr. Beauchamp, speaks urgently into his ear.

"Miss Rudnicki, you may not enter the bar of this court looking like that. You may not enter the courtroom *period*, dressed like that."

"He's alive!" she shouts, as if expecting everyone to know what this is about.

Silence, then Mr. Beauchamp speaks softly. "There was a near-drowning, an event involving our colleague, Mr. Loo."

"Yes, yes . . . the fellow without sight? Brilliant counsel. Well, I see the time is . . . We'll adjourn for the day." The judge scrambles off awkwardly.

As the court empties, Angella gives Faloon a gotcha look. Gotcha again.

◆

Arthur pries open an eye, sees a multicoloured sky. The sun's dying breath on Japanese lovers on the wall. It's 9 p.m., he's been down three hours, a needed refuelling. The bedroom door is ajar. Low conversation. Lotis Rudnicki and Hubbell Meyerson are still here. He can sense her pacing because of the ebb and flow of her distressed voice. "Todd Clear-cut! That prick!" The smell of her cigarette. "That shit-eating limousine liberal, he nearly *killed* him!"

Before Arthur took his nap, he'd talked with Selwyn by phone, in the Vancouver Island hospital where he'd been taken by helicopter. He'd swum as far as McGuff's Islet, where he was dashed against the rocks. Cuts, bruises, a twisted knee, nothing broken. "I was sincerely thinking about it, Arthur." Suicide. "But instead I just kept swimming. Then suddenly I was tossed onto the shore like a gaffed fish. I gave up. Decided to save it for a more propitious day." Still cynical, but his life force had overpowered the dark urgings of Thanatos.

We'll block the sale, Arthur vowed to him, with far more confidence than conviction.

He can hear Hubbell talking to an associate at Tragger Inglis. The terms bandied about are *breach of contract, unjust enrichment, restraining order*. Bullingham computed the cost of pro bono services, deducted that from the surge of new business its gesture will earn, offered legal aid to the Save Gwendolers.

Arthur can't remember much of his cross of Angella this afternoon, except those gruelling moments when it blew up in his face. The Whalley Wanderers, Angella's honour guard, three local merchants and a retired fire chief, standing proud in their bow ties. Arthur felt as if he were dying on his feet. Had a bottle been handy he might have ended a fifteen-year dry spell.

His former number-one suspect had given a brief reading at the Wanderlust on that last evening of March. Digital photos were taken of the literary event. Strangers bought her drinks. "Sweet Adeline," that's how the boys serenaded her from the stage. Lotis had uncovered this shatterproof alibi too late.

What, then, could account for Adeline's molecules showing up in Exhibit 52? Contamination between exhibits seems likely, Angella's DNA in accidental mix with Faloon's, a scandalous forensic error. Dr. Munni Sidhoo may not be the expert she's cracked up to be . . .

He can only pray her findings will be confirmed by Crown forensics – their DNA people are working overnight, checking her results. But then what? Did Angella engineer the murder some other way? How? Or does the answer lurk elsewhere, another paradigm?

Upon hearing Brian Pomeroy make noisy entry and smelling his steaming takeout cartons, Arthur rises, finds plates, chopsticks. Lotis is perched on the counter, morose, wiggling her flip-flops. Brian is digging into the bar, about to break his weak vow of temperance.

Hubbell protests that he's expected home, his dinner is being held. "Got your second wind, I hope. By the way, Margaret is arriving tomorrow on the noon ferry. Told her I'd pick her up and bring her here." He goes to Arthur's ear. "You won't whisper about you-know-what." Margaret's a casual friend of Hubbell's wife. Marital cheating seems fraught with complication. How can it be worth the effort?

He'll be in court when Margaret arrives, another misaligned attempt to link up. To ask her not to come would send a dangerously wrong message. Now it's too late to call her, she's early to bed, rises with the dawn. He wonders what she made of his pathetic messages of yesterday.

Lotis shouts. "Fucking Clearihue. Fucking Whalley Wanking Wanderers. Fuck *everyone!*"

Brian downs his shot of vodka and pours another. He seems somewhat in dread of her. Maybe he truly thinks she's a dryad. Maybe he suspects she sees through him.

She has shed copious tears of grief and relief for Selwyn, reinforcing Arthur's impression that her feelings are not platonic. Maybe she too is blind, denying these feelings, regarding herself as too tough to fall sway to the bourgeois concept called love. She's devastated by the failure of the Gwendolyn campaign. Arthur wants to comfort her but isn't sure how. He lacks hugging skills.

While picking at her chop suey, Lotis issues a string of epithets, crowned by a threat: "I'll *kill* that cocksucker."

"Right on, sister," Brian says. "Kill the capitalist pig." Drink has loosened the recidivist's tongue. "There's something I want to share with you, my love. I too am a kitchen communist."

"Hey, man, get therapy. Release the self-centred child within. Learn to relate to normal human beings."

"I'll *tell* you about therapy."

"Not interested." She stalks away.

Arthur makes tea, leads Brian to the living room, where Lotis is making up the couch as a bed. "Shall we presume you're staying the night?"

"Thought you'd never ask."

He regrets his formal tone, extends an invitation.

Brian is unrelenting: "You'll want to keep your bedroom door locked, Arturo, so you don't wake up with vampire bites on your neck."

She says nothing, kicks off her flip-flops, bends to her packsack, pulls out a bag of dirty clothes, proceeds to the laundry room.

"I told you, she's a loose cannon. It was *her* bright idea to test the jism for Angella's prints. That test doesn't hold up, we're tits up, Adeline will be dancing off to sign a contract with *Real Woman* for a story about how she bested you again."

He's right, if the jury thinks Arthur targeted the wrong perp, they'll suspect he's been selling false goods all along. He made the mistake of running a prosecution, not a defence. Hubris.

Arthur steels himself when Brian asks if he may bend his ear. He supposes today's session with Ms. Chow-Thomas went poorly. Here is a marriage crippled by truth and confession, too much sharing of sins.

"Caroline's *intimes* were milquetoasts. A colleague of hers, American Poets 200, a pity whore, can't get tenured, can't get published. Lasted three months. Number two was in her birding club. Three or four times a year, always out of town. They allegedly share a quality I lack called sensitivity."

Arthur slumps into a chair, feeling addiction prickles as Brian sips.

"Lila had the gall to tell me that Caroline's *relationships*, her word, were a reaction to my womanizing, also her word." His voice rising. "Womanizing! *She's* been womanized, she's infatuated with Caroline." He explodes: "Damn it, that witch sent us off on that weekend with the sole intention of ending our marriage! She wants Caroline for herself! Christ, I'd like to *strangle* the conniving . . ."

He hits the brakes, steals a look at Lotis, who has just returned. She misses this chance, an easy score into an open net. Instead, she's staring at Arthur with her wide bold eyes. Suddenly, where there was mystery, light appears. Tea goes down the wrong way. Arthur lurches from his chair coughing.

"We have to find Daisy," he says.

31

It's half past eight as Arthur sets out for his office, a vigorous walk along the shoreline. A trio of girls runs past, jostling him. "Sorry, Pops!" Arthur feels as a foreigner must, he's a rural refugee, out of place among the flashy towers, the grunting traffic of the harbour. Margaret too will find this a test, it's a poor setting for reconciliation. (About now, she's packing her suitcase . . . Will she *bring* a suitcase? Does she even plan to stay overnight?)

Despite his anxiety, he had a sustained sleep, less troubled by all the clutter of the trial. He's back on track, knows where he's going. But he isn't sure how to get there. The fingerprint on the fridge. He had almost missed that. There are so many bits and pieces. So much depends on the Crown validating Munni Sidhoo's analysis. Everything.

Christ, I'd like to strangle the conniving . . . Brian's rhetoric pointed Arthur to the cipher, the solution to the coded messages that keep getting dropped in his mailbox. What an odd sensation, that bonding of minds with Lotis. Last week's dream of Dogpatch haunts him now: daisies everywhere, beckoning, whispering. Find me. Find me.

After Brian left, Arthur and Lotis continued to talk excitedly, she pacing in her underwear while her clothes were in the washer, oblivious to her roommate's discomfort. Arthur set her tasks, directed her to contact Winters's secretary. As of this moment they should be combing through every scrap of paper in Doctor Eve's office. Locked since April 1, it may yield clues in old billings, appointment calendars, notes in desk drawers. A love letter hastily hidden between a book's pages, overlooked as Doctor Eve sought to obliterate all traces of Daisy. "You are My Sunshine" sounds, it's Lotis. "We have a name of interest. Desirée. Scribbled twice on an appointments calendar for last July, so the time is right. Nothing else, no last name or phone number. Desirée. Daisy."

An appropriate nickname for someone hobbled with Desirée, though he daren't say that to Lotis Morningstar. July, August, September, and the affair broke off in October, according to Ruth Delvechio, who bounded onto the scene very quickly after that. *The affair was so dead in the water.*

"Does the secretary remember her?"

"She thinks so. Golden-haired, poorly dressed, graceful, fragile. Came in a few times last summer, and around that time Eve stopped being a workaholic, began taking an occasional afternoon off."

Doris Isbister calls next. Arthur demands to know how to switch off the banal campfire song.

"Bring it up here, dear, and I'll install a new ring. Miss Hoover is in the waiting room. Coffee and croissants?"

"Please." He can't reach Brian Pomeroy, who's at RCMP division headquarters with a friend, an inspector, whom he's asking questions about procedures to avoid contaminating exhibits.

As Arthur packs himself into a crowded elevator, Buddy Svabo calls, falsely hearty, shouting so loudly that Arthur must hold the receiver away. "You looked kind of sick yesterday, hope it wasn't contagious." A stirring in the lift, people shifting away. "I hate to admit it, but we got a positive on Adeline. Turns out that forensics actually did find a third-person trace in the semen – this was back in April – marked it down as an unknown, and flagged the investigation team. Don't know why I wasn't informed. What's going on, Artie?"

Arthur promises to call back, relief washing over him. Sidhoo's test has held up, and Buddy is stuck with Sweet Adeline's profile in Exhibit 52, wondering how to explain that to the jury. Arthur's new paradigm is clicking into place.

On the forty-third floor, Tragger Inglis's waiting clients (stock-option holders, corporate raiders) sneak looks at the snow-white thighs of fellow entrepreneur Holly Hoover, who's reading a business magazine. Trademark mini, new hairdo, cascading curls. A cynical smile, her eyes quick today, the pupils clear – maybe it's drug-free Tuesday. That doesn't mean she won't be any less scheming and devious.

"Hey, I sold my boat. Thanks for the free advertising."

"Did you get your price?"

"On the nose." She rises and follows him. "Why am I here? – that's not a metaphysical question."

"I thought I was harsh on you in court the other day, and wanted to make amends."

"Sure you do."

✦

Sheriff Willit has to clear a path for Arthur through the crowd waiting for Court 67 to open, past the Whalley Wanderers, who scowl at him. "His Lordship is in a foul mood today, Mr. Beauchamp. Bit of a canker under his lower plate."

"The poor chap. And how is Gilbert Gilbert, have you heard?"

"Total breakdown. Not the first time. Couple of years ago he went berserk in an Italian deli when his girlfriend left him. This time his mother's trying to commit him."

"How frightful."

Arthur's thoughts fly, as they do sporadically, to Selwyn Loo. Driven not to madness but thoughts of suicide, not by bullying and shame but by a larger despair, planetary.

At counsel table, he's confronted by Buddy Svabo, whose call he forgot to return. "Fine, Artie. So don't tell me what's going on." Hurt, exasperated. "All I know is Adeline has an alibi as tight as a popcorn fart. And here comes Jasper with his cock-eyed theory."

Flynn shuffling toward them, smiling. "You mind, Buddy?"

"Tell him, already."

"Mr. Beauchamp, I'm asking myself is there maybe another paradigm."

Arthur is annoyed at his theft of this word. He'll put his paradigm up against Flynn's any day. Arthur has a bigger one. "How does your theory work, sergeant?"

"Eve Winters supported abortion rights big time. Adeline Angella hangs with an extreme crowd of pro-lifers. Writes newsletters for them. She has a history of choosing lousy friends, fringe people, fanatics. Okay? So one of them agrees to do Adeline a favour, because Doctor Eve is a pro-abortion queer. It's more than a hunch, a gut-feeling."

Ears has joined the scrum, listening, nodding like a marionette. Buddy barks, "Wipe that stupid grin off your face." Today may see the fabled eruption.

"I want to work on it, Buddy," Flynn says.

"We're sticking with the program, pal. I'm not in the market for new theories until I hear from Faloon. I got a few questions I want to ask him. You got the balls to put him on the stand, Artie?" Buddy leads him to a neutral corner, away from his rebelling seconds. "I've had it to here with that bull. He wants me to enter a *stay* against your guy."

Arthur hears that as an invitation to negotiate, and doesn't bite. The prosecution has become a cock-up, but Buddy will ask a price for a stay of proceedings – a plea to the burglaries and the escape. "Let's see how the day develops," Arthur says. He is again hungry to solve this crime. He has the old engine revved up finally, it's purring. He has a feel for the nuances of this case, how its many streams intersect.

He watches Faloon enter and look about for Claudette, who waves tentatively, a timid smile. Faloon transfers a kiss from mouth to hand to the bulletproof glass behind his chair.

Interestingly, Ruth Delvechio is in the gallery, as are her former friends, Bloom and Quong. And if Arthur's not mistaken, that's Lila Chow-Thomas back there, casual friend of Doctor Eve, the alleged marriage-breaker whom Brian proposed to strangle.

"I hope we can make up time today, gentlemen," says Kroop with a wince. The canker.

Arthur seizes this opportunity. "We can do so if we put on record that the Crown has confirmed Ms. Angella's DNA profile was found in Exhibit 52."

"Is that an agreed fact, Mr. Svabo? Otherwise I suppose we could be here to doomsday."

Buddy has little option but to consent, and Arthur files Dr. Sidhoo's report.

The sheriff leads in Angella, defiant again, shoulders up. Arthur won't give her more material for her next article. "I'm through with this witness, but I do have a few questions for Holly Hoover."

Angella looks annoyed, as if she'd been made victim of a subtle prank. As she quits the stand, she squints at Faloon, and almost bumps into Hoover coming in, then seems unable to carry on past her, as if entranced by her hip-swinging walk to the stand. Angella pats her hair, tugs at her blouse, and makes her way to the back, squeezing in with her quartet.

Except for the Topeka tax evader, the entire cast of suspects is present. Arthur may yet enjoy a chance to play the role of Perry Mason, the prosecutor stabbing a finger of guilt at the perp in the back. *It was then, Mrs. Glockenspiel, that you put the rat poison in his cereal.*

Hoover acknowledges that she's still under oath – for what it's worth – then sits as demurely as possible in so short a skirt.

"During heated debate on Friday, Ms. Hoover, you made a comment to our friend, Sergeant Flynn over there, that sounded of a threat. 'I could say a few things,' followed by an expletive. I understand you wish to clarify the remark."

"Right. I'm really rankled about being labelled an informer. I've always taken pride in keeping my customers' confidences. But if he's going to hang a sign on me, I'm going to display it. This isn't about sex – he didn't board my boat that often anyway –"

In trying to interrupt, Kroop only makes a sound deep in the throat, a growl.

"It's about how he threatened me –"

The judge finally cries, "Stop!"

She has got all this out without a peep from Buddy, who was distracted by a flash of panties as she crossed her legs, then by Flynn rushing to his ear, still occupying it.

"Mr. Prosecutor, are you just going to sit there? Have you nothing to say about this monstrous farrago of irrelevant hearsay and scandalous imputation?"

Buddy shakes Flynn off, rises. "Sorry, that caught us by surprise, it came out of nowhere." He looks reproachfully at Arthur.

"Do fundamental rules of evidence no longer apply to this trial? Mr. Beauchamp, you are under suspicion. Surely you knew what she would say."

"That Jasper Flynn threatened her? What's wrong with the jury knowing that, milord?"

Kroop can't get words out, his canker too painful. Forewoman Sueda shows matronly concern for the flailing jurist, a hand to her mouth. Finally, absurdly, Kroop sustains an objection never made.

"Then let us find another route," says Arthur. "Ms. Hoover, when did you become aware Dr. Winters was planning to visit Bamfield?"

"Just before Christmas. A bunch of us were out carolling down by the government dock, and I stopped to talk to Mr. and Mrs. Cotter —"

"I'm putting up the hearsay warning." Kroop is no longer relying on the prosecutor to do his job.

"As a result of that conversation, what were you led to believe?"

"You're walking a thin line, Mr. Beauchamp."

Arthur turns on the judge. "What she believed is not hearsay. With respect, milord, please let me do my work. This is a *murder* trial." He gives Kroop no chance to recover, quickly returns to Hoover. "What was your understanding?"

"That Dr. Winters had reserved Cotters' Cottage for the last week of March."

"And did you relay that information to anyone?"

"To a few friends. Some never heard of her, I was surprised."

"Would any of these persons happen to be in this courtroom?"

"Yeah, Jasper Flynn. He acted like he couldn't care less who she was."

No eruptions from counsel table or bench, though Kroop is twitching, holding himself back with wattle-trembling restraint. Flynn is writing furiously. In the test upcoming, Cyrano may find that Flynn remains the better dueller.

"When, where, and why did this conversation come about?"

"Early January. On the East Bam docks. One of his routine hassles. I jokingly said Doctor Eve was coming for a week to Brady Beach and he should take advantage, get a treatment for his compulsive need to bug me. He said, 'Who's she?' As if he never read a newspaper. Then he asked me how I'm doing, am I getting much action. As I was trying to tear myself away, he said, oh, by the way, did I know the exact days Doctor Eve was coming. I said, 'Why do you want to know?' and he said, 'Forget it,' and walked off."

Hoover is articulate when straight – anyone not knowing of her penchant for lying would lap this up. But she'll be an easy target for Buddy, with her long history of evasion, her motive to lie, her anger at Flynn. That's not important. The important thing is to goad Flynn back to the stand. *Motion denied, Mr. Beauchamp, you've already had two kicks at the can.*

"And was the subject raised again?"

"In April, when Jasper was threatening to lay an obstructing charge on me, I reminded him he'd seemed weirdly interested in knowing when Dr. Winters would be in town. First he said he didn't remember the conversation, then he said I was lying. Used the word *blackmail*, I don't remember the whole phrase because he was suddenly up real close, breathmint close, and he said, 'Dumpling, you spread that garbage around town, you're roadkill.'"

Martin Samples nods, pleased that this word has finally achieved status as a motif. Very European. Four stars.

Arthur sits. Buddy rises menacingly. "Okay, *Madam* Hoover, I've heard so many lies from you I've lost track, so let's start making a list."

As Buddy hunkers down to it, Arthur works his chair around, taking in the audience, Angella, Delvechio. What does Ms. Chow-Thomas think she's doing here? Meanwhile, how is Brian getting on at RCMP front office? What's keeping Lotis? Arthur needs information fast.

Meanwhile, Buddy seems to have got bogged down with Hoover, despite the leeway granted by Kroop, who is impatiently tapping his pen.

"When did you dream up this roadkill business?"

"I didn't dream it up."

"You had lots of chances to tell me earlier."

"You were never alone. Jasper was always with you."

The ever-helpful Jasper Flynn. Always there. Handling every little detail. Running the case for the Crown, spoon-feeding Buddy – but not telling him about an unknown profile in the DNA sample. One of his doodles, according to sharp-eyed Faloon, suggested fellatio. Arthur asked him if the depiction was not of a penis but a gun. Nick wasn't sure.

It no longer seems so odd that Flynn never mentioned his wife during their breezy chats on the Law Courts terraces. A diamond in the rough who preferred Daisy to Desirée. And who preferred Eve to Jasper. How tense he looked when the name Daisy was dragged out of Ruth Delvechio. *Dear Daisy, that's all I saw. Daisy was very, totally married. Rough trade, Eve called him. A jerk.*

The courtroom stirs with the panting, excited arrival of Lotis Rudnicki. She goes to his ear. "We found it, *Flynn versus Flynn*. The final decree is a month away."

The family man. A hockey dad, two strapping boys. Troubles on the home front, said Lotis two months ago, in the law library, as they examined the text he'd been reading, *Canadian Divorce Law.* Yet one must not underestimate this wily veteran of the force. A fine job of backing and filling today with his gut feeling about an anti-abortion kook. His paradigm.

"You have your shirt hanging out, my dear."

"I hate this medieval costumery." She tucks it in. "I tracked down Daisy's counsel. Grounds for the divorce are numerous bashings. Her address is embargoed on court documents – Jasper stalked her after she left him. She gave up the kids so he wouldn't contest. The lawyer wouldn't tell me any more until he talks to her."

This intense tête-à-tête is causing distraction, Flynn and Ears looking their way, the Chief Justice staring at Lotis, who seems to confound him each time she makes a guest appearance. He clearly has no idea what to make of her, has never seen a dryad in action.

Hoover continues to defend her poor reputation as Buddy dances about the ring, poking and jabbing. She's weathering it, returning an occasional barb. Buddy is shocked by her calumnies, her suggestion of sexual impropriety with the maligned officer. She shrugs. "I guess that's why they call them Mounties." A quick-witted woman, she should have chosen law. She crosses her legs again, putting Buddy in a stall.

Wilbur Kroop to the rescue: "I don't see why you're having all this difficulty, Mr. Svabo, it seems a simple matter to put the officer on the stand to refute her statement. Let the jury decide who is more reliable. I don't imagine the effort will tax them."

"Okay, I'm excusing the witness and calling Staff Sergeant Jasper Flynn."

Hoover wants to stay, to see this play out, but the room's at capacity. A gentleman gives up his chair for her. She pats him on the cheek in thanks. Arthur sends Lotis out to try to connect with Brian, it's urgent.

Flynn takes a moment, then drives himself up with a sigh. A pouting, put-upon look, he's being defamed by a cheap hustler, a pathological liar. Standing tall in the stand, with the professional, detached style of an experienced police witness, he refutes all. "No, sir, that did not happen." "No such conversation occurred." "I don't think it's for me to speculate what her motives might be."

Kroop greets that with, "Quite right. It's time we put this shameful digression aside."

"No more questions," says Buddy.

Kroop thanks Flynn, who briskly heads back to his station. "Is your case finally in, Mr. Svabo? What about these Whalley Wanderers, shouldn't they be called?" He winces, touches his lower jaw, but he's toughing it out. He can abide weakness in himself no less than in others.

Arthur tires of being ignored. "A slight housekeeping matter, milord – the usual practice is to invite opposing counsel to cross-examine."

"You don't have to be sarcastic about it. An oversight. If you have some questions of Sergeant Flynn, just say so."

"I do."

Flynn lumbers back to the stand. Arthur must go at this with utmost care.

"Sergeant, we have on record that Eve Winters reserved Cotters' Cottage in November. It wasn't any great secret. Surely somebody mentioned it to you?"

"Not at all."

"According to Ms. Hoover, when she first spoke Dr. Winters's name to you, you said, 'Who's she?'"

"That conversation never occurred."

"You had in fact heard of Doctor Eve?"

"Yes . . . I'd never met her."

"She was well known to you from her syndicated column. You might have seen her as a guest on television."

"Okay, yes. I might have read a couple of her pieces." His eyes finally leave Arthur, focus elsewhere, a hint of deceptions to come.

"You won't dispute that Holly was excited about this chance to bump into the famous Doctor Eve."

"Maybe so."

"Yet you say this loquacious young woman didn't mention it to you?"

"I'm afraid not, sir."

"Well, what in the world *did* you talk about during your many friendly chats?"

"What people were up to, the local troublemakers. General things."

"Ah, yes, and the weather, I suppose, and the latest hockey scores."

"Sometimes. Or we'd just joke about this and that."

"And she'd ask how your boys were, your two young hockey stars."

"That sort of thing." Definitely uneasy. Now release the pressure.

"You've told us that you were posted to Port Alberni – when was that, eight months ago?"

"Late October. I went there to fill in, the senior man in Major Crimes had fallen ill. And I guess I stayed." Talking fast, relieved to be off the topic of Doctor Eve.

"Before that, you worked out of RCMP division headquarters here in Vancouver." Arthur slips on his glasses, quotes from the transcript. "You testified, 'I liaised with some of the outlying detachments, co-ordinating evidence.'"

"A pretty tedious job, Mr. Beauchamp. Important, though. Major Crimes."

Pushing paper, he'd called it. Brian Pomeroy is trying to gather proof it was more than that. If necessary, he'll serve a subpoena *duces tecum*, with documents, proving the chain of possession, what officer handled what exhibit.

"You co-ordinated physical exhibits?"

"Materials for testing, cartridges, serums, paint scrapings, that sort of thing."

"How does the system work?"

"You have to make sure the item goes to the right forensics person. Then make sure it gets back to the exhibits custodian in the outlying detachment."

Lotis settles beside him, her phone calls done. She posed a solution months ago. *Someone from forensics could have planted Nick's ejaculate in Winters. Or a cop.* Arthur hadn't listened. It galls.

"Is it fair to presume you had high clearance, and with it access to the exhibit locker?"

"Here in Vancouver? No, sir, that's off-limits except for our exhibits custodian."

"However, exhibits would be signed in and out by you. They'd go through your hands."

"Packaged for delivery, sir. I never touched them. I was like a switching station."

Arthur feels a nudge, looks down to see Lotis's capitalized note: ASK ABOUT TRASHING OLD EXHIBITS. Presumably relayed from Brian.

"In closing out a file that's been through the courts, all appeals exhausted, you would destroy the exhibits, yes?"

"Records section would notify the exhibit custodian that a file has been concluded, as we call it. Some exhibits might be returned to the owner, otherwise they're destroyed locally. Blood samples, that sort of thing."

"Do you hop to it right away, or do these notices pile up?"

Hesitation. "They collect. Every once in a while, when there's some down time, my staff would aid the custodian in a housecleaning."

A sound from the bench like low, distant thunder, bad weather coming. Cross-examination shouldn't be an excuse to romp all over the playground.

Arthur will ignore him unless he says it out loud. Another note. HE WAS BACK HERE IN JANUARY.

"After your posting to Port Alberni, did you return to Vancouver headquarters from time to time? Business to clean up, that sort of thing?"

"No, not really."

"What does 'not really' mean?"

"I came back for a couple of weeks to help with a backlog, but that's all."

"When was that?"

"Mid-January . . . around there."

Kroop has been watching the clock. "I suppose you have some relevant point buried in all this, Mr. Beauchamp, but how long is it going to go on?"

"That will depend on the witness."

"We'll take ten minutes."

◆

Arthur and Lotis walk up to the seventh level, for privacy while they call Brian. On the tier below, they can see Buddy also on his cell. Getting clued in.

Brian talks fast. "I'm so coffee'd up I'm ready to scream at the next droid who asks me to be patient. This can't possibly be a secure line, our every word is being digitally analyzed, so I'll be short. No one is confirming or denying. A flying squad of Crown attorneys has arrived.

Also I hear ACU has been alerted. But that's between you and me."

"ACU?"

"Anti-Corruption Unit."

Below, heading for the exit, presumably for a smoke, are Hoover and Claudette, friendly, old transgressions forgiven. Alone in the Great Hall is Jasper Flynn, composing himself. Hoping Arthur is just sniffing around.

Buddy Svabo never really cottoned to the man, despite his meticulous preparation for this prosecution. *He had a dangerous ex-con in his jurisdiction, a thief, a rapist, and he didn't warn the community.* Flynn didn't want to scare Faloon off. He had a use for Faloon.

Arthur hopes he has it right this time. Finally, after so many blind alleys, he has a plausible chronology. Almost exactly a year ago, early summer, Desirée began seeing Eve Winters − professionally, but the relationship soon altered. At some point, she fled her husband. In October, she and Eve parted ways, and Eve took up with her graduate student. That same month, Jasper was rushed to Port Alberni to relieve the Major Crimes chief. Work was left undone, paper left unpushed. It jogged Flynn's memory − perhaps as he was checking out Faloon − that records section had "concluded" a case relating to this same infamous felon, a rape conviction.

As he summarizes this for Lotis, she nods, smiling up at him. Respect. He has her respect.

"In January, Holly lets out that Eve was planning a spring break in Bamfield. Eureka, it came to him, a plan for the perfect murder. He found a reason to come back to Vancouver briefly, to work on the backlog. Helped the exhibits custodian with a little housecleaning."

"Is that enough, do you think?"

"Enough to convict him? Doubtful. A jury will demand proof he knew of the affair between Daisy and Eve."

"Ask him. Ask him how he felt when the mother of his children got turned into a queer by her therapist."

"It's critical that we talk to Desirée. Keep after her lawyer."

◆

There's a new presence in the courtroom: a gentleman of apparent authority, crisply attired, closely shorn. If Flynn's jumpy reaction is read rightly, he's a redcoat of high rank, probably inspector. The Anti-Corruption Unit. A law degree too, because he has taken a chair in front of the bar that separates barristers from the unwashed laity.

Presumably, Buddy has talked to this officer, has been put wise, knows the defence hopes to subpoena paperwork that could tie his aide-de-camp to a coolly planned murder – one lacking any mitigating circumstance, the investigation a charade. Buddy won't be forgiving if he decides he's been duped.

Kroop, though, is not in the loop, and his baleful glare tells Arthur he doesn't want him continuing his smear campaign against a veteran officer. But his Lordship has returned to court armed with only his top teeth, as evinced by a wobbly lower lip, so his nuisance value may be limited.

Lotis is still outside on the phone. Faloon, who's quietly enjoying his redemption, has almost become the forgotten man of this trial. He could casually walk out and no one notice. Flynn is still declining to sit, though he seems tense and shaky. He's expressionless, looking straight ahead, though seemingly at nothing.

"I was pleased to hear, officer, that there's a pleasure we share. Fishing. Trolling for salmon. You do that out in the Alberni Inlet, I suppose. Barkley Sound."

"The boys and I, sometimes their friends. When I get a day off."

"A basic runabout, that's my rig. I imagine you have something snappier. With power."

"A Cormoran 850 inboard inflatable, it can get around."

"What sort of dinghy?"

"A small Zodiac."

"You have all the latest, I suppose. Up-to-date GPS. Sonar."

"That's right. I don't believe in risking lives."

"Where do you keep her?"

"Small marina just down our road."

"Hockey is another favourite sport? You're a proud hockey dad."

"The boys are pretty good at all sports."

"I'll bet they have a proud mother too."

"Well, I guess so, yes."

"But she's not at home with you."

"We're separated."

"And in the process of divorcing, I understand."

"Mr. Svabo!" Kroop cries out, demanding that this lifeless prosecutor get on the ball. Buddy complies by objecting to these personal matters, but without much heart.

Arthur reminds the court that Flynn was introduced as a man of integrity. "The Crown has put Flynn's character in issue. And with all due respect to the court, I intend to test it."

Kroop has no answer. "Please don't be all day."

"Am I right, sergeant? You're being divorced?"

"Yes, sir."

"Nothing to be ashamed of, it happens to the best of us. When did your marriage start falling into trouble?"

"It hadn't been working well for a few years. We stuck it out for the boys. It, ah, got worse last summer."

"Were you seeking help for it?"

Flynn has been holding himself from playing with his moustache – Arthur once kidded him about it during a break – but gives in, working it, buying time, as if any response might imperil him. "Frankly, I felt the problems were hers."

"Were either of you seeking help last summer?"

"Not me. I can't speak for her. Don't know what she did with her day, except she worked part-time at a drugstore."

"Ah, and where would that be?"

"I don't know. Down on Marine Drive."

Lotis is back, at Arthur's ear. "Still waiting for Daisy's lawyer to phone. I'll get a list of Marine Drive pharmacies." And she's gone again.

"You were posted to Alberni about mid-October?"

"Yes."

"What about your family?"

"I encouraged the boys to come with me, and they did. Switched schools."

"And your wife?"

"She, ah, no, she stayed in Vancouver."

"Desirée." The name hangs there, in large letters, like a lurid movie poster. Arthur is on overdrive, focused, his personal concerns stowed safely away, no longer rubbing at him. "Desirée, that's her name? Desirée Flynn?"

Flynn fingers the moustache. "Right."

"But everyone called her Daisy." Pens working at the press table, a rustling in the back.

"I called her Desi."

"But she didn't like that name either, did she?" This is a calculated guess, but Flynn seems taken aback, as if Arthur has insider knowledge. Maybe he called her Dizzy.

Flynn looks at the visiting RCMP inspector, then quickly away, and amends, "A couple of her friends called her Daisy."

"That's what she preferred?"

"Maybe, we didn't discuss it."

"Dear Daisy. That's whom we're talking about, isn't it? The diamond in the rough with the abusive husband."

"That . . . I'm sorry, but that's total nonsense, sir." It's all or nothing for Jasper now, and he rises to the occasion with dramatics, with sputtering astonishment. "I am grossly offended, sir, if you're suggesting I had something to do with the death of Dr. Winters. I didn't *know* the woman. I had no reason to dislike her."

"Surely you were aware your wife was receiving counselling from her?"

"I don't know *what* Desi was doing."

A noisy stirring in the back, as Ruth Delvechio shuffles past her seatmates and out the door, in obvious distress. Buddy is staring at Flynn with concern, fighting the realization that all along he's been running a bogus prosecution. The jury seems to be falling out of love with Flynn too. But Kroop's in denial, making sulky faces, unable to entertain the notion that a stalwart veteran of a cherished institution has committed an unpardonably evil act.

Arthur confronts the witness with Eve's old appointments calendar, the name Desirée written in twice for July. A tussle with Kroop follows over whether it can be filed as an exhibit, but the defanged jurist relents when Arthur offers to call the deceased's secretary.

He leads Flynn through the chronology: his visit to Faloon, his return to Vancouver to pilfer an exhibit that would falsely incriminate him. Flynn claims not to remember seeing a notice to conclude the old Faloon case. If there was one, the exhibit custodian would have acted on it. Documents would be on file in his office.

A switch, back to Flynn's sports boat. "Did you take your Cormoran inboard for a spin on the night of March 31?"

"No, sir, I did not."

"Where were your two boys that night?"

"They were, ah, in Vancouver for the weekend. I sent them off with tickets for a Canucks game."

"They were with their mother?"

"I assume. She has them a weekend a month. The lawyers work it out."

"You don't talk to Daisy?"

"Desirée and I do not communicate, haven't for months."

"When did you finish work on that Friday?"

"Close on to eighteen hours."

"Six p.m., then? Some of us old-timers have an aversion to the twenty-four-hour clock."

"Five-thirty, six. I had a drink with a female member, and later that evening I popped into the detachment."

"What time was that?"

"About eight."

"So maybe you had a couple of drinks with this female member."

"Okay, two drinks."

Three or four, probably. To sedate him, lower tension, give him courage, the balls to go through with his plan. "And then you went home."

"Yes."

389

"And how long does it take, going all out, for a fleet craft like yours to get from Alberni to Bamfield?"

"Ninety minutes. I would never run her all out at night, Mr. Beauchamp."

Arthur is working at a fast rhythm, allegro vivace, snapping each question after the last answer. Flynn is finding little room to sulk, to play at being wrongly accused, but he is far from being broken. Arthur has spun a sticky web, but is it enough? The jury may see this as just another example of a counsel's shifting tactics, accusing almost every witness of being Dr. Eve's assassin.

The clock nears 12:30. Arthur has more punches to throw, but no knockout blow – unless Daisy comes out of hiding. But he'll leave the jury with something to chew on over lunch.

"Officer, help me out with this difficulty. When you and Constable Beasely attended at the crime scene, you went directly to the bedroom."

"Yes, initially we saw the deceased through the window and so . . . yes, we went right to the bedroom."

"The first thing you did after looking for vital signs was to put on latex gloves?"

"That's standard, sir."

"And you kept them on as you did a cursory check of the cottage?"

"Yes, of course. To avoid contaminating evidence. Procedure is to ribbon a dwelling off after you're satisfied there's no one else inside."

"And you waited outside for the Identification team to fly in."

"Exactly."

"Then explain why your right index fingerprint was lifted from the refrigerator door."

"It . . . it was where?"

Arthur recalls to him the evidence of yesterday, the fingerprint specialist who took the lifts in Cotters' Cottage. " 'Known Individual JF, upper refrigerator door.' You are known individual JF."

"Well, I may have looked inside the fridge . . . I must've taken the glove off, they can get itchy. I'm sorry, I can't imagine why that happened."

"Try imagining you were there the previous night. Imagine you wanted a late snack."

"Don't answer that," says Kroop. "We'll take the noon break." The witness stand isn't far from the door to his chambers, where he pauses, studying Flynn, having trouble accepting this man as a bad guy, this wise, gruff cop with his fifty school visits. *We all accept that he's a sterling fellow.*

32

It's 12:30. Hubbell will have picked up Margaret by now, to escort her to the city, to his posh suite where she'll be uncomfortable, it's aseptic, inorganic, unwelcoming. The reunion will be edgy, difficult.

These fusspot thoughts are, thankfully, interrupted by Lotis, walking beside Arthur with her phone to her ear, nudging him, drawing his attention to Gilbert Gilbert. Though said to have been driven to madness, there he is, shoulders back, head high, walking up Robson Square to the Law Courts, returning to his clerkish duties.

"Good on you, Gilbert," she calls, raising a fist in salute to his gritty spirit. Gilbert walks on, expressionless, eyes distantly focused, too embarrassed to acknowledge them.

Lotis snaps her phone shut. "I'm getting the big stall. Daisy doesn't want to get involved, that's her lawyer's hidden message." B.K. Shrader, a sly divorce practitioner with a reputation for seducing the more attractive of his clientele.

"Phone him back, I'll talk to him."

Arthur doesn't want to force Desirée Flynn to court, but if he is to prove Flynn guilty, he must impale him on the sword of *scienter*, guilty knowledge of the lesbian affair that smashed his marriage. Was he motivated by powerful jealousy – or by failure, the ego-shrivelling awareness that his wife had found a better lover in a woman?

As they enter the El Beau Room to lunchtime buzz and clatter, Lotis passes the phone to Arthur, who exchanges greetings with Shrader, parries, joshes. "B.K., you still hold the record of eight decrees in one day?"

"Nine, but who's counting. I'm slowing down, the body can't keep up with the demands of my grateful clients. Thought we got rid of your ugly face – and it's a lot uglier than it used to be. Who's the little dessert treat beside you? Must be your junior, what's her name . . . Nookie. Rudnicki."

Arthur stops dead, the dessert treat running into him. He stares at the phone – where's the hidden camera? The phone speaks. "Look up."

Arthur sees him at a balcony table with, presumably, a gay divorcee, plump and pink-lipped. He's waving his phone, a crooked grin on his lumpish face. It's a mystery how a fellow like him attracts women. It must be the scent he gives off, the gonadotrophins, they cloud women's sensibilities. (What scent vents from Arthur? Something fusty, old books, worn boots, and potting soil.)

Lotis will wait at the bar with her busy phone. She has lots on her plate, including the breach-of-contract claim against Garlinc. Arthur shook hands with Clearihue. Lotis witnessed that, and will sign an affidavit. But they face a formidable problem: by ancient law, land sales must be evidenced in writing.

Upstairs, Shrader offers Arthur a chair, then encourages his companion to touch up her lips in the ladies. "No, Arthur, I won't give you Desirée Flynn, and I won't break client privilege by saying what I know. Except what's already on the record – our pleadings allege, *inter alia*, rages, beatings, murder threats. If she was scared to death of Jasper before, how do you think she feels now, with you painting him as a jealous, vengeful, murderous son of a bitch?"

"Nonsense. If he goes scot-free she's forever in danger. She'll feel safe only if he's convicted of murder. I don't ask for anything dramatic. She doesn't have to testify that Flynn threatened to kill anyone, just that he was suspicious about her goings-on with her therapist."

"What the fuck are you doing in that court? Defending or prosecuting? If you're prosecuting, you got it backwards, you're supposed to lay a charge first. You've got reasonable doubt coming out your yin-yang, you don't need Daisy. She doesn't need the lurid publicity, she's camera-shy."

"I can get an order forcing her into court."

"Give her a break, Arthur." Drawing close. "She has a new life. The lesbian adventure is over. She's going on thirty-four, an age when chances start to run out, even for the gorgeous. She's engaged to a widowed pharmacist with three kids. It looks like she can finally grab a little happiness out of life. Why steal that from her?"

He has a point. Compel her to testify, shove her before the cameras, force her to wade through the jostling throng, subject her to whispers about lesbian lovers – engagements have foundered on less. It's not Arthur's role to subject anyone to that. He rises as Shrader's client returns, lips glistening. "Okay, I'm persuaded. I'll leave her be. But, between us, did he know about the affair?"

"What do you think? He's a cop."

Arthur bids them adieu. Gone is his daydream of thrusting a Perry Mason-like forefinger at the perp, bringing him to his feet to confess in trembling vibrato, *I did it and I'm glad.* He will stop playing his hubristic role as *accusator,* he'll be generous, entrust the job to the state. Daisy may not escape attention, but let the regular authorities make their polite inquiries first.

He rejoins Lotis, who hands him her phone: it's Brian, exultant, enjoying a smoke before lunching with an inspector and a Crown attorney. "The cat is among the pigeons. The Faloon rape was closed out eighteen months ago, and a notice filed to destroy exhibits, including two vaginal swabs in a zip-lock bag. The record is initialled by the exhibits custodian – a civilian, the cops don't trust one of their own to do this job – but Flynn's initials appear too, as a witness. My informant suspects scalawaggery, the document smells of having been backdated."

"I assume Buddy has been apprised of this."

"Yup. I'm getting vibes that Jasper had been making the Force uneasy for some time. Assault complaints by his wife, handled outside the court system. Threats. It's why they bundled him off to Alberni.

Some serious stalking was going on when he came back for that two-week stint. That's why you've got Inspector Taylor of ACU sitting in the orchestra pit. After lunch, I'm coming in from the cold. See you then. Ciao."

Arthur orders a bloodless Caesar and a sandwich. It's one o'clock. Hubbell is showing Margaret through his apartment. She sees the unmade bed, the rumpled sheets. What does she think of the pillow pictures? *I can't imagine how they get into position number three, Hubbell.* Arthur phones 807 Elysian, and there's no answer. They're letting it ring . . .

◆

The Owl figured Jasper might cut ass out of town after this morning's shellacking, but here he is, the Known Individual, Flynn of the Mounted, still in boots and saddle. Maybe he just couldn't get away, maybe someone was frozen onto his tail all through lunch, for instance the man in the shiny shoes to Faloon's right.

This afternoon's performance is sold out again, you can see people lined up outside. Claudette and Holly are getting on like kissing cousins in the back row, two tough broads from the sticks. Even though the whole courtroom knows he boffed them both, Claudie isn't pissed off, she's too kind and forgiving, it's guilt-making. A wedding next month. Did he actually agree to that? What's marriage going to feel like for a dashing *boulevardier* like the Owl? Is it the right step for a man of great hidden wealth? Sebastien Plouffe, Sebastien Plouffe, I love *you* . . .

Here comes the jury settling in, here comes Father Time, and here's the disgraced copper going back into the stand. Faloon, who by now has read the transcripts twice over, is puzzling out Flynn's MO. Maybe he got advance word that the Owl and Doctor Eve made dinner reservations at the Breakers for March 31, making it an excellent night for murder. A bonus, a gift on top of the fact he had the DNA, the gob on the swab.

He probably didn't come straight into Brady Beach, instead hid his Cormoran behind one of the outcrops and rowed his dinghy in.

Maybe he had time to prowl the town. Maybe he saw that drunk condo guy. Saw Faloon! Saw him sneaking down from the Breakers. Saw him bury the zip-lock.

If thirty-one large has gone to the Sergeant Flynn Retirement Fund, easy come, easy go, it's chickenfeed. There's a thousand times more buried in Cimitière Saint Pierre.

Here comes peppery Miss Rudnicki, breezing into the courtroom like a movie star, settling in beside her learned master. The Owl always enjoys the way Beauchamp snaps his braces when he stands to cross-examine, it means he's ready, he's racked.

Flynn looks like he fuelled up at lunch, maybe a beer or two to help relax. He tries to interrupt Beauchamp with an excuse about the print on the fridge door, but he's cut off by the judge, who has gauze or something in his mouth, you get a glimpse of white sometimes.

Beauchamp begins again. "Let's try to reconstruct your movements on the eve of April Fool's Day. You went off shift, joined an officer for a drink, stopped by the detachment . . ."

"To sign off on some paperwork."

"Thank you, let me finish. And you arrived home at eight o'clock. Correct?"

"About that."

"And then what?"

"Oh, I may have unfrozen a steak dinner, watched some television. I was pretty beat. Hit the sack early."

"Can you give me the name of one person who might have seen you between 8 p.m. and dawn the next day?"

Flynn frowns, struggles, like it's almost there, a name of somebody, but no, he can't bring it home. "No."

"Ever sat around with your mates and speculated about the perfect murder?"

"I don't get your meaning."

"I'm sure we've all done it. A parlour game. I would imagine police detectives are more prone than most to indulge."

"Can't say I'm interested in parlour games, Mr. Beauchamp."

"It's always something the murderer leaves behind that does him in, isn't that the case? A footprint, a hair, a bloodstain – you've seen it all. But a tranquilized victim gagged on her own garment leaves no telltale bullets, no knife wounds, right? No blood, no clues."

The judge can't take any more of what Faloon thinks is called rhetoric. "Don't answer that question, witness. It is not a question. It is a speech with question marks."

"My question is, sergeant, did you ever consider that scenario?"

"Don't answer."

"Milord, this issue is at the very *heart* of the defence." Bellowed, he actually causes the old boy to jump.

"Are you accusing this officer of murder?"

"Your Lordship will forgive me if I haven't made that abundantly obvious."

"Staff Sergeant Flynn? Then this is a serious matter. But I see Her Majesty's consul isn't moving a muscle." The judge turns his black, vacuum-cleaner eyes to Mr. Svabo, but they can't suck him up off his chair. He's just watching, arms folded. "Proceed then. Proceed."

The great man has recovered from yesterday's reversal with Angella, a rare stumble, but what a trouper, the good don't stay down. "Sergeant, do you understand my question?"

"I don't sit around in my off hours contemplating how to get away with a crime. I want to get away *from* crime."

Flynn got off a good one, he had too much time to think. Mr. Beauchamp reacts by speeding up his questions. He puts it to the witness that he never went to bed that night, the witness denies. He waited for darkness, then took off in his boat. Denied. At Brady Beach, he anchored out, rowed in. Denied. He had some ground-up rochies on him. Denied. He had the swabs. Denied categorically.

"I'm a little vague on the specifics of your plan, sergeant. Were you hoping to catch her before she went to bed? To share a glass of wine, to talk, to complain about her unprofessional conduct, her seduction of your wife? And did matters then get out of hand?"

Flynn just looks at him.

"Or did it play out this way – there was a light on in the cottage, you saw through the windows that no one was home. You tugged the door open, you looked about. In the fridge was an open bottle of Chablis. You doctored it and hid. Outside? In the loft? Did you take a chance on the loft? I think so."

Flynn doesn't even try to get a word in, he keeps looking at the judge, waiting for cues to respond. But the old chief has turned sideways, arms folded like he's disgusted with Mr. Beauchamp, Mr. Svabo, the whole trial. The jury's got to be wondering why the prosecutor isn't tearing his hair out. It's as if he knows something.

Mr. Beauchamp bends to his assistant, who says something nice to him, and he pats her hand. She shuffles through some transcripts.

"I'm going to put a narrative to you, sergeant, and ask you to comment when I'm done. Doctor Eve returned to Cotters' Cottage about midnight, still embarrassed by the romantic faux pas with Holly Hoover. She went to the fridge, she needed a drink after that. She made a fire, had a shower, wrapped herself in a towel, poured another glass, and settled down to the little writing table by the fireplace. She pulled out her letter to Daisy, many pages long by now, to add another postscript, about her evening's doings, dinner at the Breakers, a chance meeting with a woman of the night."

Not only does Mr. Beauchamp have the whole joint mesmerized, he looks a little mesmerized himself, it's as if he's forgotten he's in a courtroom and is talking to himself. Sort of like the Owl talking in his sleep. He's squinting into space, jiggling a pencil like a baton.

"Why has she begun writing to Daisy again, after a long lull? Because events have changed. The affair had been furtive, difficult, and finally had to be abandoned. But ephemeral Desirée has since split from her husband, so why were they apart? Yes, this letter to Daisy was a work in progress, begun during the hike. She would have carried on about her disastrous affair with Ruth. And of course this is the same letter Ruth sneaked a peek at."

This provokes a nod from the assistant prosecutor, who for obvious reasons is called Ears by the other lawyers. He's stopped eating his pencil, he's being swung over by the honey-tongued lawyer.

"No doubt Eve added a note to Daisy about the quarrel, to tell her she was free of Ruth." He nods to himself, still flicking that pencil. "This is the letter, of course, that mysteriously disappeared from the cottage. Along with a little grey address book with Daisy's address."

Miss Rudnicki is looking surprised, as if it's the first time she's seen her boss kick it into high gear. The Owl's seen it many times. He did a foolish thing last night with this rookie throat, told her where the Topeka money was hidden. Did he trust her? Not a hell of a lot. She's a lawyer with no fixed address. But in the end he drew her a map of where the cedar-root hollow is. If Flynn hasn't already filched his hard-earned thirty-one grand, Miss Rudnicki can have it.

"Eve doesn't finish her final postscript. The fire, the wine, the lateness of the night have conspired to make her suddenly quite woozy. She stands, wobbly, makes her way to the bedroom, falls onto the bed. She doesn't know what's going on, she wonders if she's ill."

For no reason that Faloon can figure, Mr. Beauchamp is now beamed onto Ears. But it's like he's still talking to himself, like he doesn't really see Ears, who is just a leaning post for his eyes, a vacant spot in the room.

"She hears the stairs creaking as the intruder steps heavily down from the loft, she struggles to her feet as she sees him, a bear of a man, making his way swiftly to her. A quick, expert blow to the solar plexus." Mr. Beauchamp's fist darts forward, and Ears jerks back.

Mr. Beauchamp looks around, it's like he has just returned to the living and is startled to see everyone here. But maybe it was an act, that talking-to-himself stuff. "Wasn't it about a week ago, Mr. Stubb, as the pathologist was on the stand, that you were conscripted to play the role of helpless victim?"

"That's right," Ears says nervously.

"And do you remember Jasper Flynn coaching Mr. Svabo?" Ears nods. The scene is kind of eerie or surreal, the judge and prosecutor taking the day off work, it's like they've given up, surrendered the courtroom.

Faloon turns to see Mr. Pomeroy at the door, bringing an extra chair. But not for him, it's for a lady with him, thin, snow-white skin, real good-looking for middle age. Faloon thinks he's seen her on television . . . Mr. Beauchamp's wife, that's it.

Pomeroy sets her up at the back, then takes one of the reserved seats for lawyers.

The great defenceman doesn't notice any of this because he's reading the croaker's testimony aloud, about the victim's lower abdomen being bruised, and how a hard shot could've incapacitated her.

"I won't ask Mr. Svabo to repeat his graphic performance of straddling the victim and kneeling on her wrists, but that's exactly how it happened, isn't it? The prosecutor put it dramatically enough . . ." Another line from the transcript. "'And her horrible nightmare ends when he stuffs the panties down her throat.' Is that how you remember it, sergeant?"

"I wasn't there." Sounding like he has to honk something out of his throat. "You don't have it right, Mr. Beauchamp."

"Yes, pardon me, I have missed something. Your firearm. Your service revolver, I presume. What is it, a Smith 9 mm, I believe."

Flynn clams up again, combs his fingernails through his mighty 'stache.

"Eve Winters chipped a front tooth." Mr. Beauchamp raises his voice so loud you can almost hear the fixtures rattle. "Because she bit on the gun barrel! Because you used it to ram her panties down her throat!"

Flynn suddenly tenses and cranes forward, like he's going to bolt out of here. But no, he's looking to his left, the door of the judge's chambers, it's opening, someone's coming through it. It's that sad sack, the humiliated clerk, Gilbert.

Faloon jerks upright. Emergency. Red alert. Gilbert's got a heater and he's pointing it at the Chief Justice with two shaking hands. Flynn jumps up, roaring. "Everyone *down!*"

Gilbert takes a step back, swings the piece around, it's a snub, a belly gun, and as Flynn lunges at him, *crack*, he fires. Flynn's big body jerks as the bullet hits, but his momentum knocks Gilbert down, who disappears under him, only his hands and feet showing.

Is Faloon hallucinating? Did he just see Jasper Flynn get one in the chest? All the people yelling and shrieking and running for the exit tell him he's not in some sleepwalk nightmare, this bedlam is real.

Mr. Svabo has picked up the snub, and a couple of sheriffs are clawing Flynn off Gilbert. The jury is being hustled out, but one of them doesn't want to go, he's protesting, he doesn't want to be dragged away from this action movie. Though it looks like the last reel for Flynn, the way he's so still.

The top half of the judge's head can be seen from behind his desk, like Kilroy, just his eyes and nose. Emerging from under the counsel table come Mr. Pomeroy and Ears. But Miss Rudnicki is standing on a chair so she can see better. Sad to say, because it doesn't look very heroic, Mr. Beauchamp is suddenly making a late break for the exit, scrambling off to the back, gown flapping, climbing over a row of seats, shouldering his way through the spectators.

Cops come rushing in from a trial down the hall. Sheriffs are trying to clear the courtroom, but nobody cares a hoot about the Owl, the forgotten but totally innocent outlaw. Former outlaw, because the Owl has been inspired to make a resolution. He is going to go straight after this traumatic event. No, wait, the resolution will kick in after he digs up his fortune.

He closes his eyes, tries to replay the scene slower. He can see, on rerun, how Gilbert acted almost instinctively, like you'd do if you're jumped by a bear. But he can also see how the copper may have wanted a bullet. The cross-examination that kills. He hopes Mr. Beauchamp doesn't see it that way, it could give him bad dreams.

But where *is* his counsellor? There he is, and the Owl is ashamed for thinking he was running off like a coward. He's framed in the sunlight pouring through the big window at the back. He and his lady have their arms around each other. Tight. Real tight.

33

When Arthur shows up for his mail, he finds Nelson Forbish stuffing the latest *Bleat* into the boxes. Makepeace comes grumbling from the far reaches of the store, shooed away by Winnie Gillicuddy. "Just leave me alone to look," she calls.

There's no room for the postmaster behind the counter, the local news anchor fills every inch of space. Arthur forks over a dollar for a *Bleat*, and Nelson leans to his ear. "I have it from a reliable source that Todd Clearihue has a fetish for diapers. Wears them to bed."

"Who might this source be?"

"Not just some gullible person. A hotshot columnist from the mainstream media."

"Nelson, it's a joke."

"Oh."

Arthur takes his *Bleat* to the lounge, draws a coffee. Here's a picture of the town tonsil, walking from the ferry arm in arm with the mistress of Blunder Bay. In exuberant typeface: "Welcome back, Mr. Beauchamp! He may be a famous lawyer to some, but he's just a goat farmer to us."

A goat farmer with the dazed look of a war refugee being led to a resettlement area. Margaret maintains a tight grip on his arm, but has her face to the sun, soaking it in – Arthur was shocked at how pale was the revenant wife after two and a half months of unremitting shade.

The picture was snapped the morning after a .32-calibre bullet ended a life and a trial for murder. Not truly a trial but an elaborate sham, a nightmarish construction, brilliantly conceived – except for the flaw: an unforeseen DNA profile in Exhibit 52. In the end, Flynn was heroic or suicidal or both. Wilbur Kroop, in the face of mutterings he was provocateur to this violent scene, has taken sick leave.

Arthur left it up to Brian to sweep up the debris from the aborted trial, and he was in top form, working Kroop like a horse broken to saddle and bridle, prevailing on him to bring the jury back the next day for a directed verdict of not guilty. Forewoman Sueda was overheard to mutter, "I should hope so." The burglary charges are to be stayed. As a small gesture toward saving Her Majesty's face, Faloon will plead guilty to escape in return for three months of imprisonment, less time spent in custody.

It is Desirée Flynn who is forced to feed the media's untiring appetite for this story of same-sex seduction and the homicidal vengeance of a cuckolded cop. Her two sons are under intense emotional pressure, and she has taken them to Montreal to stay with her sister until the uproar exhausts itself. Arthur finally saw her image on the news, she and her boys being escorted by her glum fiancé into the airport. Slender, strawberry blond, wide startled eyes. Not a hint of trailer trashiness.

The lounge hosts only a few idlers today, one of them Cudworth Brown, buying drinks, celebrating an arts grant. "Twelve thousand clams, Arthur. This keeps rolling in, I can afford to get off this fucking rock. You getting it on okay with your old lady?"

"I'm flattered to know my love life is of such interest, Cud."

"Hey, man, just curious. She was pissed you weren't there for her big exit."

If the truth be told – and it won't be told here, in a bootlegger's bar – the doornail didn't need the Viagra. Somehow all the unruly emotions of the day got the blood flowing, and though the two lovers might not have matched, in acrobatic skill, the nuptial display of eagles, they were well fuelled by pent-up desire. Five stars.

They talked through the night. ("I'm supposed to throw leaflets from a hot-air balloon? Of course I love you.") They laughed, relived their time apart, the oddball things that happened. He has decided she probably does care for him deeply. But he senses demands, subtle and unspoken. He knows he has to perform. Not physically, thank God. Politically. In court. Her hero saved Faloon, now he must save Gwendolyn.

Nelson finally gives way to Makepeace, who weeds out the offers and fliers, and deals the legitimate mail like playing cards. "Invitation from Flim Flam Films to a screening."

Cud Brown from the lounge: "I put them in touch with the Sundance Film Festival. I told them to use my name."

"Postcard from Melbourne, your grandson's coming to visit. This here letter with the political sticker is from your friend Lotis. 'Be Tribal, Buy Local, No Logo.' What's that mean?"

Arthur doesn't know. How does one be tribal? He doesn't open Lotis's letter, he doesn't want to. Inexplicably, he fears it. Why would she write him? She has a phone.

As he strolls up Potter's Road, his own phone rings, with the sound of chimes – he is no longer anyone's sunshine. It's Brian, asking if he cares to hear the latest insight from Lila Chow-Thomas.

"Not really." Brian frightened Arthur with his marriage tribulations, inflamed his condition, the Annabelle Syndrome. He was too ashamed to mention his jealous imaginings to Margaret, she would have been insulted. *My God, Arthur, did you think you married a whore?*

"She says we've got to stop one-upping each other, we enjoy the drama of conflict too much, the theatre of marriage. We've begun dating, by the way. I'm feeling great, off the booze forever this time, plus I found out who pulled the panties prank. A secretary with whom, regrettably, I'd shared a weak moment. News from another front: I'm now formally retained by Gilbert Gilbert."

"How did that happen?"

"I gave my card to him as they were taking him away, before some other shyster could get his mitts on him. He's impregnable. No jury will convict him."

"Your confidence is admirable."

"Jasper didn't strike him, didn't try to knock the gun askew. He walked into the bullet. Ergo, it's a suicide not a murder."

If you've destroyed my marriage, Flynn, I hope you roast in hell! Well he may, but Arthur refuses to allow that to sit on his conscience. One person's death can never atone for another's. Suicide can never atone for grisly murder. Flynn knew he would never earn parole after so deliberate a slaying. He escaped a living hell, took his chance that a last brave act might rescue his reputation if not his soul.

"Add to that, Jasper jostled him so hard the gun went off. Accident. Lack of intent. Insanity. Self-defence. Necessity. I've got a cornucopia of defences. Got to go. Good luck in Ottawa." Where Arthur is to argue next week before the nation's court of final appeal. The Supreme Court has agreed to hear the welter of injunctions and cross-injunctions, *Garlinc versus Gwendolyn, Gwendolyn versus Garlinc.*

The arguments are complex: misrepresentation, equitable estoppel, breach of contract, unjust enrichment. But the event Arthur is gambling on is a simple handshake, witnessed, admitted by the defaulter. Ancient law demands that land deals be in writing. But if placing one's initials on a scrap of paper binds the parties, why shouldn't a vigorous handshake?

Undressed, stripped of verbiage, the issue is really about saving one of the few clumps of beauty left in the world, a microscopic green dot on a global map ... And how do you express that to a high court panel?

Arthur clumps past his gate to be greeted by a now familiar, unlovely sight. Six feet of water, a lumpy hill of clay, and a backhoe wanted by the law – these make up the abandoned engineering works of Island Landscraping. It's been noted that Stoney is a little soft on Kim Lee, and crafty Margaret intends to use that as a lever to get him to finish the job. Maybe he'll even let Arthur have the Fargo back for a while.

He enters his garden under hanging tentacles of wisteria, in riotous bloom on the trellis. There is much work to be done, that last row of beets may be beyond salvaging. He sits on the garden bench and examines Lotis's letter. Postmarked Port Alberni. What's she doing on Vancouver Island?

I don't do well at goodbyes, Cyrano. I made such a weepy, soggy mess of it with Selwyn yesterday that I can't bear a repeat. Especially with you, you lovely grumpy man. Can't find words to tell you what a pleasure it was working with you. It's been real, Arthur. I mean it. Realer than you can imagine. I'm going to do some travelling, rouse a little rabble here and there. Next stop, Tokyo, where the IMF will feel my wrath, I've been asked to help co-ordinate the protest. It's your baby now whether Gwendolyn lives or dies. Love and solidarity. Good luck in front of the Supremes.

Whoa, just like that, the Woofering Morningstar flutters off. Arthur is rather shocked by his distress. Somewhat like a father who sees his wild daughter leave home, he feels a little cheated, wishes he'd tried harder to understand her. *Many a time have great friendships sprung from bad beginnings.* On first meeting, he quoted that to her, in Latin. The hippie nymph immediately saw through the pompous dead-tongue rapper.

No return address. She left a few things at Bungle Bay, so he imagines she'll come back. He's going to worry. She hitchhikes everywhere, it's risky . . .

He sighs, looks squint-eyed at his thistles, ambles to the house to get into his coveralls. Margaret's in the kitchen, on the phone to Deborah in Melbourne, catching her up. "You couldn't *walk* into the laundry room. And of course he let Stoney loose in the yard. It looks like a damn *bomb* hit. I've ordered him and Dog to get their lazy asses back and finish the job or they're mud on this island . . . No, Arthur's incapable of dealing with those characters, they know how to get by him."

She's hasn't noticed him. Curried chicken tonight, the good smells are back.

"I don't dare wear it on the farm, I can't imagine *what* possessed him . . ." She's referring to the Piaget watch, the one Freddy Jacoby assured him wasn't hot. "Oh, you don't really think *that* . . . Arthur wouldn't have anything to feel guilty about . . . Lotis? Coming on to *Arthur?*" Helpless laughter. "Oh, he probably had thoughts, but you know him. Anyway, she said he reminded her of her favourite old pontificating uncle."

That, in the end, is how the pixie remembers him. Another Falstaff: *that stuffed cloak-bag of guts, that vanity in years.*

"No, they're not cutting yet, Deb, it's still in court. It's all up to Arthur now. I'm packing him off to Ottawa next week."

Pressure? What pressure? Arthur doesn't feel pressure.

She spots him. "Darling, can you call Reverend Al?"

He does that in his garden while thinning carrots. Al exults: "Cheese and crackers got all muddy, we've gone over the top." He means, Jesus Christ, God almighty, the Gwendolyn Society doesn't have to borrow. The public furor over Garlinc's attempt to reneg has brought in a spurt of donations.

All that remains is for Arthur to win over the Supreme Court of Canada. "We're not out of the woods yet," is how Zoller put it.

"A strange gift, anonymous, showed up this morning in the donations slot of St. John's church in Alberni," Al says. "Labelled 'For the Save Gwendolyn Society.' Thirty-one thousand smackers U.S. in a zip-lock bag. Can you see any, ah, ethical situation arising?"

"A gift from the heavens, Reverend Al. A gift from the heavens."

34

With Selwyn Loo at his elbow, Arthur enters a squat, pompous edifice hunched over the south bank of the Ottawa River. Many of the new Supremes he won't know, but he hopes they're more openhanded than those he squabbled with in the past.

The factum was authored by Selwyn with the aid of old Riley, and Selwyn will argue that part of it, the law. When it's Arthur's turn, he'll speak from the heart. He'll tell the tale of G'win d'lin, the maiden of the forest who joined her lover in the Salish sea. He'll talk about purple finches and phantom orchids and chocolate lilies. He'll talk about the bake sales and the yard sales, and about how the eagles went to nest and Doc Dooley danced a jig on the bluffs.

ERISICHTHON

The wood-nymphs, called Dryads or Hamadryads, were believed to perish with the trees which had been their abode. It was therefore an impious act wantonly to destroy a tree, and in some aggravated cases was severely punished, as in the case of Erisichthon, a profane person and a despiser of the gods.

On one occasion he presumed to violate with the axe a grove sacred to Ceres. There stood in this grove a venerable oak, so large that it seemed a wood in itself, its ancient trunk towering aloft, whereon votive garlands were often hung. Often had the Dryads danced round it hand in hand. Its trunk measured fifteen cubits round, and it overtopped the other trees. But for all that, he saw no reason why he should spare it, and he ordered his servants to cut it down. When he saw them hesitate, he snatched an axe from one and exclaimed: "I care not whether it be a tree beloved of the goddess or not; were it the goddess herself it would come down, if it stood in my way." So saying he lifted the axe, and the oak seemed to shudder and utter a groan. From the midst of the oak came a voice, "I who dwell in this tree am a nymph beloved of Ceres, and dying by your hands forewarn you that punishment awaits you." He desisted not from his crime, and at last the tree, sundered by repeated blows and drawn by ropes, fell with a crash and prostrated a great part of the grove in its fall.

The Dryads, in dismay at the loss of their companion and at seeing the pride of the forest laid low, went in a body to Ceres, all clad in mourning, and invoked punishment upon Erisichthon. She planned a punishment so dire that one would pity him, if such a culprit as he could be pitied – to deliver him over to Famine.

Famine obeyed the commands of Ceres and sped through the air to the dwelling of Erisichthon ... and found him asleep. She enfolded him with her wings and breathed herself into him, infusing her poison into his veins. When Erisichthon awoke his hunger was raging. Without a moment's delay he would have food set before him, of whatever kind earth, sea, or air produces; and complained of hunger even while he ate. What would have sufficed for a city or a nation was not enough for him. The more he ate the more he craved. His hunger was like the sea, which receives all the rivers, yet is never filled; or like fire that burns all the fuel that is heaped upon it, yet is still voracious for more.

His property rapidly diminished under the unceasing demands of his appetite, but his hunger continued unabated, At length he had spent all, and at last hunger compelled him to devour his limbs, and he strove to nourish his body by eating his body, till death relieved him of the vengeance of Ceres.

Excerpted from H.A. Guerber, *The Myths of Greece and Rome*, 1907.